CHANGED

BOOK 2 THE MADE ONES SAGA

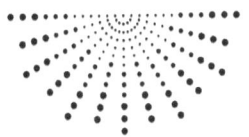

VICKI STIEFEL

❀ Created with Vellum

To Wayne Page
For your incredible friendship, support, and love

If you don't like something, change it. If you can't change it, change your attitude. —Maya Angelou

PRAISE FOR VICKI STIEFEL

ALTERED, THE MADE ONES SAGA

"*Altered* contains romance, humor, flying horses, and a playfulness that any lover of fantasy or romance will want to spend their entire weekend devouring. This superbly written and well-edited book necessitates a rating of 4 out of 4 stars." —OnlineBookClub

"*Altered* is a delightfully different book. I loved the characters and the world the author created. The whole subject of parallel universes is fascinating. It's a simple story but tugs at your heartstrings. Makes one wonder, how would I react if this happened to me?" —Cranky The Book Curmudgeon

"First things first...this was such a unique storyline and I found myself totally involved with Kit and especially Rafe." —StarAngel's Reviews

THE AFTERWORLD CHRONICLES

"This third book in the Afterworld Chronicles, *Chest of Time*, sets quite the fast pace putting them all including Larrimer and their band of followers in even more dangerous, complex, and challenging situations...enjoy this wild and intense ride. — Lynn Latimer, reviewer

"Chest of Stone is a fast-paced urban fantasy with plenty of action and eclectic, vibrant world-building. Ms Stiefel's... writing is very original, it just flows, always in the moment, always unconstrained. There was nothing formulaic about *Chest of Stone,* and I thoroughly enjoyed that. — Nocturnal Book Reviews

"Chest of Bone's writing style is innovative, the world is very interesting and provocative. It's a great story! I's a bunch of crazy, but it's GOOD crazy, with some super vivid scenes and fascinating characters." —Nocturnal Book Reviews

THE TALLY WHYTE SERIES
"This is an amazing thriller with action on almost every page. The heroine is strong, independent and sees things nobody else does... Vicki Stiefel writes a brilliant psychological thriller." —Book Review.com

"Tally is a compelling protagonist—edgy, compassionate and vulnerable—with a clipped narrating style that keeps the tricky plot in focus. She can hold her own against genre heavyweights like John Sanford and Patricia Cornwell." —Publishers Weekly

"Compelling, touching, and a pleasure to read." —Robert Parker

"Three words describe the Tally Whyte series: Intense. Addictive. Chilling. Tally's personality will draw you in as surely as the mystery does in this series." —Fresh Fiction

A WOMAN CHANGED

What if you could be young again? Would it be a dream come true or truly a nightmare?

That's the startling reality retired circus trapeze artist Breena Balážová awakens to on the world of Eleutia in her own re-engineered younger body. For a woman whose death on Earth was inches away, it seems like a second chance at life. But in this parallel world, where horses fly and animals and humans are symbionts, Bree is intended as breeding stock to balance the plummeting female birthrate.

As she searches for her missing sisters, who were pulled to Eleutia with her, Bree also must survive assassination attempts, the growing threat of war, and her unexpected attraction to the arrogant animal Clan Alpha, Gato, a man with terrible burdens and secrets.

The animal Clans join forces to combat a dark conspiracy that will shake the foundations of their world, even as Bree's search for her sisters grows more desperate and dangerous.

If Bree has any hope of finding her sisters and fulfilling her own destiny, she and Gato must carry out a perilous deception, their success or failure deciding not only their own fate, but that of all Eleutia.

CHAPTER ONE

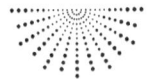

Breena Boadicea Balážová pushed up from the scratchy bed of leaves and spat out the dirt in her mouth.

Well, this sucks. Where the hell am I?

"Sybi! Kitlyn!"

Birds twittered, but her sisters remained silent.

A tendril of hair slithered from her shoulder to dangle in her face. She went to swipe it away and... "What. The. Fuck?"

She pushed to a sitting position. Everything ached. And she was hot. Then cold. Then dizzy.

Screw that. Bree grabbed a plait of hair and held it in front of her. *Red.* Fire-engine red, a horrible color. Her *natural* color. Which was ridiculous. Her hair hadn't been natural since she'd first dyed it black at fifteen.

Her nails, too? She curled her fingers. No polish, nails cut short and squared. Last week, she'd chosen blood red for her manicure.

"Kit! Sybi!" Where had they gone off to?

Bree was having some kind of out-of-body experience.

They'd been hiking in Maine's Acadia National Park, and then they'd fallen, the ledge where they'd stood giving way. No, not exactly. The ledge had *vanished.* She could still hear Sybi's screams.

With precision and deliberation, she took the monster Fear and tucked him into the box she'd crafted eons ago for her trapeze work. A panic attack now would *not* help matters.

Bree blew out a long breath and pushed to her feet, stumbling, her legs tangled in some weird fabric. She plucked at the hideous thing, an unbecoming sack of blue. The damned dress covered her from ankle to neck, shoulder to wrist.

The sun blazed high above rows of dead corn stalks, and she lifted her hand to her forehead to see where she was. Nowhere she recognized, and she began to walk, stumbling at first. Once she got her legs under her, she began to run up and down the vast sea of dead corn shouting her sisters' names. Time and again, she'd stop and listen. Only the squawk of crows answered.

Slumping to the ground, it took minutes for her breath to ease and her head to clear. They weren't here. A burning thirst got her moving again, and she strode across the field toward a distant pond, wincing at the small cuts and bruises her bare feet endured. She *could* still be in Maine. But she wasn't, that much was obvious.

If she'd been abducted, then where were her abductors?

More important, where were Sybi and Kit? Were they okay? They *had* to be. Period.

The air smelled clean and fresh, the small pond reflecting the crystalline blue sky. At the pond's edge, Bree found a spot clear of grasses and knelt, the water making her salivate. She leaned forward to scoop up a handful. And screamed.

A murder of crows startled into flight.

Bree dug her fingers into the mud and leaned above the still water. The Breena who stared back at her wasn't *her* at all. At least not 56-year-old her. She turned her face left, then right, the reflection echoing her movements, then slumped back on her haunches. Her trembling hands traced the contours of her face and throat. No extra chin. No puffy jowls. Not possible.

She leapt to her feet, checked that no one was around, and pulled up her dress. Her body. Her *body*.

The lines and curves of her twenties flowed across her flesh. She touched her taut arms, her flat belly, her curved hips. All smooth and with the firmness of her youth. Gone were the middle-aged pooch, the saggy neck, the drooping ass. Now, muscular thighs from her aerialist days flowed to strong calves and high-arched feet. Except her legs were hairy! Her hands cupped her breasts. Oh, no. They were pre-implant, pert but small, the flowers tattooed across them, gone. She pushed down the dumb dress so it covered her.

Her nails, her hair, her breasts... Her *armor* was gone. Whatever had happened, whatever had dragged her back to her pre-makeover body, whatever was going on, it was weird and horrible. She was like a turtle without its shell. She *needed* her armor.

A welcome breeze played along her body and swayed the scrim of trees edging the pond.

"Kit! Sybi!"

The silence made her heart ache and her eyes burn.

None of that, now.

A forest of conifers rimmed the large field, and beyond the forest's distant edge, smoke curled into the blazing blue sky. If she were in luck, she'd find a cabin, with people who would explain.

After a few more sips of water, Bree strode toward the smoke. Once she figured out what the hell was going on, she'd find her sisters.

Her sisters... She smiled. In the same predicament, Kit would give orders and Sybi would ponder. If they were around, she could bitch about how messed up this all was.

Nearing the smoke's source, her eyes snagged on some vertical wooden posts just inside the forest where a dirt path began. To a house, she hoped. She paused, allowing the dead stalks to screen her from view. All remained silent, and she moved forward at a trot. Soon, a yellow adobe cottage came into view, surrounded by cacti and other succulents, smoke rising from the cabin's chimney.

Shit, Toto, I'm definitely not in Maine anymore.

A flagstone path led her to the front door, and she pressed the buzzer.

Long minutes later, she swore, then began to circle the home where in the rear, she found a glass door. She cupped her hands to see inside.

A huge tan cougar slapped its dinner-plate paws onto the glass. *Fuck!* She jumped back and fell on her ass. Good thing the cat was on the inside and she was on the outside. The cougar pressed its pink nose to the window and chirped, its breath fogging the glass. It blinked its golden eyes. A pet? Who kept a mountain lion as a pet?

She froze and peered around. The cat might be inside, but something equally deadly could be outside. Exhaling a stuttering breath, she scrambled to her feet and took two steps toward the door.

The cougar stared at her, and she stared back.

It was the size of a tiger—immense, with golden eyes that appeared curious, rather than hostile. Oh, she had to be imagining things. But she pressed a hand to the glass where one of the cougar's paws rested.

A shiver arced down her spine, and she'd swear the animal *laughed*.

Oh, fuck.

She backed away from the door. What had she been thinking? That cat looked big enough to break through the glass. And laughing? Another step back, and something brushed against her head and she whirled.

A clothesline. They'd strung it from the house to a tree, and it held a dozen pants, tunics, underwear, and skirts that snapped in the breeze.

She bit her lip. She shouldn't steal. But the damned dress made her feel like she was wearing a boa constrictor. A pair of loose pants and a sleeveless tunic proved too tempting to ignore, but when she reached for the undies—no—borrowing someone else's underwear was gross.

The pants were too baggy, the sleeveless tunic too small, but both were better than the dress, which she hung on the line as a sort of apology for taking the owner's clothes.

With one eye on the cat, whose chirps had escalated, she

continued around the cabin's perimeter. That capricious Lady Luck, who in recent years had abandoned her, shined once more when she spotted a toolshed. Inside, amidst the hardware and potting soil, she discovered a pair of gardening boots. She pulled them on, wishing they were a size larger, but thankful for favors. As she left, Bree plucked a pair of pointy shears from the wall. Every girl needed a weapon, especially with that giant cat pressed against the door, drool now dripping from its open mouth.

You'd like to eat me, would you, buddy? Not today.

She still got the feeling it was laughing at her.

Cool shade enveloped Bree as she crept deeper into the forest. Ferns grew beneath massive trees so tall she could barely see their tops. Kit had visited the trees of Big Sur and Muir Woods, and these giants resembled her descriptions and photos. Redwoods. Her rational mind told her she couldn't be in California. They'd been in Maine when they'd fallen.

Her rational mind... She touched her abdomen. Still taut and firm, with a hint of abs. *Oh, boy.* Though her fear was demanding release, she clamped that internal box tight. Not yet. She couldn't freak out. Yet.

Instead, she made wide circles around the cabin, farther and deeper into the wood, calling, *looking* for her sisters.

She came upon a grove where sun dappled through the trees and small clusters of purple asters bloomed. Perhaps she had been enchanted. Sybi had told her how, long ago, people believed flowers magical. But that was ancient times. Nowadays asters symbolized love and patience. *Ha.* Her patience was as thin as tissue. Her breath hitched. A pair of monarch butterflies, Kit's favorites, lit on the flowers, reminding her asters were one of Sybi's.

Her breath hitched again, and she slapped a hand across her mouth. Put it away. For now, put *them* away, her dear ones, and find a place to hide. To think. To plan.

Her muscles ached and her eyes were scratchy with exhaustion. She climbed over a huge tree trunk that lay in her path and spotted a hollowed-out tree, its edges burnt, probably from a lightning strike. Perfect.

Bree plucked half-a-dozen ferns from the base of another living giant, then slipped inside. The hollow had to be at least twelve feet in diameter, and though the air felt closer, it was still fresh. She sat on earth littered with dead leaves and uncoiled her legs, letting them sprawl, and pressed her back against its trunk. She lay the ferns atop her for camouflage. Safe. Sort of. It would have to do.

The shaking began at her toes, creeping up her legs and torso until her entire body trembled. Fear had squirmed out of its prison, and its grip felt lethal.

"Unproductive," Sybi would say.

"Control it," Kit would encourage.

Pulling her fear tight, she once again bound it. The next hour, the next minute, the next second didn't matter. She needed to sleep.

And so she did.

Fark! Gato was disgusted after his vidcon with Fukkes as he clicked off the Alchemic feed to his den's vidscreen. The Made One Kitlyn had almost gotten herself killed by two traitors who illegally control-chipped two of their cats. Now that shoting Alchemic Fukkes said *another* Made One was in his territory, and Gato was to retrieve her.

Where? He had asked.

In your territory, Fukkes replied.

CatHome is millions of acres!

Find her, was all Fukkes' said.

With the male-female birth ratios having reached eighty-to-twenty, Eleutia had grown desperate. The Made Ones helped stave off civilization's demise with their predilection to birth females. Yet this missing one was not the first the Alchemics had lost, but the second. Something was seriously wrong with their scientists. Made Ones always arrived in luxurious surroundings, yet the Alchemics had pulled two Essences from the parallel world of Earth only to lose both—Kitlyn and now this Breena, her sister.

Gato would find the lost Made One. Naturally, he would, though the arrival of each new Made One only increased his feelings of the wrongness of stealing a woman from her home world, leaving the dead flesh, and pulling her Essence to Eleutia. The Alchemics never asked, they took, and even if those taken were near death or dying, few questioned the process. When had Eleutian ethics gone missing? When had *his*?

He knew, down to the exact minute, and it sickened him.

The Made One Kitlyn could not know that her sister was the "missing" Made One. As if he needed this, with The Challenge to win Kitlyn beginning in a few days. A Challenge he *had* to win, by orders of the Alchemics.

He'd find the lost Made One and hand her off to her makers, to Fukkes. Two Made Ones at CatHome were one too many.

Voices startled Bree awake. They spoke English, which was good, though their accents were none she'd heard before, almost Spanish, but not quite.

She froze, holding her breath, as the two men walked right past her hidey-hole inside the tree. When their voices trailed off, she loosened her death grip on the garden shears.

Once they were gone, she would find a town, a safer alternative. She relaxed back against the trunk.

Which was when a giant black puma shoved its head into her space, its frosty blue eyes gleaming like stars, its sniffing loud.

Shit. What was this place, catland? She was prey, and that big cat would *eat* her.

She scrunched tight against the farthest wall from the opening, wrestling her toxic fear, and stretched out her arms, the points of the shears aimed at the cat's face. She swallowed. "Go away. Leave me alone. I don't want to hurt you, but I will."

The panther tilted its head as if actually listening.

7

It stalked forward across the ground separating them until it stood less than two feet away. Another step, one foot. They were eyeball to eyeball.

Her hands shook holding the shears. She could kill it, stab it. The beast was close enough. Her breath stuttered. But she didn't want to kill the immense cat. Fuck.

The cat kept staring at her, and then its huge tongue snaked out and licked her bare arm.

"Ow!" Sandpaper was softer.

She made herself smaller, tucking her legs beneath her. "Leave."

The panther shook its head.

Oh, goody, she was talking to a cat who seemed to understand her.

A man's voice came from outside. "Bartholomew, do not frighten her!"

"Bartholomew?" she said.

The cat nodded.

She bit her cheek, the fear pressing for release. Yep, the cat had answered her.

Tears spilled down her cheeks. Not what she needed, dammit.

"Back up, Barth," said a deep voice outside the tree. "Let us talk with her."

The cat didn't move.

"Now, Barth," the man said.

The cat stayed put.

"Am I supposed to say something?" Bree said.

The nodding cat raised its muzzle, as if to smile or eat her. Hard to tell.

"Okay, um, I'll talk to them."

The cat tilted his head. He didn't wink, but it sure looked like he wanted to before he backed out of the tree.

A leather-clad man with a mop of blond hair poked his head and shoulders inside the tree. He had a hook nose and warm eyes. "Hello."

Bree gathered her big-top persona—the regal one with attitude

8

that had charmed crowds—squared her shoulders and raised her chin. She nodded. "Hi there."

"That was Bartholomew, one of Catamount's CatGuard."

"Oh, I see." She hadn't a clue.

"Clever, hiding out here. Without Barth, we would never have found you."

Swell. "Why are you looking for me?"

He dragged a hand across his stubbled chin. "We, ah…"

The jingling of horse equipage and, "Move!" was shouted from outside.

Relief surged across the man's face, and he backed out of the opening. With all these people arriving, not to mention the huge panther, Bree started to feel silly hunkered at the rear of the hollowed-out tree.

Her hands had grown sweaty from gripping the shears, which probably were useless at this point. Not giving them up yet, though.

Another man crouched low and entered her hidey hole, and once inside, he uncurled his hand to reveal a ball of light. Dressed in black leather, he scooched on his haunches, his emerald stare slicing through her. "I am Alpha of the Cat Clan, Náshdóítsoh."

"Nachodos… Ouch. I made it sound like nachos. Sorry about that." She kept her chin lifted, her spine straight.

"What are nachos?"

She squeezed her eyes tight, trying to shut out the man, the conversation, the tree. Reality wouldn't be held at bay, so she opened them.

"Call me Gato," he said with a lip twitch. "My birth name is a mouthful. How are you feeling?"

The strange light gave his stark features a malevolent cast. "Feeling? Not anything good."

"And…?"

"Hungry. Thirsty." Terrified.

"You arrived precipitously."

"Well, ex-cuse me."

He swept a hand across his chiseled face, with its prominent chin and lush mouth. "Your arrival was unexpected. I would like to help you, to take you to Catamount, and to explain. Will you come with me?" He held out a hand.

She raised the shears. "And I should trust you because...?"

"I mean you no harm."

That's what *he* said.

Gato's face tightened, then he said with a sigh, "Because you have no other option."

The shears glinted in the light and she held them up, widening her eyes and forcing a demonic smile to her lips. "I have these. They're an option." As much as she'd love to go someplace safe where she could learn what was going on and how the hell to find her sisters, she couldn't. Whoever these people were, they might sell her or rape her or something equally horrible. Though why they'd want some broken-down fifty-something eluded her. Except... Her body was different. And she'd seen enough to know something very strange had happened to her.

His hand shot out, and her shears vanished. She stared at her empty hands. "How dare you? They're mine!"

"True. But I wished to show you they are *not* an option."

A low-pitched hiss came from outside.

"Bartholomew is getting annoyed. We must go before the cat loses patience. As I said, my name is Gato. You are Breena, yes?"

"How did you know my name?"

"Come," he said. "At Catamount, you will know all."

Did she have a choice? Not with three men and a panther awaiting her. Fuck. "You may call me Bree for short. My sisters were with me when... I must find them *now*."

"I am afraid that is impossible." He again held out his hand.

"Why?"

His hand scraped his chin and he sighed. "Very soon. Rest assured."

Not only was he demanding she go with him, but he wasn't going to help her look for her sisters. Her limbs felt heavy, her head, muzzy, and it was increasingly difficult keeping her shoulders back and her head high. "You go first."

"All right." He handed her back the shears. "For trust." And he scooted outside.

Shears clutched in one hand, she crawled out of the tree. *Oh, my.*

CHAPTER TWO

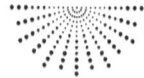

In full daylight, the pony-sized puma's massive body stunned Bree, with its huge head, pink nose, and rippling muscles. She almost giggled with terror. The cat stood beside a stocky man, while another two men sat on horses, all dressed in leather uniforms. The riders peered down at her, one holding the reins of two riderless horses.

Gato stood before her, maybe six-three, and muscled—long and lean and, she suspected, lethal.

Bree pushed to her feet and into a proud pose. "Now what?"

"We ride to Catamount," Gato said. "Can you ride, or shall you come with me?"

"I can ride just fine on my own." She'd put some snip in her voice so they knew she wasn't cowed and walked to the pale dun nibbling a tuft of grass. The other riderless horse, a huge black, had to be the Alpha's.

"Hello, boy," she said to the dun. He raised his head and began to lip her hair. A friendly sort, and she scratched behind his ears.

The four men surrounding her froze.

"Problem, gentlemen?" She arched a brow.

"He tolerates few strangers touching his face," Gato said.

She shrugged. Gato was by far the tallest of the group, a compelling man who stared at her with narrowed eyes.

"Ready?" he said.

Spine rigid, she held his stare for long moments. "My sisters could be frightened, hurt, in danger. I want to look for them now."

"Your concern is noted," Gato said. "But I suspect they are well."

"And how would you know that?"

"I am Alpha. I know things." He grinned. "You have been through much. We will discuss your situation once we return home. Now, we go. Do you need assistance to mount?"

"No." Talk about an imperious attitude. Once in the saddle, she was directed to the middle of the group, and they rode forward.

The saddle itself was strange, a combination of English and Western but with six-inch rolled and tooled cantles front and back. They proceeded in silence, while the huge panther Bartholomew paced them beside her horse.

Gato dropped back from the lead to ride alongside her. "You have a good seat."

"Thank you. Yours isn't bad, either."

He scowled, and she almost laughed aloud. In truth, his seat was perfect. Kit had honed Bree's seat over the years. All three of them had loved the "ponies" kept first by the circus and then by Kit.

An awkward silence descended, as if the man wanted to speak, but refrained. Once she got to this Catamount, he'd promised her answers to her questions, and she'd get food and a good look at herself. This was all weird.

The problem Gato held in his arms was not going away, at least not in the near future. The irritating, imperious woman had fallen asleep in the saddle. Sure she would topple, he had lifted her from her horse to ride in front of him, her sleep so deep she had not awakened.

She had hit him like a sword striking flint. Beautiful and ferocious, though fear haunted her eyes, she stirred him. That flame of sunset hair, glorious storm-gray tilted eyes, and her proud bearing had given him pause. Dangerous ground, since he was about to battle for and *win* her sister, Kitlyn. When Breena had laughed, the rich, silky sound had sparked an answering joy inside him, lately a strange and rare feeling.

The family resemblance only confirmed this Made One was Kitlyn's sister, and their bond could be used to the Cats' advantage. Kitlyn was combative, though without her sister's razor tongue. They must remain separated until after he won The Challenge, that was obvious. Together, they would wreak havoc.

Deep inside Alchemic City, within the Alchemic Clan's most secure laboratory, Calix stared down at the pod holding the Made One. He had to get her out of there. *Soon.*

Ever since he had overseen the arrival of her Essence and the creation of her flesh, she had been *his.* Yet the Alchemic Cabal wasn't Awakening her for some twisted reason. She would die.

He'd fallen in love with a shell, and now, though the Cabal had finally infused her Essence into her Made One flesh, he feared her Awakening would come too late. Each day she remained somnolent, her angelic face grew thinner, her pale blonde hair falling in tufts from her skull.

Though it was forbidden, *he* could Awaken her. He knew the procedure, though he had never performed it. He pictured her eyes opening. Would she smile up at him or scream?

His years embedded as a spy with the Alchemic Clan had warped him. Yet his longing for her felt true. He acknowledged the absurdity, even as he burned to see her animate.

Tomorrow would begin The Challenge for the Made One Kitlyn, and his time grew short. He didn't know why Kitlyn had left the Wolves and gone with the Cat Clan. Perhaps she didn't understand that the Cats hosted The Challenge, with her the prize for the last man standing.

Only yesterday, his Alchemic Mentors, Fukkes and Gabin, had talked of bringing yet another Made One to Eleutia, and here they hadn't even revived the sleeping one—no, dying one—slumbering in the pod before him. Farking idiots. As the unacknowledged rulers of Eleutia, Fukkes and many other Alchemics saw themselves as gods. May the Fates forgive him for ever thinking that a truth.

He was desperate to escape with his Made One, to save her. Yet first he must have the coordinates for where their floating Alchemic City would next land, a location known only to Fukkes' Cabal of Eleven. Calix also must remove his Watcher from the equation. He had already gathered most of the compounds needed to Awaken her. Today, he must extract two ounces of balastree. He opened the safe.

That seamlessly accomplished, he stared at the second safe on the opposite wall that held the precious palladious. So rare, only three palm prints opened the safe—Fukkes, Gabin, and Darva. He sighed, resolved to replicate Darva's print. She was a friend, and it went against his ethics and heart to deceive her. She might pay, possibly with her life.

The lab door clicked.

Calix slipped the balastree into his bag and stepped to the observation controls as Fukkes sauntered in, Darva on his heels.

Darva was beautiful, tall and slim, with long blonde plaits circling the crown of her head, her brown eyes warm and kind.

Her dimpled smile appeared. "Apprentice."

He bowed to Fukkes, then to her.

"Is anything wrong?" Darva said.

"The Made One's readings continue to slow."

"That's none of your concern, Apprentice," Fukkes said. "Leave us."

"As you wish." He bowed again, slung his pack over his shoulder, and departed. For the palm print, his target had to be Darva, and that made him sad.

· · ·

Bree awakened with the whispered word "Catamount." She started, then straightened before a strong arm gripped her tight.

"Do not fret," Gato said. " You are on my horse because you fell asleep on yours."

"You should have woken me," she snapped back.

"You needed to sleep."

"That's for *me* to decide."

"Quite the contrary one, are you not?"

"Thank you for the compliment."

"You are being nonsensical."

"And you are being a pain in my ass."

The man holding her laughed again. "A good descriptor."

Frustrating man.

The sounds of hammers and shouts peppered the air as their group rode past a large stadium. Their home must be nearing, and with it a slew of problems. And maybe some answers, too.

"There," Gato said with obvious pride, raising an arm and pointing. "Catamount."

Spectacular. That was the only word she could think of. Tucked into the side of a hill, the immense building sprawled above a town comprised of neat, colorful homes. The edifice before her evoked Frank Lloyd Wright's Fallingwater. The original enchanted her. This one, even more so. Catamount's expansive glass gave it a prime view of the village, but most striking were the pair of waterfalls cascading from beneath its overhang to plunge into the river below.

Her fingers itched to paint the scene. "Breathtaking."

"It is. Catamount is the heart of CatHome, which encompasses many villages and millions of acres. The Cats domain within the Northern Quadrant."

Whatever all of that meant. Which was when she saw a distant vehicle, like a *Star Wars* landspeeder, flying four feet above the earth. She blinked rapidly. Yup, still flying.

She squeezed her eyes tight, knowing she had to keep her shit together. She suspected this Alpha would take ten yards if she offered an inch.

A rider galloped the graveled dirt road toward them and wheeled his horse to a halt beside Gato's. The men whispered, and Gato swore and issued orders to his group as the rider departed.

He edged his horse beside her former mount. "I must go. You can ride with one of the CatGuard or on your own."

"You know the answer." Bree remounted the dun just as the wind picked up. "What's the problem?"

"Nothing to concern you, Made One."

"What did you call me?"

"I will explain later." He peeled off from the group and galloped away.

He'd explain at his convenience, no doubt.

Twenty minutes later, as the horses approached Catamount, there he was standing on a parapet, watching them like lord of the manor. Gato.

"What's an Alpha?" she said to the rider beside her.

"The head of the Clan."

As she'd thought. "How does someone become Alpha? Is it hereditary?"

The man pulled his lower lip. "Yes and no. The get of the Alpha are often the winners who in their turn become Alpha."

"Not always?"

"They, as well as any other contestants, must compete in the Alpha trials."

"The strongest guy wins."

"Strength is part of it, but the Alpha must prevail in the intellect trials, as well."

Interesting. When her eyes returned to Gato, he was gone.

After stablehands took the horses, her riding companion led her to her suite. Exhaustion dogged her steps, and she was starving and desperate for a bath.

Except Gato stood before a hall door, dismissed her escort, and led her inside.

"For you, Breena." He waved a hand at the expansive living area. "Shall we chat?"

"You'll tell me about—"

"Yes."

Instead of taking a seat, she walked to the wall of windows. Below lay the village—two rows of homes and shops bisected by a green mall and walking paths. "Pretty."

"It is," he said from behind her.

"So go on, tell me."

"Sit, please."

She didn't turn. "I'll stand."

"Come. Sit." He rested a hand on her shoulder.

She whirled, shrugging off his hand. "And what if I don't want to sit? What if I want to go home?"

He grimaced. "Ah, that would not be possible. The going home part."

"Really?" Bree slapped her hands on her hips and pasted a smile on her face. She was acting like an idiot, but he was...provoking. "And what if I say, I'll find a way?"

He snorted, eyes laughing. "You can try."

"'Do or do not, there is no try.'"

"What?"

"You've never heard of Yoda? Such a shame." She waved a hand and took a seat on the leather sofa, crossing her legs. "Why are you still standing?"

Yeah, he'd been gawping at her, that's why. He sat opposite her, legs sprawled, arm across the chair back. An obnoxious pose that made him look delicious, especially with those laughing eyes and twitching lips.

She could pose, too. But without her armor... "'The score never interested me, only the game.'" Mae West had a quip for everything.

He raised a brow. "This is not a game."

"Are you sure?" Fear nibbled. Put it away, dammit. She deliberately licked her lips, and his eyes tracked her movement. "I'm thirsty." She began to rise.

He waved her down. "Let me." He smiled, shook his head, then disappeared into what she supposed was the kitchen.

That smile. He was *something*, for sure.

"Here you are," he said, handing her a glass of water.

"Thanks." She took a long drink, while he again sprawled in the chair. "Where's your big cat?"

"Barth? Napping, as you should be."

"I should, should I? And what should you be doing?"

"Many things, the least of which is sitting here with you."

"The least?" She set the empty glass down on the table, batted her lashes and pouted. "I'm so sad I'm the least."

He guffawed, his laughter booming. "You are trouble."

"Thank you." She grinned. "So where the hell am I?"

His laughter died, his demeanor sobering. "You are on Eleutia, a parallel world that..." A soft buzz, and he took out his phone and stared, his eyes sharpening to lasers. "I must go." He rose.

She leapt up. "No way. You promised to tell me about my sisters, not babble sci-fi."

"As I said, Ma'am Breena, certain things are more important. I will see you later."

And out he went with that catlike grace of his, fluid and tempting as hell.

That man defined frustrating. Most of the lights were off, and she couldn't find any switches, but saw enough from the spill of light to pee, then locate the huge bedroom across the hall. She crawled atop the bed's soft covers, images of Gato peppering her mind, he was that vivid.

When he'd left, he should have clicked his heels or done a full-flourish bow like the imperious dude in *Princess Bride*. Dammit, what was his name? Didn't matter. Gato was a jerk. She scrunched the pillow beneath her head, getting more comfortable. A sexy jerk. Fuck, why did sexy jerks always attract her?

"Bartholomew!" Gato said, racing down the hall. The big cat appeared from the direction of the CatGuard youth compound.

Visiting his cubs, he supposed. The puma bounded beside him as he ran. "Elise and Jaron are having their child."

They ran down the steps and halls of Catamount, across the village mall to the shops and homes on the opposite side of the green.

His mobile chirped three times, and he sped up. The child was coming fast.

He prayed to The Fates, to Father Sky and Mother Terra. *Give us a girl child.*

When they arrived at the couple's Clan home, he flew through the door. "Well?"

Elise's father shook his head. "Soon."

Gato drew on his cat sense, pulling from the entire Clan, as he and Barth entered the birthing room. Elise paced in circles, her mate Jaron, the head healer, and Catamount's medical doctor looking on. Beside Elise, the Sequestered Makena held her hand and walked with her.

He froze. He had been about to hug Makena, which would upset her. She and his brother... She wore a magenta tunic and loose black pants, stars decorating the woven straw helmet masking her face. All failed to hide her lithe elegance and grace.

Each Sequestered's helmet was distinctive, though many resembled metal Peacekeepers', with eye holes and cheek guards. Some were leather, while others made them from boiled wool, which had to be beastly in the heat. Several, like Makena, wove straw ones, and all were decorated in some way or other, with wings or crests or colors. He often wanted to smile, the helmets so fantastical, but he could not. Like Makena, who paced with the pregnant Elise, the Sequestered shielded themselves from men, finding intense male attention overwhelming. Given Eleutia's male-female disparity, it often was.

The mother-to-be, Elise, looked well, her color good, her naked body glowing with health. She would do fine.

Let it be a girl child, he prayed again. "Has your water broken?"

"Yes." Elise hissed on a contraction.

Gato stepped forward and threaded his fingers through Elise's. She smiled up at him when another contraction hit.

"Breathe deep," Makena said to Elise. "That's it."

As Alpha, he poured calm and purpose into her, while the healer wove his hands in the spell to dampen pain.

"We are eager to see our newest Clan member," he said to Elise.

She snorted, grasping her belly with her free hand. "Not as eager as I, Alpha."

His laugh boomed, and the others grinned as well, except for Jaron, who gnawed his lip, eyes a hawk's on his mate.

He, Elise, and Makena walked and walked until Elise froze. "It's time."

Jaron sat on the birthing chair, arms held wide, and Elise took her seat in front of him.

Gato moved beside her, holding one hand, Makena on the other side doing the same, while the healer stood at her head, his hands working their Small Magics, and the doctor did what doctors do to help bring CatHome's newest citizen into the light.

But the Small Magics could never contain all the pain, and after long, long moments of pushing and pausing, Elise screamed.

With a final push, the child crowned, then poured from her body into the doctor's waiting hands.

"Is it a girl?" Elise said.

"A beautiful cub for the Clan to love and adore," Gato said, though his heart ached. "A handsome boy, Elise."

A bit of air went out of the room. All CatHome had hoped. There were so few female births. Too few.

Bree awakened to pitch black, disoriented, and wondering why the bathroom's nightlight wasn't on. She swung her legs over the side of the bed.

Would today be a good Huntington's day, where she functioned acceptably, or a bad one, where her mind fogged and her tremors made walking near impossible? Her inherited and always-fatal disease was both erratic and ruthless.

How *did* she feel?

Good, actually. Very good. Except her butt ached.

She reached for her trusty Apple watch, but when her hand groped the end table, it wasn't there. Odd. She fumbled for the bedside light, but that wasn't there, either. What the...

Little things began to bug her, like the bed feeling abnormally low, the fact that she was dressed in ill-fitting clothes, and that the air was scented with sandalwood and jasmine.

Stealing clothes. Hiding inside a tree. A panther. Red hair. And that man, Gato. And no Kit or Sybi.

On her feet, the cool wood floor soothing, she ran her hands across the wall searching for a light switch. She encountered a painting and then another, but no switches.

When she reached the bedroom door it felt miles from the bed. The room must be huge. Certainly not *her* bedroom.

Lights flared on, blinding her, and she stumbled back. When her vision cleared, she stared into green eyes like a cat's, like Gato's.

Before her stood a young woman, small and slim, thirty at most, with a long fall of pure white hair embellished by a braided coronet. The woman raised a singular black brow, but didn't smile. "I am Arina."

"Hi there." Bree thrust out her hand. "I'm Bree, Breena, actually."

Arina stared at it, then clasped Bree's hand and they shook.

The Peacekeepers on the ride to Catamount wore similar clothes, black knee boots and scuffed brown leather pants topped by a blue tunic with two rows of black buttons. Arina had belted the tunic with wide leather, but hers held a jeweled dagger, and she'd tied a silk bandana around her neck. Her stare was intense, a combination of disdain and curiosity.

"You're different," Bree said. "Like a pirate, but neater."

"A pirate," Arina said, her tone acerbic.

Gato had been piratical, too, especially with that swagger, but his eyes had often twinkled with humor. Not the woman facing her.

"I happen to like pirates," Bree said.

The woman's head tipped. "I see. As our Alpha's sister and CatHome's First Commander, I wished to welcome you to CatHome and Catamount."

"Thanks." The bathroom light was on, and she brushed by Arina to the mirror that covered the wall. "Holy shit."

CHAPTER THREE

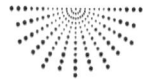

S he pulled at her flesh. It felt normal, like skin. Lifting her tunic, Bree tightened her muscles and was shocked at her four-pack. The pond's water hadn't lied. Bree looked twenty-something. But she was fifty-six. Age was just a number, right? Talk about an understatement.

Panic bubbled. Bree slammed it into the "fear box" and locked it down tight. Okay. She would gather the facts, wait, assess, and *then* she could freak out. Except she was all nerves. "'Good girls go to heaven; bad girls go everywhere else.'"

"Pardon?" Arina had followed her into the bathroom.

"Seems to me I've gone somewhere else, to quote Mae West. Guess I've been a bad girl."

"Are you feeling well, Ma'am Breena?" Arina said.

She rolled her eyes. "Perfectly peachy!"

"You are sarcastic."

"You've got to admit." She waved her arms across her body. "This is screwed up."

"Perhaps you are hungry." Arina crossed her arms, her stance wide.

"Very."

"I left a tray in the living area, as well as some clothes and a mobile."

"For phone calls?"

"Yes."

Terrific, except she had no one to call. "You sure you can't tell me what's going on?"

"The Alpha—"

"Yeah, yeah." Bree waved a hand. It would be useless to ask the myriad questions swarming her mind like buzzing bees. Except… "What do you know about my sisters? We fell, and—"

"Ask our Alpha." Arina's words were clipped.

"I'm getting really tired of you saying that, Arina."

"Is there anything else you need?"

She almost blurted *A good fuck*, but Kit's mental voice screamed *Behave*. "How do I turn on the lights?"

The mirror reflected the woman's frown. "Simply say 'on' or 'off.'"

"Off!"

Nothing.

Arina advanced on her, and Bree whirled.

"Are you positive you are feeling well?" Arina said.

"I feel fine. At least, I will once I have a bath and food. And lights."

"Bathroom off." Darkness.

"Got it. Bathroom on." And on they came. "I appreciate the help, but I'm filthy." Bree pointed to the large tub…and froze.

Worry pressed against her mind. Not *her* worry, and certainly not Arina's. The emotion was so powerful it was almost a growl. It felt alien, and she dug her nails into her thigh. Not okay. Feelings in her head were *not* okay if they weren't her own.

The feeling intensified…concern…for *her*.

"I will leave you, Made One," Arina said.

"What is a Made One?" She crossed her arms.

"It is not for me to say."

Bree threw up her hands. "This is ridiculous." It was like talking to an automaton. Bree turned on the bath taps, hoping the woman would leave.

Arina bowed again. "I will be back, Ma'am Breena."

"What is the Ma'am for?"

"An honorific." Arina said.

One question answered and a thousand to go. "I see."

"You are sure you need nothing else?"

My sisters. Information. "Not at the moment. Thank you."

She refused to think about anything but getting clean, then eating, then dressing. Then finding Sybi and Kit.

Nestled in the catacombs beneath the Keep, hidden from most Clan-folk, lay the covert WolfHome science lab. Makeshift, cobbled together by generations of the Wolves' illicit scientists, it was now run by Tilde, WolfHome's lead researcher.

The Alchemics had forbidden the practice of science by any non-Alchemics. Nonetheless, the Eleutian animal Clans persevered in advancing themselves technologically, even though it could result in death.

Deep in thought, Tilde twirled on a lab stool. Weeks ago, about to turn on the small garden hose she used for her delicate plants, she found a bug caught in a spider's web woven across the hose's nozzle. The bug turned out to be inorganic, a tiny metal dragonfly carrying the remains of a gelatinous capsule in its pincers.

The construct had mystified her, and though over weeks of observation she'd spotted maybe half-a-dozen more of the metal dragonflies, she had failed to catch one.

Fortunately, she managed to activate the bug's microscopic switch, making it fly in random circles around the room. During one test, she'd been filling a glass of water and the bug made a beeline for the flowing tap.

Running water. Its intended destination made sense—the capsule would dissolve and release its contents.

Tilde might be a scientist, but she had also been gifted with a good dose of pack magic, and her gut said the metal bugs were important. She listened, and began her experiments, but with a complete capsule, her results would be more accurate. She set her co-conspirators to trap them. So far, they'd caught several in their nets, but the bugs held nothing.

Tilde concluded the bugs were simply a delivery method for the capsules' contents, and she took several apart and put them back together, though they refused to fly afterward.

Tilde whirled 'round and 'round on the stool, thinking.

Into the lab strutted Max, a man with honied skin and sloe eyes that often gleamed with humor. A thrill rippled through her, like always. And like always, he checked that their five sound disruptors were operative.

"They're fine," she said.

Holding up a wine bottle, he grinned. "Correct!"

He was a devil, this man she loved. If he only could see her as more than a pal.

"Any luck?" he said, taking two beakers from the cabinet.

He treated the Alpha's wine cellar, which hid the lab's front door, as his personal stock.

"No joy," she said. "We have to catch the bugs in the air before they hit the water."

His brow wrinkled. "We will get it done, eventually. They're hard to spot." He poured the wine into the beakers and handed her one.

"One of these days you'll get caught stealing the Alpha's wine." The rich red slid down her throat. It was good. Very good. She bit her lip, her nerves jangly. "Um, I'm making something."

His eyes laughed. "What else is new?"

She grinned. "It's another disruptor. The idea is to scramble the bugs' computronix, and they'll crash before reaching any water. It can only scramble one or two at time, but that should be enough. If they're holding capsules, it will benefit the study."

"How?" he said. "Once we have full capsules, how can we study them without proper lab equipment or even knowing the necessary methodology and ingredients for the chemical tests?"

"Not with analysis. More for insurance." Her plan involved untainted water and mice, ones she would source from her eccentric Tortoise Clan friend who lived in the remote desert southwest of the Cats. He raised mice and opossums, their water sourced from an artesian well. Her hunch about what the chemical delivered, she'd keep to herself until the mice bore their pinkies.

She winked at Max. "Mice."

"Brilliant." His lips pursed, eyes heated, and he kissed her...on the cheek.

After sleeping most of the day, Bree awakened to laughter. "Hello?"

She searched her rooms. She was alone. The laughter hadn't been a dream, but in her head.

Damn.

No coffee in the kitchen, a sin. The drinks in the fridge smelled strange enough that she wouldn't try one for fear it contained alcohol. She took a glass of water with her, sat on the sofa, and meditated.

Thirty minutes later, her brain still felt like scrambled spaghetti. Maybe she'd been abducted by aliens, an old joke between herself and her sisters. Except it wasn't such a joke, even if the people here did look human. The place felt real enough. *She* felt real enough.

When she'd looked in the mirror, her bellybutton ring and sternum tattoo were gone. Her front teeth were perfect, too. No chip. She *loved* that chip. What she didn't love was her fucking flaming red hair.

Out the massive bank of windows, pricks of light dotted the village nestled before Catamount, but beyond that, few lights broke the darkness. The moon splashed down on acres of countryside filled with hills, scrub brush, and a few trees. No city in sight.

Maine, it wasn't.

A rise of panic gripped her throat, and she closed her eyes and evened her breathing. Better. She hadn't had a panic attack in decades, long before she'd quit drinking. They had begun with Kit's accident. That horrific accident.

Wherever her sisters were, she hoped they weren't experiencing what she was. Kit would analyze it to death to solve the problem, and Sybi...what would her younger sister do? Write down her feelings. Then boom! Sybi would come up with a brilliant idea. Bree wasn't her sisters, but whatever these people threw at her, she didn't give a shit. She would survive.

Speaking of... Her breath caught. What if Kit and Sybi were here, at Catamount? She strode across the expansive living area, past the leather couches and huge flatscreen, to the large carved door and pressed the handle. It didn't budge.

Cute.

"Door open!"

That didn't work, either.

Fuck them. She went in search of a pin.

Gato practiced his Magics in his suite, the repetition calming. He grasped the golden thread, levitating the bronze sculpture and holding it steady. He pulled a different thread, a silver one, and drew the sculpture across the room. The High Magics might be illegal under the Alchemics' edicts, but many across Eleutia continued the practice. When war came, they would be ready. How would the fiery Breena react to war?

The sculpture thumped to the carpet.

Fark!

Thoughts of that vixen of a Made One had scrambled his focus. He replaced the sculpture on its pedestal and began to pace. Kitlyn needed a final briefing, when what he really wanted was to get in the redhead's face. Rile her. Her fire had lit one in him, one he hadn't felt in years. One he wanted to feel again.

He froze. What if he took them both? Kitlyn as his partner and the redhead as his lover. He barked a laugh. They would accept that proposal when the sun froze.

The Alchemics demanded another Challenge for the redhead.

And...? Barth's mental voice, dry as Fate's Peak.

He stared down at the cat. "What? Fine. Yes, I want the redhead, and I'm acting like a hormonal teen. It will not happen, no matter how much you like her. I *must* win Kitlyn in The Challenge."

Again, the Alchemics demanded, claiming their pairing was a keystone in their ing experiments. If he didn't comply, they would hurt his younger brother, Ahanu, whom they had "conscripted" two years earlier.

Another bitter taste of blackmail he was forced to swallow.

A buzzer bleeped, and he checked his command console.

Somehow, the Made One had escaped her den.

Barth growled. *CatGuard cubs are in pain.*

Gato ran.

Bree had discovered a brooch to pick the door lock and now walked the stone halls abustle with people. Catamount was in an uproar for some reason, and with the halls jammed and the scarf she'd tied around her distinctive hair, no one paid her much mind.

Sybi and Kit could be here. But where? Bree peeked in rooms and down darkened halls.

She froze. Standing at attention across the hall was one of the Peacekeepers from her rescue. She bent down to retie her boot.

The Peacekeeper spoke with a helmeted woman who gestured wildly. Bree held her breath, her head lowered, when a blast of "worry" in her head nearly tipped her sideways. She squeezed her eyes tight, and when she opened them, the Peacekeeper had moved on.

Hooray. Bree rose to her feet, but a pressure on her mind all but leveled her. *Ow.* She stumbled into a wall, emotion flooding her —*pain.* Her breath sped up, her body cold yet sweaty, her heartbeat thundering. She pressed a hand to her breast as if to still it.

What the fuck? She wasn't in pain. Think. Think.

The agony ebbed, and her pulse and breath slowed. Bree swiped an arm across her forehead. Nothing hurt. All was normal. *She hadn't been in pain, but it had felt real.*

"Help me!"

A woman raced toward Bree.

"What can I do?" Bree said running up to her.

"The cubs and adolescents! Sky preserve us! They're all riled up, growling and screeching. I'm afraid they're going to fight each other and severely injure themselves!"

"How can I help?"

"When they're like this, Gato is the only one who can calm them. Stay with them, please, and make sure no one enters but the Alpha while I'm away."

"Whoa. I'm a stranger. They'll attack me."

The woman paused, eyes wide. "Attack you? Never. These puma are CatGuard, our protectors."

Bartholomew, the big black panther, hadn't hurt her, but could she trust the woman's words? "I'll do what I can."

"Thank you!" The woman raced away.

"Wait! Where are they?"

The woman flung an arm toward a darkened corridor. "Hurry, please!"

Bree ran, and as she grew closer, alarm pressed her mind, rising along with the growing sounds of squeaks and growls coming from the end of the hall.

When she reached the door, she flung it open and stepped inside. A wondrous jungle spread before her, complete with rocks, small hills, vegetation, and a blazing sun. She inhaled the earthy smells and froze at the cacophony of hisses and growls, whistles and screeches. She would stay by the door and guard it, and if a cat attacked, she'd have an escape route.

A shriek of pain, both audible and *inside her mind.*

She ran down the flagstone path that ended at a large area enclosed by soft mesh. Within lay a similar jungle, but with more grassy spots, and a few boulders and rocks. An adult cat could leap the five-foot fence, but not a cub or adolescent.

That cry again, the distraught feeling near choking her.

The woman said these cats were protectors, and her fuzzy memory said Bartholomew had been friendly, almost welcoming. But even cubs could badly hurt her, and their mother... But she saw no adult cougar in their enclosure.

Renewed pain splintered her mind...from inside the enclosure.

She backed down the path, took a running start, and vaulted over the fence, landing hard, and she rolled forward into a stand.

Bree raced toward the sound, branches slapping her face until she came to a small rocky hill and halted. A pale tan cub sat beside a pitch-black one sprawled on its belly. To the right, a cave of sorts, nestled into the hill. But as the black cub howled, other cats joined in to its song of misery, the sounds enough to make her want to slap her hands over her ears.

Forcing herself to ignore the howls, she inched closer to the two cubs. "Hello, kids."

The tan one's head snapped around. It growled, its muzzle baring large teeth that glistened in the soft light. Sensations of alarm were morphing into aggression.

She held out her hands, palms up. "I'm here to help."

The pair looked like older cubs inching toward adolescence, their teeth plenty big enough to cause her mortal injury.

With slow steps she moved forward to about ten feet from the cubs. The tan cub flowed to its feet, moving in front of the injured one.

"Let me help you." Bree battled her mind's panic and took a step forward. The tan cub did the same, jaws wide.

She stopped. The feelings roaring through her belonged to the cubs. How that could be she had no clue, but the fear and aggression were slowly subsiding.

Hoping there was some kind of tit for tat, as she inched closer, she projected warmth and protection. The black cub hadn't moved. But the tan cub tracked her with its eyes. Her next cautious step forward, she sidled left and saw the problem. The black cub's paw was wedged between two large rocks, with dribbles of blood dotting the soil and rock. If she could get around the tan cub, she could help the black one, who was chewing its own paw to free itself.

Another step forward.

The tan cub's muscles bunched, as if preparing to leap.

Running wasn't an option.

Bree bent her knees, eyes glued to the yellow cub, and her hand scrabbled across the soil until she found a rock. As she wrapped her fingers around it, the tan cub leapt.

Only to be knocked off course by a streak of black. The cub flew into the air, landing hard on its side. It mewed. The big black cat growled back, then its head swiveled toward Bree.

Blue eyes. A pink nose. "Bartholomew?"

The black cat nodded and padded over to her. He wrapped his jaws gently around Bree's wrist and tugged her forward. In favor of keeping her hand attached to her arm, she complied.

The tan cub joined them, pacing beside the much-larger Barth, who led her to the black cub, its sad mewling growing in volume and frequency. Barth released her wrist, and Bree dropped to her knees.

She stroked the black cub's head. "Let me fix this." She tried lifting one of the rocks wedging the black cub's paw. Too heavy.

The poor thing was in such pain, not the least because it had gnawed on its stuck paw.

"I'm going to work on this." She captured the cub's blue eyes. "I won't leave you."

The black cub's pink tongue slithered out and licked her arm.

A dizzying wave spread from her arm outward through her body, making her wobble. Feeling half drunk, she pressed her hand to the ground to steady herself. Whoa.

Bartholomew licked her face with that sandpaper tongue of his and the sensation thankfully subsided.

Shaking her head to clear it, she got back to work. With enough leverage, she could shove the large rock away. That would hurt the cub, but there was nothing for it.

The large rock pressing down on the kit was maybe four feet in diameter, and she positioned herself in front of it, braced her legs, and shoved. The rock inched away and the black cub screamed.

"I know." She stroked the cub behind his ears. "It hurts. I'm sorry."

Bartholomew nudged her.

"Yes, yes, okay."

Bracing herself again, she pushed and shoved, shouldering the rock. Not enough. Then Bartholomew pitched in, simultaneously pressing his head against the rock as she pushed. The rock wobbled, raising a cry from the cub, then tumbled backward.

The black cub snatched its paw away, its blue eyes saucers as it held up its injured paw.

Hurts!

Oh, great. Talking in her head...from the black cub. Bree slammed down hard on her bum. "Did you just talk to me?"

The black cub crawled into her lap and promptly went to sleep.

Okay, then.

Velvet rubbed her arm, the tan cub stropping her, then his black tongue lapped her face. Again, the prickly wave fanned through her, making her woozy, and the tan cub leaned against her as if to brace her.

"Oh, my," Bree said. "What's going on here?"

"I don't know, but you are inside the cubs' farking territory!"

CHAPTER FOUR

She knew that voice in all its irritation—Gato.

Woozy as she was, she gathered herself, shoulders back, chin high.

He leapt the fence with grace, then stalked to where she sat with the cubs and Barth. He was blazing mad and utterly gorgeous. He peered down at her, lips tight, jaw clenched—and in his fury, his beauty was otherworldly, like a sculpture come alive.

The woman from the hall appeared seconds later, and stared at them googly-eyed.

"*Well?*" Gato said, grinding out the word with cut-glass precision.

"Do sit down." She peered up at his looming form. "My neck hurts craning up to watch your hissy fit."

To her surprise, he folded his legs and sat, his eyes focused on the sleeping cub's injured paw.

The woman watching said, "I've sent for the vetrina."

"Good," Gato said, while petting the black cub. "Go. Tell him to hurry."

She nodded and disappeared.

"Arlo will come, little one," Gato said to the cub, stroking it.

The cub's eyes blinked open, and it purred with his petting.

"Where is their mother?" Bree asked.

His face grew solemn. "She died."

"How sad. Were they weaned?"

He nodded. "How did you get out of your suite?"

"How dare you lock me in."

"Dare? I am Alpha." He shrugged. "I needed to keep you safe."

"Bullshit. Don't you *ever* lock me in again."

He chuffed. "This is an example, coming into the cubs' and adolescents' territory, into the cubs' enclosure. *Why?*"

Though Gato's words had come out in measured tones, his face was pale, his jaw clenched. Angered? Upset? Hard to tell.

"I entered the cubs' enclosure for a sound reason," Bree said. "The black's paw was stuck, crushed between two rocks, and the cub was chewing it."

"How could you imagine you could handle our cubs, scions of the finest cats in all of CatHome?"

"I didn't imagine." Bree filled her voice with disdain. "I knew. That woman you sent off, I met her in the hall, and she said there was an urgent problem. I *felt* the little black cub's pain, and obviously I had to help. I'm not a complete fool. I grew up in the circus. Decades ago, we had wild animals perform, tigers and lions."

"The circus. *Training* wild animals to *perform?*" He sounded outraged.

"Calm down. You're agitating the tan cub."

His eyes narrowed, but he said nothing.

"We stopped showing them years ago, but when they were with us, I was drawn to the big cats, their power and beauty. After a time, they accepted me."

Gato frowned. "Did you know a cat can rip out your throat in two seconds? These cats are not like your Earthly ones."

Talk about an understatement. "I agree, they could have hurt me. But the woman said they were protectors and wouldn't." She held up a hand to halt his words. "You can see I was able to free the black one." Bree scratched behind the black cub's ears.

"Without Barth's intervention," Gato said. "The tan cub would have harmed you." Gato *growled* at her, the sound coming from deep in his throat.

Both cubs growled back at him.

"*Shote!* Stop that!" he commanded.

They immediately quieted.

"Don't yell at them," Bree hissed. "They didn't mean anything by it."

He smiled, more like a grimace, and turned narrowed eyes on her. "Oh, it means a great deal. No CatHome puma would dare growl at me unless they had *bonded* with you, Ma'am Breena."

"What? Bonded?" She swallowed hard, her dignified persona scattering like confetti. Bree suspected what it meant, and it terrified her.

Even with tiny tits and no makeup, she gathered her armor until her big-top persona settled back in place. "What do you mean?" she said in regal tones.

"The cubs licked you, correct?" he said.

"Yes, but so did Bartholomew." She peered around, but the large cat had disappeared.

Gato's chest puffed, and if anything, he was even more furious. "It matters not that Bartholomew licked you, for *he* is bonded to *me*."

Things were getting out of hand, and she desperately wanted some booze. "You realize I don't know squat. *Nothing* makes any sense. You owe me an explanation."

Gato's mouth flapped, and if flames could fly from those emerald eyes, she'd be toast. Gato's struggle to contain his fury played across his face. "I have been busy. Everyone has been busy."

She rolled her eyes as she stroked the black cub's head. "Busy? I see. Just so you understand, I've been frantic about how I have a 'new' body, why I'm hearing stuff in my head, and my sisters' whereabouts. I'm unsettled, freaking out. Can't you understand how disturbing this all is?"

He whooshed out a breath. "As I mentioned the other day, you are on Eleutia, a world parallel to your Earth."

Stars alive, he wasn't kidding. She'd heard of parallel worlds, mostly from sci-fi shows and books Kit passed on to her. Crazy, yet science considered parallel worlds a possibility. She notched her chin, nostrils flaring. "And...?"

"On Eleutia," he said. "Our Clan animals are our symbionts, our brothers and sisters. The Bear, the Falcon, the Ferret, and those shoting Wolves are merely a few of the many Eleutian Clans."

"Symbiont. That means a mutual and beneficial sharing, yes?" Breena said.

He smiled, and it was the first true smile she'd seen from him.

"Our cats offer us skills and power, energy and strength. We offer the same to them. Though not all cats living within CatHome's bounds are sentient, our brothers and sisters are, with their cat nature remaining supreme. As our human one does for us."

"Do the other cats, the non-symbionts, attack humans?"

"Never. None will deliberately hurt any human within our realm."

"So the cubs are *my* symbionts now?"

His nostrils flared. "If only it were merely that. Bonding deepens and enriches our connection. Those bonded become loyal to that individual above Clan." He leaned forward, getting in her face. "And you...you have bonded with *two*! I will have nightmares tonight because of this. The cubs are now yours, your gift and your responsibility. Farking Fates. I can't believe you've stolen two of our rare and precious CatGuard cubs."

"I didn't *steal* anything," Bree said in a calm voice, staring at the pair, the black curled up on her lap, the tan cuddled against her thigh. Easily the most beautiful and adorable creatures she'd ever seen. The tan was male, and she now "sensed" the black was female, and they were *hers*. Stars alive.

"I understand," she said in a clipped voice. "The black cub spoke in my mind."

He rolled his eyes. "Oh, yes, they are well and truly yours. Which changes everything."

"How?"

"Gato!" A man's voice boomed through the space.

The Alpha rose. "Arlo."

"Coming, coming."

A bear of a man appeared at the edge of the fence, pressed a button, and a gate yawned open.

A gate. Of course. She and Gato had leapt over the fence. They were both idiots.

The big man's rolling trot brought him to where they sat with the cubs. He bowed to her, his braided beard draping almost to the ground. "Welcome, Made One."

"Thank you." Though she didn't like the sound of that "Made One" term, his jolly round face made her smile back.

When Arlo rose, he stared at her with warmth and curiosity.

Gato cleared his throat. "The cub, Arlo?"

"Uh, yes, of course." Arlo kneeled before the black cub and peered at her injured paw. "Do they have names yet?"

"Not that I know of," Bree said.

The Alpha shot her a furious glance.

The black cub stirred. *Audacia.*

Bree jerked. She'd have to get used to that. In for a penny, etc. *Is that your name?*

Yes.

Are you female?

Yes.

Talking to a cat in her head was completely normal. Of course it was. "Her name is Audacia."

Fortis.

Another childish voice, but deeper than Audacia's. The tan cub. "That's your name?"

He nodded. *Male. Twins.*

Now she had two creatures in her head. She pointed to the tan cub. "His name is Fortis."

"Good, good," Arlo said. "Since Ma'am Breena seems to have..." Arlo cleared his throat and shot Gato a concerned frown. "You have bonded with the cubs, I see. Please assure them, Ma'am Breena, that I'm here to help. Things will go more smoothly that way."

She stared into Audacia's blue eyes, then Fortis' green ones. "You heard the man. He's here to help Audacia."

Arlo stroked the crown of Audacia's head. "What a strong and brave cub you are."

Audacia meowed.

While Arlo worked, Bree soothed the howling Audacia, while Fortis growled the entire time. When Arlo finished, he sat back, stretching out his legs and shaking them. "I'm too old for that position."

"You are but a cub in years," Gato said, scoffing.

Arlo tittered. "If only. Audacia will be fine. Nothing broken, only bruised and torn by her chewing. I've numbed, disinfected, and bandaged it, but the little one doesn't need stitches."

"Poor kit." Bree nuzzled Audacia, and she purred, sending waves of love to Breena. "Can I call you Audi, for short?"

The cub stared at her with big blue eyes.

"It's a nickname. Like, my name is Breena, but many call me Bree."

Audacia's eyes grew impossibly wider, whiskers twitching, and she sent her approval, the odd sensation like tingles. But no, more like a gentle geyser rising from Bree's toes and fingers toward her heart. "Audi it is." She nuzzled the cub, and Fortis patted her, demanding snuggles, too.

Gato rose and offered a hand to Arlo. The older man took it and groaned as he stood. "Like I said, too old." He handed Bree a jar of salve and a pack of bandages. "Twice a day, Made One. Clean the wound first. The salve will stave off infection and numb it somewhat. I'll check her again tomorrow."

"Okay." She looked between the two men.

The smile Arlo gave her was beatific. "They are yours now, Made One, and they will only permit you to care for them."

"I see. Thank you." She took the medicine, which was when she realized what the vet had called her. "What is a Made One?"

Arlo slung his bag over his shoulder. "A Made One? Why Gato—"

"Thank you, Arlo." Gato quickly steered the vet toward the fence.

She slid Audi off her lap and followed the men. "Dammit, what is a Made One, Arlo?"

The gate snicked shut behind the vet, and he bustled down the jungle path to the door.

Bree rounded on Gato, hands on hips. "Is anyone *ever* going to tell me what a Made One is?"

"The explanation is long and involved." Gato leapt over the fence. "I will come to your rooms and explain, but for now, my CatGuard will help you move the cubs to your suite. Know this, they will rip up your floors and furniture, so you must teach them to retract their claws. In addition, make one part of a wall a scratching post. You will also need…"

He piled on responsibilities about their grooming, feeding, and on and on.

"I get it," she said. "The circus, remember?"

She leaned against a boulder. Bonding. Symbionts.

A parallel world. Which didn't explain her youthful body or how she got here or what Made One meant. Why was he brushing her off before explaining things? Some purpose lay behind her being on Eleutia, but she didn't have a clue what it could be.

Without a backward look, Gato disappeared into the foliage.

She flipped her finger at his retreating back. "Pfft! Go. Tell me nothing." Creep.

When she stared at the sweet faces of Fortis and Audi, she relaxed, a warm light filling her, the joy of belonging. They were hers, and she was theirs.

Bartholomew padded from between a pair of huge ferns. *They are my get.*

Whoa. Now she had *three* cats in her head. Sure was getting crowded in there.

The cubs settled in her rooms after racing around the place like crazies, even with Audacia's hurt paw, then curled up together on an immense round pet bed brought by the Peacekeepers. It sat near her ginormous bed, and if they followed her own Sir Mouser's path, they'd crawl into her bed at night.

Imagining what her huge Maine Coon would make of Audi and Fortis, she paused. If her sisters were here, they'd talk things over, figure stuff out. She missed Mouser and all her critters, her sensei, and the three young women who'd helped out on the farm. But they weren't here. No one was here. Except for Fortis and Audacia, she was utterly alone.

Anxiety fisted her hands. If she was on this Eleutia, who would take care of their animals?

Stupid. Kit had arranged for the three Js to do just that. Bree, Sybi, and Kit had all agreed that when the Huntington's took them, the Js would get the farm and the animals. Though how they'd deal with Sybi's aggressive single-winged hawk she didn't know.

Since she was here, in a young body, were she and her siblings dead on Earth? In comas? Had they vanished?

Panic choked her again. That couldn't happen. She tried to even her breathing, relax her muscles, but she couldn't catch her breath, couldn't, no, no—

Pats on her legs, soft, like the tickle of down feathers, feelings of comfort pouring into her. Her breathing calmed, her muscles relaxing. She sighed and looked down.

Two cubs stared up at her, their expressions concerned. "Sorry for the freak out, guys. I'm okay now. Thank you."

She bent and kissed the tops of their heads, then lay down, her body melting into the mattress. Two furry bodies slunk onto the bed to nestle on either side of her. A cub sandwich.

When their purring began, waves of love wafted from the two cubs, blanketing her in a sense of well-being before sleep stole her away.

Breena awakened on a gasp, a cascade of terror choking her. *A panic attack.* No. *No.*

She panted, hands and feet tingling. Suffocating. Can't breathe. Shivers began, vision blurring. Stumbling from bed, Breena clung to the wall as the world spun.

Out of control.

A drink!

She tied a wrapper around her and staggered into the kitchen. Booze would focus her, give her the control she needed.

No.

She filled a glass of water and sipped and sipped. Empty. She gasped, throwing the stupid glass against the wall. It hadn't helped. Nothing helped but the booze.

Lies. That was addiction talking.

She slumped against the fridge, eyes tearing. The cubs were mewing, their cries desperate, and she slammed her hands over her ears. "Stop. Stop!"

What the fark?

Something slapped his face, waking him. "Gorm it all, Barth, stop hitting me."

Gato rose from the bed naked. It was the middle of the farking night. He shook his head to clear his sleep-deprived brain.

He had completed the final task for tomorrow's opening ceremony, and Kitlyn was safe in her rooms. Inside his head, Barth talked and Breena's cubs screeched.

On the wall command module an orange button pulsed. Breena's suite. Farking woman. Small favors that the red button had not gone off, alerting the entire den.

Someone might be harming her. The thought terrified him.

He threw on his pants, tossed on a shirt, and slipped his knives into their sheaths, then took his laseblaster from the hall cabinet. Insurance.

Once outside his suite, he began to run, Barth pacing him, picking up speed as the screeches in his head became screams. Dear Fates, do not let her be hurt.

"What is wrong?"

Arina's voice startled him, but he didn't slow.

"Kitlyn?" she said as she ran beside him.

"Breena."

"I will help," Arina said.

"No. Go back to bed."

"Why? Because Kitlyn does not want you, you have set your sights on her sister?"

"Ridiculous." He was panting, sweat greasing his bared chest more from fear than exertion. "Breena will be won in another Challenge."

"You will allow her to leave with two of our CatGuard cubs?"

He put on more speed. "Never."

"My point."

"Go," he said. "I am Alpha. *Go*."

Arina's lips thinned with fury. "You dare order me? Brother, I—"

"Go," he repeated.

Arina peeled away, but not before she said, "You want her. Do not take her."

He pushed himself harder to reach Breena in time.

Bree flung open kitchen drawers and doors looking for paper bags. If she breathed into one, that would help.

She slammed closed the final drawer. Nothing. But the refrigerator... Amidst the cubs' growls and screams, she opened the fridge, clinging to the door to stay vertical. "Fuck! Fuck! Fuck!"

A bottle labeled "troff" could be what she needed. One sniff told her it wasn't alcoholic. "Drass. What the hell is that?" Her hand shook as she opened the green bottle and brought it to her nose. She couldn't tell. Fuck.

Maybe there wasn't any. Maybe they didn't allow Made Ones booze. Maybe they didn't have booze.

The attack had to stop soon. *Had* to. She swiped at the tears and sweat greasing her face and screamed, making the cubs cower.

Fucking stars, make it stop.

A red bottle labeled *Kevitt*. *Try it*, screeched her addicted brain, and she again flung open drawers hunting for an opener.

"Oh, fuck it!" She slammed the bottle's neck against the stone counter. Off it flew, red liquid foaming over her hand. She jerked open a cabinet door and pulled out a glass.

The fucking kevitt smelled plenty alcoholic.

She slid down to the floor clutching the kevitt bottle and the glass.

A shriek from Fortis.

"Twenty years." She held up the glass, panting. *Please stop.* "Sober. Fuck that!"

Audacia licked her face, the sweet cub cleaning Bree's tears, her tongue tickling, the scrape against her skin like a pumice stone.

She clutched the kevitt bottle and the glass as she leaned against the cabinet, legs sprawled. Shallow breaths. Shallow breaths. If she passed out, she'd be braced and not topple over. Probably.

With hands that shook, Bree began to pour.

CHAPTER FIVE

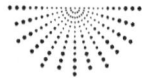

G ato rounded a corner and palm-pressed Breena's lock.
Shrieks and howls came from inside. Thank the Fates every
lock in Catamount was keyed to him.

Once inside, he slowed. Igniting his cat senses, he sniffed. Three
scents, two of which were puma. Barth concurred that no intruder
was in the suite. He relaxed a fraction, replaced his knives in their
sheaths, and headed for the kitchen.

The Made One sat on the floor in a thin robe. Fates alive, she
was stunning, but she was shaking, panting, face tear-streaked, eyes
wide, sweat beading her forehead. In one hand she poured kevitt
from a broken-necked bottle into a glass held in her quivering
hand.

"You are ill!"

Tears poured from the glazed eyes peering up at him as she
raised the glass to her lips.

"No!" He swiped the glass from her hand.

She lurched for it. "Fucking give me that!"

He kept it out of her reach as he mentally quieted Barth and the
cubs. "You are not well."

Eyes closed, Breena thumped her head back against the cabinets.

She gasped, her breath evening out and slowing, and sighed. "It's passing."

It? Gato lifted the kevitt bottle from her hand and poured the kevitt into the sink.

Bree pushed to her feet. "I'm not sick." Though he had understood Earth women to be excessively modest, she disappeared into her bedroom as if her barely there robe was not an issue. The bulge in his pants said it was.

Long minutes later, she strode into the kitchen wearing jeans and a loose storm-gray t-shirt that matched her eyes, her back poker straight, her face imperious. She cut him a sharp look and opened the coolfreeze door. Trolling for more liquor, he assumed.

He slammed the door shut, almost trapping her hand. "No."

She rounded on him. "I can't get a drink in my own apartment?"

"Alcohol is unhealthy for you."

"Fuck you. Though it's none of your business, all I want is a chilled glass of water. And for you to leave. You said when we got to Catamount, you'd tell me about my sisters, and you've said you'd explain a Made One. You've done squat. Get out."

"I am afraid I cannot do that."

"Sure you can. I'm going to take a shower. When I get out, I expect you gone."

She disappeared into the bathroom.

"Humm." He peered down at Barth. "Well?"

Pain. She is in pain.

"I know," he said to Barth. "My fault." Avoiding her because she was not easy was the coward's way, one he had taken. He cleaned the kitchen while he listened to the shower. When she exited wearing that cursed robe, he stared at her perfectly formed ass. Beautiful. Her ass, her lips, her hair—he was treating her like a set of body parts, rather than a person. Shame squeezed his throat.

Breena's body was the least of her appeal. She lit a joy in him that felt foreign.

"What are you grinning at?" she said, voice harsh. "And why are you still here?"

47

"Because I cannot resist you?" He gave her a lopsided smile.

She rolled her eyes. "How about cigarettes. Have any?"

"No. I've read about them, and they sound revolting." He opened the coolfreeze and poured her a glass of chilled water. "For you."

"Thanks," she said, her voice bitter. She stalked into the living area.

Gato blew out a long, slow breath. He was exhausted. Torn in twelve different directions, and tomorrow The Challenge for Kitlyn began. His list of urgent "to dos" kept growing, he had had little sleep, and Fukkes would expect him to greet the Alchemics in great ceremony, when what he really wished to do was murder the man.

You're the one who rose to Alpha, asshole.

He owed this Made One. She had been treated poorly, all because The Challenge—Eleutia's biggest event—was about to commence. He must keep this wild woman safe and alive. *The Fates,* Kitlyn was a pussycat compared to Breena.

He got out two glasses, a bottle of non-alcoholic troff, and headed to the living room. Barth had disappeared into the bedroom with the cubs, and he hoped they were curled up with their sire, fast asleep. Hope never got him far, though. He chuffed a laugh.

"This isn't funny," Breena said.

"No, it is not."

She sat on the edge of the sofa, back rigid, staring through the window at the starry night, and he set the bottle and glasses on the table in front of her. Her tear-streaked face was puffy, her eyelids swollen, her hands clenched. Yet her expression was serene.

What an odd, compelling woman. He wished to peer inside her, understand that whirring mind of hers. With his cat senses wide, pain radiated from her like icy shards. He must fix this.

He held out a filled glass. "Try the troff. It is delicious and non-alcoholic." The drink would warm her from the inside out.

She took the glass, and the narrowing of her eyes was the only warning before she lobbed it right at his head. He jerked sideways, missing the brunt, but cold liquid splashed his chest.

"Refreshing." He smiled.

She rounded on him, the way a snake would right before it struck. "What good is a new, young body if my sisters aren't here?" She stared at her hands, then rose. "Fuck you. I…" She disappeared into the kitchen.

He whipped off his soaking shirt and wiped his chest with it. When Bree reappeared, she pushed his hand away and began cleaning him off with a wet, and then dry towel.

Her breath was soft, her eyes intent. She took her time, and he was unsure if this was genuine concern or if she planned to throttle him next.

She is afraid. Barth. *I can feel her fear.*

Afraid? Hard to believe, but he gentled his voice as she again sat across from him. "What has frightened you?"

She snorted. "Nothing."

"Something has. Or the cubs wouldn't have been screaming loud enough to wake the den."

She looked around the room. "I don't see the den here. Only you. Leave."

"Not until we sort this out."

She stiffened, but he caught a glimpse of terror before her eyes hardened.

"My body is thirty years younger," she said. "Big cats are pals. And I've seen cars floating above the earth like landspeeders from *Star Wars.*"

"Hovercraft. The Alchemics create them. And I don't know *Star Wars.*"

"I understand nothing," she said, voice brittle. "Words are tossed about, like 'Alchemics,' and I don't even know what they are."

Fates, he needed that kevitt. He took one of the towels and dried the end of his braid. The Made One's lips were white, and she was trembling again, her hands carefully flattened on her thighs, though he suspected she wished to curl them into fists. Probably to punch him.

But she suffered.

And that rusted thing he'd once called a heart squeezed. She was more than afraid. She hurt.

He *would* fix it.

"You are doing well." He realized he was leaning forward, which she might find threatening, and he backed off, lounging against the sofa.

She rolled her eyes and returned to staring out the window.

The two cubs padded into the room, climbed onto the sofa—putting cursed holes in the leather—and nestled against her, one on either side.

She didn't reach out to pet or touch them, perhaps lost in thoughts of her Earth.

"Our Alchemic Clan..." he began, "Eleutia's scientists, brought you here. Their Clan controls the technology on Eleutia. We—"

"I don't care." She lasered him with those eyes that winged upwards, though tears hovered on the lower lids. "Just leave me alone or tell me about Kitlyn and Sybelle."

"I will, *poosha*. But no alcohol, all right?"

"What is a *poosha*?"

"A wild woman." Not even close to its meaning. Why the Fates he used that maudlin term, he did not know.

She pressed her hands on her thighs, elbows straight. "Why don't you tell me why I shouldn't get drunk. After all, it's my body and nobody else's."

"Because you were once addicted to alcohol."

"So?" Her lips quirked. "How would you, a man of Eleutia, know I'm an alcoholic?"

Fark. She made him lose all sense of caution. "I have seen your Earth medical records."

Her chest expanded, and though her breasts were diminutive, they were beautifully shaped. Dear Fates, lose those thoughts.

"How *dare* you read those?" she said. "They're private. And if you knew of my addiction, what idiot's idea was it to stock my fridge with booze?"

Because only he had seen her dossier, no other Clanmate knew.

But she was right, he should have warned the housekeepers. Another thing that had fallen through the cracks in the chaos of Kitlyn's Challenge. He would make it a point to tell them. She needed protection and comfort, not addiction. "A mistake that will be corrected."

He wished to wrap her in his arms, rest her head on his shoulder, and say he would protect her, watch over her, be there for her. Which was all wrong. He was destined to win Kitlyn, yet none of those same feelings rose in her presence. He liked Kit. A great deal, in fact. But Breena...

The three recent Made Ones, though he'd only met two, had not merely arrived in unusual manners, but were different from other Made Ones he had met, almost as if the Fates had played a hand in their arrival. Kitlyn's and Breena's personalities were unlike other Made Ones, who were more soft-tempered and gentle. Kitlyn's powerful connection with the Wolf Clan, Breena bonding with two cats—unprecedented. He toyed with his earring charm, his beloved daughter's gift, and took a deep breath. "I am sorry for your pain, Ma'am Breena. Truly sorry. You can listen to what I have to say or you can drink yourself into a stupor. Which would you prefer?"

Booze, of course. But now that her panic attack had released its death grip, Bree felt like herself again, which meant no alcohol.

There Gato sat, sprawled on her sofa, looking like sex-on-a-stick —with a bared six-pack chest and leather pants, his long ebony braid draped over a shoulder. When she'd wiped his chest, her senses had gone on high alert. She'd almost drooled. Yet his arrogance was epic, and so different from Mordecai, her love and partner both on the trapeze and off, whose large body held a gentle, considerate soul. But when Gato's face had softened and those piercing green eyes had warmed with his apology, she'd seen kindness in him, too.

"Let's hear your explanation," she said.

"Good." He took a deep breath. "I'm afraid on Earth, your flesh is dead."

"Dead?" Bree was dead. But she wasn't dead.

"Yes. Your body was dying from the Huntington's disease, which is the only way an Alchemic would take a woman's Essence from Earth."

"My *Essence?*"

"The Alchemic covenant decrees they choose only women fatally ill or near death for Made Ones. They leave the dying flesh, but bring your Essence—your mind, memories, consciousness, and soul —to Eleutia. Then they infuse that Essence into your own flesh they have recreated. Thus, you are a Made One."

She stared at her hands. Her "new" flesh felt like her own. Dead on Earth? Her deep breath was slow and calming. At least the three Js and her dojo friends would have some closure.

"My sisters...are they dead on Earth, too?"

He nodded, and he looked as if he wished to reach out and comfort her.

"You have a sister," she said. "I've met her. You should understand how desperate I am to find mine."

"I do." Gato's eyes shuttered, but she'd caught something haunted before he'd masked it.

"My body was recreated," Bree said.

"Yes," he said, "which explains your youthful appearance."

"How?"

"Only the Cabal of Eleven, the Alchemics' ruling council, knows how to accomplish that. And they do not share."

She swiped the bottle of troff off the table, rose and paced the room, swinging the bottle by its neck.

He stood. "Stop that."

Seeing him riled, eyes flashing and face taut, made her blood run fast. Stars above, he was electric. What arrogance. What passion. "Why should I stop?"

"You are impossible, woman."

"Thank you." Her smile was slow and full of snark, and she notched up her chin. "You are not the first to call me that. Nor will you be the last."

He stepped into her space and slid the bottle from her hands. "You will listen to me."

"Why should I?"

He cupped her face and took her lips with his, kissing her to shut her up.

Except...Holy shit-on-a-shingle. *Oh, my...*

His arm banded her waist, and he deepened the kiss. It was warm and comforting and thrilling. Her senses blasted rockets from her toes to her head, and she melted against him as he delved inside her, tangling his tongue with hers, drawing her even closer.

Nope. No. No. No.

She withdrew and stepped back, knew she was staring at him, but couldn't help it. Whatever that was, that was not "just" a kiss.

For long moments, they stared at one another, his face tight with shock. "Apologies. That was unexpected."

"Yes," she said.

"I was trying to shut you up." He chuckled.

She snorted. "I've had better kisses." Not that she could think of any.

"Have you?" he said, his voice a purr, an irritating smirk on his face.

The kiss might have knocked her socks off, but it had done the same to him.

"You are full of yourself." She would never admit that his confidence heightened his appeal. It was messed up that she found him fascinating.

A slow smile meandered across his face. "To paraphrase your words, you are not the first one who has called me that. You will not be the last."

His taste lingered, and when her lips had molded to his, she'd felt more from him—a gentling and a surprising protectiveness. For all his posturing, he was a dangerous man, especially to her. She took a seat and gestured for him to do the same.

He sat and again sprawled.

Her fingers twined together. "Tell me."

"First, I do not know where Sybelle is or even if she is on Eleutia."

"But you said—"

"I presume that she is here, as you and Kitlyn arrived, though the circumstances were odd."

"Odd? They were awful!"

"Sybelle must be somewhere on Eleutia, most probably within our Northwest Quadrant. If I knew where, I would tell you."

Sybi, the quietest and sweetest of sisters. She would be so afraid. "Tell me about Kit."

Gato frowned. "That is a long and tortuous tale, but all you need know is that she is here, at CatHome, and she is well."

Her heart sped up. "I need to see her now!"

"You will, soon. I am afraid now is not possible."

"You listen to me, catman, and you listen good. I *will* see my sister."

"Yes, you will see her. I promise you that."

Kitlyn was alive. Kitlyn was whole. Kitlyn was safe. Worry for Sybi gnawed, but she relaxed a fraction. "She's here at Catamount?"

His eyes hooded. A non answer, which meant yes. No reason she couldn't go find her after the Alpha left. "Is she all right?"

His eyes narrowed. "Perfectly fine, though her attitude is as poor as yours."

Go Kit. Bree clamped her jaw tight, holding in a laugh. "Excuse our attitude at being ripped from all we knew and loved!"

"You are exhausting."

"Tough shit. How dare they? How *dare* you! Why can't I see her now?"

"The time is not right," he said. "And I am Alpha."

Mr. Arrogance Personified. "Big whoop!"

He laughed and nodded. "I must confess, at times I feel the same. Kitlyn's situation is complicated."

So was he. "You're the Alpha. Un-complicate it." From his words, Bree suspected Kit was fine, though some mystery was attached to her. Gato might lounge around and laugh often, his bravado unmatched. Yet she'd caught hints of vulnerability and pain. The damned man made her curious, just like the cats he adored. "Kit is young, like me, and healthy?"

"Young and healthy. Thriving, in fact."

"But the Huntington's…it's genetic. Though I have this fine new body, is it—"

"As I said, I have seen your medical records. You and your sister no longer have the disease."

She fist pumped. "Fuck, yes!" The Balážová curse was gone.

He frowned. "You have a foul mouth."

"Sometimes." She winked, hoping to disconcert him.

"If you wish to see the medical report, that is available."

"I want to see it."

He nodded, eyes wary.

"Accepting all this as real isn't easy, you know. Cats talking in my head, like in cartoons."

"You will speak of our cats with respect. They are our brothers and sisters, as I have explained."

"And *I* bonded with two." She nodded, the regal one from her show, but had to restrain herself from sticking out her tongue. The bond with the cubs remained a warmth around her heart.

The cubs and Barth crawled beside her on the sofa and cuddled up. Long moments of petting and purring ensued, which gave her time to think—those Alchemics had done all this, conscripted her without asking if she or her sisters wanted this. Kit would be livid. Bree was annoyed, and Sybi… She would go with the flow. Given the circumstances, perhaps Sybi had the right of it. Nope. Bree was ticked. "Have you ever heard of the word 'consent?'"

His lips parted to answer, but she barreled on. "I wasn't asked if I wanted to come to Eleutia, if I wanted a new body, if I wanted any of this. Where are my scars that told the tales of my life? The chip in my tooth I loved? You Eleutians kidnapped me, changed me, and I ended up in the dirt, which—"

"Was a mistake, as was your sister surrounded by ice. Normally, Made Ones arrive to luxury."

"Luxurious kidnapping."

"It is not right." He growled low in his throat. "I feel that way. Most Eleutians do. We only take those who are sick and near death. Made Ones are necessary for our survival. "

"Survival? Talk about hyperbole."

He paled, white-knuckled hands threaded together. "We Eleutians try not to think about the ethical concerns as we go about our daily tasks, while in the back of our minds, we never forget we are dying. That *Eleutia* is dying. A mere twenty percent of our births are female."

"Twenty percent?" The statistic shocked her. That couldn't sustain life. "How did Eleutia last this long?"

"The decline began two hundred and fifty years ago, as a trickle few noticed. But as the years passed, the disparity escalated. Only with the Made Ones' help have we survived. Barely."

"What's so special about Made Ones?"

"You were enhanced, perfected. The Alchemics tolerate nothing but perfection." His words rang with bitterness. "You are healthier and stronger, and you have a predilection to birth much-desired girl children."

"Oh, goody." She sat back stunned, sorting through the implications. Finally, she smiled and hoped it was as feral as she felt. "I'm breeding stock. A career path I've always longed for."

"I would say that was sarcasm."

"And I would say you're right, catman. I'm not anyone's broodmare. I never had kids on Earth. None of us did because we all lost the lottery with our genetic disease." Yet his explanation made a horrible sort of sense, except... "How can I understand and read your language?"

"We have many languages on Eleutia, and all Made Ones are implanted with translator disks behind their ear, which allows you to speak, understand, and read Northern Eleutian."

She pressed a finger behind her right ear, but felt only skin and flesh. "How is it powered? Won't the battery die at some point?"

"No. As long as you live, so will the translator. It is powered by your blood."

"My *blood*? How?"

His smile was tight. "If I knew that, I would be an Alchemic. No animal Clan is privy to their secrets." He eyed her with skepticism. "You appear calmer. You are feeling better after your earlier discomfort on the kitchen floor?"

Her panic attack had been far more than "discomfort." Kit wouldn't have freaked out, not like she had. Bree had always been more out there with her emotions than either of her sisters. Kit would have gone into the bathroom, locked the door, and screamed. Sybi wouldn't even allow herself that much, gathering all negative emotions inside to the point where she'd vomit from the stress of her pain.

The cubs' patted her thighs with their adorable paws. Like house cats, they wanted their petting, and she stroked Audacia and Fortis. Now that he'd explained, she dared to believe the panic would subside. The unknowing had terrified her.

"I'm...better."

After a long, penetrating look, he nodded. "Good."

She controlled the tremor and steeled her voice. "*Why* can't I talk to my sister?"

CHAPTER SIX

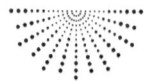

G ato threaded his fingers behind his head and leaned back, staring at the ceiling. *Why was he being so difficult about Breena seeing her sister?* He knew and it crushed him. It was not fair to Breena or to himself. As if he had a choice. Just like the Made Ones had not been given a choice.

Images of Ahanu, gone so long, flickered through his mind. His brother's laughter and pranks and innate kindness. To hold him again, to protect him as he should have that first time, to see him mature into the striking man he was destined to be—how he longed for that. He wanted Breena and Kitlyn to meet, to feel the joy of their reunion.

Kitlyn was clever, and he suspected Breena was equally so. The Wolves' Made One may have come voluntarily to CatHome, but she thwarted him at every turn. Together, what might the pair of them do?

In reality, not much. There were guards, he would be present, Breena was in pain…

They cannot meet yet, Barth messaged.

Why?

Escape.

Though he doubted that, he seldom ignored Barth's advice.

Certainly, the ceiling held no answers.

Except an oddity jumped out at him, a round shape where there should only be a corner join in the wood. Closing his eyes, he wrestled his temper until he no longer wished to punch a hole in the wall. *Those farkers.* He laughed. The Fates, how long had this gone on? He knew Catamount the way he knew his own flesh, yet he had not noticed. Until now.

He drew on his cat sense, and the room sharpened, colors brightened, hearing acute. Strength and power coursed through him.

"Gato?" Bree said.

He held up a finger. His eyes narrowed before he drew out his mobile and punched in a code and his location. When he focused on Bree, she reared back.

"You look like you want to kill someone. Slowly."

"I do. But this time, it is not you, but rather a bit of an emergency."

"Go do your thing, then."

He grimaced. "I intend to."

She arched a brow.

Gato pressed a finger to his lips. Breena nodded, padding into the kitchen, where cursing commenced while the water ran.

Minutes later, he opened the door to Taz, three Peacekeepers, and two researchers from the Cats' illicit underground lab. Three portable scanners were hooked to their belts, one man carrying a ladder. They went to work.

Do you want us to remove it? A researcher tapped to Gato on his mobile.

Someone had bugged the Made One's suite. Perhaps all of Catamount. Un-*farking*-believable. He rubbed his forehead. Those shoting Alchemics.

Taz texted, *The Anti-Made One zealots?*

No, they do not have the tech, he tapped out to his cousin. Perhaps an opposing Clan looking for intel about The Challenge. Unlikely. The CastOuts might… No. Their allies would not do such a thing.

It always came back to the duplicitous Alchemics. He nodded to Taz to remove it. *Check the entire suite, then all of Catamount.*

Taz gaped, then straightened and raised his palm to his forehead, saluting.

When Bree closed the door behind Gato and the last Peacekeeper, she pressed her back against the warm wood. *Shit*, whoever had placed the bugs had heard her meltdown and could use it against her.

Did she care that "they" had heard her panic attack? They'd tell her family, her friends. Right. She wasn't easily embarrassed, and she had no friends on Eleutia, which was great in this instance.

She sat cross-legged on the couch, closed her eyes, and searched for that meditative state, one of the tools she used to keep her panic attacks at bay. Fifteen minutes later, she unfolded her legs and opened her eyes to find two concerned cubs staring up at her.

"It's okay, guys," she said as she petted them. "I was finding my center."

Fortis nodded and Audi licked her arm. Joy flowed from her heart outward, and the final tight coil in her gut relaxed.

Her arrival on Eleutia made a strange sort of sense. Had Kit accepted that they'd been "reconstituted?" Eventually. But dear heart-on-her-sleeve Sybi. Her reaction was worrisome.

Eleutia sounded desperate for females, but these Eleutians needed another think if they imagined she'd be their personal broodmare.

If she could only find her sisters. Though she had to admit, she wasn't sure how.

No global internet existed, though there was web connectivity throughout CatHome's vast acres. One of their tablets could help. The phone made sense to her, and if she knew Kit's number, she could call.

Flipping the phone open, she said, "Call Kitlyn." Nothing happened. "Call Kit!" Nope.

She sighed, wrung out. Her panic attack had been bad, and she could almost taste that drink. She wanted it, the wanting as familiar as an old shawl. Her drunken, promiscuous years were a pleasant haze, their appeal strong—forget the trauma, ignore the problem, mask the pain. Fortis let out a snore, and she stared at the cubs dozing beside her, a head resting on each thigh.

No, she would not take a drink.

Resolve firmly in place, she went to find Kit.

An hour later, Bree flipped another page of *Flora and Fauna of Eleutia*. She had forced herself to wait before continuing the hunt for Kit. Her first expedition had been a bust. Now, as she stared at an illustrated horror captioned *Battle Beetle*, she didn't quite believe what she saw. The bug was huge, maybe two-feet long, with disgusting legs and pincers. And it flew. Ugh.

When she had looked for Kit earlier, she'd followed the right-hand corridor, keeping track of time with the phone Arina had given her. On her search, she'd passed regular people, Peacekeepers, and a woman in a painted straw helmet. Her search had ended when she'd peeked around a corner to see a throng of Peacekeepers barreling toward her.

Hightailing it back to her suite, she'd vowed to look again in fifteen minutes. She'd eased the adrenaline rush first with some stretches and exercises, then grabbed some cheese and troff to quiet her growling stomach.

Ten minutes to go before she searched another corridor.

Good thing *Flora and Fauna* had pictures, because her concentration was zero. The next page showed a brown bear that looked much like Earth grizzlies. The caption said many were symbionts to the Bear Clan. She checked the mobile. Only two minutes had passed. Another page and...

She laughed aloud. A fairytale book, for she stared at a phoenix bird. The text said they lived in the western regions of Eleutia and were nearly extinct, having been hunted near to death. The big beetles she could believe, but a phoenix? Next would be a unicorn.

Bree turned the page. *Holy shit!* A flying horse. The text called them mistrals and described their coats, their feed, and where they preferred to graze. And that their bones were the strongest element on Eleutia, their wings folding into their bodies to vanish. Physics-wise, flying horses seemed impossible. But they were real here on Eleutia. Bree couldn't wait to see one.

She reached for her troff, while the cubs paced the living area.
Out.

Out. What the... Ah. "Time for walkies, kids?" She could multi-task and look for Kit, too. She changed into a sarong-type skirt and t-shirt, and covered her hair with a poorly knit beanie.

They walked down a corridor flanked by acres of glass that over-looked the small town to their left, and on their right, myriad gardens. Everyone stared, though Bree suspected it was the two cubs flanking her they were ogling. When a lone person would pass, Bree would stop them to ask about Kit. They all gave the same, tired response, "Ask the Alpha."

A greenspace stretched to the bluff, and she opened the slider for the cubs and followed as they bounded out and began sniffing the grass and shrubs like bloodhounds. Both peed, Fortis several times, and she'd again forgotten to ask if Catamount had poop bags. Dense trees that capped the plateau high above seemed to reach the clouds. Redwoods. Another time, she would explore. The cubs raced around, tumbled, and played, and when they ran back to her, they wore exhausted, toothy grins.

Audi mewed, and a string of drool leaked from Fortis' jaw. "I'm guessing you're hungry."

Back inside, the food scents drifting down the corridor made her stomach rumble. They must be near a dining room or kitchen. Kit could be there, too. "Let's get something to eat."

The cubs ears perked.

They rounded a corner to find a clump of men standing in the hall, all staring at something Gato was holding. The men's heads bobbed up to stare at her. Gato rolled his eyes, of course. She was getting used to that expression.

"Why are you here?" he said.

"What's going on?" she said.

Gato shoved from the crowd and stalked toward her. The cubs began to growl, and she loved that.

"You are more frustrating than a moregul," he said as he neared.

Bree pinched her skirt and curtsied. "I aim to please, m'lord."

"Enough!" He threw up his hands, one holding a matte-black ball, faceted like a golf ball. How strange. She wanted a closer look. "What's that?"

"A deactivated listening device. We are clearing the den of them."

"Who bugged you?"

"We are unsure," he said, and held out his palm for her to look at it.

She held up the ball. "I'd swear I've seen something like this before, except I can't remember where."

"Sadly, there appear to be many around Catamount to fire your memory."

"I don't mean that. I mean on Earth. Holy shit." Her eyes snagged on tiny engraved silver letters.

"What do you see?" Gato said.

"One sec." She pulled the ball close to make sure she'd read the word correctly. Oconus, preceded by the U.S. copyright symbol.

She had dated a guy who worked for a private military company. He'd said OCONUS meant Outside the Continental United States.

"Is that an Eleutian symbol?" She pointed to the copyright.

"Not one I have ever seen, Made One."

Was it possible? Then again, *she* was brought here from Earth. Why not stuff, too? "It's an Earthly symbol that means copyright, like ownership." She explained the meaning of OCONUS. "Is this from Earth?"

His face hardened to an impassive mask. "Possibly. Go eat. Your cubs are drooling all over the floor."

"That's it?" she said.

He gave her sleepy eyes and a husky voice. "For now."

Frustrating man.

Gato glared at the dull black ball in his hand. The listening device from Earth. He turned to Taz, his newly promoted chief of security. "Hand me another one."

Taz reached into his shoulder sack and gave him the device. That one, too, had the same strange symbol and name. His nostrils flared. The Alchemics had bugged Catamount with an Earthly object. Only their science Clan had the ability to pull objects to Eleutia. Most were harmless toys or tools sold covertly.

But this was no toy. Yet another breach of their covenant with the animal Clans.

Fury blinded him. He could do nothing to bring them to task. The pathetic Council of Clans now bowed in service to the Alchemics. Compass True, the rebel alliance bent on ridding Eleutia of their stranglehold, was already speeding toward war. Confronting Fukkes would merely prompt that shote's laughter.

The Fates, he wished to fark them all to Nixana. Their warrior goddess of Death would know exactly what to do with them.

He curled his hand tight around the ball. If he squeezed, he would destroy the device. But there were plenty more.

Calling a convene of Compass True would affect The Challenge, which must take place without interruption. The rebel alliance could use these devices. Something to ponder *after* The Challenge.

The ball in his hand made a satisfying crack, startling Taz. He dropped the ball into his cousin's bag. "Continue with Catamount's debugging."

"I will, cousin, but—"

"Yes?"

"Is the Made One safe?"

"As chief of security, I should be asking you that."

"Not what I mean." He scratched his chin. "What I am trying to say is that…well, perhaps she is a spy."

"For the Alchemics?"

His cousin nodded, hand on the hilt of his sword. Ah, Taz, ever seeking conspiracies where there were none. Perhaps he had made a mistake in elevating his relative to security chief. No, Taz deserved the appointment, had earned it. Gato drew him away from the others, an arm slung over his shoulder. "The Made One is not a spy, though she is desperate to find her missing sister, Sybelle."

"I have been searching, as you asked." He shook his head. "I have found nothing so far on the sister."

He snapped a nod. "Continue with the search."

"But you should consider her being—"

"She has asked to talk with the Alchemics about her sister, and they have refused." Intrigue was catnip for his cousin.

Taz scoffed. "A ruse. Let me investigate her."

Gato's patience, never his strongest suit, had thinned. "Leave it, Taz. I will see you in the command center this afternoon."

As Gato strode off to steal a few precious moments of privacy, Taz's eyes darkened with uncharacteristic anger. Gato made a note to find out why.

Back in his den, Gato stared blindly out the windows toward the town square below, hands threaded behind his back. All of CatHome and its people were his to keep safe. Occasionally, the weight of responsibility rested feather-light. Most days, it pressed him until he could barely breathe.

His eyes went to the portrait above the hearth. Ahanu… Fifty years younger than Gato and always smiling or laughing. More than two years earlier, his little brother had been conscripted by the Alchemics. Most believed Ahanu was at a university down south. A few knew the truth—that Ahanu's "conscription" was a kidnapping, the ploy to place Gato under Fukkes' thumb. And effective one, for he deeply loved his little brother.

In the square down below, five of the Sequestered waved up at him as they walked the path, their colorful pants, tunics, and dresses flapping in the northerly breeze. Each wore their distinctive helmets. His lips twitched at one woman's scarlet crest atop hers. Quite the statement, one he admired. He waved back to the women, though it hurt.

Having chosen to hide themselves, each eventually either revealed herself as open to courting or remained "other" forever. In the scheme of things, the Sequestered were but a small tragedy, yet he never ceased trying to coax them into the reveal. They were wanted, desperately, both as mates and as citizens.

Enough. He buried his melancholia and focused on the immediate problem. Dashing off a text to Compass True about the listening devices on his second mobile, the secure and illegal one, he then texted Calix, the Alchemic/Falcon and one of their spies in the Alchemic stronghold.

He might be unable to bring the Alchemics to task, but he could twist their devices to Compass True's advantage. Calix would help.

Weeks had passed since Calix had heard that conversation about bringing yet *another* Made One to Eleutia, and time was growing short for him to save the woman lying in the pod. His beautiful Made One.

He had been forced to wait, the Watcher they'd set on him clever, but Calix was more so. He'd been tempted to take the Watcher out, but to do so before the day they escaped would raise too many questions.

His frustration built and built. How ironic was it that in those weeks, he'd learned the shocking truth of the Cabal's ultimate plan?

He sat on the balcony outside his living area, a sweet breeze blowing from the west, his legs resting on the rail, and a ball of twine in his lap. He cut off a large length of string, tied it off, and began to build his Cat's Cradle, a game he learned from watching vids of Earth. Though it was a two-person game, he had found a solo version. The game soothed him and allowed him to think. He made his first move weaving the twine.

Should he notify Compass True about what he had learned or not?

Notification might precipitate war, which could prevent him from liberating his beloved Made One.

What to do?

He fumbled the twine and began again to build his Cat's Cradle.

Made Ones were created by taking Essences from Earthly women who were dying or severely aged and debilitated. Yet the process, in place long before his birth, troubled his ethics.

Deep in his soul, he agreed that the dying or infirm deserved the same bodily autonomy as young people in good health did.

Nevertheless, he went along with their conscription. All Eleutia did, except for the Anti-Made Ones, though their reasoning that Made Ones were an evil curse was absurd.

But recently, Calix had discovered the Cabal of Eleven was stealing *unsanctioned* Essences from Earth—healthy, vital humans.

Anathema. Forbidden. Horrific.

He had passed along the intel to Compass True's council leaders, but they could do nothing. Nor could he. The rebellion simply wasn't ready to confront the Alchemics. They didn't have the firepower.

The Cabal stored the stolen Essences in the secret vault known only to them and now to Calix and Neela, another Compass True spy. The thought shook him, and he tangled his Cat's Cradle again. He began anew.

Using these Stolen Ones' Essences, the Alchemics didn't plan to create Made Ones. No, each Cabal member was acquiring a single Stolen One's memories, skills, attributes, and the emotional outlook needed to understand how that person thought, felt, walked, and talked. To mimic them.

They'd taken one country's president, another's religious leader, and yet another's corporate titan. On and on. Eleven souls stolen. Eleven Earthly luminaries. Unlike the Made Ones' flesh, which was dead on Earth, the luminaries' comatose flesh remained alive. The Cabal planned to transfer their own Essences into the Stolen Ones' comatose flesh. Then they would arise.

Though within they were Alchemics, outwardly they would appear as the human leaders on Earth. The Cabal would become Earthly Alphas, men and women who ruled the planet. Diabolical.

Why the Alchemics wanted to rule Earth, Calix had no idea. Nor did he care. Their reasoning mattered little, their behavior not only unethical and cruel, but forbidden by the Alchemical Code. The bigger questions—if the Alchemic leaders left Eleutia with their hoard of technological secrets, would Eleutia herself be condemned to death?

CHAPTER SEVEN

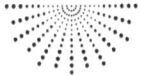

A server in the dining hall took Bree's order and said not one word about the two cubs lounging on either side of her chair. She ordered meat for them, as well.

Art lined the walls of the dining hall—frescos depicting the Cats' lives—while cloth dressed the tables and lit stars spangled the ceiling. Subtle music flowed quietly from speakers.

As the many tables in the hall began to fill, her eyes searched for Kit to no avail. A shadow darkened the table, and Bree looked up to see a tall woman—at least six-foot-three—with a muscular physique, a blond braid to her hips, and twilight-violet eyes.

The woman frowned. "Forgive me for staring."

Bree smiled, hoping to put the woman at ease. "Hello. I'm Breena. And you are...?"

The woman mumbled something even her new, acute hearing couldn't catch.

The Amazon cleared her throat, *smelled* Breena, and straightened her shoulders. "I am Fudge. My birth name is Malen'kiy, which means small, but no one calls me that. The nickname began when I was a cub." She shrugged. "It stuck."

Bree grinned. "You are no longer small, but epic. I might be jealous. No, I *am* jealous. Come, sit with me." She pulled out a chair.

The Amazon wrapped her hands around the chair back, but didn't move. "I am small compared to other Bear Clan women."

Bree could only imagine the other women's size. "You're a Bear?"

Fudge still didn't sit. "Yes. I am mated to a Cat, which some resent." Her smile transformed Fudge's face to radiant . "My mate, Axayacatl, is perfect. He has a nickname, too—Ax."

Mates and mating? She had a lot to learn. "Please join me, Fudge."

"I should not."

"Why?"

"You are the Made One. I didn't realize at first, not until I smelled you. Your cubs are beautiful."

Bree tapped the chair she'd pulled out. "I'd love if you ate with me."

Fudge peered around the room, nodded, and thumped into the seat. "Do *you* smell *me*?"

Odd. She sniffed. Soap, rosemary, horse. "You smell nice."

Fudge nodded. "That is good. Some Cats say I smell pungent."

"Whoever said that is rude." Bree put her napkin in her lap as the server placed her cactus soup on the table, then crouched down with plates of meat for the cubs.

Fudge leaned forward. "Order the sandwich, too. It is a new thing we learned from the Wolves before going to war."

"War?"

"Called off." Fudge waved over a server and ordered four sandwiches. "One is for you."

"Thank you." She tasted the cactus soup flavored with chilies, lime, and a hint of cilantro. "The soup's delicious."

Fudge shrugged. "I'm not fond of cilantro."

People came and went, and she tracked them all, hoping for sight of her sister. Tables filled and emptied, yet theirs, with eight chairs, remained empty except for herself and Fudge.

The server placed the platter of sandwiches on the table.

"Now this is good," Fudge said with a grin as she bit into a sandwich.

"It is," Bree said after she did the same.

The dining hall was now jammed, yet she didn't get why no one had joined them. Were they avoiding herself or Fudge?

Bree took another bite of her sandwich. "Have you met my sister, Kitlyn?"

Fudge's eyes widened. "No."

"You'd like her. You've seen her, though?"

"I *have*." Her face split into a smile. "She is very beautiful."

"Where did you see her?" Bree said.

Fudge stared at the table, her fingers fidgeting. "I cannot say. My Alpha…"

"It's okay." Others had seen Kit, and that meant everything. She didn't care what Gato said, Bree would find her, dammit. Together, she and Kit were unstoppable. They'd find Sybi, and… She wasn't quite sure what came next. "Kit *is* beautiful, inside and out."

Fudge chewed her mouthful of sandwich. "You are more so."

"We are attractive in different ways." Much of Kit's beauty was her solid belief in herself, whereas Bree's confidence was mostly fake, aided by plastic breasts, dyed hair, and glamorous clothes that had formed her big-top persona—assertive, skilled, assured. Without her armor…

"Your sister will be gone after The Challenge, unless Gato wins her."

"The Challenge?"

"It's the biggest event on all Eleutia," Fudge said with enthusiasm. "A Made One is offered up as the victor's prize."

"You're kidding. The prize? A *person* is the prize?"

Fudge stared at her plate. "I know it sounds bad, but Made Ones are our salvation. So The Challenge is held in order to distribute the Made Ones fairly."

"Distribute?"

"I can feel your anger." Fudge raised her head. "Sometimes, if I think hard about it, I get angry, too, that we are reduced to such. But without Challenges, wars would be fought over Made Ones, many would die, and…"

71

"Human beings are not possessions."

"No," Fudge said softly. "They are not."

Gato left Kitlyn's rooms satisfied the bugs were cleared from her suite, and once again surprised at how much he liked the woman. She was intelligent, competent, and determined, qualities he admired, not to mention she was a little wild. That appealed to him, too. Kit would be a fine partner.

Which was what he kept telling himself over and over.

As he walked, the scent of roasting beef and spices made him hungry. Mid-day meal had begun, and he was thankful the bug removal crew had cleared the hall earlier. With little scientific knowledge or equipment—only that which was pieced together—the Cats' research lab beneath Catamount would have to scramble to understand the workings of these devices.

"Hello, brother." A smiling Arina strode down the hall, stood on tiptoe, and kissed his cheek, which he returned with a hug.

"Good to see you, sister," he said. "How goes the debugging?"

"Well. The CatGuard and adolescent areas are secure, as are the classrooms and child-care rooms."

"Excellent." He clasped his hands behind his back and kept walking. "What about the Command Center?"

Arina slipped into stride beside him, hooking an arm through his. "Cleared, according to the text I received from Taz. Catamount will be free of listening devices by nightfall. This is all tiring, to be focused on these bugs. With The Challenge tomorrow, you should rest."

He barked a laugh. "Rest? When cats fly like mistrals."

"You mean they cannot?" Arina said with a quirk to her lips.

The sister he loved stared up at him, her green eyes a mirror of his.

Arina frowned at his sigh. "Not up for humor today?"

"Always!" He forced a grin.

She tilted her head, that secret smile she occasionally wore touching her lips. "You still plan to win Kitlyn?"

"Of course."

"What about this new one, this Breena?"

"A wildcat. She is proving to be a large pain in my ass."

Arina tilted her head. "Yet I have not seen you look at any woman the way you look at her. Not since..." She trailed off.

His sister almost voiced the name of his much-loved partner, Derula, long dead. "That look is frustration. This new Made One is beyond annoying."

"And Kitlyn is not?"

He laughed. "Amazing how two women can find their own individual ways to frustrate. I see their resemblance, but their natures are quite different."

His sister gave him a solemn, penetrating stare. "You are faking your attraction to Kitlyn, are you not?"

Staring into Arina's eyes, he saw wariness. "I admire her strength and courage, but she does not appeal to me in that way."

"A partner in name only?"

He knew where her words were going. "No, she will be my partner in full and produce a girl child. Perhaps, two. And you will be an auntie again!"

"The Fates, I had not thought of that." She chuckled, smiling up at him. "I would like that. Where are you headed?"

"The Great Hall," he said.

"I will come with you. I am hungry." Her eyes gleamed.

"You're always hungry, sister, yet you remain tiny as an elf."

"What is an elf?"

"From several Earth books I have read, elves appear to be small magical creatures."

She snorted. "I do not care for the small, but the magical I like."

He laughed. "I was sure you would."

The dining hall quieted as Gato and Arina entered the room, and diners nodded to the couple now threading their way through the tables.

Fudge placed her napkin on the table and backed out her chair. "I must leave."

"Why? You said dessert was the best part."

"It is, and may you enjoy it, Made One."

"Whoa." She rested a hand on Fudge's forearm.

"You...touched me."

Bree snatched her hand away. "Is that a bad thing?"

"No, I...thank you."

"Stay for dessert."

Fudge peered ahead, her face tightening as Gato and his sister approached their table. When they arrived, Fudge nodded, first to the Alpha, then to Arina. "Alpha. Commander."

"Leave," Arina said.

Fudge scraped back her chair and stood.

"No way," Bree stood as well, shoulders thrown back, chin raised, face autocratic. "Why should Fudge leave?"

"She is not one of us," Arina said.

"Neither am I." It would take more than Arina's burning eyes to frighten Bree.

"True," Arina said. "But you are an exceptional case."

Why wasn't Gato saying anything? "I was enjoying a delightful lunch with Fudge. I see no reason why you should spoil that."

"You do not understand our ways, Made One." Arina crossed her arms.

"So far, the ones I do understand, I don't much care for."

Gato speared her with a look. "Made One, Malen'kiy was a CastOut when Ax met her. By the orders of the Alchemics, they are rejected by their native Clans and cloistered. We allowed her to mate with Axayacatl and join us, but she remains separate from the Cats."

CastOuts...cloistered...*rejects*. "That's horrible. Even their name, the CastOuts. It's inhuman and inhumane."

Gato's smile was pained. "We are not human, Breena, but we *are* humane."

"She goes," Bree said. "I go."

"Good," Arina said.

"Sister, no," Gato said.

"It would please me if they left." Arina's eyes softened when she peered up at her brother.

The long look he gave Arina betrayed nothing, but then he shook his head and pulled out a chair. "I cannot." He sat at their table, his eyes on Bree, who again took her seat. "Fudge?"

Her Amazonian friend's stare took in Arina and Gato, her lips trembling. A gentle soul in an epic body.

Gato waved a hand. "Sit, Malen'kiy. Sit Arina."

"I find I am no longer hungry, brother." Arina whirled and left the hall.

"Join us, Fudge." Bree smiled up at her. "Dessert, remember?"

Fudge's eyes never left Gato's, as he offered her a smile that reached his eyes, his warmth compelling.

"I've never been this close to you, Alpha," Fudge said as she took her seat. "You have pretty eyes."

Gato started. "Thank you, Malen'kiy. Now what's to eat for midday?"

Bree was shocked when Gato went against his sister's wishes, even more surprised to find that while they ate their dessert, and Gato his meal, their conversation was rich, the laughter abundant. Other Cats took notice, a few stopping by their table for a word with their Alpha, where he proceeded to introduce both Bree *and* Fudge, which pleased her greatly. Several Peacekeepers stopped by.

"My first cousin, Taz," Gato said. "Our chief of security."

"Nice to meet you," Bree said. "Though I've seen you before."

He nodded. "That you have, Ma'am Breena."

A serious man, brown-haired and stocky, who looked nothing like Gato.

The Alpha rose, arm extended. "And this is Sir Ambrose."

After Bree greeted the older man with a goatee and salt-and-pepper hair, Gato explained that his "Sir" was an honorific for retired Peacekeeper officers. Gato embraced Sir Ambrose, and they slapped backs.

"How have you been, old man?" Gato said.

Ambrose's brows beetled. "Old man? Ha! I can still best you in a claws contest, you young cub."

When the pair moved on, Gato said Sir Ambrose would be her claws trainer, which sounded interesting. Perhaps something to enhance her martial arts skills.

"Ambrose is a brilliant fighter, one of our most lauded." Gato leaned close and pitched his voice low. "My sitting here, a small gesture regarding Fudge. For you, Made One."

As Fudge spoke with a flamboyant man wearing a sarong and dangly earring, Bree tilted her head toward Gato's and whispered. "A kindness for Fudge, Gato. Why don't the other Cats mingle with her?"

"Though now of our Clan, Fudge was born a Bear, and many fear her CastOut gifts."

"They have gifts?"

His eyes went to Fudge, who smiled at him. "You must ask her. We keep her origin secret from the Alchemics. Too dangerous."

Bree smirked. "Isn't 'danger' your middle name?"

"Of course!" He laughed, and his eyes darkened, but she'd swear behind the swagger, she saw sorrow. Perhaps Audi felt it, too, for she placed a paw on his thigh and peered up at him with her big blue eyes.

Gato scratched behind Audi's ear, eliciting a purr. "When the time is right, Ma'am Breena. When the time is right."

With those cryptic words, he stood, bowed to them, and departed.

She wondered what made a powerful Alpha like Gato so sad.

After mid-day, Bree and the cubs continued their search of Catamount for Kit until Fortis' paw tapped her leg.

Go!

"Where, Fortis?"

He notched his head toward the vast acreage outside the window and his paw landed on her thigh. *Out!*

Of course. Time to pee.

She donned the fuzzy jacket she'd brought and out they went, walking the stone paths of the many-acred curated plot filled with meandering trails and orchards of exotic trees that would blossom in spring. The sun was warmer than Bree had expected, and she tugged off her jacket, tying its arms around her waist.

As they wandered, Fortis and Audi roughhoused, chasing each other, drifting leaves, and waving grasses, Fortis peeing on every bush and tree. Bartholomew bounded over and began playing like a cub himself. In the distance, Bree saw Gato talking to a Peacekeeper.

Minutes later, Audi pooped, and Bree trolled her pocket for the kitchen rag she'd brought for just that occurrence. A soft buzzing began beneath Audi's scat, and the earth began to writhe.

"Eeep!" She stumbled backward.

The cubs and Barth stared at her.

From behind came the sound of soft laughter, and she whirled. "What's so funny?"

"Your eeep," Gato said as he sauntered closer.

She pointed to the churning earth. "What the hell is that?"

Gato stood beside the foot-sized clump of humming dirt, the earth churning as if by Rotorooter until it gradually subsided. "That was one of the strangest things I've ever seen."

"This park." Gato waved an arm. "It is a primary area for our Catamount cats to defecate."

"I still don't get it."

"Come. The sun is warm and that shade tree and bench look appealing. I will teach you all about tiger beetles."

Once seated, Gato began to speak. "Down in the southern continent, perhaps 500 years ago, the Alchemic Clan engineered tiger beetles, named so because those southern Alchemics are most associated with the Tiger Clans.

"Tiger Clans? Are the tigers the size of Barth?"

"The animals or the Clansmen?" he said, lips twitching.

"You are such a wiseass. Animals, of course!"

He chuckled. "Symbiont tigers are twice Bartholomew's size."

Picturing it boggled her mind. "I'd love to see one."

"I am sure someday you will."

In the distance, a couple hurried toward them carrying an infant. Gato grinned. "That's Jaron and Elise and their new babe. I will introduce you." He stood, as did she.

But when the couple closed on them, they weren't smiling. Both bowed their heads. "Alpha, Made One."

The fuzzy-haired infant was adorable, waving a wooden rattle as he peered at the world with wide eyes.

"How can I help?" Gato said to them, running his finger down the little one's cheek.

Jaron's lips thinned.

"Jaron?" Gato said. "Elise?"

The mother's eyes slid to Bree, but she said nothing.

"Excuse me," Bree said, sensing she was inhibiting conversation.

"Stay," Gato said, though he kept his eyes on the couple.

"But I—"

"Stay. What is the problem, Jaron?"

Bree tried to tune them out by wiggling her fingers in front of the infant. "Hello there." She looked up at the couple. "What's his name?"

Elise's smile was shy. "Kustaa."

"A strong name," Gato said.

A flush rose beneath the infant's cinnamon skin.

"No," Jaron said, fear in his eyes.

The rattle the baby held rose into the air and touched Bree's nose. It hovered for a moment, then fell to the ground.

Shooting stars. Levitation?

Everyone froze but Bree and the child. And, yes, the babe had done something really weird, which she guessed was freaking them all out.

"No!" Jaron said. "Kustaa must not—"

Gato laid a hand on Jaron's shoulder. "He must, and you know that or you would not have brought him to me. He will be kept safe and he will be loved. Their Alpha has assured me this, and I have seen such with my own eyes."

Elise was quietly weeping, and though Bree wasn't sure what was going on, she knew it must be bad.

"Take the time you need to accept this," Gato said. "Once you are prepared, we will then make arrangements. *They* see and hear. If Kustaa does not go, the consequences..."

"We know," Jaron said, stoic-faced. "We *know*. We will do what must be done."

Gato hugged them both, took the child in his arms, and kissed his cheek. He returned Kustaa to his mother. "Someday no child—"

"Soon, Alpha," Elise said with a plea. "Make it soon."

The trio left, Jaron stiff-backed and Elise weeping. The rattle rose once again, and Jaron snatched it from the air.

Gato slumped onto the bench and watched the family until they disappeared.

Bree sat beside him, and though she had at least a million questions, she asked none of them. When his eyes found hers, she expected to see sorrow. Instead, twin flames turned his emerald eyes bright with fury.

Bree reared back. "What just happened?"

He stuttered in a breath through clenched teeth. "Kustaa must join the CastOuts or he will be killed by the Alchemics."

"What? *Killed?*"

His hands scrubbed his face. "The Alchemics are shotes."

"The whole Clan can't be—"

"Oh, but they can. Understand this, Made One. The Clan once did much good." He left the bench and stalked to a clump of flowers waving in the breeze, returning with a yellow snapdragon. "Beauty for beauty."

"Thank you. Please explain?"

"The Alchemic Clan innovated healthy food for our plants and trees, immunizations, and even our mobile communication devices."

"My translator?" She pointed to the skin behind her ear.

Gato's face darkened, his brow thunderous. "A more recent innovation. With the advent of the first Made Ones two hundred or so years ago, the Clan has grown more and more insular." He frowned.

"Now they focus on their experiments, reproduction research, and the creation of Made Ones. They have distanced themselves from the larger world, their literal detachment increasing when they built their flying city."

"A flying city?"

"Yes. If a child is born with High Magics abilities, he or she must be cast out."

She harrumphed. "That's ridiculous. And if you don't do as they say?"

"If the child is not cast out, the Alchemics kill it."

She reeled. "But—"

"No but. It is law. No exceptions."

Bree tried to process what he was saying, but it sounded unreal, impossible. Who would kill that sweet infant because he lifted a rattle?

"The Alchemics were always different," Gato said. "The one clan unaligned with an animal, but they were accepted, even admired. As our women declined, and the Alchemics failed to solve the problem, they began creating Made Ones. Their power increased, as did their demands on the animal Clans. Days gone by, it was common for them to partner, even mate into our Clans and vice versa. Now, no Alchemic would think of partnering with one of us. They have piled laws upon laws to control us, including the death of any child differing from the norm."

"I can't conceive of..." She sputtered.

"No one of any conscience can." He heaved a breath. "Enough of this. I wish to hear more about your life in the circus and on the farm."

"But—"

"Please." His eyes softened.

Feelings like electric ribbons ran between them, pulling them closer and pulsing with energy. "Where to begin?"

"At the beginning, of course." His piratical laugh echoed through the garden.

Tingles skittered up her arms, and she smiled. "I was born

beneath a circus tent, during a show that my mother was performing in."

"Pregnant?"

She laughed. "You couldn't stop her."

His grin said it all. "This does not surprise me. Her act was…?"

"She was an equestrian, like Kit. So was my father."

"I see. You put in your first circus performance at birth."

"That I did!" Bree stared at her hands minus the calluses she always wore from her trapeze work. So many complex reasons for her choice, but really, it came down to one thing. "I chose the trapeze because I wanted to be different."

"From your parents." He placed a finger beneath her chin and raised her face to his. "I fought against becoming Alpha, my father's and grandsire's roles with the Clan."

"Same reason?" she said.

He nodded. "But in the end…" He spread his arms wide. "I had no choice. The Fates chose for me."

"Do you really believe that?"

He quirked his lips. "Perhaps. Or perhaps I am just that good."

She laughed, punching him lightly on his shoulder. "Were they as arrogant as you?"

His laughter boomed. "Not even close."

"I'm not sure I believe that."

"Wait," he whispered.

Taz stood watching them and signaled for Gato, who sighed. "I must go. Tell no one of Kustaa."

"I would never say a word."

"Thank you, Breena. For me, your presence was a comfort, a moment out of time." He bowed, then jogged toward Taz.

What a terrible and surprising conversation. Her heart ached for the family about to be ripped apart, and for Gato's pain. He'd been deeply affected, his feelings open wide. The man had been compelling before, but today she'd seen someone to admire, a man she could grow to like very much.

Darkness began its descent, Fortis took care of his business, the tiger beetles did their work, and they returned to the halls of Catamount. Though they searched for Kit, it was to no avail.

Back home, she lay on her bed trying to process the awful concept of killing imperfect children. That might have happened on Earth in the distant past, but now? If that were true, people like Stephen Hawking would never have proposed his brilliant theories and the great humanitarian Helen Keller would not have astonished the world. The utter ruthlessness of it floored her. Though their name was a debasement, she thanked the stars for the CastOuts who took in and nurtured those "flawed" children.

Tired and saddened, yet restless, she trolled the suite, finding a glow globe like Gato's in a closet, which delighted her, and a bottle of Kamla, which she didn't dare taste. And in a kitchen drawer, she discovered a sheet listing all her suite's verbal commands, which finally explained why her T.V. wouldn't turn on. One small victory in a strange and distressing day.

She flopped onto the couch. "Vidscreen on," and the T.V. blared. "Volume down!"

Down it went, and she listened to a reporter tout The Challenge, which he said would be broadcast in its entirety beginning at eight a.m. the following day. Videos of prior Challenges began to play onscreen.

Stars afire! Within the coliseum, what looked like Rome's gladiator games took place. Fortunately, nobody seemed to die, just get beaten to a pulp. The fighters were strong and clever, but really? A Made One as the *prize*?

Kit must be having fits. Her sister would not go gently, that much she knew for sure. Bree wished she knew what Kit was planning.

Later that evening, about to climb into bed, she lifted the folded note propped on her pillow, her name written in a bold scrawl.

She unfolded it—*As promised, you will see your sister tomorrow.*

For a single brief moment, excitement flooded her. And then she saw the underline beneath the word *see*. "Fuck."

She would *see* her sister, all right. *On T.V!*

Damn that self-important, egotistical prick of a man.

CHAPTER EIGHT

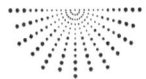

The Challenge commenced, and Fudge joined her to watch the games in her suite while Ax worked. When she first spotted Kit on T.V., she screamed her name, a wave of relief sweeping over her. She fist-pumped, too, which Fudge found entertaining.

Seeing Kit dolled up like some prize on *Let's Make a Deal* made her want to throw things. She imagined her sister fighting the whole process and was shocked when Fudge said Kit had come willingly to the Cats.

Whether Kit was a reluctant prize or an accepting one, Bree remained glued to the television. During the opening ceremonies, plenty of grandeur and marching took place before the dignitaries' grandstand.

"No!" Bree leapt to her feet.

A contestant shouted "Kill the Made One!" and threw two knives. The first missed Kit, but—*heavens stars!*—the other flew toward her sister's heart.

Arina shoved Kit away, taking the blade in her own shoulder.

Holy shit. Bree dropped back down on the couch, fingers fisting the cushions. Arina had saved Kit's life. Bree would make a bigger effort to warm up to the Cats' First Commander.

Fudge stared at her, eyes wide.

"Arina saved my sister," Bree said with awe.

Fudge squeezed her hand. "That she did, and I am not surprised. Our First Commander is CatHome's first defense, and a threat against your sister is one to CatHome, as well."

Over the subsequent three days of The Challenge, Bree saw blood, sweat, and lots of near-naked males fighting for the privilege of owning Kit. Barbaric, ridiculous, and thrilling, the event was like a combination of MMA fighting and ancient Roman gladiatorial competitions.

The men's honed bodies were exquisite—some elegant and others brawny—at least they were before they started bleeding. She watched Gato's bouts with both horror and fascination. His lean musculature and elegant movements were beautiful, his leaps and twists sinuous and electric. The only man close to his poetry of motion was the Wolf who'd attacked Kit's would-be assassin.

As an athlete, Bree appreciated the beauty and skill of the games, but as each day passed, her outrage grew at the thought her beloved sister was not only placed in danger, but treated as an object.

Fiery stars, was *she* to be a prize in The Challenge, too? That would suck.

If she only were at the games in person. Dammit, she had to talk to Kit.

But Gato had repeatedly refused, though he'd been regretful. Then went from regret to a quiet fury as he'd pointed out the Alchemic contingent in the dignitaries' grandstand.

She'd asked Gato to speak to them about Sybi, but when he'd done so, the Alchemics had shut him down with no word of her sister. What pricks.

Watching the spectacle, it became obvious Kit knew the Wolf. How interesting. Kit had been thrilled when he'd arrived on a *flying horse.*

The final day, Fudge again joined her. Amidst one of the contests, her friend raised her hand to wave at something out the window.

Another flying horse soared overhead, too high to see its rider. "So incredibly beautiful. How can you see who it is?"

"I can't," Fudge said, "But I recognize the mistral. I helped train her and know her rider well."

"You *train* mistrals?"

"Sometimes. I have always had a way with them. It is a hobby."

"Wow. Talk about a hobby."

When only three fighters remained, one being the Wolf and another Gato, Kit disappeared from her seat.

Odd. But…she'd bet the stars and the moon Kit had some plan in place.

"Would you like more troff?" Fudge said, refilling her glass.

"No, thank you," Bree said.

Holy shit!

A new participant entered the arena dressed in white leather and wearing a hood. *Oh, ho!* Bree began to laugh like a maniac.

"What is so funny?" Fudge said.

"You'll see. I don't want to spoil the surprise."

Fudge gave her a "you crazy?" look and shrugged.

Neither the crowd nor the judges recognized Kit. Her brilliant, beautiful sister was going to fight for herself. How cool was that?

"The white combatant will pick the Wolf next," Fudge said. "The weakest of the two remaining."

But Kit chose Gato to fight first. Her sister definitely liked that Wolf.

"That makes no sense," Fudge said. "Why would he pick the stronger of the two?"

"Not sure 'he' is a he," she mumbled.

The pair engaged, and Kit threw Gato with a judo move, followed by a karate chop. Ouch. Taekwondo, krav maga, capoeira—Kit drew from the many skills learned over decades at the dojo. Gato was getting creamed, and her twinge of sympathy for the Alpha surprised her.

"What is the white fighter doing?" Fudge said.

"Earthly fighting styles called martial arts."

But Fudge wasn't paying attention to her, only the bout, which enthralled them both. Bree began to clap, the cubs picking up on her excitement and mewing.

Ohhh. Ouch! Oh, dear. Wow! "Yes!"

"He won," Fudge said with awe. "He beat our Alpha."

"Whoohoo!" shouted Bree. "Just you wait, Fudge!"

And when Kit pulled off her mask, both Fudge and the crowd gasped.

"I am the victor of the Made One Challenge," Kit said as the crowd hushed. "I am Kitlyn, the Made One, and I get to choose. I choose me. I choose the freedom to have a choice. I deserve it, and I have won it. No Made One should be forced into commitment, rather than having a choice.

"You are a fair and just people. A good people. Heed my words. I choose *me*."

Bree hugged Fudge, laughing aloud.

Kit had flipped their fucking Challenge on its ass. *Go, Kit!*

Now her sister was walking toward that Wolf, her steps purposeful.

"Come!"

Bree whirled. She'd been so absorbed, she hadn't heard Arina enter. Gato's sister sported a sling and a scowl, and Bree leapt up and hugged her, careful of her injury. "Thank you for saving my sister."

Arina stiffened, patted Bree's shoulder, then pushed her away. "I was happy to do your sister that service." Arina nodded. "Come. You are to see your sister in the flesh. My brother insists."

Gato had lost. He was not used to losing. That bastard Rafe, now cozying up to Kitlyn, must be laughing his head off. Gato had lost to a woman.

And yet, he should not be surprised by that fact. For centuries Eleutia's women had fought beside their men, had been courageous, often heroic in battle, with some attaining the position of Alpha. The lack of female births had changed everything.

He had one more card to play to keep Kitlyn. A dirty one so loathsome he shied away from it, even as he knew in his bones he had no choice. The Alchemics would hurt his brother.

It was time. He signaled the guards.

Arina demanded Bree change into a formal blue gown, spangled with what looked like topaz and sapphires, the hem trimmed in gold.

"These are paste, right?" she pointed to a sapphire.

"Paste? No, they are gems from Mother Terra."

She was wearing a fortune in jewels. The irony hit her, and she laughed and twirled, the jewels sparkling. The gown flowed around her, allowing movement, though the low bodice gaped. Since the dress had been crafted for someone with greater assets, she stuffed toilet paper down there so she wouldn't look totally ridiculous.

Now, she sat in an absurd throne-like chair, three guards shielding her view of the stadium ground.

"If you rise," Arina said. "If you speak or move toward your sister, Kitlyn's guards will hurt her."

"My ass, they will. This is ridiculous. Why can't I talk to her?"

Arina didn't answer.

Hurting Kit was probably a bluff, this being some choreographed play she suspected Gato had cooked up. But Bree wouldn't test it. It didn't matter. She had a secret, one she would use when she saw Kit.

Some signal must have gone off, because two of Bree's guards stepped aside to flank Arina, with the one remaining beside her.

Kit!

Bree gripped the curved arms of the chair so she didn't bolt toward her, but she kicked her leg out, striking the remaining guard in the shin, she was that pissed. He didn't even grunt, damn him.

Kit was running toward Bree when Gato grabbed her, except Kit whirled on the Cat, and then the Wolf punched Gato in the face.

Bree flinched. She didn't like the Wolf hitting Gato, whose lip was bleeding. Damn that Wolf.

The two men argued, but Bree's eyes remained on Kit. Only Kit. Now what? Her sister and Gato were talking. Bree caught the word "choose" and Kit's subsequent fury. Seriously? Gato was making Kit choose something?

The Wolf had again moved close to Kit, and he bent and spoke low. She wished she could hear. Bree's anger felt like a boil inside her that was about to burst.

Kit placed a hand on the Wolf's cheek. Oh, wow, Kitlyn's feelings for the Wolf were deep.

If Gato was making Kit choose between Breena and the Wolf, she would shoot him.

Time for action. She erased her guard's smirk by socking him in the solar plexus, then caught Kit's eye, and winked.

Now, for their ace in the hole.

Bree began to speak, not with her voice but with her hands, signing the ASL they'd all learned to communicate with their youngest sister. Impish Marie might be long gone, but her memory and their knowledge of hand-talking remained.

Go, she signed. *I've got this.*

No, Kit replied in rapid ASL. *You must come with us to WolfHome.*

Accompanying Kit now... Alluring. She'd bet Kit had a plan for Bree's escape, too. But the Cats would fight it. Gato would fight it. If she fled, from what Fudge had told her, there would be war. People dying, others hurting. Nope.

If Kit wanted that Wolf, she should have him, and not on a funeral bier.

Bree centered herself and signed.

I want to stay. Don't worry. I'll be ruling CatHome before I'm done. She grinned.

This isn't a joke, Kit signed.

Who said I was joking? Her big sister could be deeply serious, taking the world on for either Bree or Sybi, or both. Not today, dear one. Bree made a brushing motion, winked, and mouthed *Go!*

Kit lifted a hand to her heart and yelled, "Love you, Bree!"

Bree returned their time-honored sisterly gesture. *Ha!* Gato was pissed.

Kit's group had moved closer, and she heard her sister say, "I choose Rafe."

Ah, Kit's Wolf was named Rafe. Bree liked it. Beneath the bruises and blood, she could see he was pretty darned hot, though not blessed with the elegance of the Cat Alpha.

The Wolf gave Kit a searing kiss, which Kit answered with great enthusiasm.

Not being with her sister hurt, yet joy filled her at Kit's happiness.

Arina bustled her out of the grandstand and down the steps, again shielded by the guards. A whooshing of air, the beating of wings, and in the sky, a flying horse, black as Hades, with wild eyes and a gleaming coat. Bree shoved at the guards, but they didn't budge.

By standing on tiptoe, she could see enough. A judge ran from the stands and started waving his arms and babbling at Kit. Bree grinned. Her sister was having none of it as she helped Rafe onto the black mistral.

A scream from above, and a second mistral flew high in the sky, a marvelous, curly coated one with silver hooves, its black mane and tail flying.

A hand banded her upper arm.

"We go now," Arina said.

"One more minute." She wanted to see Kit safe out of CatHome.

"Now. My brother is furious, and you will bear the brunt of that fury."

As if she cared. She snatched her arm away, warm thoughts of Arina evaporating. "I can live with that."

A movement high above, and Bree cupped a hand over her eyes to watch Kit and Rafe soar high atop the two mistrals. Good for them. She raised a hand and waved, then stalked back to Catamount.

Bring it on, catman. Bring it on.

Minutes later, Bree hung up the blue dress with much difficulty, the swarming cubs bumping and rubbing her, blasting their glee as if she'd been gone days, rather than an hour. Silly kits.

After feeding the cubs, she made a plate of cheese, bread, and grapes. Perhaps food would soften Gato's anger. She got out glasses and chilled water, then brought it all into the living room, eager for Gato to bulldoze in and rail at her. She'd give him the tussle he was looking for.

But Gato never came.

The expected call came a day later, and Gato snapped on the vidscreen. Fukkes stared back at him, those crystal teeth flashing in a smile, but his eyes seethed with anger.

"You lost," Fukkes said.

Gato wouldn't bow to this man. "I did, in a fair fight."

"That, we saw. Nonetheless, you lost Kitlyn. Bring him," he said to a man off camera.

A guard led in Ahanu, his wrists manacled, hair plaited, face stoic.

"You dare bind my brother!" Gato said.

"Dare? Oh, ho, we dare much more, *friend.*"

Another guard entered to flank his brother, and each gripped a shoulder and shoved Ahanu into a chair beside Fukkes.

"Such a fine kitty cat," Fukkes said, and ran a finger down Ahanu's face.

Gato nearly exploded. A terrible thing was about to happen, and he wanted to scream and rail and reach through the vidscreen to steal Ahanu away. Instead, his cat sense at the fore, he gathered the strength and power to remain still and silent no matter the cost.

A knife flashed, and Fukkes sliced off Ahanu's right ear.

Gato's scream never left his lips.

Just as Ahanu had done. He had neither moved nor uttered a cry, his rapid blinking his only sign of pain.

Bright red blood flowed down his brother's neck as Fukkes held up the amputated ear. Gato drew more strength from Clan and cats, enabling him to remain still amidst his howling fury and grief.

"An important thing, an ear," Fukkes said. "You will note, I gave you a boon. I could have taken a hand, a tongue, an eye. Do not disobey us again."

In slow measured tones, Gato said, "You will pay a price for maiming my brother."

Fukkes shrugged. "Whereas, you have already paid."

"Vidscreen off!" Gato screamed.

At WolfHome's underground lab, Tilde bubbled with excitement as she fine-tuned their newest scramblers.

The Challenge had been incredible, Kit's victory amazing. And she'd appreciated that her mice had waited to give birth until she had returned from CatHome.

Her disrupter had only worked on a single dragonfly, from which they'd retrieved a full capsule before her creation caught fire, a failure she'd have to rectify later. Today's project was to sext the baby mice.

Weeks earlier, she'd set up splendid multi-level cages for the three pregnant mice and given them straw and toilet paper to build their nests. One, Two, and Three had birthed litters containing ten, seven, and nine pinkie mice. The mouse named Two ate several of her pinkies before Tilde noticed. Unfortunate. She also thought it was gross, but that was unscientific and she'd never tell.

Today was the sixth since their birth, and the twenty-two remaining now-furry pinkies had begun climbing into their food dish and drank from the water bottles. Old enough to be handled, which was the only way to reveal their sex, she messaged Rafe, Kit, and Max.

Gender was hard to tell with baby mice, but she'd been tutored by her Tortoise friend, a master.

Rafe arrived sweaty from physical therapy, as he'd been badly damaged in The Challenge. Kit and Max appeared together, and

Rafe immediately swooped in to kiss his love. Tilde forced herself to look anywhere but at the romantic duo, except when she caught Max's eyes, his were devouring her.

The confounding man had never embraced her that way, like a lover. Not once. "Best get started," she said in a too-cheery voice, nerves prickling her skin.

She placed a gray baby mouse from Three into her palm and raised its tail, its back legs off the ground. "The small hole beneath the tail is their anus. A female mouse's vagina is just beneath its anus, while you should see the baggy scrotum on the males. The mouse I'm holding is male. Now pick a mouse and do the same and we can compare. I've set up magnifying glass stations and printed images to guide your assessment."

Max rolled his eyes. "Why do we even need to do this? Looking at a mouse's butthole?"

"Cut it out, Max," Rafe said.

"It's important," Tilde said with a huff. "We must determine their sex. Period. Let's look at our mice." She placed the pinkie in a cage separate from its mother, made a note about its sex, and lifted another pinkie from Three's cage. "It's hard, sexting."

Kit giggled.

"What?" Tilde said, poking the bridge of her glasses.

"On Earth," Kit said, "sexting means sending explicit sexual images of yourself to someone by mobile or computer."

Rafe shook his head. "Why would anyone do that?"

"People are more sexually conservative on Earth," Kit said. "And it's titillating."

"I think my mouse just shote in my hand," Max said.

"You'll live," Tilde said.

"Thank you," Max said. "Miss Science Smartypants."

"Go fark yourself," Tilde said with a grin.

Max smiled slow and hot. "Not nearly as much fun as—"

Rafe growled. "Back on track everyone."

"Ready?" Tilde said.

They took their mice to their stations and raised their tails.

"This makes sense, but..." Max stared at his mouse. "Why does this matter? Don't all the mice in WolfHome drink the same water?"

Tilde nodded. "True. But not Three." She pointed to the third cage that held a gray-and-white mother and babies. "I ended up buying bottled water from a mom-and-pop company above the northern Pellopines."

"Whoa," Max said. "That stuff is pricey. Their ad copy says it's got lots of good minerals and vitamins."

"It *is* pricey," Tilde said. "I originally hoped to source it from my Tortoise friend, but his spring unfortunately dried up. Since the bugs' purpose seems to affect the Wolves's water, untainted water is essential to the test."

"Let us have at it," Rafe said.

Their first round produced four males.

The second round, the same.

The third round, three males and a female from Three.

The fourth round, three males and a female from Two.

The fifth round, four males.

Two baby mice remained.

By the time they got to the final two pinkies, Tilde had trouble containing her excitement. One more female and... She and Rafe cupped a pinkie each, One and Three's get.

"Male," Rafe said.

"I've got..." Tilde pulled up the tail from the Three pinkie, and her hope deflated. "Male."

They placed the mice back in their nesting cages.

"It's easy to get the sexes wrong," Tilde said. "We'll check them again in a week. We can see the nipples then. The males don't have any, but the females have ten. They'll look like little indentations."

"You are discouraged," Rafe said.

She pasted on a bright smile and quipped, "The nature of science. But I've ordered six opossums, three females, three males, from my Tortoise friend."

"Why?" Max said.

"They gestate in twelve to thirteen days and have twelve-to-twenty joeys each."

"Joeys are babies?" Kit said. "An Earth term."

Tilde grinned. "It is. I read the name in a book our historical scribe gave me!"

In the midst of washing his hands, Rafe paused. "You told Yuan?"

"I did *not*." Tilde had felt failure before, but she was an optimist and had a dollop of hope left. "The opossums' different biology may produce different results."

Rafe looked grim. "This is taking too much time. Your findings must be ready for the fair's Compass True meeting. How can you possibly be?"

"Persistence," Tilde said.

CHAPTER NINE

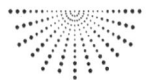

Weeks passed where Bree's frustration grew as she was shuttled around Catamount like a UPS package. She should have gone with Kit.

No, her decision was sound, and to her surprise, Gato permitted them to talk on the phone and vidscreen. She and Kit discussed everything, including what each was doing to find Sybi.

WolfHome had sent scouts throughout the Northwest Quadrant, hunting for information, and Gato had assured her he had done the same. So far, no luck. Bree had also gotten a list of Alphas from Gato, who'd agreed to her writing them about Sybi, and she anticipated their replies with fingers crossed.

Though she loved her conversations with Kit, she ached to see her in the flesh, to talk face to face, to hug her.

That didn't happen. According to Gato, it was too dangerous for them to either visit WolfHome or to host Kit here. She'd seen how Kit had been attacked at the games, and he told her about the Anti-Made Ones, men and women who opposed Made Ones' creation. They had become increasingly violent, injuring a Bear Made One and killing a Made One of the Ferret Clan.

Instead of a visit to her sister, she was hauled to the library, where she studied Eleutian history, and though it fascinated her, she'd never let on. Two guards accompanied her daily to the armory, where her rigorous arms training proceeded with knives and bows. As Gato had said, Sir Ambrose taught her to fight with the claws, weapons she strapped to the backs of her hands. She loved the arms training, which honed her muscles and sharpened her reflexes, not to mention teaching her the use of weaponry. Though she made sure to complain—she was in essence a prisoner—from the looks the trainers and Gato threw her, she suspected they knew she enjoyed her workouts, too.

The days passed swiftly, and she'd write notes to Gato, the old-fashioned kind, asking to see her sister and if he'd had any word of Sybi from his scouts. To say his replies were terse was laughable.

No and No was his daily response.

He was being his imperious self, and she believed him about the danger to herself and Kit, and that he knew nothing of Sybi's where-abouts. From what she'd seen, he had never lied to her.

Bree would scan Catamount's daily newsletter on her new tablet, but no hint of another found Made One was mentioned, nor did CatHome's intranet offer any answers. The Alchemics had to know, and yet each time she asked to vidscreen with them, they refused.

"They are like this," Gato had said. "They act like the gods they are not, caring little for our world or its inhabitants."

"It's their world, too."

"True. But their Comstat Fukkes heads their Cabal of Eleven. The Cabal makes all decisions for the Alchemics. I am sorry, Made One, truly sorry. I know what it is to long for a loved one."

He turned away, and she rested a hand on his shoulder. "What's wrong? Is someone holding something over you?"

"Ha!" He threw up his hands. "Who could hold something over the most powerful Alpha on Eleutia, eh?"

Sure. But she could only press him so far. "Then what's wrong?"

He walked to the window. "Nothing you can fix, Breena. It is unimportant."

She came up behind him. "Whatever it is, I'm sorry."

He faced her. "Why?"

"Because I've watched you around Catamount. You're a kind and decent guy."

"Decent? I'd like to think so, but kind?" He grimaced. "I am not kind."

"I saw the time you helped that teen in the library with his homework."

He shrugged. "I had nothing better to do."

"Of course you didn't. What about when you adjudicated a dispute between a Cat and a Falcon over a female Cat? I could see it was hard, but you found for the Falcon."

"Naturally. He had the right of it. That does not make me kind."

"The time you helped that family raise the barn behind their home?"

"It is a community effort. Why do these things matter?"

"Or when I watched you begin the children's arms training the first day?"

"That is my duty."

Bree shrugged. "All true. But I've come to know you a bit, and I've watched your face during those and other times. Your love and care for your people shines."

His eyes narrowed. "Naturally I love my people."

"And do all Alphas behave as you do?"

"You are being ridiculous."

"You always deflect when you don't want to answer me. Who has a hold over you, Gato?"

He threw up his hands and stalked off.

"You do that, too," she hollered. "All. The. Time!"

When the cubs turned four months, Gato added CatGuard training for them and Breena. The elite military of CatHome consisted both of men and cougars. Bree used hand signals and voice commands, and the practice was a hoot for her. Less thrilled were her cubs, who complained loudly when they returned to the suite.

She saw little of Arina, but Gato was a frequent presence when he wasn't off Alpha-ing. They ate together often, and even watched several vidshows about Eleutia, with him explaining in detail what she didn't understand. He mentioned wanting to learn Kit's fighting style and the "hand signals" she'd used with Kit.

She would never teach him ASL, but she might teach him a few Taekwondo moves. Someday. But she couldn't help admiring his curiosity.

Gato was a font of knowledge, a student of Eleutian history, and he grew animated explaining historical culture, politics, and battles. Equally fascinated with Earth, he asked numerous questions and often made her laugh with his shock at her descriptions of reality T.V., zip lining, and Las Vegas, among other things. At a party celebrating the birth of a CatGuard's child, they danced several dances evoking contra, Scottish country, and old French-style court dances.

Afterward, Gato accompanied her to her suite. Though they were both sweaty and tired, the blood in her veins sang, and she invited him in.

"Shall we share some troff?" he said.

"What about kamla? I found some in the fridge and Fudge said it was rare and unfermented."

"It's delicious, the non-alcoholic version of ilaberry wine. The ilaberry bush grows high in the Pellopines, and harvesting the berries is a perilous undertaking. I thought you would enjoy it. Sit. You look to drop where you stand. I will get it."

When he returned with the bottle of kamla and two glasses, placing them on the table, she was still standing.

"I have an idea. I'd like to teach you the waltz."

He arched a brow.

"It's an Earth dance." She didn't know why she wanted to waltz with him, yet she did. Very much.

"You haven't had enough dancing?" He grinned.

"Never." She held out her arms in the waltz position and showed him the steps. "Well? Come on."

He walked into her embrace.

"Normally, the man leads, but I will until you learn."

"Ah, now I see." His grin was devilish. "This is all about you leading me around."

She answered his irresistible smile with a smile of her own. "Of course it is. Vidscreen on. Play the music I requested at three-quarter time, with the strong accent on the first beat of the measure."

"Ready?" she said to Gato. "It's a simple movement. *One*-two-three, *one*-two-three. Here we go."

His sinuous elegance delighted her, his body moving in harmony with hers. And after about five minutes, he stole the lead, and it was as heavenly as she had imagined. When he drew her close and whirled her around the room, her belly coiled tight.

The music stopped.

"That was great," she said, breathless. "Did you like it?"

"A dangerous dance," he said, face serious. "One that I confess I enjoy. We will teach the Clan." His head bent toward hers, and she tilted her face up to those sculpted lips she wished to kiss.

He studied her, his emerald eyes darkening. What did he see? In him, she read desire and longing and… His eyes shuttered, and he squeezed her hand and stepped back. "I could use some of that kamla right now."

"I could, too." She hid her disappointment with a curtsy. "Thank you for the dance."

"I thank *you*, Made One, for opening my eyes to new ways."

"It was just a dance," she said, still missing his embrace.

"Was it?"

Even as Bree grew more and more beguiled by the Cat Alpha, she needed an escape plan. Just in case. She tried three potential routes, and while she was turned back each time, she found the strongest possibility in the mesa above Catamount. But with reluctance, she admitted she was torn about leaving. Catamount was becoming home.

Her pursuit of Sybi was a daily frustration, but she persevered, while her friendship with Fudge solidified. Some days, Ax joined them at mid-day meal, as did Gato, Sir Ambrose, and Taz. Fudge and Ax made an interesting couple, his volubility a contrast to Fudge's quiet nature. Sir Ambrose was jovial, except when he was training her, and quiet, taciturn Taz watched all with intense focus. When various Cats stopped by their table to talk or pet the cubs, Bree made a point of introducing Fudge and schmoozing, and surprisingly, the Cats began to warm to both of them.

But not Arina, who either ignored her or was painfully formal when she deigned to speak. Bree was okay with that.

When alone, she practiced her martial arts and gymnastics, which was satisfying. Oddly, this new flesh demanded she set up a rig and fly. So strange because she'd lost all heart for the trapeze when she'd watched Mordecai plummet to earth. Her love was dead in seconds, as was her love for aerial work.

Yet she longed for a fly bar, the call of the catcher and the moment the return began, when she'd do an angel or a flip or a double-double to hit the bar with confidence. The urge was so strong, some days she'd swear she heard Mordecai's "Gotcha!"

That Tuesday, when she returned to her suite to get her claws for training, she got Gato instead. He stormed in like a dust devil, accompanied by Barth, carrying a large box he set on the sofa table.

"What the hell?" she said.

The big panther herded his cubs into the bedroom.

Gato rounded on her, and she stumbled backward.

"What has frightened you?" He moved slow, palms open, eyes soft.

"You. I was once punched in the face, and I've never forgotten it. You had that same look in your eyes."

With care, he cupped her cheek. "Hit you? *Never*. And if anyone dared do so, he would not survive." He stepped back, his expression mischievous. "Strangle you, perhaps. You have tried to escape three times with our cubs."

"No I haven't. I've been dipping my toe in the waters, is all. If I want to leave, your guards will never know."

"Why are your lips so red? As if you have kissed—"

"No one. The color's from berries. Duh."

"Berries?"

She sighed. "Because I wanted some lipstick."

He tilted his head. "Why? Your lips are perfect."

They were? "Never mind about my lips. I am a prisoner, and I have the right to escape."

"You are no prisoner. Understand, the Anti-Made Ones are vicious. And on your explorations, you took our cubs. They must stay at CatHome. You do understand this?"

"Not exactly," she said. "We're bonded. Don't they go where I go?"

He shot her a sour look. "They are also CatGuard and of the Clan."

"Ah. Let me get this clear. I can't leave without Fortis and Audi, who are now part of my being, or I can leave without the cubs, something I could never do. Which says I am nothing but a prisoner."

"You are not," he said, voice husky. "You are more, far more."

"So I can go to the Wolves and my sister?"

"Do not." He drew in a deep breath. "Please."

He'd shocked her.

When he clasped her to him, she was stunned into stillness. Their breaths mingled, his hot and scented with cinnamon. His eyes burned, and she desperately wanted his lips on hers. Her bones melted, and she pressed closer, his flesh steel beneath his clothes, his cock insistent. He bent forward as if to devour her, and yet he kept those damnably appealing lips from hers. Her hands clasped his stubbled cheeks, and she stood on tiptoe.

"Ma'am Breena, did you forget..." Sir Ambrose stood framed in the doorway, red-faced. "Oh, apologies. Deepest apologies." He bowed, then whirled and vanished.

Gato rested his forehead on hers. "I should not touch you. Never touch you."

"Why? Because I'm meant for The Challenge? To be handed off to some stranger, to leave CatHome? You? My cubs?"

He stepped back from their embrace and shook his head. "We will see."

Bree snorted. "I'll never stand for it." She grabbed her tablet and walked to the couch focused on the screen, because she couldn't let her burning eyes reveal how much his words hurt. When she felt him near, she glanced up. He wore his damned detached Alpha mask.

"Explain how she did it?" he said as he sat across from her.

"Who and did what? I'm going to get some troff." She padded to the kitchen. She should be furious. The Challenge? No way in hell. Yet Gato was torn. That was obvious. It almost seemed as if he didn't want to put her up for the Challenge any more than she wanted to be a prize. If that were true, who could pressure him into it and why? They'd talked about it, but he'd deflected.

Bree took two bottles of troff from the fridge and opened them.

Whether he was the most powerful Alpha on Eleutia or not, it would take incredible force to compel Gato to do anything. For something as large as The Challenge, an expensive and time-consuming event, few could exert that pressure.

Arina?

Another Alpha?

The Alchemics?

From all she'd heard, those scientists liked control. They were patronizing and demanding, and they dominated the animal clans via technology.

She set the bottles of troff and glasses on the sofa table. "Gato?"

"Hum?" His eyes turned from the window toward her.

"What are the Alchemics holding over you?"

He reached into a vest pocket, pulled out a silver flask, and arched a brow. "Nothing."

Truth or lie—she couldn't tell when he wore that stoic mask. Pressure him now, and he'd dig in his heels. She pointed to his flask. "What are you drinking?"

"Kevitt."

"That's alcoholic. Pretty rude."

His brow furrowed, but he screwed the top on and replaced the flask in his pocket. "You are right, of course. Forgive me." She poured him a mug of troff.

"Thank you." He took his drink. "How did your sister defeat me?"

Bree laughed. "That's something Kit will have to tell you." With the Eleutians unschooled in the martial arts, Kit had been unstoppable. Little did he know Bree and Sybi were her equals.

"You could." He drank, staring at her over the rim of his mug. "I would bet my mistrals on it."

"Ask Kit."

He sat back on the sofa and spread an arm across the back. "I expected that would be your answer. Fine. If you want to see your sister, you will tell me."

She didn't get him. He wanted her, yet he restrained himself. He was often considerate, yet he could be so damned demanding, too. She sipped some troff. It might not be alcoholic, but it was delicious.

"Do you always use blackmail to get what you want?" she said.

His lips quirked. "Often."

"Prickface."

His bellowed laugh made her insides fizz. He *was* a prickface. Unfortunately, he was also warmhearted, tender, and appealing. Fuck.

"You will teach me," he said, nodding as if it were a *fait accompli*.

Ha. "No, I won't."

"In a week, your sister and the Wolf are having their mating ceremony. Before then, I will know some of those moves, and then Arina, you, and I will go to the mating."

Mated to a Wolf. Happiness burst inside her, and she nearly teared up. Kit was in love, the only way she'd agree to a ceremony like that. Stars alive.

Perhaps she could teach Gato some martial arts. She wasn't a sensei, but she could show him some moves. He would be adept at them, given his strength and the way he moved. Sure, he was blackmailing her, so she'd mollify him and get to see Kit. Not that she would make this request easy for him. *Maybe* I'll teach you."

"If you teach me well, I will also bring you to the fair."

"And I should care about some fair because...?"

"You will see jugglers and fire breathers."

"Which we had in the circus."

"Mistrals, as well."

"Eh." She shrugged, though that would be a thrill.

"There is dancing and food and..." He paused, letting his smile grow. "And trapeze artists."

The idea of flying again... No. She shrugged. "I've seen many."

He held up a hand, index finger raised. "Oh, and Kitlyn will attend the fair with her mate."

She batted his hand away. Baiting her, that's what he was doing, and he'd saved the juiciest lure for last.

Gato leaned forward. "Teach me to fight as she did." His eyes softened. "I would be in your debt."

When he was open and honest, he undid her. This man. *This man.*

"I will teach you." Bree had studied for years. Gato would take years, too. "As long as you promise not to use the arts against me, my sisters, or Kitlyn's mate."

His face tightened. "Why do you care about the Wolf?"

"Duh. He's going to be my brother-in-law. Kitlyn loves him. You can be a bully, you know. You orchestrate everything to come out the way you choose, without thinking of the other person's feelings. Sometimes, you're a selfish, self-centered bully."

She expected a sneer, instead she got a frown and a sigh. "I am all that and more."

"Why? You are good to your people. An honorable and humane leader. Arrogant, yes, but not mean-spirited. Why do you bully me? Why twist and turn Kitlyn to your own desires? You're not power-hungry. You don't need money. Why? "

CHAPTER TEN

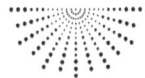

"**E**xcuse me," Gato said. "I must use your facilities."

He strode into the bath as if chased by goddarts and sat on the edge of the tub.

If Breena only knew. Terror had streaked from Gato's gut when she had asked about the Alchemics' hold over him. Fortunately, she knew nothing. And he could not tell her. The lives at stake mattered, including his brother's.

Night after night, he saw again his brother's ear cleaved from his head. His hands squeezed into fists. Fukkes taking Ahanu's ear was a gauntlet thrown down, one that said "we rule you." And yet, the move hinted at desperation as well.

Why?

The Clan had once been Eleutia's scientific saviors, admired men and women who invented mobile phones and vidscreens, discovered the rampage death cure and the vaccine for sarsanoma fever. What had changed?

The people themselves. No, not quite. As the Cabal of Eleven ascended to power the Clan's insularity, coupled with their demands on the animal Clans, had increased. He had ideas as to why, as he would bet Rafe, once like a brother, did as well. These Alchemic's escalations drove him to near madness, and he missed Ahanu's calming presence now more than ever.

And that woman. She was his bane and his bliss. He longed to touch her, to know her, to understand her.

Their sublime almost-kiss had turned disastrous when Sir Ambrose had walked in on them.

The Made One was a sorceress who kindled his mind, stirred his soul, and fired his blood. He chuckled. Not to mention his cock. Her potent allure could prove deadly for Ahanu.

Yet Breena shined so bright, her colors painted in bold strokes. He wished to hold tight to that combustible, contrary creature who seldom left his mind and plagued his dreams. Each time the urge came to claim her, he again saw Ahanu's stoic face, the blood. And the pain. *The Fates.*

A soft knock at the door. "Are you okay?"

He scraped his hands across his face. "Of course!" He flushed the toilet, washed his hands, and pulled open the door. "Can't a man take care of business?"

"Uh, yeah. But you were gone for a half hour. I thought you fell in."

He winked. "I did not. I am pleased you will teach me that fighting style. When we return from the fair, we will set a date for your Challenge."

"Like hell we will." The contrary woman crossed her arms and snorted. "I will not participate in a contest to win me like some carnival prize."

"I am afraid you have no say in this." He returned to the living room and took a sip of troff.

Bree thumped back down across from him and sat forward, her mouth firmed with resolution, her long braid swinging across her shoulder. Her eyes narrowed.

Farking Fates, all he wanted was to haul her into his arms and kiss her senseless.

"I have no say?" she said with a smirk. "If you think that, you're a fool. You heard Kit's words. Made Ones deserve to choose for *them-*

selves. And you saw what she can do as a fighter. Wait until you see my skills."

"Your sister surprised us all," he said. "You will not."

Her brilliant smile promised warmth, openness. He wanted those for himself. He wanted *her*. Did she know what he was thinking? How much he desired her?

Breena winked.

"May the Sky welcome you." Calix peered down at the man he had just killed. The Watcher had not been a bad sort, and if Fukkes and Gabin hadn't set him on Calix, he would still be alive. Calix draped his bloody lab coat over the dead man.

Having secured the final Awakening ingredient, the essential palladious, he switched the Made One's pod to hover mode, the attached portable breather automatically turning on. He pushed the floating pod through the disposal chamber's door, down the dusty corridor, past the evac extractor, and outside. His next breath smelled of pine and freedom.

Guiding the pod to his cart, Calix slid it onto the bed, and switched off the hover mode. The pod settled with a satisfying whoosh, and he covered it with dead corn stalks, tossing a large tarp over the whole thing. He untied the horses and clambered onto the driver's seat, placing his precious case in the box behind him. The padded container looked like a potato crate, but was bolted to the wagon bed and contained the Awakening reagents he'd stolen.

He eyed the chamber's exit door a final time. Any minute, hordes of Watchers could pour into the clearing. Though the day was chilly, sweat slid down his spine.

Not only must he get the Made One to safety, but he had to alert Compass True to the Alchemics' true plan. They would unlawfully steal healthy Essences from Earth, their intentions monstrous—to destroy those human Essences and transfer themselves into the empty flesh. They intended to rule Earth.

His coordinates confirmed the city had come to rest over the bluffs of BearHome. He wiped his sweaty hands on his tunic, then took up the reins. "Move on, boys."

He clucked, snapped the reins, and headed down the slope to his cabin. To safety and the Made One's resurrection.

Breena walked with Gato to the gym, a massive enclosure with two cavernous rooms and many smaller ones. They passed men sparring naked, in loincloths, and in full leathers, the air pungent with sweat, while shouts and grunts echoed. Beyond the large room, they headed down a corridor.

Beginning his training in a relaxed environment hadn't appealed to Gato, who insisted on getting right to it. Bree had conceded, her role a challenge, but she would do her best to emulate her sensei.

At the training room door, they slipped off their boots and Gato tucked his braid beneath his tunic as she preceded him inside. She'd insisted on loose clothes, and he'd already asked questions about their apparel, his interest in every aspect of training impressing her.

The well-lit room sported off-white walls and was covered in a large, cushioned mat of cotton batting. It would do.

She walked to the mat's center and sat.

"What are you doing?" he said with irritation.

"We talk first." She braced herself for his railing about not beginning to work out.

"Why?" he said, fingering his earring.

His calm surprised her. "Much of these disciplines are internal, and it's important you understand where they came from and how they operate."

"All right." He folded his body onto his knees and sat across from her.

"You're doing it right, but your hands should relax on your knees."

"But you do not sit that way."

"My left knee kills if I do."

His eyes lit with humor. "Try."

She tilted her head, then she got it. She assumed the position and laughed. "Of course. My new body doesn't have a bad knee."

"It does not."

Once their positions mirrored one another, she began. "Most martial arts have Asian roots."

"Asian? That is west, across the Titanus sea?"

"Yes, the sea we call Pacific. If you sailed west on Earth from California, you would come to Asia—Japan, China, and other countries."

He nodded, and she took stock. To her surprise, the atmosphere surrounding them was one of attention and promise. Good.

"The many arts include Taekwondo, the most ancient and the one we will begin with."

He began to rise, and she flapped a hand. "Not yet. We have a ways to go."

When he sat again, she continued. "Karate, a Japanese art, involves kicks, punches, and open-handed chops. Jujitsu, evolving from both China and Japan, is the forerunner of Japanese aikido and judo. It involves grappling and the idea of fighting in close proximity. But as I mentioned, much of martial arts involves what's going on within you."

"How a warrior prepares for battle," he said.

"Yes, and no. For example, aikido means "the way for harmony." It's meant to unify your spiritual energy or ki with the physical and use your opponent's momentum and strength to achieve your objective. Brazilian style uses choking and fighting on the ground. Hapkido, Korean, uses weapons, and the Chinese art of kung fu applies various fighting styles, like high kicks and other acrobatics. Brazilian Capoeira is acrobatic, as well, and Israeli Krav Maga employs ordinary objects as weapons, along with grappling and hand strikes."

As she spoke, he listened with profound focus, his posture relaxed, yet intent.

"Any questions yet?" she said.

"No."

"Tai chi, Chinese, is quite spiritual with its slow-motion postures. It's believed the art was created by a Chinese monk using Taoist breathing techniques."

"Taoist?"

"An ancient Chinese philosophy. Finally, the Korean Taekwondo is where we will start. Kicking is emphasized, though it also uses joint locks, throws, hand strikes, and punches."

"Tell me the origin."

His question pleased her. "Taekwondo means 'the way of the fist.' It's old, at least two thousand years."

She rose, and he mirrored her movement, his eyes hawk-bright.

"You care about the past," he said.

Bree thought for a moment. "I do, and the way it can inform the future. Let's begin. I'm going to bow to you and you do the same. The purpose is to show respect and gratitude for your sparring partner. In a way, it's a promise."

"And what do you promise me, Breena?"

His question was more, and had little to do with their sparring. When Gato faced her, she pressed her hands together and bowed. He mimicked her.

"We start in the Joon Bi or ready stance, facing forward, feet planted about a shoulder length apart. Let your arms hang down, but slightly bent, your hands lightly fisted out."

She demonstrated, he did as asked, and she adjusted his arms. "Your fists should be down around waist level. There. Taegeuk il jang is the first of eight forms."

"Forms?"

"Movements, actions. Each taegeuk form is represented by a trigram, a divination symbol derived from the I Ching, a book... Long story. The trigram for Taegeuk Il Jang is three solid horizontal lines, and it represents a keon or symbol. Taegeuk represents the sky. I thought you would like that, given Sky is one of your five religious elements."

"Thank you," he said with sincerity.

"For what?"

"For acknowledging the truth of our way."

Speaking as they were, a mantle of peace and focus between them, it was as if they shared the same head space. She saw inside him, past layers of artifice, to the man himself and his deep connection with his world.

"Come, let me explain the form," she said waving a hand. "Each form is a series of movements. Turn left ninety degrees into a walking stance, left foot forward. Yes, good."

His supple body moved as she instructed, and she demonstrated how the actions flowed one into another, creating the complete form.

By the end of ninety minutes, they were sweating more from focus and intensity, than activity. Gato's grin when he tossed her a clean towel to wipe her face pleased her immensely.

"That was not difficult," he said.

She chuckled. "No, it wasn't. But you see, each form requires perfection, which equals patience on both our parts. The techniques aren't hard to learn. But each movement must become fixed in your memory."

"Fixed?"

"You must own it, know it in your soul. To master any martial art, ask yourself: Can I execute every move with perfect precision? Can I load every punch with power? Can my high sidekick linger long enough to demonstrate mastery? To answer questions like those and others with a yes takes hours of practice, hard work, and repetition. It's easy enough for you to do the form, but to understand it, according to my sensei or teacher, there is the challenge. See what I mean?"

"You are my sensei."

"No. I wouldn't dare use that term for myself. I'm still a student."

"You have the patience of a teacher."

In that moment, crystalline in its perfection, a current ran between them, one of promise. Of hope.

"I...try," Bree said.

"'Do or do not, there is no try.'" Gato quirked a brow.

She giggled. "You remembered Yoda!"

The door swung open, and two laughing men entered.

"Shote," the hefty one said as he spotted them. "Alpha, apologies."

"None needed," Gato rested a hand on her elbow. "We are finished here."

Bree was excited enough to jump out of her skin. For Kit's mating ceremony, six matched bays pulled their carriage on the three-day trip to WolfHome. Conversation with Gato and Arina may have been desultory, but the rolling landscape and the book Bree had brought provided entertainment and kept her nerves under control. In a few days, she would hug her sister.

The Mediterranean topography of CatHome gave way to rolling hills and pine forests, and as the elevation rose, her memories of Maine and home did as well.

Their group arrived late, the ceremony begun, and she and Arina stayed in the shadows with Barth on guard, while Gato searched for a table. She would have time with Kit and didn't want their reunion interrupting the ceremony. It wasn't hard to stay secret, as the hall, round like other buildings at WolfHome and larger than Catamount's hall, was bursting with people and animal symbionts. Flowers adorned the tables and wove around pillars and roof beams, their jasmine and wisteria scents perfuming the air.

In minutes, Gato signaled them to a table far from the dais, where Kit, Rafe, and the Alpha couple sat. Food was served as people performed in the semi-circle before the dais. To Bree's astonishment, four wolves howled a song so beautiful it made her heart race. But it was the aftermath of the song that had her weeping.

The entire party moved outside as her beloved sister performed acrobatic tricks atop her mistral, Moonrise. Those same tricks had crippled and nearly killed Kit. That her sister had the courage to perform them awed Bree. Unlike the day of the accident, Kit was perfection. Hence the embarrassing tears.

"Are you well?" Gato bent his head close and asked with a whisper.

She nodded and explained about Kit's accident. "They're tears of joy."

"Ah. The best kind."

After Kit's amazing ride, the ensuing party was raucous, and at the tail end, the Wolf Alpha shocked everyone by announcing his pending abdication. Though he was Rafe's father and put his son up for Alpha, Gato explained that attaining Alpha wasn't hereditary. Many competed, the trials both physical and mental contests.

"Do you film them?" she asked.

"Of course. If accusations of cheating arise, the vids help determine the truth."

"I meant as a show."

"No contestant wants to be splashed across a vidscreen, not unless he's the winner."

Bree wished she could show him reality T.V.

A receiving line formed, and Gato made his way toward it. She moved to follow, but Arina held her back. "Wait, Made One."

Stuck behind the crowd, she couldn't see the mated couple. What was Gato doing?

Bree stepped forward, a hard shove to her shoulder, and she stumbled to the ground. Face to face with a furry wolf's butt. His head snapped around, teeth flashing, and predatory blue eyes locked on hers. *Shit.*

The wolf blinked, and those huge jaws widened into a grin, his black tongue lolling from his mouth.

She had the terrible urge to giggle, which might get her bitten. The wolf's persona was adorable and funny and far different from Barth, who kept his dignity at all times. *His* tongue would never loll.

She dared to scratch the wolf's chin, his eyes drooping closed.

A hand wrapped around her arm and lifted. "Now we move."

"Yes, yes, Arina, I'm coming."

Kit and Gato stood before the dais, her sister speaking fast and furious to the Cat Alpha. But then Kit spotted Bree closing in on the group.

Rafe notched his chin at Gato. "Is Ahanu down from university?"

Gato's head snapped around. "Why?" He growled.

The air grew charged, as if electricity arced between the two men. Voices muted, and the Wolf Alfa standing beside Rafe tensed.

Kit rested a hand on Rafe's forearm, and a virtual balloon popped, sound returned, people laughing and drinks clinking.

Rafe shrugged. "I assumed my Skyson would find the time to accompany you for his Skyfather's mating."

"Unfortunately," Gato said. "Ahanu had exams, though he told me he tried."

"It has been years since he's called or written any kind of meaningful letter," Rafe said. "Why is that, do you suppose?"

Gato brows rose. "Perhaps you have angered him."

"Fark that," Rafe said. "I have not."

Taking advantage of the two arguing men, Kit ran toward Bree. "Sister!"

Bree rushed forward, too. *Shit*. Kit was about to cry. Kit never cried, and Bree couldn't handle it. She'd start crying too, loud, noisy stuff and very undignified.

Bree clasped Kit to her, intending to never let her go. Her sister's embrace was strong, stronger than she'd been in many years, and they both wept. Feeling Kit's strength and vigor after decades of pain and debilitation was pure pleasure.

"I'm so happy for you," Bree said. "Rafe, WolfHome, your mistral. And your riding! That was the best."

Kit closed her eyes, inhaling deeply. "I am blessed, Bree."

"You deserve it, sis!"

"Is Gato forcing you to stay?" Kit said. "Being cruel? Demanding things?"

Bree grinned. It was impossible not to. "I'm fine, Kit. Fine." Over and over again she reassured her sister.

"Are you sure?" Kit said yet again.

"I haven't had this much fun in years."

"We Wolves offer you sanctuary," Kit said. "Stay here with me and Rafe. You would be loved, honored, and we'd have so much fun. Stay."

Bree wanted to. "We could hunt for Sybi together."

"We could, except... Rafe will be competing for Alpha." She blew out a breath. "I can't leave him during the trials. But Sybi is on Eleutia. I know it. Rafe has sent out scouts and messengers to other Clans, as has his father."

"Gato has as well, but every time I ask him to vidscreen with the Alchemics, they continue to refuse. They also denied meeting with me during the Challenge." They *have* to know something about Sybi.

Kit's lips thinned. "They're bastards. I've done the same, with the same results."

"Creeps." Bree scanned Kit's eyes and saw love and hope and their decades-long history. She smiled. "I'll stay."

They hugged yet again, laughing the whole time.

When they stepped back, Bree took a deep breath. She'd chosen. Except. Damn. She'd forgotten the most important part of CatHome. "My CatGuard cubs." Kit knew about Audi and Fortis. "They're mine. I'm theirs. We are...connected."

Kit drew away, her face solemn. "I'd forgotten your cubs."

"They're so wonderful and—"

"You can't take them from CatHome."

"Sure I can." Bree grinned, faking it, knowing her fight with Gato would be epic.

"No, you can't." Kit hooked an arm through Bree's and steered her to a quiet corner of the hall. "Were you to take them from CatHome and we to accept them at WolfHome, the Cats would start a war. Their symbiont cats are sacred to them, as our wolves are to us."

"But war? My friend Fudge said the same. Are you sure?"

"The Clans nearly went to war over me. That's why I ran away to CatHome for the Challenge."

"But..."

"Clan wars happen easily and often," Kit said. "It's awful. Rafe said they're a ripple effect of the female decline. Male tempers mount swiftly, and even slights and insults can provoke deadly consequences."

War. No, Bree and the cubs were not worth a war. If she abandoned her cubs, she'd have to break the bond. Was that even possible? If it were, her heart would be crushed, but she'd survive. She didn't know if Audi and Fortis would. They were so young. Even if they survived, the break could badly damage them. "The bond isn't a small thing." She pressed a hand to her head and heart. "It's here and here."

"I've seen it with Gato and his cat. And Paulo, the coywolf." She grinned. "You know, the one you met when you landed on your knees, which was pretty funny. If we left, he..." Kit shook her head.

"I can't abandon them. Not yet. For now I have to stay at CatHome."

Kit agreed, and they hugged and talked and laughed for long minutes as people began to leave. After prolonged farewells, Bree rejoined Gato and Arina and the Alpha steered them out. Bree turned back to Kit, smiled, and signed. *Love you, sis! See you soon!*

A promise she'd keep, even if it was via vidscreen.

She turned in a swirl of skirts because she didn't want Kit to see her sorrow.

CHAPTER ELEVEN

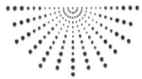

Bree had three days to stew as the carriage sped back to CatHome. The final day on the road, after long hours of driving, Bree's lids grew heavy. Arina was already asleep, with Bartholomew sprawled across their feet.

Gato slid through the carriage window. Bored, he'd been driving the team, and now he was windblown, flushed, and grinning. He was, she had to admit, edible.

"Who is Ahanu?" she said as he took the seat beside her.

He laughed. "My younger brother. Far handsomer than I."

His *brother?* Rafe had called him "Skyson," which must be like a godson. "Where is he?"

"At university."

"Where?"

"Down south. A fine school, and he excels, of course." Gato tilted his head back and closed his eyes. "You will like him when you meet. He is nothing like me, but rather a kind and gentle soul with joy in his heart."

"What is he studying."

"Poetry and literature."

"Sybi's favorites. Did you hear…?"

"At the ceremony, I spoke with several of Rafe's scouts." He sighed. "It is as if your sister vanished into the ether. Strange, as a Made One's arrival is always a big event."

"Mine sure wasn't."

"No, but once we found you, everyone at CatHome knew, and soon your arrival was known by all in the Northwest Quadrant. Not one whisper of Sybelle has come to our ears."

Bree stared out the window at nothing, blinking fast, trying to keep her shit together.

"We will be home tonight," he said.

"I'm glad. I miss the cubs." She leaned her head on Gato's shoulder, allowing sleep to creep in.

Bree jerked awake with a yip. The carriage had sped up, flying over ruts and bumps, and landing hard.

Gato held up a finger while pressing a device in his ear, nodding. He released it.

"What's wrong?" Bree said.

His lips thinned. "Our driver says six riders are on our trail."

Arina reached beneath the seat to pull out her sword.

Riders chasing them... At least Bree had changed into her jeans, a white tunic, and cloak. "I need a weapon. A knife."

Gato, who'd retrieved his own sword, stared at her for long moments.

"Well?" she held out her hand.

He slapped a dagger into her palm. "You do as I say. Clear?"

"Crystal."

"They may have laseblasters," Arina said.

"Doubtful," Gato said. "The weapons are chipped and monitored by the Alchemics. Too traceable."

Bartholomew had risen as well, his growls soft beneath the thunder of hooves and clatter of wheels.

Gato pulled himself halfway out of the carriage, then dropped back inside. He pressed his ear device. "Up ahead, that copse of trees, pull in and unhitch the team."

"Do we have time?" Arina said.

"We must. Those men behind us are no bandits."

"Then who are they?" Bree said.

"Anti-Made Ones."

The carriage barreled onward, swaying madly as it took a curve, then forging ahead until minutes later, it came to an abrupt halt.

"Out!" Gato said.

They poured from the carriage, and Gato ran to help the driver free the six horses, while Bartholomew prowled circles around Bree and Arina.

"They want me, don't they?" she asked Arina with a whisper.

Arina stared into the darkness. "Yes."

"Hurry!" barked Gato.

They raced to where he stood beside the horses, and he took Bree's waist and flung her onto the back of a big bay. "Ride!"

She grabbed the reins, checked the harness strap, tightened her legs, and kicked.

Light flared beside her, and she'd swear it singed the hair on her arms.

"Stop, Breena!" Gato shouted. "They have laseblasters, fark them. Their range is short. Into the trees and climb."

But it wasn't to be, for they were instantly surrounded by six men dressed in black and wearing cloth balaclavas. Each held a lase-blaster pointed at them, Barth, and their driver.

Arina and Gato raised their swords, but it was all for show.

A man nudged his horse forward. "Give us the Made One and you live."

Nothing about this situation was good, and beneath her cloak, Bree slipped the knife into the small of her back. Not very safe, but it would have to do.

Gato chuckled. "Are you sure you wish to die tonight?"

Bree was dragged off her horse by one of the men, and none too gently. She staggered to the ground but managed to jab an elbow in his face.

"Fark you, woman!" He backhanded her.

She reeled, her mouth pooling with blood. She spat at him.

Gato went nuts, flinging the knife that had appeared in his hand straight for the leader's throat.

She took a running start, vaulted onto a horse, and kicked.

As she hoped, the bastards galloped after her.

Calix had traveled for days with the Made One, pressing onward though his lack of sleep had begun to catch up with him. They had made it to NoLand, a large swath of land between the Northwest Cats' and Wolves' territories. His cabin sat on a ridge, a good vantage point, and he'd carefully prepared it for their arrival.

He halted the wagon, allowing the horses a moment's rest, and reached inside his carry bin for a hunk of cheese and some water. Down the slope lights flickered, followed by puffs of smoke. Some fools were using laseblasters in the middle of the night.

He slipped on his infrared goggles. A woman bent low on a galloping horse, her cloak billowing behind, followed by five riders gaining on her.

That didn't seem fair at all.

He slipped from the wagon and tied the horses, making sure both wagon and horses were hidden by the screen of trees. From the wagon's bed, he hefted the stolen lasepipe, its tracker dismantled. A beam of moonlight pierced the clouds, splashing across the woman and her pursuers.

That hair. He'd swear… But why would pursuers fire blasters at a Made One?

Not that it mattered. He shouldered the lasepipe and ran down the hill.

A huge man stepped from the trees, raised sword in hand. "Halt."

Calix stopped so abruptly, he almost toppled. "They are attacking a Made One!"

"You wish to kill her."

"No! I am going to help her. Move!" Calix caught the man's profile, saw the fall of rust and slate-blue hair. He gasped. "You were—"

"Yes. I am CastOut Clan."

He knew of only one Eleutian with that hair, a Falcon Clan infant he had seen in old photos. "Not possible. You were tiny, weighed a pound at birth. You *died*."

The CastOut threw back his head and laughed.

"Kestrel!" called a voice from the wood.

The large man glanced over his shoulder.

Down below, the woman's horse was flagging, the five riders closing in, their laseblasts peppering the night.

"Fire!" Kes said.

Arrows flew.

Perhaps this was the stupidest thing Bree had ever done. Her enemy's horses were fresher, their mounts sleeker, while hers was tiring.

They planned to kill her. Not right away, maybe, but she'd seen the hatred in their eyes. Gato had told her about the Anti-Made-One faction. They'd already killed a Made One. Fuck them.

Now what, Miss Bravado?

They fired at her, but as Gato said, the laser blasts had a short range and dissipated before reaching her. So far. But they'd soon be in range. She had to do something radical.

Her jaw squeezed tight.

Kit's trick, as Bree called it. Her sister's perfect execution was nothing like Bree's semi-competent display. But it could work.

Not that they could see or hear her, but for the hell of it she gave them the finger. "Watch this, fuckers!"

Holding the reins one-handed, she gripped the ties of her heavy cloak and tugged, while making sure the thing didn't fly off, and clamped the ties between her teeth. The cloak flapped when she released it, and she muscled it closer to the leather harness surrounding the horse's withers.

The thunder of hooves grew louder.

Burn seared her hip and she almost grunted. Instead, she tightened her jaw. The first blast of pain lessened, and she released the reins, squeezing with her thighs and heels, and took the ties from her mouth and knotted them to the left and right harness straps, the fabric bunched in front of her. The cloak secure, she wrapped both hands around the right strap and slid sideways toward the flank, one leg remaining atop the horse's back.

The animal panicked, picking up speed, and the ground blurred, his hooves kicking up dirt and divots of grass. If she didn't time this right, she'd be toast.

They galloped around a bend. She swallowed hard, then simultaneously flung her right leg outward and released her hold on the leather. Airborne, she twisted, spiraled, and landed with a roll on the ground, rolling until she rose to a wobbly crouch.

Ow.

Her horse galloped onward toward home, her cloak flapping.

Would the deception be enough? She stumbled behind a tree.

If she had fooled them, they'd pursue her horse. If not...

She couldn't see, couldn't tell.

The clouds cleared, bathing the night in cool light. Damn, her white shirt glowed like a beacon. She remained in her crouch in case they saw her and she had to sprint away. Sprint? Ha.

They were close, thundering toward her hiding spot. Two men had pulled off their masks, and their teeth gleamed, their grins hungry.

Which was when arrows flew through the sky, and her pursuers toppled from their mounts like autumn leaves from trees.

Calix watched the five pursuers topple from their horses, yet not a single arrow had touched an animal. The Made One's horse was long gone. She was safe. He rested the lasepipe on the ground and peered up at the man still holding a sword aimed at his heart. He was their leader, of that Calix had no doubt.

"Now what?" he said to Kestrel. Nothing made sense. The Cast-Outs… These men could not be CastOuts, broken, deformed, and enfeebled men and women according to the Cabal. "Who are you? *What* are you and them?"

The man peered down at him, raptor-black eyes boring into his. Another man approached, but Kes's eyes lingered though he lowered his sword. "Marcos."

"All set," Marcos said. "Are you done, Kes?"

The leader didn't answer, never taking his eyes off Calix.

"I'd like to leave," Calix said.

"Where?" Kes said.

"Away," Calix said.

"Where?" Kes repeated.

The other man chuffed. "The Kestrel won't let you leave until you tell him where you are going."

He had never been the focus of such intense scrutiny, not even from Fukkes. It was as if those black eyes punched through his soul.

The infant culled from the Falcon Clan had that same-colored hair. Though he didn't see how it was possible that child survived, a tiny infant, underweight and malformed, with feathers sprouting from his flesh. Yet here he stood, this man with his unique kestrel hair and eyes black as death, the son of two mated Falcons, a muscled and massive commanding leader.

If Fukkes knew, it would terrify him. The Fates, how he wished to tell Fukkes and watch the fear grow in his eyes.

"Where?" Kes said.

It was a risk, but… "To my cabin. Down the glen and up the rise. I'm escaping from the Alchemics."

"I know your cabin," Marcos said. "It is on our land."

"It's in NoLand," Calix said.

"*Our* land." Kestrel didn't even blink. "Go."

Calix blanched.

"He means," Marcos said, "we will allow you to go to your cabin."

Relief washed through Calix like a spring rain, and he leaned on the lasepipe to steady himself.

"We know of your place," Marcos said. "Do not venture far from it, or we will kill you."

"As you wish," Calix said.

"We will be watching," Kestrel said.

Who *were* these people?

Bree hunkered behind the tree, arrows arcing from higher up the mountain and toppling her pursuers.

Her hip hurt like crazy, and her mouth from that backhand, and her calf where, at some point, she'd been cut deep enough to soak her jeans.

Using her teeth, she ripped off a hunk of shirt and bound her calf. The archers could help her, and she opened her mouth to call out. She closed it. They'd saved her, but for all she knew, they would kidnap her, too.

The arrows stopped. Silence, except for the wind's murmur through the trees, making her shiver. She rose pulling on the tree trunk and began her limp back to the carriage.

Passing the bodies, she paused. Moonlight shined on the bloodied men. She hated touching dead flesh, but she checked. Not a single pulse. What a waste.

Barth loped out of the darkness, and a thrill of relief staggered her. Then Gato appeared atop one of the carriage horses. He vaulted off and enfolded her in a gentle hug, as he breathed in great gulps of air. He pushed her back and examined her head to toe, swearing the entire time.

"They hurt you, Made One." Lines of exhaustion carved his face, his eyes dark with concern.

She got all weepy, which was dumb, but she smiled. "I survived."

Face tight, he closed himself up like a magic cabinet. "Yes, you did."

Careful of her burnt flesh, he gripped her waist and tossed her atop the horse.

"I'm not a sack of flour!" she said.

"No," he said. "You are much heavier."

Gurrrr.

He stepped to the bodies of her attackers. "Did you see who shot the arrows?"

"No. It just…happened." She pointed to the forest. "They came from there."

He peered up the mountain, then gathered the reins of the pursuers' horses that hadn't fled. "This is NoLand. A large tract that exists between CatHome and WolfHome."

"Gato?" Feeling woozy, she gripped the leather harness, but the world went black.

Bree was humiliated. She never fainted, never passed out. But this was the second time she'd awakened in Gato's arms. They were back in the coach, daylight blazing through the windows, and she wasn't in pain.

She pushed herself up, taking the seat beside him. Why didn't she hurt? Her hip must be a mess. "My hip—"

"Healers at the inn saw to that, as well as your face and leg."

"The inn?" She sounded breathy, weak. *Fuck.* "Where are we?"

"A few hours from Catamount," Gato said.

The bruising beneath his eyes bothered her, and she suspected he hadn't slept. "Go on."

"You've been unconscious for two days. We stayed at a village on the edge of CatHome until the healers deemed it acceptable to continue."

"Arina's not here."

"She took a fresh horse and several Peacekeepers to deal with the bodies."

Those men had hurt her, shot her, but she wished they weren't dead. They probably had families, children, friends. Villains had loved ones, too. "They were Anti-Made Ones?"

Gato's face darkened. "Yes. They despise you and all your kin, seeing you as a blight upon Eleutia. Along with disposal of the bodies, Arina is looking for proof that they are, indeed, from that cult. Their laseblasters will tell the story."

Her jaw tightened. "They were trying to kill me."

"Perhaps. Or they hoped to capture you. For years, they were pranksters and protesters. They have changed to deadly adversaries."

He leaned back against the seat, arms raised to cup his head, and closed his eyes.

"You haven't slept," she said.

"I am used to it."

"Lie down." She peered outside. Three outriders and Barth accompanied them. "I'm wide awake. We have guards. Sleep."

He went to move to the bench across from them, but Bree reached for him. "Here. Use my lap as a pillow."

Though he arched a brow, he curled up on the seat, placing his head in her lap. She laid his cloak over him, and he inhaled deeply. Soon, his bones melted into relaxation and his lips parted, a soft snore whooshing from his mouth.

She touched his hair, that gorgeous fall of black he so often wore plaited. He'd tied it back with a leather thong, and she wove its silky mass through her fingers. The great Cat Alpha asleep in her lap. Even in sleep, he looked fierce.

The carriage's rhythm was soothing, and her own lids began to droop.

She liked him, far more than the legion of lovers she'd taken to escape the pain of Mordecai's death. They'd been placeholders, men she'd never connected with. Yet for some reason, with this domineering prickly man, she did.

The connection confused her, her desire mostly one-sided. No, that wasn't exactly right. He seemed to desire her, yet he wasn't pursuing her, not romantically. He'd made that clear.

A lock of hair drifted across her face, and she tucked it behind her ear. He even found her hair attractive. *Humm.* If what she believed was right, whatever the Alchemics were holding over him—and it must be powerful—was compelling him to stage her Challenge and to not pursue her himself.

Or was her conclusion a fantasy because she'd begun to think of Gato as hers?

CHAPTER TWELVE

Tilde worked alone, settling the six opossums in their large cages and setting up the pure water for Opi 3 to drink. To appease a niggle, she used desalinated sea water, rather than the bottled, having lost faith in the Pellopine water.

She hadn't told the others that the opossums arrived, hoping to avoid their disappointment if she again failed.

Days later, she watched them mate. All three females had reacted to the clicking males used to attract them and went at it. Today, she checked the females and all were pregnant. Finally, something had gone well.

She sat down hard on a stool and twirled, letting out a long breath.

Now, the wait, which wasn't that long. Ten to fourteen days, then another week to identify the joeys' sex.

Twelve days later, her eye caught an odd movement from the opossum cages. Tilde raced over. All three females were giving birth, and she grabbed her tablet and waited.

Hours later, she was tired, though all she'd done was jot notes while watching fifty-two joeys being born. Tilde had been fascinated as the tiny and blind, pea-sized creatures journeyed from beneath their mother's tail, fighting through the hair on her belly in search of her pouch, where her teats with milk awaited.

The lab was warm, but the joeys had no fur and must be cold, poor things, and they couldn't even see or hear. She'd observed their mighty efforts scaling their mother's belly to reach her pouch. Several had fallen off, and she'd reached to help them. She stopped herself. Each opossum mother had only thirteen teats and the joeys that fell was Mother Terra culling the herd. She'd slumped back on the stool, sighed, and let them be.

One week to go before she could sext the joeys.

Eight days later, Tilde arrived at Rafe and Kit's stable in a flurry. Max and Kit were already there, as was Rafe, who looked awful. Tilde got chills seeing his battered face. He had endured another Alpha trial the previous day, squeaking out another victory against two separate challengers.

"Why don't we go to the healers first?" she told Rafe as he led Nightfall from his stall. The mistral's clip-clopping hooves echoed through the barn.

"After our ride," he said, scratching Nightfall's forehead.

Kit's lips thinned, but she didn't speak, and when Tilde opened her mouth, Kit shook her head. Rafe's mate was determined to support him in his bid for Alpha, but feared he would break beneath the weight of the trials, his First Commander duties, and his leadership of Compass True.

"I have lots to tell you guys!" Tilde said.

"As do we." And though he smiled, his eyes said to wait. "Let's ride to our picnic spot first, shall we?"

"Great idea," Max said.

Once they arrived at the glade, they laid out their picnic on emerald grass surrounded by pine and aspen. She and Kit unpacked the basket of WolfHome cheese, drass, beef sandwiches, and a fluffy ilaberry pie, while Max and Rafe activated the four portable disruptors. Though it was unlikely the Alchemics had bugged the wilderness area, the two men trusted nothing to chance.

Tilde was gathering her thoughts when Kit nodded to Rafe.

"Kit has been reading the histories," Rafe said. "Including the censured ones our librarian keeps hidden. She has come up with a radical idea, one I see as a very real possibility."

Rafe's usual resolve seemed tempered by an odd discomfort.

"What's wrong, Rafe?" Tilde said.

His lips tilted into a chagrinned smile and he arched a brow. "What if the Alchemics are not Eleutian?"

Tilde almost blurted *you're crazy*, which was not the thing to say.

Max shook his head. "I know several born and bred."

Kit held up a hand. "I've met one or two as well. Though my darling mate, per usual, has cut to the chase, let's begin earlier, about two-hundred-and-fifty years ago. As I read, a pattern emerged. The *tone* of the Alchemics changed."

"Tone?" Tilde said. "You know I am not that subtle."

Kit laughed. "You'll get what I mean. Prior to the early 1770s, the articles noted the Alchemics' transparency and accessibility. The Clan wasn't secretive at all, and they mingled freely with the animal Clans."

"What were you reading, some social calendar?" Max said.

"In one sense, yes. I read the usual dry tomes, but also several novels, glitzy books, and periodicals."

"'Glitzy?'" Rafe laughed.

Kit grinned. "You know, um, stuff about celebrities and such. Periodicals. Tell-alls. Biographies. I was trying to understand them as people, more than scientists. From what I got, the Clan's behaviors were different from now."

"Different how?" Tilde said.

"They intermarried with animal Clans," Kit said. "Alchemics had affairs with non-Alchemics. One female Alchemic even fought a duel over a Bear Clan male. Though their Cabal of Eleven came into being around the 1200s, along with the rise of Clan Alphas, the tenor of the Cabal changed in the 1700s. That's when the Clan became more secretive."

"Specifics, please." Max shoved a hunk of bread into his mouth.

Tilde elbowed Max. "Don't be so snippy."

"They used to hold open meetings and seminars," Kit said. "Meetings which Clansfolk from Eleutia could attend. Now, those meetings are closed and only the results become public. Even more interesting, two hundred and fifty years ago was when the eleven members of the Cabal were replaced by new Cabal leaders. Every single one."

"No council changes all members at once," Rafe said.

Kit nodded. "The Alchemic's did, which was when new communication restrictions were put in place. Simultaneously, they constructed a whole new block of labs. Their food changed too, dishes no one had ever tasted before appeared, like Abrulo Stew, darjingo, and even drass."

"We've drunk drass forever," Max said with a scoff.

"No, you haven't, actually," Kit said. "I asked the Wolf Alpha, who blustered that Eleutians always drank drass."

"Blustered?" Rafe laughed. "Pure Da."

"Except." Kit held up a finger. "When I insisted Ulfr think about it, he said I was right. I know, shocking. He remembered first tasting drass as a young man. Given his age in the upper two-hundreds, it meshes with the two-hundred-and-fifty-year timeline."

"But the Made One program didn't begin for another seventy years or so," Tilde said. "I remember reading the first Made One was introduced a hundred and eighty years ago."

"Correct," Kit said. "But what if it took seventy years for them to perfect Made Ones? Think about it. In the early days of female decline, the slide in their births wasn't noticeable."

Max snorted. "You sure did a lot of reading, Kit."

She grimaced. "Some of it was so boring, I thought I'd scream. But I found nuggets, too. One in particular." Kit hugged her knees and smiled. "I saved the best for last. For almost seven hundred years, Alchemic City was built into the bedrock atop a mountain far north of WolfHome. Yet two-hundred-and-thirty years ago, the city —somehow—began to float and change location."

"Are you sure?" Max said. "I thought it was much earlier than that, like in the 1600s."

"It wasn't. I triple checked my sources, one of which was a novel. The city was stationary until then, and...poof."

"The High Magics could move the city," Max said.

Rafe shook his head. "I've been to Alchemic City, and I would have felt any use of High Magics. There were none."

Kit looked from Tilde to Max, her eyes warming when she stared at Rafe and he nodded back. "What if the Cabal is comprised of eleven aliens from a parallel world or another planet? Men and women whose purpose is to use other worlds as, well, like a petri dish experiment?"

"Petri dish?" Max said.

"We call them glassine dishes," Tilde said.

Max gawped looking at Kit. "You're saying our world is their petri dish?"

Rafe leapt to his feet and paced. "Yes, as if the eleven Cabal members see Eleutia as a giant laboratory. Months ago, Calix hinted that something had changed. Something big he was investigating."

"He wasn't specific?" Max said.

Rafe shot him a dark look. "No, and in subsequent calls, he got oddly secretive. Of late, I have been unable to contact him. The call goes through, but he does not answer. I talked to Neela, and she does not know where he is, either, or what he meant by the Cabal changing. Neela has not heard from him."

"What about the Falcons, his original Clan?"

"Not a word."

"Aliens," Tilde said, her voice awed. "I wonder... All the restrictions about our Clans studying science came about—"

"Post-two-fifty," Kit said. "The same is true for their rules regarding magic, as well as adding pages of other rules. There's more. Within that same time frame, they began killing mistrals for their bones. I also noted an increase in missing women and children from the animal Clans."

"Missing women and children?" Tilde said.

"Not many," Rafe said. "But enough that the percentages increased from point two to one-point-five percent. Though small, the change is a disturbing one and could be connected to the others." Rafe turned to Tilde. "Have the opossums arrived?"

Oh, dear. All the alien talk had scattered her focus. "Um. Yes?"

"What's that mean?" Max said.

"It's the water!" Tilde blurted, unable to wait a second longer.

Max took a bite of pear. "Clarify 'the water,' Tilde."

"I tested the opossums and—"

"Without us?" Kit said, incredulous.

Tilde stared at her wine glass, the ruby liquid dark and lush, and she took a slow sip. "I did... I'm sorry, Kit, but I didn't want to fail you guys again."

Kit rested a hand on hers. "You never fail us, Tilde."

"That's kind, but I saw your faces with the mice results. I suspect why they disappointed, and later I'll test my theory."

"Tilde, what exactly are you saying, sweetheart?" Max said with a surprising gentleness.

"Right. Sorry. The results—the two females who drank our Wolf-Home water produced thirty-five joeys, of which twenty were males and one was female.

"That doesn't add up," Rafe said.

Tilde got sad all over again. "The rest died. They fell off their mamas and..." She explained. "I checked the corpses. Twelve were male and two, female. Sorry, I... I should have included them in the total."

"Tilde, it's okay," Rafe said, squeezing her hand. "So in other words, of the thirty-five joeys, only three were females. What about the third female opossum?"

"Woohoo!" Tilde's embarrassing shout made her bite her lip. "The third female drank desalinated ocean water. She produced fifteen joeys, three of whom died."

Max waved a hand. "Come on, come on!"

"She had eight females and seven males! Squee!"

Her three friends' shocked faces mirrored one another.

"It's true," Tilde said. "You see, the females have these pouches and the males bifurcated penises and—"

"Farking Fates!" Max said. "Our water is poisoned."

"I suspect all Eleutia's is," Rafe said.

"Our water," Tilde said with confidence, "is contaminated with a chemical suppressant—most likely a synthetic hormone—which inhibits female births."

"Our water," Kit said, awe in her voice.

Tilde grinned. "All we need to do is purify our water, and we are all set."

"For the entire planet?" Rafe's expression was grim. "The decline is worldwide. This hormone must be in all the animal Clans' potable water. In other words, we have to fix *all* the world's water to balance the birthrate."

"That's impossible," Max poured wine to the glass brim and downed it in one gulp.

"This is horrible," Kit said, looking equally glum.

"We *can* do this," Tilde said. "Now that we know the cause, we can find a solution."

Rafe arched a brow, twirling a dandelion. "What choice do we have? We need to know how to fix our water before the Alchemics realize we have discovered what they are doing."

"We can," Tilde said. "Other Clan researchers beside myself will work on it."

"I know what you're going to say, Rafe." Max fisted a hand.

Tilde shivered at Rafe's slow grin. "War. Once we know how to purify our water, we rid ourselves of the Alchemic blight. We destroy them."

On Bree's return to Catamount from her assault, the Clan healers gave her an acceptable bill of health, and she was back in her suite, the cubs bouncing around in ecstasy.

Those men would have killed her for simply being a Made One, though she'd had no say in the change.

Home on Earth, she'd read mystery novels and thrillers, watched action movies, and seen true crime shows—none truly captured how it felt to be prey. A cocktail of terror, fury, and bewilderment twisted her gut.

But she'd been determined, too, and had managed to win the day, assisted by a rain of falling arrows. She was proud of herself.

She lit an incense stick, turned on the bath, and warmed a mug of troff. Bree slipped into the bath with her mug. She would find friendship and love at WolfHome with Kit. Two heads peeked over the rim of the tub, nudging her for more pets.

"I would never leave you two." Two pair of ears perked. "After my bath, kiddos, we'll go for a walk and have some playtime. Deal?"

The two bounced with glee, Audi mouthing a ball that was in serious need of replacing. What was it doing in the bathroom? She felt their excitement, and their urging her to hurry. She chuckled.

"I won't be long." The water eased her aches, the troff her belly, and the little beasties did the same for her heart. She smiled, and Audi licked her arm. She would never ever leave her cubs.

The following morning, she found an intricately carved wooden spoon beside her bed. Smooth as Audi's coat, its elaborate designs swirled across the handle, embellished with flowers and a cat mid-leap. No note, though a sigil of some kind was carved on the spoon's back. What a treasure. She'd bet Kit had sent it.

Later that day, she walked with Fudge to the mesa above Catamount, looking forward to deepening their friendship and a mellow afternoon with Audi and Fortis. Two Peacekeepers followed at a discrete distance, the same pair who trailed her everywhere since the attack.

The cool air cleared her mind, bringing thoughts of Sybi and her sister's affinity with all growing things. How she would love this otherworldly redwood forest that felt mysterious in ways different from Earth.

Wherever Sybi was, she hoped... The cubs bounded off.

"Don't go far, you two!" She smiled up at Fudge. "They're full of joy and such rascals."

"Like bear cubs, both Clansfolk and animal."

"Do you miss your bear symbionts."

"Sometimes." Fudge chuckled. "But I meet bear roaming CatHome's wilds. They are not my symbionts, but they recognize me for Bear. We have fun."

"Can you talk to the cats like you can to your bear symbionts?"

"No, but when they look at me a certain way, I swear they are trying to tell me things. And sometimes, I know what they are thinking." She laughed. "At least, I pretend I do. But they are simply cats to me, and I love them." Her smiling face turned solemn. "You look tired, Breena. How are you feeling?"

Bree detailed the chase and the arrows that had saved her. "I'm still jangled. Honestly, I'm amazed I'm not dead."

Open-mouthed horror crossed Fudge's face, and she enfolded Bree in a quiet hug. "You are safe here."

"I do feel safe, especially with those two following us." But she couldn't quite forget that Anti-Made Ones hid in plain sight.

The forest had grown quiet, though a breeze blew like a ribbon through the trees.

"What did you think of WolfHome?" Fudge said.

"I liked it. The people and wolves seemed warm and friendly. I loved the round houses and buildings, and the mating ceremony was beautiful. It felt so good to hug my sister."

"I am sure it did." Fudge smiled. "From what I hear, WolfHome is a good place, safe for people like me."

"People like you?"

Fudge raised a shoulder. "Different."

Bree hooked an arm through Fudge's. "We're all different, my friend. All quirky and odd in some way."

"You know what I mean."

"I do. And I'm not making light of it." She resented that Fudge had been marginalized and made to feel diminished, when she was nothing of the sort. Her friend had yet to tell her what her gift was, but she wanted Fudge to volunteer that info. Gato had said one's gift was private and shared with few.

"Will you tell me about the CastOuts?" Bree said.

"They are more powerful and more dangerous than anyone knows," Fudge whispered in Bree's ear.

"The Alpha does."

Fudge nodded. "He is good friends with our leader, Kestrel. The Cat Alpha is one of the few normals the CastOuts trust."

Could Gato have been lying about his brother? "Ahanu's not a CastOut, is he?"

"No!" Fudge froze, covered her mouth, and walked on.

Bree rushed to catch up to the tall woman's gigantic strides. "Gato said he was at university."

"Ahanu is very smart, or so I've been told. I have never met him." Fudge strode across a moss-covered trunk Bree had to leap over.

Her friend finally halted, looking uncomfortable. "Gato, the Cats, they have been good to me, Breena."

"I'm glad." She was tempted to push. Fudge would tell her. But their friendship mattered more, and bruising her kind soul was unacceptable. "It's okay. CatHome has many secrets. I sense whispers beneath the surface. As if a weight…"

"Yes, like everyone is expecting a snap," Fudge said.

"It makes me curious, and don't say I shouldn't be."

Fudge's laugh boomed. "That would be like telling a cat not to play."

"Exactly!" She laughed, too, and they walked on.

A troop of chattering birds high in a tree caught her eye, large, green birds. "Are those *parrots*?"

"We call them immies, because they can imitate our words. They come up from the south and seem to like it here, especially in the reds."

"I wish Gato were here to see them."

The laughter in Fudge's eyes faded. "Our Alpha has many burdens."

"I feel it, like a stone pressing his chest."

"Most Cats do not talk of such in front of me. But over the past few years, I have seen the Alpha change from a laughing, joyful, unshakable man to someone squeezed by that which is not of his making."

"I've thought the same about him being pressured."

Bree would put money on the Alchemics doing the pressuring.

The hush surrounding them deepened, as if the forest was holding its breath. Bree checked her phone. The cubs had been gone for a while. Too long.

"Fortis! Audacia!"

No cubs bounded from the trees. She chewed her lip, then turned to the Peacekeepers. "Help us find the cubs?"

The four spread out, calling, and walked deeper into the forest, though her guards were still in eyeshot. Her mouth dried and sweat ran down her back as she raced through the trees, hollering for the pair over and over until she tumbled over a log.

Bree gasped, eyes squeezed tight, she lay half on the log, half on the mossy earth. She was panicked. No panic attack would happen. No it would *not*. That would spell disaster for Fortis and Audi. Searing stars, why had she ever let them out of her sight? They needed leashes, trackers, anything to keep them nearby and safe.

On shaky legs, she pushed to her feet, her only injury a scraped elbow.

Maybe Audi was hurt, just like when she'd first found them. Or they could both be dead, attacked by a bear or... "Fuck!"

Deep breaths. Again. Bree cleared her mind, and though she'd never done it before, she mentally called Barth. He often spoke to her, mind-to-mind, right? *I can't find the cubs!* Calm. She must be calm. *We are in the plateau forest. Come! Hurry!*

Breath stuttering, she ran again. "Audi! Fortis!"

But they did not come.

She hadn't been looking up. She should have looked up. They might have climbed high in the redwoods and gotten stuck. She twirled and twirled, shouted, and twirled. Dizzy, she leaned against a giant red, tears of frustration mingling with sweat.

She phoned Fudge. It rang and rang. Next she dialed Gato. He didn't answer, either.

Call the cubs mentally, you idiot.

Duh.

A deep breath, and she steadied herself. Then with calm and precision, she yanked that bastard Fear and slammed him into his box.

Audi! Fortis! I need you. Come to me. Find me now.

A rustling made her whirl. Barth bounded from the trees to stand before her, Gato hard on his heels.

"I can't find them!" she said.

The human cat's purposeful strides put him before her in seconds. "Hush. All is well."

"No, all is not well!" she practically screamed.

He slid an arm around her waist and led her to a small glade where the sun shined on a circle of grass. "Cubs do this. Disobey, go off on jaunts. It is natural. In our wood, no creature would dare touch them."

"Remember how I found Audi hurt? One might be stuck or an accident or—"

"We will find them." He pressed his forehead to hers. "Barth feels them. Can you not?"

She cleared her mind, and tried and tried and... She sensed them. They were running, happy and tired, and they were close.

Relief made her turn away from Gato, her fist clamped to her mouth so he wouldn't hear her sob. From behind, hands banded her shoulders, and Gato pulled her back against his chest. But he said nothing.

The solidity of Gato anchored her, and a deep breath later, her mind easily "found" both cubs—happy and playful. She'd overreacted, yet he hadn't made fun or yelled, but said all the right things. He was such a protector, with a bravado cloaking a deeply sensitive and caring nature. If she flew, she suspected he would always catch her.

The cubs' excitement as they raced toward her was surprising. "They're on their way back." Bree squeezed her hands and turned. "Thank you."

He nodded. "An Alpha's duty. No thanks needed."

His face was serious, but his eyes held a warm smile. "Be well."

He and Barth loped off as Audi bounded out of the woods, minus her twin. "Fortis!" she hollered.

The cub appeared seconds later.

She dropped to her knees, about to hug them, when she noticed something dangling in their mouths.

Each held a dead mouse, which they dropped at her feet.

Gifts. An apology. Thank the stars they were safe.

Sorry. Audi.

Fortis mewed.

She hugged them. "It's okay. I got scared, is all. Thank you. You are both mighty hunters. You got your prey, and I'm proud. Go on, they're all yours."

Fudge and the two Peacekeepers appeared as Fortis and Audi devoured their mice. Done, Fortis preened, while Audi leapt at Bree. They toppled onto the grass, laughing and rolling around as the cubs licked and nuzzled her. Then the pair flopped down as if to curl up for a nap.

"No napping until we're home!"

They retraced their steps, Fudge in the lead, when a large tan mountain lion flowed from the wood and bowed to Fortis, Audi, and Bree. The cougar stropped Bree's thigh, and she stroked its soft pelt, recalling the huge cat in the cottage when she'd arrived. The memory felt like years, not months ago. "Why did he bow, Fudge?"

"Your cubs are CatGuard," Fudge said, "and you are bonded."

They reached the stairs for the climb down to Catamount, but Fudge halted her. "I saw our Alpha with you."

"He came because of the cubs."

Fudge shook her head. "He came because he has feelings for you."

"Sure he does," she said, her voice laced with sarcasm. "I'm his ticket to holding the next Challenge."

Fudge eyes grew soft. "It is more than that, Breena."

Perhaps. She hoped. Or, it could be Fudge's romantic nature coming to the fore.

CHAPTER THIRTEEN

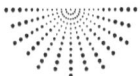

Calix maneuvered the hovercart into the cabin. He was starving, but he must take care of the Made One first. The place was rough, merely a shack with no running water, bath, or kitchen. But the well outside would serve their needs. When he Awakened her, she would have a powerful thirst.

He pushed the cart beneath the window, where it settled nicely. Though the hover took up much of the wall, enough space remained for him to maneuver. To Awaken her, he would move the pod outside, but being near the window would give her some much-needed sunshine. He checked the tube threading into the pod, its source canister, and the calibration dial. All perfect.

The back of his neck ached, his temples throbbing. His obsession was unhealthy. He knew that. Could he temper his longing when he Awakened her? The question circled his brain around and around and around. Stupid to worry. All that mattered was that she was alive and awake.

Setting his bag with the Awakening chemicals aside, he unloaded the rest of the wagon and placed their provisions on the scarred table. His friend Darva had packed the provisions, enough food—apples and pears, cheese and bread—for several days, as well as a kit to make potable water, a jug of troff, and a skin holding drass. He needed that drass. When supplies ran out, he'd forage. A Falcon never forgot his hunting skills. But those days ended when he and his sister joined the Alchemic Clan, a disastrous move that had led to Hyla's death and his spying and desertion.

As Calix lifted the infuser to calibrate the elixir, a twig snapped outside. His Falcon sense rose, and with care, he laid the infuser on the linen cloth, strapped on his claws, and lifted his laseblaster.

A rustle of leaves. He pushed the hovercart into the corner and peered out the window. Nothing. Creeping to the door, he cracked it and slipped outside, careful to stand in the overhang's shade.

Ah. The edge of a boot and a cowlick of red hair behind the boulder to his right. Two men, the sounds of separate breaths not in sync. One whispered to the other, and he recognized the voice.

"Come out, you idiots!" He stepped from the overhang. "I can hear and see you."

The pair skulked into view. Keplar and Prosa were pseudo-friends who sometimes acted as the Alchemics' minions, as well as for Compass True, and others—mercenaries for hire. Not the brightest ones.

"What do you want?" Calix said approaching them.

Keplar, the taller of the two, held up a sack. "We brought you some food. We thought you might need it."

"Who sent you?" He didn't raise his blaster, but kept it in plain sight.

Prosa's eyes widened. "No one. We heard you left the city and we knew of this shack."

"I see. Thank you." He took the sack, knowing full well they had not brought him food out of the goodness of their hearts. Calix didn't want to kill either man, small players in a big game, but he would if necessary. "The CastOuts may kill you."

Prosa, the shorter and more belligerent of the two, shrugged. "We're not afraid of some ragtag band of losers."

They had no idea.

"C'mon," Keplar said. "At least share a bottle of drass with us in your cabin."

"Only one chair. The day is lovely and we can sit here." Calix pointed to the rocks that encircled the campfire area.

They drank and talked, the two idiots blabbering on for hours until the sun began to set.

Too dark for Awakening. *Shote*. Their farking fault.

Keplar pointed to the cabin. "Can we come in?"

"Why?" Calix struggled to keep the anger from his voice.

Prosa shrugged. "Never mind."

Fark. They *knew* about his Made One. Perhaps tried to get him drunk and steal her. His Compass True training corralled his panic. Barely.

"I've had a long journey," Calix said. "Come back another day."

Prosa, to his surprise, saluted him with two fingers. "Will do."

They *would* return, gorm them. He must find the Made One another refuge before he Awakened her. He would begin tomorrow, checking maps and using the infrared seeker.

That evening, Calix rested. He dreaded the chore before him, but he was resolute. Kepler and Prosa might be brainless, but they were dogged, curse them.

The following morning, he felt poorly, his mind muzzy, and he chalked it up to the previous day's events. He heated some troff, which didn't help, then pulled up the maps on his secure tablet. The screen wavered, and he blinked. Perhaps he had a virus. NoLand's dark and dangerous wood was full of odd creatures, old magic, and CastOuts.

With reluctance, he opened the pod, the gaseous nutrient mix swirling like smoke, and injected the Made One with the elixir to halt her deterioration. A simple procedure once he understood the solution's components. That the Alchemics had allowed her decay made no sense.

He pressed his hand to her cheek before sealing the pod again.

Tomorrow. He would search for a new nest tomorrow.

. . .

For days, Gato had tried to contact Calix with no success, growing more frustrated with each unanswered call. Curse him. How ironic. He could not get in touch with his own spy.

Fark him, and fark the Alchemics. Soon. Soon they would rid Eleutia of the Alchemic infestation.

He stared at his mobile, hating the thing. It was yet another tool Fukkes used to control Eleutians. He slid the small mobile into his pocket, and after switching on the sound scramblers, he walked to the wall safe and unlocked it with his palm. He drew out a lead box the size of a thick book, opened it, and lifted a mobile almost as large as its container.

Locking his bedroom door, he removed the device made by his underground tech troop. In secret, Eleutia's hidden labs strived to create the tech needed to circumvent the science clan. Each animal Clan had several such phones. If the Alchemics ever learned of the project, all the participants would die.

The number for the Wolf had never changed. Not in the forty years since they'd fought dakos atop mistrals, side-by-side, the Wolf once his blood-brother. Everything else *had* changed—Ahanu taken. Gato's subjugation. None of which the Wolf knew. All of which had corrupted their bond until they could barely talk without drawing blood. He hoped Rafe would accede to his request, though he doubted it.

He dialed, and said, "Grambaux here."

"Rivaux here."

Compass True protocol.

"I cannot get in touch with the Bird," Gato said, referring to Calix.

"Nor can I," Rafe said.

"I need the name of another operative."

A pause, then, "That is stretching the rules, Grambaux."

"I *need* another contact." He must know how his brother was faring.

"Have faith. I will call you back." Rafe hung up.

As his only contact within Alchemic City, Calix fed Gato information and kept him apprised of Ahanu's mental and physical well-being. Ahanu... It felt as if he'd been taken a hundred years ago, rather than two. The past week was the longest he and Calix had ever been out of touch, and it was *too long*.

He snagged a bottle of drass and a glass, thunked them onto the table, and peered out the window. Below, two Sequestered walked the path to the library. A man hugged a pile of sticks to his chest, and three Peacekeepers sauntered along, laughing.

A normal day. One like any other.

He pressed his forehead to the window, the cool glass soothing. When had it all gone wrong? When had the world changed so he barely understood its landscape or its many deadly pitfalls?

How long could he sustain being pulled in myriad directions—Ahanu, The Challenge, Breena, her cubs. The world felt fuzzy and undefined, with choices that were not choices, but directives.

Breena could not leave with the cubs.

But The Challenge must be held.

Breena would leave with the cubs.

Unless he defied the Alchemics and won her.

Disgusted, Gato retrieved three heavy lacros balls and elevated them with the gold thread. Calling on the silver threads, he began to juggle the balls using the High Magics.

A week ago, Ahanu had been safe in Alchemic City. But was he safe now? He feared the Alchemics would do worse things to his brother unless he appeased their relentless demands. Without a contact like Calix within the city, he'd never know.

His daughter Luciana could ask her trees if... But she was not here, the CastOut child he was forbidden to love.

As he was forbidden from loving the Made One. *The Fates*, love could not be proscribed, and he ached for Breena. She turned his world topsy-turvy, made him feel like the man he once was.

Honorable. Ethical. Truthful.

But The Challenge must be held.

Fark! Perhaps Kes could help. Kestrel was brilliant, a fine man and warrior who had become near like a brother. They had shared truths and fears and secrets, and Kestrel had many powerful ones. The man himself was a power, a hidden one. What if...

A pulse to the High Magics, and he lowered the three balls to the floor. An idea, small and radical bloomed and he used the same illicit mobile to call Kestrel, and they talked for fifteen minutes before another call interrupted.

"I approve the idea of a trade," Kes said.

"Good. Our first salvo in the war."

"I am eager," Kes said.

"As am I," Gato said. "But we must think deeply about this and not be precipitous."

Kes chuckled. "My friend, you are the impetuous one, not I."

Signing off, Gato answered the call. "Grambaux here."

"Rivaux here. I will text you some information." *Contact Neela within Alchemic City. Use 'effrontery' in a sentence when you speak with her.*

Gato memorized the number and deleted the text.

"Good luck," Rafe said.

"Thank you, old friend." And for the first time in decades, he said those words without irony.

Gabin was disgusted. Fukkes' absurd outfit—striped pants, purple velvet vest, and red jacket—hung on a clothes rack while Fukkes subjected his body to the spray of the air tan.

"Get out," Fukkes said. "Can't you see I'm tanning?"

Gabin walked to the rack and flicked Fukkes' striped pants. "These are your clothes."

"Aren't they delightful?"

"When are you going to stop dressing like an Earthly clown for the Eleutian natives?"

"Never. Their reactions entertain me enormously."

Fukkes' tanning was something he did every day to bring a glow to his milky white skin and, he claimed, to think. He sat in the center of the room, the tanning spray misting down, reclining on his lounge chair, yet another unsanctioned transport from Earth. Even worse, the chair was covered in that repulsive Earthly plastic. When they arrived on Earth, they would fix things.

Fukkes was predictable. Once his timer went off, he'd move to his belly to give his back an equal chance. Fukkes and vanity were synonymous.

His leader held up a hairy arm. To Gabin's eyes, he was looking a little orange. "Next session you need to adjust the spray. You're looking a bit like an orangutan."

"What in the Fates name is that?" Fukkes said.

"Now you're spouting Eleutian drivel," Gabin said. "The Fates? Really. An orangutan is an Earthly monkey."

"I can easily adjust the color. But perhaps I'll keep it as is. It pleases me." Fukkes sighed and melted into the comfort of the chair. "Why are you here?"

"We need more than drones to search for Calix and the Made One. But only you can approve the use of Watchers."

Fukkes smiled. "And I will not approve it. I am hearing rumbles from the animal Clans, our test subjects. We need the Watchers here. Now get out."

The vidscreen chimed, and a blonde woman appeared. She saluted Fukkes, who faced the screen in his tanning chair.

"Hello, Fukkes," she said.

"Hello, Inga."

Gabin recognized the Wolf. She had left her Clan over some problem, he'd thought with the Anti-Made Ones. Which made her call with Fukkes disturbing.

Fukkes flicked a hand. "Leave, Gabin. Now."

Sweaty from claws training—Sir Ambrose had figuratively ripped her to shreds—Bree showered, dressed in a purple tunic and loose green pants, and began to prepare the cubs mid-morning treat. Her phone dinged—a text from Gato requesting she meet him in his suite for a mistral ride. She squealed aloud. He said to wear jeans and bring her leather jacket. A map to his rooms accompanied the text, which was thoughtful.

His map showed the layout of the huge building, and he'd drawn a tiny mistral above his rooms, which he highlighted with a large arrow. Funny man. His home appeared to be the largest in the den, set away from the other apartments and suites.

"That's Gato's, all right. Big ego, big suite."

Audi and Fortis bounced around making chirping sounds, hoping for an adventure.

She bent down. "I'm sorry, kids. But I'm going on a mistral ride, so you can't join me."

Bree swiftly changed, buckled on her waist belt, and slipped her knife into its sheath. Sir Ambrose insisted she always carry one. She left treats out and numerous toys for the cubs, crouched down, and kissed each on the nose. "Use the scratch wall, okay?" The thing was getting threadbare and was scheduled to be replaced next week.

Walking toward Gato's rooms, her hip ached, a lingering pain from her wound. She sat on a bench beside a small courtyard waterfall, its spray refreshing, and massaged it. Life in the circus meant numerous bumps and bruises. Her recent ones, however, felt bone deep, soul deep, a rootless feeling nearly bringing her to tears.

She should have gone to Kit.

But she wouldn't leave her cubs. Not ever.

Worse, she didn't want to leave Gato.

With that dark thought, she continued on to the Alpha's rooms.

Three corridors later, Bree knocked on a heavy door carved with cats gamboling in the grass and lurking high in the trees. A door suitable for an Alpha.

No one answered her knock, but the door was unlocked and she eased it open. "Gato?"

The suite's entry led to a large living room with a high ceiling, carvings on the doors and moldings, and a blue-and-gold woven carpet.

"Gato!" Where was the blasted Alpha?

Black couches and chairs dotted the pristine room and a display of weapons covered an entire wall. Another held a near-life-size painting of Gato, Arina, and a white-haired youth who had to be Ahanu.

In the portrait, Arina sat on a high-backed chair, a sword across her lap, Gato directly behind her, with his one hand on her shoulder and another on the teen standing beside him. All three were smiling, though Ahanu's grin was cocky, his left hand on the knife hilt at his waist. He looked as if he were saying *I'm a man now*. A handsome portrait.

A man's home told his story, especially if he was single.

Gato felt a little messy to her, like he might toss a jacket onto a chair. Yet his home was orderly to the point of perfection. Bree stepped toward the curved fireplace that resembled Southwestern kivas.

The thick wood mantle held half-a-dozen photos—Arina in battle gear, Gato dressed the same, an older couple, probably their parents given the man could be Gato's older twin.

More photos, and a miniature alter with a piece of gold silk, a blue druzy crystal, and an empty bowl. Gato had shown her some of the Clans' alters, which honored The Fates and their five elements— Earth, Air, Sky, Water, and Sorcere.

"How dare you enter my home uninvited?" Arina said.

Bree pivoted to find Arina standing with her hand on her sword pommel, eyes flashing.

Arina stepped closer. "How dare you?"

"I'm as surprised as you are," Bree said, wishing she had room to back up, to maneuver. "Gato sent me a message to meet in his rooms. He even sent a map."

"Show me."

Bree bristled. "You don't believe me."

Arina's eyeroll was followed by "please" gritted out between clamped teeth.

She handed Arina the phone. "See for yourself."

Arina's finger scrolled through Bree's messages. "I see nothing."

Bree swiped the phone back and checked. Gato's message. The map. They were gone.

"I don't understand," Bree said. "Gato sent me a text about taking me on a mistral ride. His map of Catamount was detailed and pointed to these rooms."

"Quite inventive, Ma'am Breena," Arina said. "Why were you spying on me?" Arina's eyes turned fevered as she drew her dagger, held low, as if to thrust it up into Bree's chest.

"Think, Arina. What do I have to spy on?" Bree slid sideways and slipped her hand to the handle of her knife beneath her jacket.

"My secrets," Arina said.

Breena goggled. "Why the fuck would I care about your secrets?"

"Arina, I cannot find the Made..." Gato's voice trailed off as he took in the room, his eyes going half-lidded. "Ah. It seems you have found her."

"She was snooping," Arina said.

"Not true," Bree said with a calm she wasn't feeling.

Gato pressed Arina's arm downward until she lowered the knife. "Snooping?"

"She entered my rooms," Arina said. "Without my permission."

"Worthy of a gutting, dear sister?"

Arina twirled the knife, then sheathed it. "Perhaps."

Gato's laugh rang dark as chocolate.

Their cozy brother-sister banter ticked her off. "I'm leaving."

Gato halted her with a hand on her shoulder. "I would also like to know why you were here, Made One."

She went through the whole message thing again, and his eyes held hers for long moments.

"She is telling the truth, Rina," Gato said.

Arina snorted. "So where did this alleged message go?"

He gave his sister a fierce scowl. "Obviously the one who sent it, deleted it."

"And how could this alleged person use your number, eh?" Arina said. "And why send her here?"

He glanced at her sheathed knife. "You would have cut her. Maybe more."

"I would not have," Arina said.

He arched a brow. "No?"

"Not badly, anyway." Her lips twitched.

"Perhaps. I'm more concerned about this mysterious message." Gato held out his hand to Bree. "May I keep your phone? I will get you another."

She thrust the phone at him and stalked out, knowing any minute she'd feel the Cat Alpha's hand on her arm.

And there it was. She whirled. "What?"

"I thought to escort you home." Gato walked beside her down the hall, hands clasped behind his back. "That incident was unfortunate."

"No, it was deliberate and creepy. Your sister has a short fuse."

"Only with you."

The day had darkened, ominous clouds skating across the sky, while dust swirled and smaller trees swayed in the increasing gale. It had rained seldom since she'd arrived in CatHome, and it would be welcome.

Lightning flared, a surreal brightness flashing the hall and courtyard.

"I really was looking for your rooms," she said. "Not hers. The door was unlocked."

Gato stopped. "The message may have been a prank."

Bree halted, too. "Or it was meant to harm me? Why?"

He blew out a long breath. "The Anti-Made Ones is a possibility."

"They are among us, at Catamount?"

"The Antis are few," he said. "But their impact grows."

The "prank" didn't feel like one, but more underhanded and insidious. "What if it wasn't them?"

"Rest assured, Taz will thoroughly investigate. You are safe, Breena."

A harmless prank. The Anti-Made Ones. Or perhaps a different motive entirely. If she persisted, Gato would put guards on her, the last thing she wanted. She nodded. "The painting in Arina's rooms was beautiful, the one with you and your sister and brother. Ahanu is handsome."

"That he is." Gato clamped his hands on her shoulders, anger and hunger pulsing from his stiffened body. He smiled, and it was the smarmy one he used right before he shot a zinger. "Any time you wish to examine my rooms, please do not hesitate to ask. I would be more than accommodating."

She punched his hands off her shoulders and walked away. When she felt his presence behind her, she swept her leg out to tumble him.

Except he danced away, she lost her balance, and landed on the floor.

"Damn it!"

Laughing, Gato held out a hand and hoisted her to her feet. "Are you hurt?"

Only her pride. "No."

"Our Taekwondo sessions have been effective," he said. "And I am a fast learner."

She studied his face, and his concern and sadness squeezed her heart. No matter what pained him, he had a resolute will.

"You're still going to hold my Challenge, yes?" she said.

A beat, then, "Of course."

"A friend wouldn't do that."

"I am your guardian and protector."

Bree needed a friend more. She held his eyes for long moments until a Peacekeeper hailed Gato, and she strode off to retrieve the cubs for mid-day meal.

CHAPTER FOURTEEN

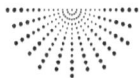

Gato let her walk away. She was distancing herself from him. Not that it should matter. But it did. *She* did.

No, they were not friends. Rather, a part of him hoped they could be much more. Unlike all who saw him as Alpha, she treated him as a man, one worth knowing.

He rubbed the back of his neck, his muscles aching. The sad humor in the situation hit him hard. The prank had worked. His sister had unknowingly gotten what she'd wanted, a distance between himself and Breena. Arina would be thrilled.

After talking with the Peacekeeper, he returned to his den and punched out Fukkes' number on his mobile. He could not face the Alchemic on the vidscreen today.

"Hello, Kitty," Fukkes said.

"Send my brother home."

"But Ahanu is so dear to me." He chuckled. "You did not win the Made One Kitlyn, nor have you scheduled the Challenge for the Made One Breena."

"Kitlyn was unfortunate. The Challenge for Ma'am Breena will happen, as you know. It is a massive event needing much coordination."

"Make the event a reality. At present, your efforts are subpar."

He waited, playing Fukkes' game. The schemes, the posturing—Gato barely recalled when he had been forthright and open, once his hallmark. He slumped on the couch. Fukkes always won these battles, the fight exhausting.

"I have a new task," Fukkes said.

"No." The word popped out, bitter and harsh.

"An Apprentice, a man named Calix, has taken something valuable from us to NoLand. We want you to find Calix, kill him, and return the item."

The growl began low in his belly, and he fought until he wrestled it into a silent howl. How dare Fukkes ask him to murder. Calix's escape explained the Bird's silence.

"You have never asked me to kill before," Gato said.

"What is one more? You have killed many."

"In battle."

"Do you renege?"

"No, I do not." No threat, not even on Ahanu's life, would make him unjustly kill another. Fortunately, Fukkes did not know that. "If I must do this, I will speak with my brother first."

"As usual," Fukkes said. "I anticipate your every wish."

A pause, then, "Brother?"

Ahanu's voice was hoarse, a mere shadow of the melodious tenor that had thrilled audiences in CatHome and beyond. "How are you?" He had to ask, though the answer would be false. It always was.

"Well." Ahanu cleared his throat. "I am well, brother."

"And do the birds still sing for you?" The line from the play Ahanu had once performed meant many things to both of them. He hoped his brother remembered.

"Only until the last note is sung."

Good.

Crackle on the other end, then Fukkes' oily voice came back on the line. "What did that mean?"

"We were reciting lines from a play my brother and I are fond of. A memory we both enjoy."

"Bring me Calix and the package. Then we will talk about releasing your brother."

"As you wish." Gato disconnected, unwilling, *unable* to continue. Yes, they would *talk* about freeing his brother. But they never would.

He pounded his fist into the couch until feathers exploded everywhere.

In her small cubicle within Alchemic City, Neela drank drass and continued calling Calix. Each time the call went to voicemail, her worry escalated.

When Calix told her his plan to steal the Made One, Neela said he should not, that their mission would be compromised. He had ignored her, the fervor in his eyes disturbing.

He had stolen the Made One. Yet when he was safe away, he had failed to call her as promised. She *should* tell Rivaux, her contact and Compass True's leader. Rivaux needed to know about Calix. And yet she could not, was not ready. If she revealed Calix had left the city, and that he had stolen a Made One, she would become point for Compass True. The idea terrified her.

Bree had lived in CatHome for months, through the winter, where snow never fell and time feathered gently over the senses. Yet she felt the promise of spring a few days before the fair. Winter wasn't quite done with them yet, but Bree scented the change on the breeze.

She'd see Kit soon, and she was fizzy with excitement. Days had passed since she'd seen either Arina or Gato, the last time their confrontation in Arina's rooms. Though she wasn't sure what to bring to the fair, she'd begun packing. No one had told her what to do with the cubs, either, as the Alpha had done for Kit's mating. Were they to come or stay in the den? If they stayed, who would watch them?

Twenty minutes later, she and the cubs found the Alpha in the command center, its banks of computer screens manned by three Peacekeepers. Gato stood by a viewing console before several enormous vidscreens, legs spread, arms crossed, focused on the two-story building where the Sequestered lived. Taz clicked keys, while the camera changed angles.

"There has been much activity at the Sequestered's den," Taz said.

A woman in a long orange dress breezed through the front door, the helmet covering her head and face bearing a painted female warrior.

Gato squeezed Taz's shoulder. "Keep an eye, but I expect they're simply aflutter about the fair."

"Perhaps." Taz said, swiveling his chair to look at the Alpha. "How many of them are attending?"

"I believe three," Gato said.

Taz pointed to another screen. "A stranger entered the pub yesterday."

"Prete's cousin was coming for a visit."

"He is from the South, correct? I will check that the stranger is, in fact, Prete's cousin."

"Look into is if he is not," Gato said.

"Will do."

Bree walked toward the two men.

"What do you need, Made One?" Gato said, scratching each cub behind an ear. He stood, pivoting to face her, his sexy-sleepy eyes eating her up.

Really? After their discussion and the days-long silent treatment?

Both Fortis and Audi leaned against her legs, as impatient as she. Bree would swear they'd gained five pounds since yesterday.

"While I'm at the fair," she said. "Who will take care of these guys?"

"No one," he said in a casual voice. "You will not be going."

"I have to. Kit will be there."

"Most likely she will. You will not, however. It is too dangerous."

Taz made no secret that he was watching and listening, and though she liked the guy, her words weren't for public consumption.

She moved closer. "Can we talk about this somewhere more private?"

"No. I regret you will not see your sister, but after the attack on our return from WolfHome, travel for you has become too dangerous. That is final."

She nodded, as if she would actually comply with his edict. "I see."

"There will be other fairs, Made One." He looked genuinely penitent.

"I'm sure there will."

She made certain he didn't hear her snort as she left. Obviously she was going to the fair. She'd find her own way, that's all.

Later that day, Bree and Fudge stood before the stadium arena, Fudge explaining further details of The Challenge. Bree brought up the fair. Fudge would bring the rugs she'd woven, as well as smaller items such as table runners and coasters. Having seen Fudge's exquisite work, she suspected they'd be in big demand.

"Gato said I could go to the fair," Bree said. "Now he says I can't. Can you sneak me in with your group?"

Her friend's eyes widened. "That would be impossible."

"I need to see my sister."

"I understand," Fudge said, taking her hand. "But I go with the Alfa's group. He will see you, I will get into much trouble, and he will send you back."

"I could disguise myself."

Fudge's eyes were mournful. "You want to leave us, to go to WolfHome."

"No." She hugged Fudge tight. "I'm staying here. Promise."

"I want to help, but..."

"No worries, okay?" Bree would still find a way to the fair.

Fukkes had turned off his music and closed the blackout shades. Sitting naked in his tanning chair, he welcomed silence to ponder the transfer to Earth.

Though the Cabal had agreed on a timetable, events such as the Clans' restlessness, the Anti-Made Ones' attacks, and Calix's ridiculous theft of the Made One had derailed that. He must move the Earthly exchange closer, before the Authority, his world's governing body, got wind of it. That would be disastrous.

A Cardinal at the Vatican, the United States president, the UK's House of Lords leader, a Japanese minister of state, and other business, political, and religious leaders were a good fit, though they needed to shift the reality star and the German writer to two other luminaries. Time-consuming research would be involved, and their best researcher had...

The door banged wide. "We found it!"

Fukkes forced his eyes open and glared at Gabin, the wild-haired man he called colleague. Idiot was more fitting.

Neela flew in, saw Fukkes' was naked, and squeaked. "Forgive me, Comstat. I was looking to stop Gabin from intruding."

"I'm right here, Neela," Gabin said, his voice dripping with annoyance.

She whirled and squeaked again. "I didn't see you. But you know you should not enter when the Comstat is tanning."

Gabin pushed her aside and approached Fukkes. "We found Calix. His hidey-hole. We can retrieve the Made One."

Gabin and Neela—two monkeys who blathered on and on. Didn't they see their lunatic behavior? Foolish, especially given Gabin was from Fukkes' world and not this cursed one.

Neela was other. She'd been born into the Alchemic Clan, true, but she acted more like animal Clanfolk. Gabin's behavior... More and more emotions leaked into his actions, ruling him. He even had a sweet spot for the timorous Neela. Fukkes couldn't see why.

Fukkes flicked off the tanning spray, picked up the Japanese fan, and waved it across his body. The sensation pleasured him.

"Gabin," he said. "My foolish friend. We care about this because...?"

Gabin gaped. "To retrieve the unique Made One, of course."

Fukkes waved his hand "She is dead."

"Not if Calix calibrated her correctly."

"Ah, yes." Fukkes waved an arm. "But that's unlikely. You see, I suspected his traitorous tendencies, and had Darva salt the food and drink for his little journey with our favorite psychedelic, aritico."

"That will kill him," Gabin said.

"Yes." Fukkes smiled. "Eventually. It's quite slow acting. A fitting end for a traitor. If by chance he emerges from his hallucinogenic haze, it will be far too late for the Made One."

Gabin's face paled. "But the time and effort we took crafting her into something special."

"A waste. But she is dead, and Calix will be dead soon as well. There are others. Or there will be. Now leave." Fukkes flicked a hand. These discussions were tiresome.

Neela backed out of the room on silent feet. Gabin, on the other hand, flapped his lips like a beached fish. When he finally collected himself he asked the unexpected. "How exactly did you know to put the drugs in his food?"

"He was planning to 'liberate' the Made One. Or at least try. It was obvious, the way he looked at her, behaved around her. How did you not see? His obsession amused me, thus I let it unfold."

"Fark, Fukkes, what a waste. Pitiful."

Fukkes straightened his shoulders. "You dare speak that way to *me*?"

Gabin bowed. "As you say, Comstat."

Oh, how disappointing. Fukkes had hoped for pleading. Perhaps a little begging. No, Gabin just deflated and fell back in line.

How he would love to leave Gabin on Eleutia. But Gabin was one of them, and he would become one of Earth's leaders along with the rest of the Cabal.

Hope bubbled as Bree approached the Sequestered's front door and knocked. A slender woman wearing a turquoise tunic, umber pants, and a woven-straw helmet decorated with stars answered. The Sequestered woman projected style, with a capital S.

"How can I help you, Made One?" she said in a confident voice.

"May I come in?"

"Of course." The woman widened the door and gestured Bree to a large open room with several seating areas, a flat vidscreen, and a bar. "Please sit. I will send the mistress to you. Would you care for any refreshments?"

"That would be lovely."

The Sequestered disappeared down a hall, only to return in minutes with an un-helmeted woman wearing jeans and a blue tank top. Earthy and sharp-featured, the woman looked about forty-something, with graying hair, burnt ochre skin, and light gray eyes that softened when she spotted Bree.

Bree stood and held out a hand.

The mistress took it in both of hers. "It is a great privilege to meet a Made One. Are you well?"

"I'm good, thank you. And please call me Bree."

"Forgive my bad manners. My name is Jocelyn, and I have been mistress at Sequestered House for sixty years. How can I be of service?"

Sixty years? Bree took the couch, while Jocelyn sat across from her. "Sorry, but I'm confused. You look...maybe forty? How could you run Sequestered Home that long?"

Jocelyn grinned. "My understanding is that we Eleutians age differently from those on Earth."

"*How* differently?"

"Slower."

The Sequestered who'd greeted her returned minus her helmet, and carried a tray with a platter of small cakes and glasses bearing troff's minty scent. Her ebony skin glistened, her lips lush, her high-cheekboned face cut along fierce lines, with wild curly hair as striking as her ice-blue eyes. A stunner.

She set the tray down on the coffee table.

"Thank you," Bree said.

A smile turned her face from intense to loving. "I am Makena. May I join you?"

"I'd love that. And I'm Bree."

Once they were settled and nibbling, Jocelyn answered Bree's question. "I am one hundred-and-eighty-eight years old. I am sure you have noticed our days and years correspond to those on your Earth."

Holy shit. All she knew shifted. She had no idea how old Gato was or Fudge or anyone she'd met on Eleutia.

"How old is the Alpha?" Bree said.

"Seventy-eight."

He was more than twenty years older than her fifty-six Earthly years, when she'd imagined him years younger. "Your memory amazes me."

Jocelyn shook her head. "We had a huge celebration when our Alpha's first child was born. A memorable occasion."

"I bet it was. Gato has a younger brother, Ahanu. Do you know much about him?"

The woman's cheeks flushed. "That is not for me to speak of."

Out of the corner of her eye, Makena curled her hands into fists.

For a kid away at college, Bree was bothered by all the hush-hush surrounding him. Which begged the question—why was everyone clam-like about Ahanu, including his brother who deflected all her questions? If the boy was the cause of what troubled Gato...

She sat up straighter. "I have a request, Jocelyn. May I accompany the Sequestered to the fair tomorrow?"

A smile brightened her face. "We would be honored. We will need the Alpha's permission, naturally."

"That's the thing. He doesn't want me to go."

"I see."

"My sister lives with the Wolves and she'll be there. I need to see her."

Jocelyn's sigh gave Bree her answer.

"That I understand," Jocelyn said. "I would miss my brother terribly if I didn't see him every day." Her eyes unfocused and her face softened, as if she were delving deep into memory. Then she took a deep breath. "We would love to help you, Made One, but we cannot without our Alpha's agreement. You are too important."

"I'm not."

"Please understand. Cats are one of the few Clans with Sequestered. That right was given to us by the Clan and by our Alpha. If we broke that trust, we would leave ourselves open to having our rights withdrawn. Gato would fight for us, I am sure of it, but even an Alpha cannot control all the citizenry, nor does he wish to. Breaking the trust would be the wedge some need to steal our rights. Many men want *all* women available to them. No longer would we be allowed to shield ourselves. As mistress, I cannot risk it. Our women are often shy, some damaged. I am very sorry."

Though Bree was disappointed, she got it, having had enough annoying advances during her lifetime. She admired these women who took control of their own lives and made a stand.

"I, too, am sorry, Ma'am Bree." Makena leaned forward holding a steaming carafe. "Would you care for more troff, Mistress? Bree?"

"Thank you, no." Bree stood. "You've been most hospitable and forthright, and I'm truly glad to have met you both." She could ask them not to tell Gato of her request, but it wouldn't affect whether they did or not. Bree didn't bother with useless words.

She chewed her lip as she headed home, past cacti and succulents, the air fragrant and sweet. Who else wore clothes that hid their identities? A leaf drifted to the stone steps, an iridescent bright blue. She reached down and cradled it in her palm.

Someone cleared a throat. "Ma'am Breena, good day!" Taz stood ramrod straight, helmet tucked beneath his arm, sword at his side. But those eagle eyes never stopped moving.

"What kind of leaf is this?" she said. "It's beautiful."

"An ilaberry leaf, though I cannot imagine how it got here. The Fates' gift of a heavenly wine." He frowned. "You have not tasted it, have you?"

He knew about her drinking, which bothered her more than it should. Though she'd almost succumbed, she'd been stalwart since her panic attack

"I have not, Taz. Nor will I." Ouch. She hadn't meant to sound snippy. "But I love kamla. That's from the ilaberry, too, right?"

He nodded, lips pursed. "It is."

The phone clipped to his belt buzzed, and he bowed, slipped on his helmet, and strode off, golden in the day's light as he jogged across the green. The man defined the word "soldier."

A soldier. Who wore a helmet. That could work if she dressed as a Peacekeeper. Their leather armor, especially the helmet, would disguise her well.

CHAPTER FIFTEEN

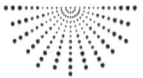

Fudge thought her idea brilliant and helped Bree gather gear for her disguise as a Peacekeeper. Euphoric, now she walked across the concourse, scanning the houses and stores lining the green. The cubs pranced beside her, excited about the "adventure" outdoors and the new toys she'd promised them, which would also allow her to get a gift for Kit with her funds from the Made Ones' Trust.

As with many Earth villages, the stores of CatHome marched beside homes, offices, and Sequestered House, the buildings styled like Southwest adobe or Wright's Usonian ones. All used native materials, many with courtyards or shelters out front and acres of nature out back. The small, often intimate shops made picturing a BestBuy on Eleutia impossible. All blended with the Mediterranean landscape, as if the buildings and land were one harmonious creation.

She paused. What little she'd seen of CatHome looked pretty utopian, yet she'd felt enough anger, watched enough behavior, both good and bad, to know it was as real as any Earthly town.

The cubs left the path to hunt "big game."

"You two, don't wander off." She headed for a small shop with a red roof, a breeze rippling her tunic and the unbound hair that now almost reached her waist.

The cubs joined her in a few shops, but more often played outside. She'd yet to find toys for them or a gift for Kit, until a fabric salesperson suggested the sport store at the end of the block.

"You will like Sir Ambrose," he said.

"I know him! He's my claws trainer."

The young man grinned. "A fine one. The sport store is his, ever since his retirement."

A bell jingled, and Taz entered the store, halting in surprise when he saw her. "Are you following me, Made One?" He grinned, and it turned his craggy face handsome.

"You should smile more often, Taz," she said. "Of course I'm following you. Gotta keep our chief of security in line." She quirked a lip, and he chuckled.

"Your new cloak is ready," the clerk said to Taz.

"Excellent."

"We're off," Bree said. "Errands. Careful, Taz, I might be a spy!"

The men were laughing as she left.

Swinging open the brown door of the sporting goods shop, she entered a large, dark room lined with shelf after shelf of weapons, tools, notions, toys, and more. Like those old-fashioned general stores on Earth, it filled everyone's wants and needs. Perfect.

She waved to Sir Ambrose, who waved back, the gray-haired man's stance poker straight as usual.

"Good to see you, Made One. Excellent timing."

"How come?"

"I have just gotten in a slew of new orders."

"I'm terrified. You're looking to part me from my money."

"I want those gifted korot in my till." He grinned.

She hadn't ever seen him grin—the man barely smiled—and it was almost diabolical. How very un-Ambrose like. *Gifted* korot? She never thought of her trust money that way, not that she spent much. She should examine that.

"I am teasing, Made One. Please. Explore, enjoy."

"Will do!" She raised her palm to her forehead, elbow out straight, and gave the CatHome salute.

His smile widened, though his eyes didn't laugh, perhaps remembering his Peacekeeper days.

Audi distracted her, and then she spotted a small flying mistral hanging from the rafters and raced over.

Sir Ambrose must have been watching because he walked to the silver mistral, pulled the string dangling from its belly, and its wings flapped.

"I love it!" she said. "Would you put it aside for me?"

"Of course," he said, his smile vivid.

She found a basket and slung it on her arm. First, she loaded two large food bowls, which the cubs needed, and when Fortis began rubbing her leg, she reached down to scratch his ear. She paused. Their life forces hummed within her, a quiet presence and a fierce comfort. She kneeled and hugged them both, their motor-boat purrs rumbling. "I love you guys."

Love. You.

They used words more often now, and each time gave her a thrill. After that moment of harmony, they dashed off to explore.

Funny cubs. Though she browsed, she failed to find any stuffed or rubber pet toys, which the cubs would tear apart in seconds, anyway. What she did find were bones as long as her forearm, which she added to her basket, and balls in a bin beneath a hanging row of spears. The balls looked like they were for bocce and sturdy enough for play.

A few aisles over, the cubs growled at something. "Behave, guys."

She dropped the two "bocce" balls into her basket and moved on.

Her devils reappeared, a ball in each mouth. "Guys!"

Both Fortis and Audi began tossing them in the air. Guess she was buying those, too. She put on a stern face and waggled a finger. "Don't you dare take anything else. Understood?"

They nodded, all solemn.

In the middle of the next aisle—the cubs trailing, bocce balls clamped in their jaws—she stopped dead.

Three huge bins held Spalding basketballs, complete with the official NBA insignia. What the hell?

At the counter, the mistral for Kit sat wrapped in clear paper, and she unloaded her basket, including a basketball.

"I found goodies. Are you having a good day, Sir Ambrose?"

He straightened his spine further, his smile sweet. "Very."

Yet his brown eyes probed like a hot poker, a look she'd never seen in the many days he'd trained her. Disturbing. Nerves a-jangle, she fussed with her purchases to mask her withdrawal. Time to pay and leave, and she drew korot from her bag.

"I see you have discovered our newest offering," he said.

"Where did you get the basketballs?" She slid the korot across the counter. "Time to get these guys back for their nap."

"You call them basketballs, eh?" he said. "I purchased them from a trader. Our more unusual goods typically come from them."

"These are from Earth." Because of the Made Ones' existence, all Eleutians knew of parallel worlds.

"They are. Quite the coup for us to get them. Anything that appears from Earth is heavily sought after."

"Appears? How did they get here? I mean to Eleutia."

He shrugged and leaned his elbows on the counter. "Do you know the game these are used for on your world?"

"I do." She laughed, except her eyes started to burn. "My sister knows it better. She's a fanatical basketball fan." Her heart stuttered whenever she thought of Sybi. Though it hurt, she used her slender knowledge and explained basketball to Sir Ambrose.

His grin broke wide, and he leaned forward. "Your basketball sounds like an excellent game. One I think we Eleutians would enjoy. You'll have to give me all the details, such as the court size, the height of the baskets, the lines on the court floor, and especially the rules."

A cub nudged her. "If only I could. I haven't a clue. If Sybi were here, she could tell you all that stuff." The cub nudged again and she leaned down. "What?"

Fortis gave her teeth. *Bone.*

167

"You can have the bone when we return to our suite." She straightened. "How..." Her words trailed off at the laseblaster pointed at her face.

The cubs' emotions burst with aggression, and they began to growl. *Shit.* She repeated the mantra as she pressed a hand to each cub, hoping what she wasn't sure. Where the fuck was Taz when she needed him?

"You've pulled a gun on me, Sir Ambrose. Why?" The blaster's fat round barrel was aimed at her face. No one had ever pointed a gun at her up close, and her heart stuttered, her palms sweaty. Control and calm.

Like when she'd flown the trapeze, terrified of the moment before a performance, when she first gripped the bar. But she'd conquered that fear, and a rush of icy calm flooded her veins, sweeping away everything but cool thought.

Ambrose could have already killed her, which said he wanted or needed something from her before pulling the trigger.

He blinked.

She'd obviously surprised him with her measured question. Perhaps he thought she'd break into hysterics?

"You are an abomination," Ambrose said in a voice both even and reasonable.

"How can you say that and teach me every day?" she said.

"Go." He wagged the gun toward a door that she assumed led to a back room. Bree wasn't about to walk blithely to her death. If someone walked into the store, they'd distract him.

"You're an Anti-Made One, aren't you?" She rested her hands on the counter, leaned forward, bending her knees, and braced for a jump. "Why do this? You might see me as an abomination, but I think and feel. I have a heart and a soul."

His face flushed. "You have no soul. You are a false construct." He waved the gun again toward the door. "Move."

He would kill her, just not in the middle of his store, the fire in his eyes and clipped voice spoke of his commitment. He really did hate her.

With her martial arts, she could disarm him. But the moves were tricky given the counter separating them, and if the laser hit the cubs...

"I can do it here." And the bastard smiled. "But it will make a mess. I like things neat and tidy. Go."

My ass. She liked the idea of a mess upsetting him. It gave her more time to plan. Flying into him over the counter was an option, but it would be better if she could get him out from behind...

Movement to her left. Fortis and Audi...slinking toward the counter's end. Fear rippled through her, and she locked her jaw. *No, no, no.* The cubs were going after him. He would hurt them, kill them.

The risk. She must take it.

A wonderful peace stole over her, her sensei's teachings.

Ambrose waggled the gun and ground out, "*Now!*"

She nodded, seized the laser's muzzle and pushed it away—Ambrose gawping at her—her other hand clasping the grip, and she wrenched it out of his hand. "Fuck you!"

The blaster fired.

It missed the cubs, and she near collapsed with relief.

Holy shit.

The cubs' speed was incredible, a literal blur.

A screeching din as she raced around the counter, the sounds of ripping and tearing horrifying.

The front door flew open with a bang, and Gato, a dozen Peacekeepers, and three mature cats poured inside. But they were too late, at least for Sir Ambrose.

"Stop!" she yelled at the cubs, who were gnawing at Ambrose's face and gut, *eating* him. That might be a part of their nature, but... "No!"

The pair looked up at her, eyes wide, muzzles bloody. "He was such a shit, he'll probably poison you."

She was all the more surprised she didn't find it shocking. "That's right, you two. You did great, really great. But we don't eat people."

They padded toward her, but they didn't understand. She

couldn't blame them and she would explain later. Or maybe Bartholomew would save her the trouble. No, he might encourage them.

The cubs sat before her, their heads hung low.

She hunkered down and faced two bloody muzzles and a string of guts dangling from Fortis' jaw. Bree swallowed hard. *Not gonna upchuck here.*

"You were terrific, guys. You saved my life." Though they were covered in Sir Ambrose's glop, she pet them and hugged them. "I'm very proud of you both."

"As am I." Gato prowled over. "Exceptionally proud. You are fine CatGuard, fine sons of your sire." He leaned against the counter and sighed.

The dreaded lecture was coming, and she had no intention of waiting for it.

Gato helped her rise. "Thank you," she said. "For that and your timely entrance."

A brow quirked, his frown deepening. "Timely? I think not. We were late. Ambrose… He was once a great warrior, feted by the Clan, and I have been blinded by his care of me all these years. When my father died, it was Ambrose who assumed the job of teaching and training me. Ambrose who…" He cleared his throat and stared at Ambrose's remains.

"I'm sorry, not that he's dead, but for your loss."

"Loss? He betrayed us all." He squeezed his eyes tight and sighed. "Can you not stay put?"

"Why should I?"

"Gah!" The hand he banded around her upper arm shook. But he wasn't angry. Rather, his whole body trembled.

"What's wrong?"

"Other than you nearly getting blasted to the Sky?" His hug was fierce and tight, and as he held her, his trembling subsided. He took her hand and led her from the store, the cubs and Bartholomew padding behind them.

"Wait! I want my stuff."

Gato signaled to a Peacekeeper to retrieve her goods, and he took the basket in hand. "We are returning to your suite. You will shower, and we will talk."

"*You* are a tyrant," she said, her voice soft, the adrenaline rush receding and leaving her shaky. She was covered in blood and gunk, and a man she considered a friend had tried to kill her.

"Of course, I am." Gato waggled his brows. "I am Alpha, and you will do as I say."

"Always." She didn't even have the energy to snort.

Gato stared at her, incredulous. The woman *never* relented. Today, she caved like a deflated tent. He didn't like it. She must be more shaken than she appeared.

Curse Ambrose. His mentor had been such a great friend, Gato had put Breena with him for claws training.

The betrayal stung, true, but his brain had exploded when he saw the laseblaster pointed at Breena's face. His fear-fury had matched what he felt when Fukkes' had taken his brother's ear. But Bree was no Ahanu, and yet... *Fark.*

He led Bree across the greensward, but because of the cubs, he took her a different route home, the mischief-making pair staying as close and quiet as the Fates' messengers. Sadly, ones who stank. Time for their first outdoor swim. That would be interesting. Perhaps even fun.

Breena, on the other hand, was not fun. She had closed up tight as a sealed barrel of kevitt, her skin chalk, her freckles in stark relief.

She was traumatized, but if he put his arms around her for comfort, she would spit at him like a wounded puma. The Fates. Breena mattered to him too much.

He led them beneath Catamount's overhang and down a gentle slope to the river. The Afródis meandered through CatHome and beyond the mountains to the sea, her waterfall sprays sparking rainbows. Idyllic, other than the cubs' stench and Breena's passivity.

At the river's edge, he turned to Bree. "Tell Fortis and Audi to swim and clean off."

She blinked a couple times before answering. "You do it."

Her apathetic voice chilled him. "No. It must be you." He leaned closer and whispered. "As part of their training."

"I see," she said in that same detached voice. "Fortis, Audacia, go in the river, swim, get clean."

Like infants who loathed bath time, the kids mewed and protested. In other circumstances, he would have laughed. "Demand they do it."

She waved over the two kits and bent down. "Sit, please. We cannot go home until you are clean. You won't get the bones or the balls until you wash off all the blood and guts in that river. Got it?"

The cubs nodded.

"Now go!"

They padded off, slower than snails, reluctance in each step, but when they reached the river, they slid in like seals. Gato remained by the bank to make sure the current did not trouble them.

A splash. Bree. Could she even swim?

Seconds later she burst through the surface and his breath froze. Silver water sluiced down her body, a woman reborn.

He dropped the boot he had removed to rescue her and stared. She was Theris, a goddess of the sea who was everything beautiful and kind. Watching Breena's long, even strokes back and forth across the river, he relaxed.

The cubs were fine, too, having discovered swimming fun, and had begun a game of hide-and-seek.

He thumped down onto the bank. His day had gone from bad to a shote-storm, and he scrubbed his face, trying to wipe that image of the blaster aimed at Breena from his mind. His Bree.

No. She was *not* his Bree. She wasn't. Even if when he saw her, his heart fluttered like a teen's. Even if he thought about her hours a day. Even if he dreamed of her. His temple throbbed.

A woman meant for The Challenge could not be his.

But as she swam laps, his mouth dried. She made him ache for a closeness, to know all of her, and for her to know him. He had not felt those desires in eons, and now feelings hummed between them that felt strong as a mistral's bones.

They could not be.

Or… He could find a way.

He leapt to his feet and cupped his hands around his mouth. "We go!"

Bree paddled across the river, lifting herself onto the bank, when he would have helped her. She stood before him, dripping, her eyes dull and unfocused.

"Call the cubs, Made One."

Three tries later, they responded, typical of both puma and human cubs. Bree had pulled on her boots by the time the pair emerged, shaking themselves, thus blessing him with an unneeded bath. But they were clean and minus that rancid smell.

Breena walked across the bridge.

"Wait, Made One," he said.

She whipped around. "Why should I?"

"You are upset."

"Am I?"

CHAPTER SIXTEEN

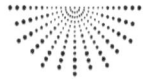

Upset. Ha! That didn't begin to describe Bree's feelings. Death and danger plagued Eleutia. She couldn't even walk into a store without almost getting killed. Was that how the people in war zones felt? A target, hunted and haunted.

When impending death from Huntington's had loomed, their world had been calm and measured. As their end drew near, they knew what to expect and how to deal with it. At the 7-Eleven, they hadn't worried about being chased on horseback or a gun thrust in their face.

But there was no going back. Her lips twitched—dear Sybi would call that the understatement of the year.

"Yes," she said. "Let's return to the security of my prison."

Gato frowned. "Catamount is no prison."

She flopped on the ground, legs crossed, head in her hands. "I didn't live this way on Earth. Always in danger. Always threatened. I feel..."

He lifted her from the ground and hugged her close, his arms warm and strong. Instead of confining, he felt comforting, safe and protective, and she allowed herself to relax.

Gato pressed her head beneath his chin and stroked her wet hair.

"I cannot imagine it, Breena. Being brought to another world where I am alone and unknown. Do you miss your Earth terribly?"

A hollowness inside her. "I should. But I don't, which upsets me." Her laugh was bitter. "My animals, the girls who worked for us, my sensei, but...there's no one else."

"Your circus friends?" he said.

"I've missed them for years, long before we were pulled to Eleutia. We left them, not the other way around."

"I am sorry."

"Don't be. It was our fault, distancing ourselves because of Kit's accident, Mordecai's death, and the Huntington's. I miss our animals most of all. Here, even though I've seen Kit and know she's here, I feel unmoored, like a cork bobbing in a vast unfamiliar sea."

"You are not alone. I swear on the Fates, I am here. I will always be here for you."

"I wish..." To stay at CatHome, with him and the others. To explore the feelings building between them, thin filaments of emotion that wove back and forth, like the warm ties that bound one person to another. She wanted...

"What do you wish?" he said, his breath warm against her cheek.

She tilted back her head to stare up at him. "I wish..." You. "I'll leave CatHome after The Challenge, right?"

Only his eyes spoke, and they said she was correct, no matter the sorrow she saw there as well.

She stiffened and pushed away. If her attachment to him and CatHome deepened, her heart would splinter when she was forced to leave. No more Gato or Fudge or Ax or...

She would fight. Run away. Run to Kit. No, not there, not war, but even if she was hauled back to CatHome, she would fight until the Challenge victor shouted "Mine!" And then she would keep on fighting.

Gato put on that stoic Alpha mask as he unpinned the ornamental sigil of the CatGuard from his shoulder. Plain bronze, all CatGuard wore them, but as she looked closer, two emerald eyes winked from the cat's face. Gato's eyes.

"For you," he said. "Send this. I will always come."

"In other words, when I'm with some other Clan, and I'm in trouble, I'm to send for you?"

"Yes."

She shook her head. "A beautiful gift, but I can't accept it." She folded his fingers around the sigil. "I'm sorry, but you don't understand at all."

She broke free and walked toward the steps rising to Catamount. She needed Kit, to see her, to ground herself once again. At the fair, she could do that. And she would.

Calix crouched before the small fire he'd built and turned the spit, making sure to brown the rabbit evenly. Darva had packed the wrong food and nutrient drinks, that was certain. His gums had begun to bleed, and he was exhausted, his mind increasingly foggy. His mother's voice chirped in his head, so he made a point to pick some edible greens. Straightening, he remembered how Hyla always scooped her greens onto his plate, and his mood soured further. He thought about his dead sister into the night.

The day of the fair dawned sunny and unusually hot, the road dusty. Bree's CatGuard uniform, with its leather cuirass and suffocating helmet, itched from sweat. Fudge had heard about Sir Ambrose, and it was she who insisted Bree go as CatGuard, rather than Peacekeeper, as the latter would stand out in Gato's cohort. Only Fudge, who walked beside her, knew of her deception.

The sun beat down on them. She had cut her long hair for two reasons, first to fit beneath her helmet and second because it would piss off Gato. Yet the process had shocked her. Bree expected to be gleeful, ridding herself of the hated red, and yet as the locks fell one after another, she found herself staring at the many shades, some near blonde, others a rich red. Almost pretty.

When she was eight, she'd begun to loathe her hair and all the names the kids called her. Comparing it to Kit's rich auburn was a constant source of misery.

Furious and annoyed when she stared in the mirror at the hacked-off mess, she'd shaved her head into a mohawk. *That's right, goddammit, a mohawk.* She cringed. Her anger at her hair, a longtime companion, was elusive, as if she'd clung to it out of habit. She'd run her hand across the bristles. "I'm a warrior!" she said, staring at the flaming crest in the mirror.

Lucky stars, she looked hideous. Gato would have fits, and she laughed. As her mom always said, it would grow back.

Wind blew dust in her face, the breeze as warm as the surrounding air. One thing was certain, her mohawk helped with the heat, even if this whole soldier business was damned hard work.

Leading the group, Gato and Arina rode magnificent stallions. Two CatGuard outriders accompanied their group, along with eight additional CatGuard and three Sequestered, their bright clothes and dramatic helmets in striking contrast to the CatGuard's uniformity. Behind the Sequestered, a heavily laden wagon pulled by two mules lumbered forward containing trade goods for the fair. Bartholomew and three tan pumas accompanied them, and she could picture Audi and Fortis prancing beside her. Next year, her cubs would be old enough to come, and she'd told them that when she'd left them in the CatGuard nursery.

Barth knew she was here, and he might tell Gato, or he might not, the four-legged cat's way of thinking different from human ones. She bit her lip. Even if he told Gato, Bree wasn't returning to CatHome, and each mile they traversed cemented that determination.

Fudge and Bree marched at the rear of the group. Her friend said the main body of CatHome's fair attendees were taking a different, overland route with the bulk of goods in that caravan. When she'd asked Fudge why, she'd had no idea.

"Are your rugs in the wagon ahead of us?" Bree said.

"Yes. It holds all my trade goods, as well as others' pottery and jewelry, specialties of our Clan and highly sought after. Perhaps some spoon carvings, though we seldom sell those to outsiders."

"Was it you who left the spoon by my bed?"

Fudge chuckled. "No. "

"Why are you smiling?"

"It is a courting gift."

"I can't think of anyone who'd leave that."

"Can't you?"

"No! What about the animals? Do all Clans bring their symbionts?"

"The leaders, always."

"They don't fight with each other?"

A laugh burst from Fudge. "Sometimes. More often, the men get into it. Peacekeepers assigned to the fair stop things from getting out of hand." She shook her head. "Mostly."

"The fair's a big deal then."

"It is. A four-times yearly event no Clan in the Northwest Quadrant would miss."

Gato signaled the CatGuard to move beside the wagon and Sequestered when a cloud of multicolored butterflies shimmered from the trees, their wings iridescent in the light.

"Beautiful," Fudge said.

"Yes."

She and Fudge dropped back, while Ax and three other CatGuard Bree didn't know moved beside the wagon and Sequestered.

"Are we almost there?" she asked Fudge after the soldiers left.

"No. You sound like a newly weaned cub."

She did, but she wasn't used to hiking for hours, not in this body or armor. Her thighs quivered, her shoulders ached, and her scalp itched.

"What's the fair like?" she said.

Fudge gave her an odd look. "Do you not have fairs on Earth?"

"We do. But I've never been to an Eleutian one."

"The fair is set up as a spiral, with the center holding the gathering hall and its outbuildings. That's where the auctions take place and contests are held, as well as dancing and evening feasts." Fudge's animation grew along with her description, her hands gesturing to illustrate. "As the spiral moves outward, numerous stalls are set up with goods and services for sale, along with drinking and eating kiosks and areas for dining."

"It sounds a lot like our fairs, though without the spiral layout," Bree said.

"Really?" Fudge said. "The spiral's outer part holds the animal pens, with horses, sheep, and other animals for sale. If any mistrals are up for auction, they will be housed there, too."

As she listened to Fudge, Bree's fatigue slipped away. She would see Kit soon and the fair sounded exciting. "On Earth we have contests for the best animals and baked goods and such."

"We have that, too," Fudge said, circling a large pothole in the dirt road. "With the fair taking place over seven days, there is much to do and see. And eat!" Fudge grinned.

Bree could almost taste the fried dough topped with powdered sugar and honey. One of her weaknesses. Right now, her mouth was gritty, and she swigged some water from her pouch and spat.

Gato held up a hand to halt the group. "At ease!"

Thick pine and spruce flanked the road, while moss and sprigs of grass lined the edge, the air filled with rich forest scents.

They took a seat in the shade, and Fudge leaned close, lowering her voice. "We are crossing NoLand, home to the CastOuts, though that is unofficial."

"Why did we stop?"

Fudge shrugged.

"You lived up here, in the mountains?" Bree said.

"I did." Fudge ducked her head, as if embarrassed. "It is not something I talk much about, Bree."

"I wish you would, so I could understand."

Fudge peered into the dense screen of trees, as if searching for her old home. "Many say CastOuts are dangerous oddities. Wild men and women with no laws, no inhibitions, no real community. Some know that they are fearsome fighters."

"Were you one of the fighters?"

Fudge nodded. "Only once. CastOuts have laws and inhibitions, just as other Clans do, but our society is structured differently. The Alchemics see us as imperfect, and they do not tolerate imperfection. Some of those infants and children die, but many are found and grow to maturity as a CastOut. The Alchemics know, and we are allowed to exist, separate and never equal."

"That's horrible to tear children from their family and Clan." Bree thought of meeting Kustaa, Jaron and Elise's infant. That adorable child would soon be a CastOut. The tragedy of it sickened her. From what Gato had said, Kustaa would be safe and loved. But his parents' pain... Devastating.

"Yet," Fudge said. "CastOuts have many exceptional gifts."

"Yours is... I'm sorry, I shouldn't ask."

Fudge frowned, eyes darkening. "It is all right. I would like you to know since we are friends, and I might get angry or excited or..."

Bree touched Fudge's arm. "I don't need to—"

"I breathe fire."

Though Bree almost sputtered, she caught herself. "I see."

Fudge laughed. "No you do not. But you are trying to act normal. For me. That is a kindness."

"I, um...I never knew anyone who breathed real fire before. You do mean like dragons, right?"

"Our dakos? Like them. Yes." Fudge smiled, but the darkness in her eyes returned. "As a newborn, when I scorched my mother's arm, they knew. My parents tried to hide it. They loved me. But newborns get angry and agitated easily. When they failed to conceal me, my world changed."

"You lost your parents, your Clan. I'm so sorry, Fudge."

"Thank you."

"But how does a person breathe fire?"

"It is not easy." Fudge chuckled, her eyes up ahead on the trees, as if she were waiting for something or someone. "I am the lone fire breather, as far as I know. Many CastOuts have one-of-a-kind gifts. One friend has three arms, another can help things grow, another has skin strong as steel. At least one can fly."

"That's so cool." Bree had imagined flying, truly soaring through the air, many, many times. The CastOuts sounded like X-Men, rejected because they were different, which to some equaled scary. "We don't have people on Earth who can breathe fire, fly, or any of the other things you mentioned, though I'm not sure about the person with three arms."

Fudge bent to whisper. "It is rumored the Alchemics experimented with our symbiont DNA. We speak in whispers because the idea that they would do such a thing..." Fudge shook her head.

Horrific, and deeply disturbing. Even worse, these Alchemics ostracized the very people they may have created.

"Could my sister, Sybelle, be there, at the CastOut encampment?"

"Not as far as I know."

"But maybe?" Bree said.

A few yards away, Gato stiffened, his head tilted as if listening for something. He straightened in the saddle as a man stepped from the buffer of trees.

The stranger was huge—tall, muscled, and fit, with an odd fall of rust and slate-blue hair tied back in a queue. He wore a large sword strapped to his hip above leather pants, a t-shirt, and an embroidered vest. Two smaller men followed, wearing similar pants, plain vests, and carrying bows and arrows.

Gato dismounted and walked to greet them.

"Do you know them?" she asked Fudge.

"They're CastOuts. The one with the striped hair is our leader."

A woman slipped from the forest, her long black hair swinging as she ran toward Gato and hurled herself into his arms.

Fury took Bree by surprise. Not anger. Jealousy. Yeah, she had it bad. Considering the length of their hug, her feelings might be justified. At least they didn't kiss. The woman was younger than she'd first thought, a beauty with olive skin and wide blue eyes, her generous mouth breaking into a smile at something Gato said.

"Who is she?" Bree said.

"Luciana."

"A beautiful name for a beautiful woman."

"She is that," Fudge said. "In spirit, as well."

"How are she and Gato friends?"

Fudge shook her head. "I cannot say. You will have to ask the Alpha."

Bree would once she no longer needed her disguise, though she might not like his answer.

"Take thirty minutes," Gato said to the troop. "Eat. Relax." Then he and the woman moved off the road to sit on a boulder. No one said a word, though Arina's sad expression spoke volumes.

She and Fudge ate some tasteless rations while the pair talked. When the time was up, Gato and the black-haired beauty clung to each other in a desperate hug, the woman's tears plainly visible.

They once again marched off, but Gato turned in the saddle to watch the CastOuts melt back into the woods. Arina leaned toward Gato, speaking rapidly, and her tone was angry, though her words were too soft to hear.

What an odd meeting. And while Bree retained that prick of jealousy, she didn't think Gato and the woman were lovers. But they were more than friends.

Calix sat on a stump.

Why was he out here?

He should be doing something, but he couldn't...

A chipmunk! Good food. He leapt.

Opening his eyes inside the cabin, Calix knew he had again lost track of time. He stretched, touching his toes, then reaching up high. Today he felt more himself. A better day. He rose to prepare the Awakening serum.

Water burbled on the stove, and he blinked, then laid out his tools in a neat row, the vials lined up like little Peacekeepers.

He tottered over to her, lost his balance, and caught himself on the Made One's clear prison. Her angelic face had filled out, her hair grown lush. She was holding on, the elixir staving off her deterioration. For now.

He needed to do something. But he...

A rustle outside. He staggered over and opened the door on those idiots Keplar and Prosa. They looked funny, their heads big as watermelons on teeny-tiny bodies.

He had forgotten to find another cabin.

"It's been weeks, Calix," Keplar said.

"Weeks?" Calix said.

"Let us inside," Prosa said.

"Come on in!" He raised the blaster and pointed it at Prosa. "Or maybe I'll end you." He giggled.

Keplar took a step forward. "Put it down."

"No!" He waved the blaster.

The two watermelon heads looked at each other and vanished. He scratched his chest. He needed a bath.

Was he just talking to someone?

CHAPTER SEVENTEEN

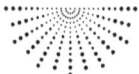

Bree was dusty and tired, but her heart leapt at the sight of hundreds of colorful tents rising up the mountain bowl's sides. Ochre and cinnabar, crimson and sunny yellow, turquoise, violet, and deep green—glorious. A remembered joy when they'd returned to the circus after the winter hiatus. On her left, cliffs fell to the roiling sea far below, and in the chill breeze scents of ocean mingled with pine, the wild fragrance bracing.

Moments later, the entire bowl came into view, wound with the spiral Fudge had described. Huge wooden buildings sat at the center, buzzing with activity, while the throngs entered the bowl, some setting up tents, others wandering the stalls. Bree wanted to see everything.

They followed Gato as he led them down the dirt track at a measured pace, and they soon wove through people and animals, who scurried off the path. Down and down they went until they came to a large green space where Gato halted their troop.

The Sequestered didn't wait for Gato's orders but began setting up their tents.

Bree leaned toward Fudge. "Do CatGuard have a separate tent?"

"Yes," Fudge said. "But you cannot sleep there."

"Right. Okay if I stay with you?"

"That would be good, except... My helpers and apprentices will see you."

"Better than CatGuard seeing me." She grinned. "If we're discovered, I'll say I snuck along."

Fudge rolled her eyes. "Gato will surely believe that one."

"I'll figure something out."

"This was a very bad plan. You will be found out."

Bree shrugged. "I don't give a shit. I had to come."

"I know." Fudge patted Bree's shoulder. "I know."

In the hullabaloo of setting up, Bree snuck away and changed her clothes behind a small stand of birch. She'd brought jeans and a bunch of upper layers to keep warm, along with a hat to hide her flaming mohawk. She'd also banded her breasts, not that she needed to.

Bree searched the fairgrounds for Kit, who she learned wouldn't arrive with her Wolf mate until the following day. *Damn.*

The sun was setting, the air chilly, and she was played out and starving.

A breeze made her shiver, and she hugged her heavy quilted jacket tighter. Sitting on the grass behind Fudge's tent, she bit into the gyro-style wrap. *Stars*, that tasted good.

Fecund scents and sounds, of animals and people and pine, lulled her. Nearby, a few cheerful campfires glowed as folks cooked their evening meal. The distant whoosh of waves, of giddy laughter and musicians practicing, tore her back to the circus, the sublime time before it all went to hell.

She longed for a jigger of scotch and a pack of Marlboros as she sipped her troff. She shouldn't go back there, back to that time with her parents, her sisters, her circus family. And Mordecai. Oh, how he'd loved her, and she, him. She loved them all of course. And flying —soaring through the air, twirling, spinning knowing Mordecai would catch her each time, his large hands gripping her wrists with authority. He never slipped, never let go, not even once, until that day his fly bar had broken and he'd tumbled down and down and down. The thud when he'd slammed onto the sawdust floor. The crowds' screams. Her own, matching the agony in her heart. It had felt like her death, as well.

Yet though his passing was terrible, Kit's injuries felt worse, their horrific effects rippling through the years.

A shadow fell across her lap, and she peered up. Gato glared down at her, hands on hips, Barth at his side.

Even rigid with fury, he sent sparks flying through her belly. Thank the stars she was wearing her hat.

She reached out a hand to pet Barth's chin, then patted the grass beside her. "Have a seat."

His nostrils flared. "Have a seat?"

"Sure." He was trying hard not to yell. Poor fella. "Take a load off."

"I do not even know what that means," he muttered.

Barth nudged her chin for another pet, and she wished her cubs were beside her. At least Barth wasn't mad at her like his brother Cat. Gato had found her too soon. She could really use that scotch.

He chuffed, then folded his body to sit beside her, his breath hot on her ear. "You were to stay at Catamount, where you would be *safe*."

"Safety is overrated, to quote Kit." Did she dare when he was so pissed off? Oh, what the hell. "Who was the woman you met on our way here?"

"Luciana," he said, brows raised. "Why?"

"You seem very fond of her."

A flash of pain, his chuckle bitter. "Fond? I love her more than life."

That shut her up.

"I know that look," he said. "You misunderstand, *poosha*. Luciana is my daughter."

"Daughter?" she said. "She looks old enough to be your wife."

He sighed. "That was Derula, my partner, and we are getting off the subject of your disobedience."

His daughter a CastOut. He hurt, and the million questions in her head could wait. "You know I'm not the obedient kind."

His eyes iced over. "You leave in the morning."

"I'm afraid not. I *will* see Kitlyn."

His fire burst through the ice. "*I* am your *Alpha*."

His face might be a mask of ferocity, but his eyes told the story. He knew she would stay, but he would make it hard for her. Gato performing his Alpha-ness. "I may be your Made One, but you're not the boss of me."

He grunted, then mumbled, "I'll have my Peacekeepers escort you."

She smiled and kissed his cheek. "Sure you will. And won't everyone be agog by the fuss I make when you force a Made One to leave. My epic scene will be fun…for me."

He ground his teeth. "Why must you be so contrary!"

"Because I have to see my sister."

"They haven't even arrived yet."

"So I learned." In for a penny… She removed her hat.

"*The farking Fates!*" He raised his hand, then dropped it. "What have you done?"

He was literally shaking. Didn't the queen say "Keep calm and carry on?" Bree grinned, though she felt like running. "For my disguise."

"You look like a member of the Hyena Clan!"

"I'll take that as a compliment." She peered at him, face serious.

He stared back at her, equally serious, his earring glinting in the firelight, but his lips twitched.

She smiled, and they both began to laugh.

He wrapped her in his arms. "What am I to do with you, Breena?"

Love me? "Don't fuss about me staying."

They parted. "I will try, *poosha*. Our donkeys have hair like that as well."

"Hyena or donkey," she said, her finger tapping her cheek. "Such a hard choice."

His laugh bellowed around the campsite before he quieted, his words slow in coming. "I only wish to keep you safe."

"Dear, frustrating man, I know that. And I appreciate it. But even before you sat down, you knew I wouldn't leave."

Barth slid his head onto her thigh, its weight warm and solid. She stroked him, his vibrating purr tickling her.

Gato stared at the stars canopied across the sky. "It is beautiful, no?"

"Very." This high in the mountains, the air was crystal and cool, the scents rich with life. All background music to this man. This one man who affected her like no other. He was arrogant, paternalistic, and imperious—she shouldn't have found any of that attractive—yet he moved her more deeply even than Mordecai.

She clasped his face. "Why are you sad?"

Again his laughter boomed. "Sad? Do not be absurd."

Her hands fell away. "Someday, catman, you'll tell me." She rose to her feet.

"Wait. Stay." Gato grabbed her hand.

"Why should I?" She wanted to. Very much.

"Please."

That damned word.

Once seated, she faced him, and he cupped her chin. His breath was warm on her lips, while a mixture of hunger and despair leaked from his eyes.

"You confound me," he said.

"Back atcha, fella."

"You make me want more," he said. "You make me forget my purpose, my duty." He closed his eyes and pressed his cheek to hers.

And all her wiseass comebacks vanished. His sorrow and need suffused her with a wish to comfort and an answering desire for more as well. Their embrace was deeper, holding the promise of something rich and meaningful. It whispered of what might be.

She wrapped her arms around him and held on tight.

He pulled her closer still, the world dissolving to heat and want. To touch his skin, to weave his hair with her fingers, to press her lips to his. Instead, she breathed him in, reveling in the moment's intimacy. When they parted, his eyes glittered with fire. He turned her, so her back rested against his chest, his arms banding her waist, his breathing synced to hers. Or was it hers to his?

Bree relished the pleasure and comfort of him holding her. His muscled forearms were warm beneath her hands, and she stared at the stars as if they would answer the mystery of this relentless attraction.

Attraction. Who was she kidding?

Each day at CatHome, her feelings had deepened, growing branches, spreading through all of her like kudzu. A male friend once said she was the best casual lover he'd ever had. She did casual well. Her emotions for Gato were anything but.

He pressed a kiss to her cheek. "I want you."

"I know. The feeling is mutual."

"Come, *poosha*." He rose, pulling her with him.

She stepped back. A joke. She could steamroller this with a joke. "You're too old for me, catman. You're over seventy, while I'm a mere fifty-six."

He raised that arrogant Alpha brow. "Irrelevant."

No more games. "I can't, Gato."

He pulled her tight to him again, a grin on his face. "Of course you can."

She smoothed her hand down the sharp angle of his cheek, felt the scruff bristling his chin. "You are putting me up for The Challenge, and I can't make love with a man who plans to give me away. How could I?"

His face tightened. "Because we want each other. It's not impor—"

"It *is*, Gato. Desire used to be good enough for me. Not with you, it isn't. I want more than a fuck. And you don't. Or can't."

Bree pulled her hand from his and walked toward the tent, not wanting him to see how much rejecting him cost her.

Come after me. Let me share your burdens. Say you won't put me up for The Challenge.

He did none of those things. And she was alone. Again.

· · ·

Gato lay naked on his bedroll, his hand fisted around his cock, thankful the Clan Alpha shared a tent with no one. Breena had given him a cockstand to surpass any other, and he stroked the blasted member for release knowing it would not be enough. It would never be enough until he buried himself deep inside that confounding, frustrating, remarkable woman who thwarted him at every turn.

He pictured her naked beneath him, laving her breasts, pounding into her, loving her as no man ever had before. She was his, and the longing inside him would be assuaged by nothing less.

Breena wanted his truths. That was not possible until Ahanu was safe. Then no Challenge would happen, and he would keep Breena for himself. For *them*selves, partners, perhaps even mates.

He jerked his hand up and down his cock, faster, tighter, back arching, straining for completion as he pictured Breena's smile, heard her voice, saw her pleasure.

Ahhh.

He melted into the bedroll, reaching for his worn t-shirt and cleaning himself up.

Not his hand, not another woman, nothing and no one would satisfy him but Breena.

"Fark!"

He dressed and strode from the tent, his steps fast, and faster still, until he ran through camp, a demon on his heels.

Fark.

He was Alpha, head of the most powerful Clan on Eleutia. For Clan, Breena would be The Challenge prize. Nothing mattered more than Clan.

Gasping, he halted abruptly and bent at the waist, hands on hips, breathing as if he had run a race and lost.

His lies, those arrogant lies, were hypocrisy.

Twenty minutes later, Gato slid onto his belly beneath a pine, its branches an additional cloak in the night. Barth laid beside him, ever vigilant. The inky dark meant little to his cat senses, and he saw perfectly well.

Down below, two Peacekeepers guarded the entrance to the

double-sized tent set beside a cluster of Madronis trees. Additional Peacekeepers belonging to each attendee surrounded the tent, though he didn't see Axayacatl or Taz. But they were there, he sensed their presence through Barth. Others entered the tent, all cloaked and hooded. Members of Compass True were a cautious lot.

After a good fifteen minutes, he whispered, "All clear?" to Barth.

Yes.

Gato checked his mobile one last time, then he and Barth approached the tent. The two men guarding its entryway sat on stools by the tent flaps, laughing and drinking while playing that new chess game. They appeared relaxed and inattentive, a deception he approved of. No one would suspect that the most important meeting of the fair, perhaps on all of Eleutia, was about to take place.

As he walked toward them, the men rose, their jokes and intoxication falling away like a costume. He whispered the password into a Peacekeeper's ear, and the pair lifted the double-canvassed tent flaps, their thickness preventing any light from bleeding through.

Hovering in the doorway, he sized up the room. Six men and three women sat at a large round table set with bottles of drass, cups, plates, and food, with a small brazier burning at the table's center. Several sound disrupters sat on the table, as well as around the tent's edge, while rich rugs sprawled across the earthen floor, evidence someone had a flair for the lavish. Probably the Falcon, who loved his creature comforts. No recording devices were present, and the single notebook belonged to a young woman at a side table, furiously scribbling across the pages and ignored by the members talking in low voices.

As he stepped inside, leaving his weapons in the designated spot, the room went silent. He spotted Rafe, and his discomfort warred with his pleasure.

Gato nodded to the members and took the seat across from Rafe's to tweak him. He didn't doubt the man's blood pressure had risen a notch or two at his entrance. His good friend Kestrel sat to Rafe's right. He gave Kes a nod, which was returned. To Rafe's left, the sharp-faced Falcon Alpha wore a worried look, perhaps concern for his Clanmate, Calix. The ancient female Bear Alpha, the excessively young Deer First Commander, and the slippery Ferret Chief Armorer were also present. He didn't recognize the remaining two men, one with a massive tiger beside him and the other with a small monkey perched on his shoulder. Nor had he met the new Sequestered councilor, not a Cat, her helmet painted with wings.

As Gato poured himself some drass, Rafe rose, nodded to the group, and pointed to the little redhead. "We called this meeting for a specific purpose. Tilde, our lead scientist, has discovered something that is outlandish enough as to seem impossible. But we have done tests, which Tilde will tell you about. Our purpose this week is to discuss and find a solution to our discovery. Tilde?"

The woman stood, pale, lips tight, eyes wide. Terrified, obviously. He smiled at her, hoping to reassure the girl that they wouldn't eat her.

Tilde drew a long breath, poked her glasses up her nose, and began.

"For how long I don't know, though I postulate it has been years, centuries. What I *do* know is that the Alchemics have been poisoning our water."

Murmurs around the room, but no one spoke.

"They have been poisoning our water," she said, "with a drug that affects a woman's reproductive system. The drug causes our women to give birth primarily to male children, rather than a balance of fifty/fifty, male to female." Tilde huffed, a large sound coming from a very small person. "In other words, rather than help us with the declining female birthrate by creating Made Ones, the Alchemics themselves have caused this horrible, farking situation where women give birth to only twenty females per one hundred births. Sorry for the swear." She sat back in her seat and crossed her arms.

Had he heard right? No. The Alchemics would not do that. They were everything logical, and this fantastical idea made no sense. But he, like the rest in the room, remained silent. Eleutia was *dying*. The male/female disparity was not merely killing the planet, it had twisted its males, birthed the Sequestered, decimated families, caused inter-Clan wars, and more. That the Alchemics had engineered it was too twisted, too vile to comprehend.

The Falcon Alpha opened his mouth to speak, but Rafe stood and said, "Falcon, hold that thought. Please present your evidence, Tilde."

Tilde again rose. She explained how she'd found a tiny drone, and where that discovery had led her. "You see, we couldn't test it on women because of the nine-month gestation. Instead, I found mice."

"Mice!" said the Ferret Chief Armorer. "They drink the same water as we do. How would that be valid?"

Tilde enumerated the experiments, the failure of the first one with mice and success of the second with opossums. "After the mice failure, instead of the original bottled water, I repeated the tests on different mice and opossums with desalinated sea water."

On fire, she continued. "Of the 40 litters, 263 pinkie and joey births, for the control group—those who drank Clan water—54 female mice and opossums were born to 209 males. Of purified seawater groups, with a total of 78 litters and 468 total pinkies and joeys, 240 females were born, with 228 males. To translate, the two seawater groups produced approximately a 50-50 parity, male and female. The control group produced 20 to 80 ratio, female to male."

She slumped in her seat, cheeks flushed, and took a long sip of drass.

The faces around the table were either the palest white or a blistering red. Even the Falcon's ebony cheeks had turned a dark russet. Fists were clenched, jaws tightened, yet no one spoke.

What was there to say? The idea that a Clan had set out to essentially destroy Eleutia and its inhabitants was so big, so appalling, he floundered processing it. "Why?" His voice was a rasp and he firmed it. "Why would they do this? They are Eleutians."

"Are they?" Rafe said, lips thinning.

"What is that supposed to mean?" Gato said.

"Let us stay on track," Rafe said. "We must find a way to solve this without alerting the Alchemics. Immediately."

"Can we purify our water, what we now use?" the Deer First Commander asked.

"No," Tilde said. "Our lakes, rivers, and streams are all interconnected. All of our potable water is infected. We would need resources, chemistry, and techniques we don't posses to create a counteragent. If that is even possible. We don't even have the resources to understand the drug's makeup."

A cacophony ensued, including the symbiont animals growling and yipping. Gato tuned it to background noise until the Bear Alpha crooked her finger. Gato leaned forward.

"How is Fudge, then?" the Bear Alpha said.

"Well. Content in her mating and better since making friends with our Made One, Breena."

"I am glad." The Bear Alpha said, her lined face pleating into a smile. "Fudge was such a sweet, gentle child. She remains precious to us, even though we were forced to abandon her to the CastOuts."

As he and Derula had been forced to abandon Luciana.

The ever-perceptive Kes chimed in, a man of few words and great insight. "We value Fudge, as well."

The Bear Alpha squeezed her eyes and nodded.

Rafe used a bowl as a makeshift gavel and banged the table.

Gato arched a brow. "A cheese bowl?"

Rafe grinned. And for that moment, they were in harmony. It wouldn't last, it never did, though Gato wished for their friendship as it once was. But he had drastically changed, become an arrogant prick. He suspected Rafe did not long for the mending of their bond.

"We cannot determine how to cleanse our water tonight," Rafe said. "It is vital we remain circumspect, as I have no doubt Alchemic spies are here at the fair. Tilde is working with her counterparts in your Clans. Subtlety is essential. As part of our multi-pronged offensives against the Alchemics, we continue to seek ways to pin down Alchemic City.".

"It's a floating city, Rafe!"

Rafe's jaw bunched. "I have noticed, Tiger. I should say I am working on how to determine where the city will alight next."

"How is that possible? From our spies in the city, only the Cabal knows where."

"I am getting closer, but Calix's absence from Alchemic City is a loss. Neela is good, but she hasn't Calix's experience or his ruthless determination. It is late. We will reconvene tomorrow evening." Rafe looked around the table. "Agreed?"

With nods and yeses, the meeting disbanded, the participants leaving in ones and twos, so as not to raise suspicion. Gato lingered while Rafe spoke with Kes, until the CastOut leader exited with Tilde, giving her a safe escort, no doubt.

"Rafe," he said, gathering his weapons.

"What?" Rafe growled as he did the same. "We arrived minutes before the meeting and my mate awaits."

"That is quite the black eye," Gato said.

"Alpha trials," Rafe replied.

"Are they going well?"

Rafe shrugged. "It is a long road, as you know."

Gato nodded. "That I do. Your mate's sister is here."

"Is she?"

"She was forbidden but came anyway." He slid his knife into his boot.

The Wolf laughed, straightening. "Of course she did. She is Kitlyn's sister, after all." He sobered. "What changed?"

That came out of nowhere, and the meeting tent was not the place to share with the Wolf. "You have never asked me that before."

"Why have you shut me out?" Hope crossed Rafe's features, quickly shuttered when Gato remained silent. "I will see you tomorrow evening, Alpha."

He wished… "Tomorrow."

CHAPTER EIGHTEEN

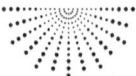

Bartholomew at his side, he was eager to return to their camp, to seek a way to untie the knots binding him. Ax and Taz joined him as he exited the tent.

"Go," he said, not in the mood for company.

"You sure?" Taz said.

"Get a drink or something, cousin. Relax for once. You are off duty."

"You got it." The men grinned and trotted toward the food and drink stands clustered closer to the spiral's center.

Only Gato's grim thoughts kept him company as he walked up the hill. The idea of poisoning their water was so large, his brain had trouble comprehending what the Alchemics had done. Or why. They could decimate his world with their laseblasters and cannons, with bombs that flattened an entire village. Fast. Powerful. Why the water? Yet he believed Rafe and the redhead. The why mattered little.

Loud, slurred voices interrupted his musings. Three too-jovial men headed up the path. By the smell of them, two were unknown Ferrets and one a Bear named Garland. The Bear hailed him, and he returned the man's smile with a weary one of his own. He wasn't in the mood for conversation, especially with a drunk Bear.

Garland ambled over. "What's gotten you looking glum, my friend?"

"I've lost out on a horse I bid on." Gato shook his head. "A Deer scooped him up."

He's hunting, Bartholomew said in his mind. *Beware.*

Farking spies were everywhere. He turned toward the Cat encampment.

"I'll walk with you," Garland said. "I'm meeting up with a Cat."

And the moon was made of blue cheese. "Who would that be?"

"Taz."

Hunting, eh? "He went for a drink with Ax."

"That's fine. He said to meet him at his tent. I will wait for him there."

Gato shrugged and kept walking, trying to shut out the big dumb Bear tagging after him.

"Aren't private auctions forbidden at the fair?" Garland said.

"Of course."

"But you just said—"

"I did. Feel free to report it."

"Gato, I didn't mean anything by it."

Garland's hand might be raised in a placating way, but his eyes told the truth. He would find no treasure here, but perhaps... "What have you been doing at the fair?"

"Eating!" Garland patted his stomach. "Hoping to meet a woman. Any woman."

"Seen any Alchemics in your travels?"

Garland spat onto the dirt. "Fortunately, not."

He could be with the Anti-Made Ones. "Nor have I. Also fortunately. Women, eh? You know we'll be holding a Challenge for the newest Made One."

"Really? Is she attractive?"

"She is. Would you like to meet her? I'm sure she's—"

"No. I'd be too nervous."

Barth?

He is nervous. There is more. Anger and...

Gato's hand slid to the knife at his waist. The hilt was ornamental, but the blade lethal.

"Too nervous, eh? Ma'am Breena is quite..." He couldn't stop his grin. Fates, she made him feel alive. "Unique."

The Bear's face hardened, and though he tried to smile, it looked more like a grimace. "No, thank you. I guess I'll go down to the food tents to find Taz."

"Ho, there!" Shouts.

Garland eyes widened, and he ran.

Two immense Bears barreled into him before he got far. The trio collapsed in a heap, and as they stood, the two large Bears each had a hand wrapped around Garland's upper arms. They hauled him off.

Gato rubbed his forehead. His world continued to get stranger and stranger. One spy down. Hundreds to go.

The following day dawned clear and chilly. Gato sent a message saying Kit had arrived, and Bree found her sister in the barns tending her and Rafe's horses, as well as their stud mistral, Daybreak. Their reunion, though brief, was wonderful. Kit had much to prepare for the auctions, and though she declined Bree's help, they agreed to meet up after Daybreak's auction when they'd be at more leisure.

Their chat left Bree with a joyful glow as she, Fudge, and her helpers set up Fudge's fair booth. Though the booth wasn't large, there was enough room for an artful display of the handwoven rugs, wall hangings, and embroidered tapestries, the bulk of Fudge's wares. Finishing up, they shared a mug of kamla.

"Hey, Fudge, who's this pretty lady?"

The woman approaching had a tall, lithe body and wore a t-shirt with a colorful wraparound skirt.

"Loni!" Fudge said. "I thought you were meeting up with that Peacekeeper."

Loni cast a black look at Fudge. "He was bad. Very, very bad. I'm done with him."

Fudge introduced them, and the surprisingly strong Loni pulled her to her feet, then dove in for a hug. Loni wore makeup, the first Bree had seen on Eleutia. But though she had breasts, *she* felt like a *he*, including the impending scruff on her chin. Bree wasn't going to ask. Not about that, at least.

"Do you know where I can get some hair dye?" Bree said.

Loni's peals of laughter rang through the air. "You do not have much left to dye, but what is left is a gorgeous shade."

"Well..." She combed fingers through her mohawk. "Um, I'm not a fan."

"Your color is spectacular," Loni said, and turned to Fudge. "The woman's moon-mad."

Her friend snorted. "Get lost. See you in an hour for your shift."

Loni kissed Fudge on the cheek, gave Bree a wave, and trotted off.

"She isn't like anyone I've met at CatHome," Bree said.

"There are others like Loni, and she is a he."

No surprise. "A Cat?"

Her friend nodded. "After Ax, Loni was my first friend at CatHome. He runs the apothecary in town."

"You called him a 'he,' but he looks transgender." The kamla went down smooth. "Is he?"

Fudge tilted her head inquisitively.

"When a person identifies as female, though his biological gender is male."

"No, Loni identifies as male and prefers women, though he services both sexes. But some Eleutians do prefer love and sex with their same gender, too. With the decline, men like Loni provide a service, as our males have both sexual and intimacy needs." She leaned closer and winked. "Do not for a minute think he does not enjoy his avocation. I would watch out. Loni cannot resist a redhead, even one with a hideous haircut." Fudge winked.

"I wish everyone would stop yapping about my mohawk."

"It will grow back, as my papa used to say." Fudge sobered. "Why did you cut it?"

Bree stared up the hill to the colorful tents and pennants flapping above them. Her fingers threaded together, twisting into a knot. "Objectively? I had to cut it for the CatGuard helmet. Couldn't have a bright red ponytail hanging out, could I? But I've always hated my hair color. I was angry, and I...it just felt right to make it mine again."

"I would give my left breast for your hair," Fudge said.

"It's not even worth one of my tiny ones." Bree's laughter died. "Dyeing my hair was part of my armor. I painted my nails, had my breasts enlarged, and I once wore beautiful clothes to highlight my assets. I was noticed."

"Noticed? That sounds more like camouflage to me," Fudge said.

Bree sat stunned. Camouflage? She had nothing to hide from. Except... Instead of the armed warrior she'd always imagined herself, was she really creating a smokescreen? No one had ever called her armor camouflage. No one had dared. Not Kit or Sybi. Not her circus family, either. Perhaps because she used her razor-sharp tongue often and, she admitted, at times indiscriminately. Only Fudge had dared. Soaring stars.

"Give me a minute." She strode off toward Fudge's display tent, her eyes burning.

The sun was lighting the bowl, shining across the hundreds of tents, Eleutians bustling to and fro. Few women were present, some had guards, others were in pairs, but all were watched like prey.

Not armor, huh? Perhaps it wasn't. Perhaps all her affectations *were* camouflage, to hide that she wasn't good enough.

Ridiculous—she was an accomplished trapeze artist, one of the circus' stars.

And yet... She'd always compared herself to Kit, who was infinitely more wise and talented. And Sybi, who was the most brilliant of the three, her intelligence only trumped by a heart that encompassed all.

Distracted, she lifted a small tapestry and unrolled it on the table.

If she thought about it, she was the prettiest of the sisters, but the least confident, and she'd compensated with the boobs and hair and makeup. Both her sisters were beautiful as they were, and yet Bree had chosen the shallowest way to stand apart. She'd also used alcohol, the easiest way to bury her feelings.

The small tapestry she'd been absent-mindedly holding depicted a scene with mistrals and men battling flying snake-like lizards. The tapestry was so vivid, she shivered. On looking closer, she saw two of the "men" were actually two *women* dressed in full battle gear, swords in hand.

Before the decline, women had greater parity with men. Bree was surprised, yet pleased, as well. She'd come to like this world and its people, at least most of them. Her lips twitched. She liked having her young body back—who wouldn't?—and the adventure of the place, too. Of the three sisters, she'd always been the most flamboyant and daring. True, no one on Earth had tried to assassinate her. Both times she'd been blind with fear, yet she'd risen to those occasions, instead of caving. That made her proud. She'd also done the extraordinary by bonding with Audi and Fortis.

Her sisters were exceptional, spectacular. Maybe she could be too, once she found her true self buried beneath the detritus of her insecurities. Even without her armor, she might actually be better here on Eleutia.

"Are you all right, Breena?" Fudge peered down at her, concern written in every line of her face. "Did I say something to hurt your feelings?"

"No! Not at all. You got me thinking." She reached out a hand and squeezed Fudge's. "And that's a good thing."

Fudge cupped a hand over her eyes, looking toward the field. Gato approached, his pace swift and determined.

"Alpha, greetings," Fudge said as he reached them.

"Fudge, Made One. Do you need additional help with your booth?"

"We have plenty of people and are almost ready to open," Fudge said. "Thank you."

"I've been working with the seed vendors, who are in chaos," he said. "Their tent is already mobbed, and they are not even set up yet. Can you spare a worker?"

"Yes." Fudge grinned. "I can give you two."

"Excellent!"

After Fudge assigned two of her people to Gato, she returned to Breena and bent close. "You burn when you look at our Alpha, my friend."

Bree's stomach dropped. "Because he's a pain in my ass."

"I guess you are the same to him, because he burns, as well." Laughing, Fudge slapped her knees. "Though I would say the pain was elsewhere, Ma'am Breena."

The dreaded blush heated her face. Not going to think about that. Right. Bree pretty much thought about it, about *him*, 24/7. "He can be mean."

"He's more often kind."

"True." She knew that intimately. The teen in the library, the barn raising, that time in the garden he'd helped a child find his ball. He was a good man, damn him.

"Our Alpha has many burdens." Fudge rose from her seat and arched her back in a stretch.

"He does." Too many.

Fudge stared at Breena and leaned close, voice a whisper. "No squealing or screaming, Made One. I have a secret to tell you."

Bree looked up, concerned.

"I am pregnant." Fudge grinned.

"Holy shit," Bree whispered, teeth clamped tight because squeal was exactly what she wanted to do. Instead, she grabbed Fudge in a mighty hug. "I'm absolutely giddy for you and Ax!"

"Not too loud!" Fudge laughed.

"I'm a good secret-keeper." Bree nodded, all serious.

Fudge wrapped herself around Bree and squeezed.

A literal bearhug. Bree felt loved.

"Give our Alpha a chance," Fudge said. "He is worth it."

· · ·

Bree walked toward the Cats' tents, hurrying to wash up before lunch and the auction where Gato would bid on the rights to Daybreak. Kit wouldn't miss it. She wanted to see Gato win them.

"Made One!" Arina stepped toward Bree from a cluster of tents, raising a hand as she trotted over. "I would like to show you something."

"Cool. What is it?"

"You will see." Arina and Bree jogged up the bowl to a grassy level field. What Bree saw stole her breath. In the distance, two men were practicing on a trapeze, the two platforms hammered into opposing trees, and a bar dangling from wires strung above.

"A good surprise?" Arina said.

"The best."

"I will see you later."

"Thank you!" Bree said.

With a grin, Arina jogged off, her smile making the whole encounter even stranger.

Bree raced toward the green space where they practiced. Wisely, they had set up a net beneath the trapeze, and she watched rapt as the man on the left platform shouted "Hup!" and the man on the right leapt and did a half turn before the catcher grabbed his wrists and swung.

The catcher had good form. Both men did. Perhaps not as polished as she'd been in her heyday, but they knew their stuff. Their equipment looked strong and well-maintained, too.

With the grass still wet with morning dew, she draped her cloak over a boulder. Her boots and socks flew off next, and she tossed them beside her cloak. Taking a deep centering breath, she ran her hands down her jeans, wiping off her nervous sweat.

Once she leapt, her nerves would vanish, replaced by a cold certainty. The jeans she wore were supple enough. And though this new body came with no aerialist calluses, she didn't care.

She had to fly.

Cupping her hands around her mouth, she hollered, "Mind if I climb up?"

"Not a smart idea, ma'am," an aerialist answered.

"I've climbed before, and flown."

"If you say so." The man on the right grinned down at her. "And if you dare!"

Ha! As she began to climb the rope ladder hanging from the left platform, she shivered with excitement. Atop the platform, the thinner man waited, his smile as cocky as his partner's.

"You are crazy, lady," he said.

"I may be that, but I'm an aerialist, too, a professional one who always checks her equipment." She raised a brow.

He snorted. "Triple check, you mean. We have the best equipment on Eleutia."

"Give me a shot?"

"You cannot perform with us."

"When do you go on?"

"Three days. You gonna come?"

"Of course! But I don't want to perform, just fly." She hollered across to the stocky catcher. "Will you catch me?"

The man looked down at the net and back at her, his smile a Cheshire-cat's. "Sure."

Could she trust him to catch her? If he was playing a trick, so what. All she'd do was land in the net. That was fun, too.

She was glad she worked out daily, and though she might not be in top form, she was in decent enough shape to fly. And fly she would.

"How good a catcher is he?" She asked the thin man.

A lock of blond hair slipped onto his forehead. "The best. You are really going try this?"

"Not try, but *do*. My name is Breena, and I'm with the Cat Clan."

He did a half bow. "I am Torval and that..." he pointed to the stocky man. "That is Roghaar. We are of the Ferret Clan. Pleased to meet you, although I am still skeptical."

That earned him a sassy wink. "Aren't we all?" She dipped her hands in the resin bowl, then faced the catcher on the opposite platform. "Ready?"

"All set."

A frisson of excitement shot through her. She wanted to impress them, and she knew that impulse could be disastrous, so she went for simple. "I'm going to do a single flip." It was obvious both men expected her to plummet to the net.

She unclipped the bar and wrapped her hands around the wood. "Ready!"

The catcher yelled, "Hup!"

And Bree flew.

CHAPTER NINETEEN

Gato gaped at what he was seeing, that spiked red hair a beacon. Fear overcame fury, and he ran.

When he reached the trees, Breena stood atop the platform beside one of the Ferret aerialists. She held the bar as if she were going to take off.

Shote. Shote. Shote!

She would miss, fall, and even with the net, might break an arm or her neck.

As Gato reached for the rope ladder, Bree launched herself.

He white-knuckled the rope, biting off the word "Stop!"

She swung back and forth twice, legs pumping the air, speeding faster and faster, and the Ferret catcher mimicked her swings, his legs hooked over the bar, arms outstretched.

Bree released her bar, and Gato almost closed his eyes.

She somersaulted, then stretched out her arms for the Ferret catcher.

The man would miss. Breena would fall.

Gato would be sick.

The Ferret caught her wrists, and she his, and he swung her back and forth twice. Then he released her into the air, and she did another somersault, and Gato died once again.

His crazy woman was laughing.

Dearest Fates. Laughing.

She caught the bar the thin Ferret had swung toward her, her laughter continuing, a rich, beautiful sound unlike any he had heard before. Sky be still, he needed to hear that laughter again. Many times again.

The urge to climb up, to grip her around the waist, to haul her back to earth was strong enough he clamped his hands tighter on the ladder. He could flay her for risking her neck, for trusting that Ferret to catch her. He wanted to shake her until she saw sense.

Were he to do any of those things, she would murder him. Worse, his lack of faith would deeply hurt her.

He got his trembling body under control, shaped his face into a calm mask, and stepped onto the grass beside the ladder to wait patiently for the woman who was becoming necessary to his life.

As Bree climbed down, she saw Gato staring up at her, too far away to see his expression. She could picture it easily enough. He'd yell at her or haul her off like a sack of grain, embarrassing her in front of the aerialists.

She leapt off the final rung, straightened her spine, and raised her chin for his dressing down.

"You were beautiful," he said.

Wait, what? "Beautiful?"

"The way you flew through the air. The somersaults. Incredible. Magnificent. Poetry."

"Where is Gato and what have you done with him? Because I'm not sure I recognize this guy complimenting me."

His eyes warmed. "Perhaps I'm turning over a newer, calmer leaf. Come. I wish to show you something special."

"Um, sure, but I need to wash up first. I can meet you—"

"I will accompany you."

She lifted her discarded cloak and waved to the two aerialists, hoping she'd see them again. On the walk back to the tents a melancholy colored Gato's words, one she'd felt more and more. Yet another "something" had been added to his burdens, their dark whispers more insistent. Maybe she couldn't solve his problems, but sharing helped.

"Something new is worrying you."

"A meeting. And *poosha*, aside from nearly losing my mind watching you soar through the air, I'm handling it."

When would his burdens become so heavy he snapped? Bree ducked beneath the tent flap. "I'll be quick."

Showers in short supply, she washed up with cloth and bowl, then donned fresh jeans and slipped a turquoise tunic over her head as Gato walked into the tent. Or rather, sauntered.

The man had several modes of entering a room. He'd often glide, prowling like the Cat he was. And then there was swagger mode, which alternated between flamboyant Zorro and taciturn Neo.

Today, she got Neo, stoic-faced and intense.

"Knocking is appreciated," she said.

"I am Alpha." He crossed his arms.

She burst out laughing. "Get a grip, catman, or you will become a legend in your own mind. Then again, maybe you already are."

"After my surprise," he said. "You will accompany me to lunch and to the auction."

No asking. What an autocrat, but that was Gato in all his arrogant glory. Irresistible.

The stare she gave him should burn him to his toes.

"Please," he said. "A request."

After she picked herself up from her virtual faint, she smiled. "I'd be delighted. Let me just fix my hair."

He growled. "What's left of it."

"It'll grow back. You know I don't like the color. As soon as I get some dye, I'll—"

"Do nothing." He got in her face, close enough she could see the puma stamped on his black buttons. His hand stroked the top of her mohawk. "Your hair is the color of sunset. Magnificent. It reflects who you are—fire and light and warmth."

The poetry of his words... He saw things in her that didn't exist. Yet he made her feel beautiful, not just skin beautiful, but deep inside. "Thank you."

After she ran the brush through the thick spikes, he held out a hand, and she took it.

"Come. I'm eager to show you my treasure."

Her mind went wild at that one.

Atop the bowl's hill, Bree accompanied Gato to a the same huge, rectangular barn where she'd met Kit. For a stable used quarterly, it was impressive, with wide aisles and clean, good-sized stalls holding all manner of horses. Some were as large as Belgians, others petite like Arabians, and everything in between. As they walked the aisle, the place bustled with stable boys, owners, and prospective buyers examining stock.

In a blink, she was back in their small barn at home. She inhaled deeply. What fun they'd had as kids during the circus' winter hiatus, when they'd retreat to the farm and be like other people for four months.

In Maine, she, Kit, and Sybi went to a regular school, with regular hours. They did homework, and weekends were for fun. Marie was alive back then, and they'd send secret messages to one another. They'd planted a ridiculously huge garden that turned brown, except for Sybi's plot. She took it seriously, talking to the vegetables and flowers like they were people. But by then, Marie was gone. She sighed.

"Breena?" Gato reached for her.

She raised a hand, her smile strained. "I'm fine and eager to see your surprise."

He ran his hand up and down her arm, nodded, then said, "Come."

They held hands as they walked through the stable to a canvas-topped corridor and into a smaller barn. Here, the stalls were three times as large, the horses' names embroidered on each webbed door, some dozen in all. Guards with swords and laseblasters sat at each door to the stable, the nearest one nodding to Gato.

"These are mistrals from the Northwest Quadrant," Gato said. "Eleutia's treasure. Three are for sale, two others are here for show, and the remaining are stallions up for stud-fee auctions."

Since she'd arrived on Eleutia, she'd seen mistrals in the sky. They had wings. These did not, and even though she knew their massive wings vanished into their bodies, it still seemed impossible.

Gato stopped at a stall holding a gorgeous dapple-gray mare with a curling silver mane and tail, her silver hooves complemented by dark stockings. The embroidered name on the stall door read "Pegasa," and she tossed her head when she spotted Gato. He grinned, reaching out to scratch her beneath her chin.

"Pegasa is my treasure," he said. "Sister to Bellerophon, my stallion. I say they're mine, but no one truly owns a mistral. They accept you or not."

"Hello, girl," Bree said.

The mistral apparently loved attention, for she reached over the half-barrier to strop Bree's chest with her head. When she drew away, Pegasa circled the stall prancing, tail raised, neck proud and steps high, showing off her beauty.

"She's wonderful," Bree said.

"She is a devil." But his smile was warm.

"I've seen them fly. I've read about them, too. But seeing one up close—she looks like a normal horse, albeit a huge one. It's strange, unbelievable."

Gato's eyes lit with laughter. "But true. Watching their wings emerge from their bodies as they prepare to fly is...describing it doesn't do the process justice."

"It doesn't make sense," she said.

Pegasa returned to the stall door and Gato slipped her a carrot.

"It does not," he said. "They are magic."

"Magic." The book she'd read hadn't used that term.

"Yes. That which our Eleutian science does not understand, we call magic. No one has discovered precisely how mistrals work, an endless frustration for the Alchemics." Eyes dancing, hands on hips, he paced, as if he couldn't contain his energy. "We do know their bones are incredibly light, yet they are the strongest material on Eleutia. Unbreakable, yet supple. Long ago, hunters poached mistrals for their bones. They almost died out and hunting them has been banned for centuries. An immediate death sentence if caught. Yet poachers remain."

"How awful to kill these beautiful creatures. What other magic—"

"Hush." He bent close and whispered. "I should not have spoken in this exposed place. Though the Alchemics permit Small Magics for healing, starting a campfire, and such, they forbid High Magics under penalty of death. Enforcement is random, but mercy is seldom offered. Even discussing the High Magics can result in severe reprimands."

"Who *are* these people? These Alchemics."

"That is the question of the day. Let it be. Pegasa is one of the reasons we came to the fair."

The mare snuffled, and Bree scratched her chin. "Pretty girl. At the auction, you hope to win stud rights from Daybreak, Rafe's mistral?"

"Yes. Pegasa is here for Rafe to examine her. She will be bred at his stable. Daybreak has sired all Rafe's mistrals, and many say Daybreak is Eleutia's greatest living mistral." He pointed to an empty stall, the door stitched with his name.

"Your mistrals, Pegasa and Bellerophon, why do they have Earth names?"

He winked. "I am just that clever."

She punched his shoulder. "You're that ridiculous."

He threw back his head and laughed. "Many years ago, a Made One belonged to our Clan, and she told me tales of your world, including the story of your Pegasus. How could I name them anything else?"

Pegasa had returned to the half-door, and Bree blew in her nose, petting her, while the mistral's long-lashed eyes drooped. "She's glorious."

"I expect she will permit you to ride her someday. She likes you," Gato said. "Mistrals are mercurial creatures who show their dislikes swiftly."

"I can't wait to ride her."

"Once we make love, you will." He held out his hand for Bree.

She folded her arms. "Seriously? Blackmail doesn't become you."

His sensuous smile made her bones ache. "Blackmail? No. Merely incentive. Come." He took her hand. "Lunch, then the auction."

She was still annoyed as they headed down to the dining tents. When she smelled the fried dough, her mouth watered. Lunch was delicious, the dough exquisite. Heaven on Earth. Nope. Heaven on Eleutia.

As they approached the auction building near the center of the spiral, Gato dared lick a corner of her lips. "Powdered sugar."

"Right."

"I do not see why you like that dough."

"Your palette is unrefined, catman. Someday you will."

Gato paid the participation fee, retrieved his bidding paddle, and led her inside where scents of people, horses, and sawdust mingled. Set up like a small half-arena, Rafe would display Daybreak at the very center where fresh sawdust covered the floor. Down front, the bench stadium seating gave way to a flat section with rows of chairs most likely for deep pockets and dignitaries. The whole set up, so like the circus, gave her goosebumps.

As the stands filled, Gato surprised her by heading for a bleacher near the top, rather than courtside. Knowing the Cat's circuitous mind, she'd bet he had some strategy in place.

"I'm going to find Kit," Bree said.

"After the auction."

"But...you're right."

"Let me explain." Gato sat and unceremoniously pulled her down beside him. "Kitlyn will be helping the Wolf with Daybreak. After the auction, I've arranged your meeting with your sister."

She and Kit had already planned to meet, but his thoughtful gesture touched her. "Thank you."

Gato appeared relaxed, loose-limbed, almost disinterested. Yet he vibrated with tension, his hand fisting the paddle in a white-knuckled grip. Winning these stud rights mattered more than simply getting Pegasa with foal. It was about Rafe.

The crowd filtering in was high spirited, and soon hawkers selling programs and drinks climbed the rows. No cotton candy, though. Disappointing. The attendees were mostly male, with only a few women sprinkled through the stands. Too few.

"What was it like when male-female births were equal?" she said.

He shrugged. "Before my time."

"You're a student of Eleutian history."

"I am, and while it fascinates me, I prefer to focus on the future, one where Eleutia is healthy and women birth males and females equally."

Lights flared on, spotlighting the semicircle down front. The crowd hushed, the side curtain parted, and Rafe strode out followed by the biggest horse or mistral she'd ever seen. Golden in color, and at least twenty-one-plus hands high, he towered over Rafe, who was well over six feet. Daybreak followed Rafe wearing no bridle, no lead. Nothing. Wow.

A woman slipped through a side door. *Kit!* She was followed by a large blond man bristling with weapons, and both took seats in the front row. Murmurs of "Made One" and "Champion" flowed around the room. "Why does my sister have a bodyguard?"

"The Anti-Made Ones have attacked Kitlyn in the past. You have see how persistent they are."

"They're trying to kill Kit, too?"

He nodded.

"You haven't assigned me a bodyguard here."

He winked. "Not one you've seen, *poosha*. Today, *I* am your bodyguard."

Oh.

Rafe raised his arms, and the hall hushed. "You are here to bid on stud rights for Daybreak. I will hold six auctions, the winner of each having the right to Daybreak's stud services with a mistral of your choosing and my approval. Ulfr, the Wolf Clan's Alpha is today's auctioneer." Rafe bowed to the stands, then led Daybreak around the semi-circle once, twice, and exited the arena.

Ulfr took center stage, and electricity surged through the air. The bidding began.

Half the time she couldn't see, with people popping up in front of her to bid. A man who looked to be about Ulfr's age, his samurai bearing enhanced by a mane of white hair, took the first stud right. A young man down in the second row took the second. Gato had yet to bid.

A hawker climbed the aisle, and she pulled some coins out and purchased programs and drinks for them.

"I wished to purchase those for us," Gato said, disgruntled.

"I did instead. So what?"

"I am Alpha. I am—"

"A Neanderthal? That's sweet, but we're all set." She handed Gato his drink and program. After opening hers, she turned to Daybreak's page. Pictures and text told the story of Rafe's farm and Daybreak, who'd been a battle horse. A painting of two men riding mistrals fighting a snaky dragon made her take a second look. Daybreak's rider was clearly Rafe, but she'd swear the second man astride a gray mistral was Gato.

"This is you, fighting with Rafe."

He glanced at the program and nodded. "A great battle against the dakos. Vicious creatures from the high mountains far to the east."

Curious that Rafe submitted this specific painting for the program.

The third auction's bidding began, with bids ping-ponging around the room.

"One hundred korot."

"One-fifty."

"Three hundred."

Gato stood and raised his paddle. "One thousand."

The room hushed. Even Ulfr paused, then said with a growl, "Repeat that bid, Alpha."

"One thousand korot."

Silence. The caller scanned the arena. "One thousand korot is on the table for Daybreak's third slot. Are there any other bids?"

Still standing, Gato crossed his arms. He wore his Alpha mask, looking lethal, as if he'd cut off the arm of anyone who raised a paddle.

"Last call," Ulfr said.

Silence.

Down below, Rafe peered up at Gato, hands on hips, shaking his head and wearing a grin.

"Sold," the caller shouted in a booming voice. "To Gato, Cat Clan Alpha."

"Yes!" Bree jumped up and pumped her fist, much to her instant embarrassment. Gato laughed and hugged her.

"Now, we go find Kitlyn." Gato had won, and victory was almost as sweet as Breena's lips. Almost. When Rafe had stood, he was certain the Wolf Commander would naysay him, as he'd done every other year. Something had changed, something powerful enough for Rafe to permit Gato's win.

If Rafe had learned the truth of those blackmailing Alchemics...

He pressed his forehead to Bree's. Had he not done the same to his *poosha*, tried to force her with the lure of riding Pegasa to make love with him? To *love* him?

Absurd. He needed to fark her, to get her out of his system. That, and no more.

He peered down at the woman in his arms, who stared up at him wearing a smile, her eyes alight with joy. For him.

Delightful. He had begun lying not only to others, but to himself. Breena was no casual fark. She had breathed life into his hollow heart and anchored herself inside him.

The Alchemics and Ahanu's loss had twisted him into a Cat he no longer recognized, one without truth or honor.

"You look so serious." Bree's berry lips bowed into a frown. "Everything okay?"

He nodded, unable to speak.

Breena turned her head and looked for Kit.

"She will be out back," Gato said. "Waiting for you, Breena."

"You are the most confusing, frustrating... I don't understand you. One minute you're bribing me and the next you're acting thoughtful. I want to understand you, I truly do, but I don't."

"At times, I don't understand myself either," he said with a bitter laugh. "Your eyes are like storm clouds over the Pellopines."

"Gahhh! You'll drive me back to drink!"

"You would not do that."

"No," she said. "I wouldn't."

"Come. I will go give that Wolf my money while you meet with your sister."

CHAPTER TWENTY

L ater, they sat outside Rafe's and Kit's tent, Bree sipping troff, the others, drass, while they talked horses. A few awkward moments had passed, but now Rafe shared a memory of that very battle she'd seen pictured, Rafe on Daybreak and Gato atop Bellerophon. The two joked about ugly flying lizards, and Gato's taciturn demeanor had fled as the pair playfully argued about who got in more strikes.

The two finding common ground delighted Bree. Gato had few close friends, and seeing the distance close between the two men felt like the finish of a long tiring race.

The sun cast its fading rays across the fair, the day turning golden. Cooking scents wafted on the breeze that fluttered the green-and-yellow pennants atop Rafe's tent. Both men were well pleased with the day's events. It was the most relaxed she'd seen Gato in…ever.

"Want to walk around the tent?" she said to Kit.

"Let's." Kit turned to the two men and grinned. "You guys won't kill each other, right?"

"Us?" Rafe said, brows raised.

Gato chuckled. "Never."

She and Kit hooked arms and walked.

"Have you learned anything new about Sybi?" Bree said.

Kit shook her head. "No. Our scouts have found nothing. So far, no joy."

"I've asked around, too. Gato, of course, and Peacekeepers, friends at CatHome. Nothing. I told you I wrote to the Clan Alphas about Sybi."

"And...?"

"Their responses were all negative. Gato spoke to the Alchemics about her again, but they dismissed all his questions."

"And you believe him?"

"I do."

"He's a good Alpha," Kit said with a smile.

"What?" Breena said. "You beat him to a pulp in the arena."

Kit gave that secret smile of hers. "I wanted Rafe."

"La, la. I would never have guessed."

"The Alpha watches you like a hawk, you know," Kit said.

Bree snorted. "Yeah, because he doesn't want me to run off."

"The heat in his eyes says something different, sister."

"It's complicated."

"When isn't it?"

Bree shook her head. "I can tell you're happy."

"Deliriously so," Kit's brilliant smile said it all.

"I'm glad. So glad. You deserve happiness, Kit."

Kit poked her chest. "So do you."

She wished for... rainbows and fucking unicorns. "Gato insists I be presented at a Challenge."

Kit rolled her eyes. "It won't happen. I'd take bets on that one."

Bree chuckled. "And you plan to stop it how?"

"Oh, it won't be me stopping it. The Cat will. His eyes say he wants to tuck you away and feast on you all by himself."

If only. But Bree enjoyed a shiver of pleasure imagining it. "Though we've talked, I didn't tell you about my panic attack, where I almost took... I almost had a drink."

"Oh, Bree." Kit's eyes melted with sympathy. "How awful. What stopped you?"

"The cubs. Gato. It was a bad attack, but I haven't had another one. And I haven't had a damned drink, either. I won't."

"My lucky stars." Kit hugged her, and for moments Bree was back on Earth.

Their years of struggle and illness, of laughter and love, of joy and tragedy infused her with all that had gone before. Not a single Eleutian knew her past, and she remembered Mama's laughter and Mordecai's kisses and a million points in time that made her who she was.

"I wish I'd been there for you that day," Kit said when they parted.

"You're always in my heart, kiddo, and in my head." She groaned. "I swear, sometimes I hear you ordering me this way or that."

"Bossy, am I?"

"Only in that loving, big-sister way of yours. I've felt naked here, without my big boobs, my black hair, my—"

"Of course you miss that," Kit said with dry sarcasm. "After all, they were expensive."

Bree punched her in the arm. "You know what I mean."

"Those superficial things, your armor. You don't need them, Bree. You *never* did."

Kit had said that before, many times. "Please don't faint, but I'm starting to see you might be right. My friend Fudge called it camouflage. I think... Maybe she's right, Kit, and I was too scared to look at who I really was."

"Who you really *were*," Kit deadpanned. "How about brave? Funny? Caring?"

"Annoying?"

"That, too!" Kit laughed. "Nothing's wrong with your camouflage if it gives you confidence, but the real you is better and far more interesting. I'm so happy you're beginning to see that."

"I guess," Bree said. "But, boy, was I pissed when I arrived here and didn't have any say in the matter."

"Ditto," Kit said, her face serious. "Be wary, Bree. The men who brought us here are devious and deadly. I met Fukkes, our maker."

"He's their leader, right?"

"He saved Rafe's life using my blood, so I should be thankful. But he's creepy, calculating, and highly intelligent."

"I can't wait to meet him."

"Knowing you, you'll punch him in the face."

"Ah, the temptation."

They neared a stream burbling on the forest's edge and Kit paused. "I love you, Bree, far beyond sisterly love. After my accident, you were so amazing. I…" She sighed.

Bree clasped her big sister's hand. "Sybi and I love you so much. Now you're well and whole, and you've grown beyond anything I ever dreamed of."

Kit kissed the back of Bree's hand and they walked on.

"What do you know about Gato and Rafe's troubled friendship?" Bree said.

"Some, but not all," Kit said. "From what Rafe has said, they were besties." She laughed. "Not that Rafe would ever use that word."

Bree rolled her eyes. "The Cat would be horrified. 'Besties' is way beneath his dignity. What happened between them?"

"Rafe doesn't know, but he said Gato changed about two or so years ago, that he became secretive and aggressive. Short-tempered enough that they dealt with each other almost as enemies. Rafe worries he did or said something to offend the Cat, but he can't think of what. Do you have any idea?"

"None. Gato often curses Rafe, and yet I see longing and sorrow whenever he speaks of him." A nightbird's haunting trill echoed and for some reason it gave her chills. Bree hooked her arm through Kit's.

"You know," Kit said. "Their estrangement makes Rafe sad, too. He misses his friend."

"I suspect Gato feels the same."

. . .

Gato finished the bottle of ale and tossed it into the recycle barrel. Across the small campfire, Rafe took a pull on his drink. Twilight approached, and the air had grown cold. But the fire was warm as it shot sparks into the night. A moment of contemplation. And perhaps rapprochement?

He blew out a long, slow breath. "At the meeting, you asked me what changed. Why ask me now, after years of estrangement?"

Rafe's eyes lifted from the campfire to Gato. "Because I have learned things. Things about my Skyson, for example."

"Such as?" Gato forced his voice to stay casual.

"I checked with many universities, particularly down south."

Typical Rafe. "It seems you have time on your hands, even with the Alpha trials."

"I made time." Rafe leaned forward, eyes narrowed. "It appears Ahanu is attending none of those universities, which begs the question—"

"Do not voice it."

Rafe clasped his hands behind his head and leaned back. "War is coming, my friend, and we cannot fight the Alchemics until our water is under our control and restored. Many of us will die in this war, but without the balance, all Eleutia will die. I have had no better comrade than you, both on and off the field of battle."

Nor had Gato. The loss of the Wolf's friendship had gutted him. He would not say the words about Ahanu aloud, yet... "There is a problem, and I must deal with this alone, Radulfr."

"I see," Rafe stared at him, his voice dry as the Death desert.

Gato's eyes bored into Rafe's, willing him to understand. "But I apologize for allowing our antagonism to grow and fester. My fault. Though I cannot speak of my brother now, you will know soon."

Rafe held his gaze, but said nothing.

"Trust me," Gato said.

Rafe pulled another bottle from the cooler, and minutes ticked by where Gato felt like a fish on a hook.

Rafe nodded. "I do." And he lifted the bottle toward Gato. "I always have. Another ale?"

Thank the Fates, the Wolf would not interfere. Gato snorted. "You have to ask?"

The Wolf uncapped it and handed over the bottle. "Though you turned into a farking asshole, you have never broken my trust."

"Nor will I." He forced himself not to twist the bottle in his hands. "Notice I ignored the 'asshole' comment. See? I am always diplomatic."

"Oh, yes, as you were when you stole my Kitlyn."

"I did *not* steal your mate, as you well know."

"But it was you who declared war."

"Fark, Rafe, I—"

"Your friendship has always mattered to me."

"And yours to me," Gato said.

Rafe lips twitched. "At times, your assholery is endearing."

Gato laughed. "'Assholery?' 'Endearing'?"

"Yep." Rafe took another swig, eyes laughing.

Gato grinned. "We are good, then, Sir Almost Alpha."

Rafe spewed ale across the fire, his laughter ringing through the camp, but his words were serious. "We are better."

It was enough.

After clasping forearms and thumping backs, their talk veered toward horses and mistrals and magic. Fireworks blazed the sky and singing commenced a few tents over. People streamed by the tent, including a redhead, which spiked a longing for Breena. Though knowing she was on the other side of the tent, he missed her.

He was doomed.

Bree paused their meandering at the rear of the tent. The nearby wood rose to the crest of the cliff, and beyond that, the sea, with its briny scent and crashing waves and cawing gulls. "I love the smell of the sea." It evoked...

A movement amongst the pine. An odd one. Bree stepped between Kit and the wood. "Do you ever miss Earth?"

"No," Kit said. "Not much, anyway. Let's face it, we don't have a ton to miss. I think we were wrong, Bree."

Bree turned a casual eye to the wood. Nothing. "Wrong about what?"

"The way we cut everyone off back on Earth. Our circus family, friends who tried to remain close. We shouldn't have."

Bree took a minute, then nodded, distracted by the sense of eyes on them. She began to stroll toward the front of the tent, her hand holding Kit's. "I agree. But we can't change it."

"We can't. What we can do is find our beloved Sybi."

"She *must* be here, right?" Bree said.

"I believe that."

"So do I. What if someone is hiding her?"

"What will you do with Breena?" Rafe said.

He notched his chin, voice firm. "She must stand for The Challenge."

"Not if you claim her first."

"Claim her? No one will claim Breena without her consent."

"Will you compete?"

Fukkes forbid it. Gato tacked on a smile. "She would thrash me the way your Kitlyn did."

Rafe's eyes warmed. "My beauty would have taken me down, as well."

"Instead she won and took you for herself."

"Breena could do the same. And choose you."

Bree's nova lit Gato's life. If she chose him...

"I see the hope in your eyes," Rafe said. "It has been years since I have seen that look on your face."

Hope. He took a long pull of ale and caught the eye of a Peacekeeper watching Breena and Kitlyn. He nodded. All was well. At least with their women.

"What bodes ill?" Gato said.

"'Bodes ill'? Seriously?" Rafe said.

"You are being evasive."

"I need your help. What we said at the council, there is much they are not ready to hear. You are. Kitlyn and I do not believe the Alchemics are Eleutian."

"Of course they're—"

Rafe held up a hand. "Many, yes. Born and bred. But the Cabal leaders are different. They know things and do things highly un-Eleutian. Have you noticed how swiftly their tech advanced in the past two hundred years? How today we seldom mingle with any Alchemics but the Cabal? How they seldom ever leave their city?"

"Some of it, I have considered. But not that they are off-worlders." Had his inner demons blinded him to what an Alpha should see?

"We had not, either. The worst of the rumors say they manipulate the DNA on both Eleutians and our symbionts to produce CastOuts?"

Bile rose. "Yes. Kestrel believes it to be true. And because of that, you believe they are off-worlders?"

"Yuan, the Fates Paladin, began to speculate."

"Your former armorer?"

Rafe nodded. "Her word was 'unnatural.'"

"It is too big a leap." Gato shook his head. "You have always seen conspiracies where there are none. You were sure the dakos last attack was a diversion."

"I still believe that. I also believe the farking Cabal is from another world. Think, my friend. If they are off-worlders, examine how many of their actions makes sense."

Gato considered how they orchestrated him, an unnatural thing for an Alchemic to do. The torture of his brother, atypical as well.

"Off-worlders would not care for Mother Terra, her land or her creatures. Not as we do."

The fire crackled, sparks flying. Gato lifted his face to the night sky and wove together the disparate elements the Wolf had presented. "It is possible."

"Shote, Gato, yes. All of our research points to their arrival two-hundred-and-fifty years ago. *That* is when it all changed."

He opened his mouth to speak.

Trouble. Barth.

"The women!" he shouted. "To me, Peacekeepers! To me!"

Gato ran.

A sound. A flash. Bree shoved Kit to the ground. But as she landed atop her sister, pain seared her arm.

"What the hell, Breena?" came Kit's muffled words.

The pain was tolerable, but whatever hit her was making her woozy. *Dammit*. The world grew distant. Yet in her head, she heard crunching leaves and footsteps nearing. "Call Gato and Rafe." No energy to do it herself. She closed her eyes.

It was as if she were two people. One covered her sister and was in pain. The other heard crunching leaves and heavy footfalls and... Someone approached, masked and carrying a bow, getting closer.

Bree's eyes were shut. How... The cubs did stuff like that, showed her pictures. But they were far away.

Fuck. Bree hadn't the strength to roll off Kit and give her a chance to run. She didn't seem able to move at all. They would die. Was that Kit speaking to her?

The man came closer. He was small, his hair blond, his eyes blue. He stalked nearer, and she swallowed. "Push me off. Run."

Kit struggled, and Bree tried to help, but her limbs, her torso, wouldn't respond.

"You're too heavy," Kit said. "I can't."

"You must." She panted. "A killer is coming."

Kit shoved at Bree, but pain shot through her and she groaned. Kit froze.

In Bree's mind, she screamed for Barth, who'd never arrive in time.

She gritted her teeth and forced her lips to move. "Kit."

"We'll pretend we're hurt," Kit said.

"I am hurt." Her words sounded slurred, like she was drunk. If only.

How ironic. Rafe, Gato, Peacekeepers, right on the other side of the tent, but her mind saw the shooter. Almost on top of them. Why hadn't he fired another arrow? Many arrows?

The booted feet stopped by her head, mask lowered.

Kit's eyes widened. "Inga."

Bree knew the name, a Wolf who had betrayed Kit and Rafe.

Their enemy's lips parted into a slow smile as she dropped to one knee and drew a knife from her boot. "Payback is sweet, isn't it, Ma'am Kitlyn? You stole Rafe from me. Now I get to finish this close and personal, to see your face when I kill your sister. Then I will run my knife slowly across your throat and watch you struggle for air and choke on your own blood."

The blonde was fixated on Kit, to Bree's advantage.

Inching her fingers, she found her knife's solid hilt. Struggling to wrap her hand around it, she finally managed and clenched it tight. With slow, deliberate movements, she drew it from its sheath.

Bree thrust her arm wide, swinging the blade in a sloppy arc toward the blonde's thigh.

Before it struck, a slash of black crashed into the assassin.

The woman shrieked, and men poured from around the tent led by Gato and Rafe. The killer's screams died, replaced by the sounds of Barth's savaging the woman.

CHAPTER TWENTY-ONE

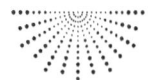

Someone lifted Bree off Kit. "Gato."

"The Fates!" he said. "You foolish woman, you have an arrow in your arm."

He cradled her with care. "I'm okay. Not that bad."

"You have been *shot*," Gato said. "It is bad."

"No it's *not*," Bree said.

"Must you always argue?"

"That's my sister," Kit said with obvious pride. "You know, I'm sick of people shooting at us."

Rafe and Gato growled in tandem.

"Wanna see Barth," Bree said.

"No," Gato said.

"Please!"

"Farking Fates." But Gato angled his body so Bree could see. She gasped and closed her eyes.

The woman was in *parts*, Barth chewing a leg.

Bree couldn't blame the puma. It had been Barth all along, showing Bree those pictures in her mind.

"Where are you hurt?" Rafe said to Kit.

"I'm not." But the rest of Kit's words were a whisper except for "Inga."

Rafe paled. With care, he stood Kit on her feet and stepped to what was left of the assassin. Barth growled.

"Quiet!" Rafe's Alpha stare silenced the big cat, and he crouched beside Inga. When he rose, he turned to face the trees.

Kit leaned in. "They were once close. They grew up together, and she loved him."

"No, she didn't!" Rafe spat without turning. "I was an object to acquire, a trophy."

Kit walked to her mate and wrapped her arms around him. He bent his head.

"We go to get you fixed," Gato said to Bree.

"The remains...?"

"Peacekeepers will attend to them."

"Rafe may want to do that," Kit said.

"I am aware."

Bree harrumphed. "I can walk."

To her surprise, he stood her on her feet, but his arm remained around her waist. She wobbled, straightened, and blew out a long breath. "Let's go."

Inside Rafe's tent, a doctor cleaned, sewed, and bandaged Bree's wound, while a healer used "Small Magics" to muffle the pain. The wound wasn't severe, but her arm throbbed and she was still woozy. By the time Kit and Rafe reappeared, Bree sat on a stool, her mind in a haze.

Kit wound an arm around her shoulders and leaned in close. "Rafe and the Peacekeepers took care of Inga."

"We buried her," Rafe said, his voice thick with pain. "What was left. She did not deserve a pyre."

Gato crossed his arms as he stood before her. "We return home."

He would expect an argument. She hadn't the energy to give him one.

. . .

Neela tiptoed into Fukkes' suite carrying a supper tray. He hated noise, at least noise *he* didn't make. She slipped down the suite's hall to the large living area. Empty, as was the dining area and kitchen. Odd. Fukkes was always here.

She tapped her pocket to make sure she'd brought the stalker. Good. The few times she'd caught him talking to himself, he'd unwittingly supplied good intel, though it was Calix who always managed to bring Compass True the most meaningful information.

The rebellion saw her as less than Calix, and she would prove them wrong when she discovered something of worth.

The floor vibrated. She set the tray on the dining table and checked her watch. They were moving the City. Always such a secret. Alerting Rivaux of their changing location, she tapped code into her watch using the rebellion's newly adjusted timepiece. The frequency was untraceable, and she was proud to be one of the watch's first testers.

Neela shivered, and pushed her bangs from her sweaty forehead. If Fukkes discovered her, she would say she had brought him dinner. Simple.

The Comstat might be in his private lab, so she padded to the door and cracked it open. Empty, but for a beaker puffing green steam. Linens lay behind the second hall door, while the third door revealed an enormous bathroom. Such luxury. The skylight made the all-marble room glow.

Far, far to the east, Neela's home sat at the base of the Skytouch Mountains, the lakes crystalline, the rivers rich with fish, their peaks capped with snow year-round. Bighorn sheep were her Clan's symbiont, and she missed them, their companionship, protection, and especially their humor.

A sigh almost burst from her lips.

She followed the corridor as it jogged left. Fukkes was speaking to someone.

Creeping closer, mouse-quiet, Neela took the stalker from her pocket and screwed the segmented wand into her observation goggles. Once she slipped them on, she turned on its recorder and slid the stalker through the cracked door.

Fukkes sat slumped on a bed that hugged the wall. He raked his fingers down his cheeks, and they came away smeared with makeup. She'd never seen him look defeated before, his bravado doused.

Turning the wand's eye, she viewed a sterile room devoid of personal items and artifacts, an odd thing for a man who wore crystal teeth and clownish clothes. Fukkes leaned forward, pulling a chain from beneath his shirt. He fingered a charm at the end, then crossed the room to retrieve a large, carved box from the dresser.

Neela pressed a small lever, activating the telephoto, eager to see what was inside the box.

He unlocked it with the necklace charm, then his hands dove inside to lift an object draped in maroon velvet, round on the bottom, but jagged on top. Tossing off the cover, he revealed a broken Essence globe. He lifted it with reverence, the jagged edges sealed with serusplas.

Neela stilled. Lights floated and mist swirled through the half globe. Unlike the usual Essence multicolor swirls, these were a murky gray with two gray lights bobbing aimlessly around the space.

Two Essences in a single globe. It shouldn't be possible. It shouldn't be done. She'd learned at university that placing two Essences in the same globe would inevitably force them to combine, forming a strange, unnatural Essence.

Fukkes pressed his forehead to the glass. "Mari. Xenon. I have missed you."

Perhaps he held one of those memory balls she had read about, ones that held fragments of a person's life and thoughts, their images and vids. Yet aside from their color, the two lights looked and acted like Essences. Whatever the thing was, its contents were beloved to Fukkes.

"My love. Ah, there you are. And there's our boy, our Xenon, romping in circles on his pretend pony." Fukkes laughed, and it was creepy as shote. "You are both very funny."

Fukkes leaned back against the wall, the ball pillowed in his lap. "I'm tired, Mari, tired of this absurd pose I play on this cursed planet. For the first time in my thousand-year life, I am weary."

A thousand years old?

A creak from the corridor. Neela stepped back and raised the goggles. She was a scared rabbit. Another creak. The sound was the coolfreeze, that was all. The Fates, she wanted to run.

She could not. She *would not*.

Again she slid the stalker's eye through the door, but the room was empty. Seconds later Fukkes reappeared, ball in hand, and sat on the bed.

"Where has my energy gone, eh Mari? I've always been up for the challenge, the fight, the exhilaration of conflict. Victory was all that much sweeter. Maybe I should enter the mist."

Neela had no idea what "the mist" was.

"You will be delighted, my dear Mari, that I have finally set in motion my plan to decimate those cursed Anti-Made Ones who destroyed you and our beloved Xenon."

Shocked, Neela couldn't fathom how the Antis had penetrated the City, no less destroyed Fukkes' family. Horrible.

"The Authority learned of it, as well as their destruction of dozens more Essences. They *forbade* me from taking revenge. Forbade me! How dare they!"

He looked off in space, his hands shook. "Once I confirm the third sister's death, I will move."

Stunned, Neela rocked back on her heels.

He shifted the globe, cradling it like an infant. "My time nears to leave this cursed place, but not before I've crushed this planet and decimated these barely sentient insects crawling across Eleutia. Imagine being connected to beasts. Disgusting."

Fukkes stiffened, and his eyes cut to the opposite wall.

The Fates. Fukkes saw them as *insects*? She would shock Compass True when she told them.

Neela backed down the corridor toward the outer door, fear and excitement making her tremble as she reached for the knob.

Her fingers touched the metal, then a click, soft and terrifying.

The handle wouldn't budge.

"Don't go." Fukkes stood in the hall. "I must thank you for bringing my supper, Neela."

The trail was dusty and the night dark, Breena draped across his lap asleep, her head resting on his shoulder. They rode toward CatHome, and he was grateful.

Gato had been in conflict too long. He had lied both to others and to himself.

He could never let Breena go.

Not for The Challenge. Not for the Alchemics. Not for his sanity. She had become the spark of his life, his tether as the world spun into chaos and war.

The arrow was his tipping point. When he had seen it embedded in her arm, the wild fear near leveled him. No more indecision. No more dishonesty.

She was his, and he, hers.

He would court her, with all the beauty and consideration she deserved. Would she accept him?

Before the Alchemics learned of his defiance, it was crucial he bring Ahanu home. He could do it. After all, he was Alpha of Eleutia's greatest clan.

He bent his head and inhaled Bree's cinnamon-spice scent.

"How is the Made One?" Arina said, riding up beside him.

"Asleep."

"Your arms must be tired. Let one of the men carry her."

He almost spat "never!" but stopped in time. "My arms are not tired, and I would trust few with her after recent events."

"These are your people, Gato. They would never hurt the Made One."

"The woman, Inga, was once one of Rafe's people. Sir Ambrose was one of *ours*."

"That is different."

"How?"

Arina sighed and peeled her horse off toward the back of the line.

He watched her go, but his *poosha* slept on, her face that of an angel. He chuckled. She would find that descriptor laughable. His heart lifted, though his patience had thinned. He wanted her awake *now*.

He stifled the impulse to laugh aloud. Though he was Alpha, he was acting like a lovesick cub. So be it. He warmed further to the idea of courting her and wondered if she had found the spoon he had carved. Though he had left it beside her bed, she never mentioned it, and why he had carved it those many weeks ago had been a mystery. Now he understood.

He settled into the saddle, more comfortable than he had been in years, his mind set on contriving Ahanu's escape.

Comforting scents surrounded Bree—pine and horse and Gato. The rocking made her nestle closer into his soothing warmth, content. Noise intruded. Too much noise.

Bree opened her eyes to see their entire party on the road to what she suspected was CatHome.

"Everyone left the fair? Why?"

Gato didn't look down at her, his eyes scanning the countryside. "It became too dangerous for us to remain."

"Aren't you overreacting?"

"Overreacting? Me?" he said in that sarcastic tone she found both annoying and endearing.

She mustn't be badly injured or he wouldn't be giving her snark. "Wasn't our murder-attempt quota filled for that venue?"

"Only *one* threat was eliminated." He smiled. "And nothing else untoward is likely to happen, especially to you, as you've been such a compliant and effortless guest."

"Your sarcasm underwhelms me."

"Ha! First you bond with our CatGuard cubs. Then you nearly die on the road and at the hands of Sir Ambrose. Oh, and you disguised yourself as CatGuard and snuck into the fair. Finally, the ilaberry on the cake, you got yourself shot. Yes, I am overreacting."

Quite the sermon, and she might admit, lumped together like that, it sounded pretty awful, except the sneaking in part. "Okay, you're right." She tried to swing her leg over to a sitting position, but Gato clamped her to him.

"Dammit, let me sit up," she said.

"No. The healer said you must ride home this way."

"Why not send me home with some Peacekeepers?"

"We all go. I protect what is mine."

Gato was saying that to piss her off. She sighed. He saw her as his personal burden, when he already had too many. "What about Fudge and the others who depend on the fair for their livelihood?"

His face hardened. "There will be other fairs. And the Clan will supplement their income for the ensuing months until the next one."

"What if *I* want to return to the fair?"

He grinned. "Now you're taunting me."

"Maybe."

"We almost lost you and Kitlyn. Rafe has left for WolfHome, as well."

"Kit's attack seemed very personal."

"To a point it was, but Inga was also acting on some scheme of either the Alchemics or the Anti-Made Ones. Bartholomew using her as a chew toy means we couldn't discover which."

"Does it matter?"

"It is possible the Alchemics are manipulating the Antis in some twisted way—they've done it before, with the goddarts."

"But why would the Alchemics want Kit or me dead?"

"I doubt they do, though they may have been testing your and Kitlyn's reflexes or...fark! They live for experimentation and I seldom comprehend their thinking."

Her hand brushed his cheek rough with stubble. "I'm not easy to kill."

"Perhaps not." He turned his face and kissed her palm. "But I will keep you safe at CatHome."

A chill slithered down her spine. "You can't watch me 24/7."

"Wait and see."

On their return, the cubs bounced like pogo sticks around the living area, and it took both Barth and Gato to make sure they didn't bounce all over her. Though her arm ached fiercely, she was so damned glad to see the cubs she let them nuzzle and lick until her skin was nearly raw. She hadn't realized how much she'd missed the mischievous pair, and she smiled when the little beasties curled up and fell asleep beside Bartholomew.

Oh, how she'd love to sleep. As soon as she had her bath. The next thing she knew, Gato had called Fudge to assist her. "I don't need —"

"*Poosha*," Gato said, his eyes alight with humor. "You could drown. How would that look? Imagine the headlines: Alpha allows Made One to drown in her own bathtub. It would be a scandal."

"You are such a drama queen," she said.

Gato frowned. "Drama king. If anything, I'm a drama *king*."

She stood on tiptoe and kissed his cheek, even if he had upped his paternalistic ante.

After her bath, she melted into bed. Fudge had gone and Gato was talking to two Peacekeepers.

Oh, joy. Peacekeepers. Her new guards.

CHAPTER TWENTY-TWO

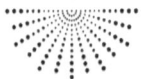

After a week of being forced to stay in bed by a pain-in-the-ass Alpha, Bree started physical therapy. She staved off boredom by reading *The Book of the Fates* that Arina and her brother had given her after performing something called The Fates Healing ceremony. Reading the book wasn't easy, but she found "the Heavens' guide to life" compelling. Along with healers and a medical doctor, Fudge, Jocelyn, Taz, and Makena had visited. Even Arina stopped by to check on her, and a handsome blond healer brought her a daily healing herbal tea.

Arina remained a mystery, as changeable as the breeze. One minute she was solicitous, the next angry, at what Bree didn't know. Gato had an earthiness and exuberance Arina lacked, her somber nature hovering like a storm cloud. Though her attentions felt more like a duty, Bree caught an occasional look of fear clouding Arina's eyes. But nothing Bree did could open a crack in her stoic façade. Even the taciturn Taz showed a softer side when he visited or conferred with the healer on security matters.

Though Gato was a constant, appearing often, checking on her health, bringing the occasional treat or flowers, he'd leave as swiftly as he'd come, putting a distance between them Bree didn't understand and couldn't seem to breach.

Two weeks after being shot, Bree saddled Bristol, a large gray with a calm presence and a sweet demeanor, and though her arm ached, it was worth it. She'd escaped her prison, the disgruntled Audi and Fortis remaining behind. But their constant communication with Bartholomew meant they'd tell Barth her location, and he'd tell Gato, and…voilà, no jaunt. After her ride, she'd promised them a swim in the Afródis.

Finished tacking up, she leaned against the saddle. She always bristled with energy, but ever since she'd been shot, each day was more enervating than the last, like the viral pneumonia she'd had as a kid.

She was doing all the right stuff, seeing the doc, the healers, drinking her tea, walking, and doing PT. Her energy would return.

The hand she ran across her mohawk shook. The shaved part was growing in, the bristle longer, now more like a flop-hawk. She'd really done a job on herself with that haircut.

She gathered the reins and lifted her foot into the stirrup.

"And where might you be off to?"

Fuck. Gato truly walked like a cat. "I don't know where I'm going, but I'm sick of sitting in my room." She swung into the saddle and peered down at him.

Bristol turned her head and rubbed it against Gato's chest. "Yes, little girl, you are a good mare. I hate to disappoint you, but your lady friend is going on a different kind of ride today."

"I am, am I?" She pictured another kind of ride, one where they both were naked. Damn, she was horny for him to the point of obsession.

He pursed his lips. "I thought you might like to join me on Pegasa."

"Oh." To ride a *mistral.* "I'd love to, but…" She couldn't make this too easy for him and patted the mare's neck. "Bristol's excited about our ride."

His slow smile scrambled her brains. *Damn that man.*

"Our Bristol will be equally pleased with extra carrots and a few peppermints to soothe her disappointment. Shall we fly?"

She shot him a grin. "If you insist."

Bree sat in front of Gato atop Pegasa, her heart beating in time to the mistral's wings. She had never, *never*, experienced anything as amazing, not even flying the trapeze. They climbed high enough for the air to cool, and Gato had wrapped her in his jacket. With one of his arms snugged around her, she was toasty warm.

Pegasa ate up the skies above CatHome, and now headed toward an ocean blue enough to hurt her eyes.

"We wear goggles in battle," he said, his warm breath tickling her ear. "Today, we take it slow and easy."

It didn't feel slow or easy as the mare dipped and soared. Soon they flew above the waves, dropping lower still until the mistral appeared to dance on the crests, the ocean spray flecking Bree's cheeks. She laughed for the joy of it, the freedom of it, and she wanted to fling her arms around Gato, press her hands to his cheeks, and take those snarky, sensitive lips with hers. She wanted to tell him he'd stolen her heart and to love him fully. And yet...The Challenge. The fucking Challenge.

She sighed.

"Are you tired?" She turned her face and brushed a hand across his cheek. He stiffened. He always stiffened nowadays, and not in the good way.

Pegasa wheeled around, heading back to shore. "Must we return? I could fly forever, fly into infinity to see what was next."

"The Fates seldom give up their secrets."

"Neither do you."

He remained stubbornly silent. She melted against him, reveling in the pleasure of his warmth and strength, that she was always safe with him. And then, for all the thrill of being sky high, she dozed.

A week after their ride on Pegasa, Gato was frustrated, furious, a touch panicked. "Fark!" As the days passed, Bree's color had grayed, plum stains of exhaustion beneath her eyes. She was not healing from the arrow, not properly, and the healers and medics still had no idea what poison was on the arrow's tip. Not Goddart's Sting or Breena would be dead, yet he knew of no other venom that would affect her so severely.

When they had returned to CatHome, the healers had assured him she would recover swiftly and well.

He stalked into the healers' den, his mood vile. "So? What have you discovered?"

The Master Healer raised heavy lids and rose from his desk. He bowed. "Alpha. I have reviewed ours and the medica notes on the Made One."

"Her name is Breena."

"Nothing detectable in Ma'am Breena's system indicates anything but a wound to her arm. That should be healed by now."

Gato waved a hand. "The wound itself is sufficiently healed. But she is pale and exhausted all the time, each day worse than the previous."

The healer shrugged. "Our Small Magics cannot accomplish more."

He was not so stupid as to ask about the High Magics. The farker would never risk it. Would that healing was his magical area of expertise. Instead, he smiled, thanked the healer, and left. The healers had given a mighty effort. He had seen with his own eyes. Yet he sensed lies woven through the Master Healer's words, why or about what he couldn't guess.

Confronting a healer was a tricky thing, one that tangled politics with religion, which he was loath to do without hard evidence. He would get to the bottom of this.

He spoke with their lead doctor, as well, and he achieved the same result but without the lying.

"I shall request the Alchemics test Ma'am Breena's blood," the doctor said.

"No. They would not agree, but instead insist on visiting CatHome. We cannot have that. Fukkes is too dangerous."

"I agree," the doctor said. "To have him sniff out our labs would be disastrous. Contact the southern Cats."

But it was too risky. There would be chatter, which would produce the same result—the Alchemics on CatHome land. *Fark.* Every move felt more precarious than the last, each moment fraught with danger and discovery.

He had devised and set in motion a plan to free Ahanu, but Breena's health had put that on hold. More waiting. His hand fisted. He would not break. Could not break. He drew on his Alpha essence and feline strength, bolstering his purpose. He would not falter.

He set Ax on following the Master Healer, and Taz investigating him. And then...

Desperation made him reach for his Compass True mobile.

"Rivaux here."

"Grambaux here." Rafe had healed his friend Max with High Magics. He hoped he could heal Breena, as well. "I heard what you did for your friend who was ill."

Silence at the other end.

"If what I heard is correct, I need your help."

"Too dangerous, my friend."

Rafe was right, given the punishment for using the High Magics. "For the Made One. For Breena."

A whoosh of breath. "Fark. Because of the trials, I am constantly scrutinized. I will work out a way to make it possible."

The hawks had watched Gato during his Alpha trials. "It is urgent."

"Let me think, and I will get back to you."

"*Soon,*" Gato said.

"As soon as possible, I will come." Rafe hung up.

Which might not be soon enough for Bree.

Bree dreamed of riding the hills behind their Maine home. Of picnics with her sisters and PB&Js and s'mores. The images darkened, blackened with pain, Sybi's pain. The dark slithered inside her, eating her from inside out. Devouring her.

Her eyes snapped open, heart pounding, recalling the dream in all its ugly vividness. As much memory as dream, Sybi's sorrow had been from her boyfriend's betrayal.

Bree began to cry, head throbbing in time with her aching heart. Sybelle had to be here, on Eleutia. Why couldn't they find her?

The cubs patted her thighs, their love a soothing blanket. She sniffled, running her wrists across her eyes, and nuzzled them. "Thanks, guys. Fudge brought a new toy. Let's get it!"

After giving them the new pull toy, she staggered back to bed. The last week had sucked. Her joints ached, her mouth perpetually dry. And if she were any more lethargic, she'd be dead.

Early on, she'd begun a painting of the cubs. But by day three, she could barely lift the brush. Though she spoke with Kit several times, she never mentioned her weakening condition. That was the last thing Kit needed since Rafe came home exhausted each night, and each morning faced yet another Alpha competitor. Kit said they kept coming and coming.

A knock at the door had her scrambling from bed. She pressed her fingers to the end table to stop swaying, then her stomach insisted she race to the porcelain throne. Again.

"Coming! Give me a sec." She rinsed her mouth, brushed her teeth, tugged on a robe, and hurried to the door, the word "hurried" being subjective. More like teetered.

"Come in, Oliver." The blond healer held Bree's steaming cup of herbal tea, his smile equally welcome.

"I thought you were Gato," Bree said. "He takes the cubs for their CatGuard exercises around this time."

"How are you feeling today, Ma'am Breena?" He handed her the mug, and she took a sip.

"Mediocre to lousy, which sucks." She hadn't told Gato, but the healed skin on her wound had split.

"May you feel well soon, Ma'am Breena," he bowed and turned to leave.

"Wait. I need you to do some healing for me and to not tell Gato."

Oliver's forehead crinkled. "And why not tell our Alpha?"

"He'll fuss. You know how he is."

A twinkle in Oliver's eyes. "That I do. But my appointment..." He checked his phone. "I have ten minutes."

"It won't even take that long," she said.

"The Alpha will be angry."

She snorted. "Let me take care of the Alpha. C'mon."

"As you wish," he said, twitching at his robe.

Oliver healed her split skin using his Small Magics, tut-tutting the entire time.

"Fortunately," Oliver said, "the split was small and wasn't infected, though I agree that perhaps the Alpha should not hear of this."

"What shouldn't I hear of?" Gato said as he breezed in.

The cubs bounced around him, and he slipped each a treat.

"I know your palm opens all Catamount's doors," Bree said. "But I wish you'd knock."

"I will make the effort," Gato said. "Good day, Oliver. Fortis, Audacia, we go."

Walking back to the living room on jelly legs, her heart pounded. Damn the man for looking so handsome, even in his daily outfit of black jeans, black boots, and black long-sleeved T-shirt. His underwear was probably black, too. Or maybe he went commando.

Stop it.

He was trying to herd the cubs out the door, looking perfectly adorable as he struggled to maintain his stoic face while the kits ran circles around the room.

Bree slumped into the chair and reached for her tea. "Damn." The mug lay on the floor, the liquid puddled on the table.

The cubs had tipped it over again, and she was beginning to think they'd made up a game called Knock the Cup. She went to make more tea from the leaves in the cabinet.

Gato frowned. His Breena looked even worse than when he'd seen her earlier. "Wait. What is wrong?"

"The cubs keep knocking my tea over," she said. "I think its their new game."

"Apologies, Alpha, Ma'am, I must go." The healer bowed and made for the door.

"Stay," Gato said, keeping his eyes on Bree.

"I really must—"

Gato cut his eyes to the healer. "Your Alpha asks you to wait one farking minute."

The healer stiffened. "Of course, Alpha."

"Oliver," he said, walking toward the healer. "We last met at Taz's birthday celebration, didn't we?"

"We did. I will make more tea for Ma'am Breena." He disappeared into the kitchen.

Oliver. Ollie, that is what Taz called him. They were chums from university, he believed. Yes, both had traveled to the Bears for schooling. But there was another memory of them, one he could not quite grasp.

The cubs circled, near tripping him, and he laughed, giving in to their antics by petting them both. "I suspect you villains spilled the healer's tea. That was for your Breena."

Oliver bustled back into the room carrying a fresh mug.

Bartholomew raised his head and growled. At the *healer*.

Why? he thought.

Smell.

Gato took a long, low breath, remaining silent as he walked to where Breena sat. He took a knee so they were eye to eye. "How are you?"

She smiled. "Okay. I'll feel better once I've had my tea." She eyeballed the cubs. "No more games, kids!"

"They have deliberately spilled things?" Gato said.

"The tea's been their worst victim. They're going through the terrible twos, even though they're less than a year old. They knock into things, bump stuff out of my hand. I wear my tea more than I drink it."

A smile teased his lips, but he snagged the mug Oliver was handing her.

"Hey!" Bree said.

He widened his smile. "It's nothing, *poosha*. I just want a sip." He sniffed, and the glass mug shattered, his hand dripping blood onto the carpet.

"What have you done, Alpha!" Oliver leapt to his feet. "I'll get some bandages and—"

Gato pierced the healer with a stare.

Oliver tilted his head, as if confused, then said, "Bandages." He trotted down the hall to the bathroom.

Bree cradled Gato's hand in hers, palm up. The cut was deep and mean. "Oh, my love."

"It is nothing." He ripped off his shirt and wrapped it around his hand. After Bree tied the ends off, he pulled out his mobile and made several calls, speaking too low for even Breena's enhanced hearing.

"What put you in such a tizzy?" she asked.

His anger boiled, and he growled.

"Stop it," she said. "You're scaring the cubs." Barth's fur was on end, as well, and the kits were mewing. "I'll go see what's taking the healer so long with the bandages." She rose, and he snaked an arm around her waist. His bare chest pressed against her back, warming her, soothing her, and she sagged against him. "Did Oliver do something to me? Tell me, he'll be back in a sec."

"He won't. The healer is gone."

"He's in the bathroom."

"No. He went out the window."

"We're forty feet in the air, Gato."

"Claws. I have met Oliver several times, though it took me a bit to recall why his name startled me. He is Taz's good friend and Sir Ambrose's nephew. I had forgotten the latter. I assume he used the claws his uncle was so adept at. They make excellent tools for climbing up or down walls." He muttered a swear word.

Bree twisted to face him. "What did Oliver do, Gato?"

He lifted his *poosha* and laid her on the sofa, setting her lengthwise against the arm and placing a pillow behind her head. He crouched down, hating what he had to tell her.

"Not simply Oliver," he said.

"Gato?" She cupped his cheek.

"Oliver's…"

The door flew open, and Arina and a dozen Peacekeepers flowed inside. "Alpha." She bowed. "Ax has apprehended the healer."

"Good. Have you found the security chief?"

Arina shook her head.

"Taz?" Bree said. "But he's your cousin. Your friend."

"Sir Ambrose was a friend as well," Gato said. "This is not about you. Trust me." He kissed Bree's palm and rose. "I must go, love. You called me that, you know."

"But—"

"I must leave. And no more tea."

CHAPTER TWENTY-THREE

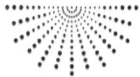

Bree lay in bed, per orders from a healer she hadn't recognized. She tried to push herself up on her elbows but hadn't the strength. Before falling asleep, she'd watched the Peacekeepers range themselves around her suite, all twelve of them. Talk about crowded.

Taz and Oliver had tried to hurt her. They must be Anti-Made Ones, though Gato said it wasn't about her. Yet no one would explain, perhaps because Gato's cousin was involved. Shooting stars, he was chief of Catamount's security.

Fortis and Audi lay beside her, with Barth sprawled before the door. Her phone said she'd slept for three hours, yet she felt as tired as before.

Another healer appeared, panting, red-faced, his cobalt robes swinging as if he'd run a marathon.

"May I enter?" He stared down at Barth.

"Yes," she said.

The healer stepped over the sprawled Barth and approached the bed with tentative steps. He was young, with a shock of red hair and sea-blue eyes that were warmed by some inner joy. He held out his hands. "Shall we try this again?"

"I'll try anything. I feel lousy."

He laughed. "I would, too, in your situation."

"And what might that be?"

"Let us get to work." As he raised his hands inches above her body, she gripped one of his wrists. "Wait. It's my body and my life, and I want to know what was done to me."

He kneeled and sat back on his heels. "I have been ordered not to."

"By whom?"

He remained silent.

"Leave." She pointed to the door.

"Ma'am Breena, is that wise?"

She narrowed her eyes. "I have never been wise, only determined. Now leave."

Bartholomew rose and stepped away from the door, his blue eyes tracking the retreating healer.

Minutes later, angry voices came from the living room, then the word "Go!" was shouted by Fudge, of all people. Within seconds, the healer reappeared, his sheepish face telling the tale.

"Apologies Ma'am Breena. I must do my work, if even from a distance." He swallowed, tripped over Bartholomew's paw, and landed flat on his face.

Secrets, secrets, secrets. It was all about secrets. Twice a day, she was fussed over by healers and prodded by doctors, and still felt like crap. But she had to admit, better crap, well enough to do something about those secrets.

Bree had had enough.

Using the cane Fudge gave her, she could make it around her suite without help. When Gato appeared, his eyes lit with joy, probably because she was vertical. It certainly wasn't her looks. She wouldn't ask if they'd caught Taz because she had a plan, one that meant being alone with the Alpha.

The following day, feeling stronger still, she whispered to the cubs, explaining the importance of their role in her "play." Once they agreed, she left them on the bed and signaled Barth to follow. Her protectors were down to five Peacekeepers and Fudge, which was better than twelve. In the living area, Fudge was talking with one of the men.

"Fudge, would you get Arlo? Fortis and Audi aren't feeling well." Everyone scrambled in a panic to help the cubs. Two went with Fudge to find the vetrina, and another went into her bedroom to guard the sleeping Fortis and Audi. Time to get rid of the final two.

"Would you mind getting me some troff?" She opened a drawer in the living room credenza and handed the Peacekeeper a key. "I think I'm out, but there's more in my storage closet at the back of the kitchen."

And then there was one.

Bree gasped. "Bartholomew says there's someone in the bathroom."

The Peacekeeper raced off, and she and Barth slipped out of the suite. Bree thumped down the hall as fast as her cane would carry her, then scooted around a corner. "Barth, we need to find Gato."

The cat's eyes iced over, and he stared at her for long moments, finally nodding.

They padded through Catamount's halls until they came to a door that opened on a series of stairs leading up, up, up. Watery light draped the staircase. Bree set her jaw and gripped the rail to pull herself up one stair at a time. She paused at the first landing to catch her breath. And onward.

By the time they reached the top landing, she was woozy and panting. Perhaps time to reconsider her "brilliant" plan.

Barth leaned against her hip, and energy—like a soft electric charge—fanned inward. She staggered, then shook her head like a dog. "Whew. You can do that?"

I can.

"Why haven't you done that before?"

Too ill. Might have killed you.

"Thank you." She cupped his muzzle and kissed his nose. "Now let's find our catman."

They walked down the hall, Bree careful of the cane's thump. No windows, and only dim bulbs bathed scraps of space, while murky shadows ate any true light. From this high up, the view would be spectacular, yet the hall was gloomier than any government building. Creepier, too.

A sound echoed, and she started, but they kept going. Around another corner, and a few steps down the hall, a shorter corridor opened to her right, a dead-end.

Barth stopped and sat, facing it.

Four doors flanked the short hall, their upper halves, steel bars. *A prison.*

Barth padded to the solid door facing the main corridor and sat again. A narrow vertical slot opened near the top.

On tiptoe, Bree peered through the slot, but the stygian light showed her nothing. Then she heard Gato's voice

"I ask you again, Taz. Why?"

A pause. "I've been here for five days, and yet you ask when you know the answer." Taz voice was bright with anger. "You *know.*"

"I do not," Gato said.

Bree rested against the wall. *She* didn't know, either. Taz's poisoning must have been prompted by something terrible.

Her mind felt clear, able to put pieces together.

"Cousin—" Gato's voice was full of so much pain.

"I am older. I was your best friend. You knew how much I loved Arina."

Gato scoffed. "Decades ago."

"My love has never wavered," Taz said. "You forbid us to be together."

A pause, then, "It is not allowed. I had no alternative."

"You had a choice! We all have a choice."

A sigh. "I am sorry."

"Arina and I should be together," Taz said, sounding weary. "We *belong* together."

"And because you could not, you chose to hurt the Made One."

"Why should you have your love when I cannot have mine?"

"The Made One is not my love," Gato said.

Pain squeezed Bree's chest. He'd said it with such conviction.

"Proclaim that if you will, Gato," Taz said. "But to all it is obvious how much you care for her."

"I have cared for many women over the years."

Taz's soft laughter echoed. "Not like this Made One."

"You were Breena's friend." Gato's voice rose. "She trusted you."

"She did." Taz hissed. "I was killing her slowly because watching you grow more frantic each day was a pleasure."

"Why you farking—"

"Will you hit a chained man, Alpha?"

A rustling, and Bree peered through the slit. They'd moved beneath the single bulb's pale light. Gato's body was stiff, his fists clenched, his face taut. Taz was laughing..

Gato pushed him hard enough for Bree to hear a thump on the wall.

"The Made One will die," Taz said. "Perhaps not by my hand, but many wish to see her end. I may have failed. Others will succeed."

Long moments passed in silence.

"I return tomorrow with the council's verdict," Gato said.

Bree backed away from the door and hobbled down the corridor. Once Bartholomew was clear of the short hall, she stopped. Gato would see her when he turned the corner. And then what?

Bree kneeled by Bartholomew and hugged him. What a mess. Gato was in pain. Taz must be in pain, too. A constant for both of them.

The cell door clanged, the lock clicked. But no footsteps. Bree pictured him standing there, face slack, eyes haunted, hurting. He loved his people so.

Footsteps sounded, and she rose and rubbed her palms down her jeans.

Gato rounded the corner, and his eyes narrowed. He laughed—

not a pleasant sound—shaking his head. "Your scent carried to the cell, Made One. Taz and I were both aware. Why are you here?"

"Fark you, Gato!" screamed Taz.

He squeezed his eyes, then stalked past Bree. "How have I been so blind?"

She scrambled forward and brushed his arm. "Blind? How was it *your* blindness? Taz poisoned me because he's screwed up and in pain."

The air stank of bitterness and sorrow. He leaned back against a corridor wall, crossing one booted ankle over the other, wearing that sardonic, smiling mask of his.

"Forget about this." He hugged her to him, then set her aside, storming down the hall toward the stairs.

She staggered after him. "Wait!"

He walked down the stairs, ignoring her, and she hobbled after him.

He abruptly halted and whirled on her, and she bounced into him. He steadied her. "Say nothing to my sister. This wasn't just about Arina, for all Taz says it was. He tried for Alpha, as well. He was older, bigger, stronger. Many expected him to rise to the position. But I won, and I believed he accepted that. We were brothers once."

"None of this is about *you*," she said. "Or even me. Stop trying to make everyone's burdens and mistaken choices your own."

He towered over her, fists curled at his side, his fury a cold, terrible thing. Except it wasn't directed at her, not really. He was hurting, and this was how he coped.

"I am Alpha. The Clan's burdens are mine."

"Not this one." She raised her chin and stared him in the eye.

His eyes sparked with anger, but the lurking bleakness cut her deep. His fists uncurled, and he took her hand, leading her down the stairs. They walked through the halls, and though he was going slowly, she was flagging, her head foggy, her body breaking into a sweat. Now was not the time to pass out. "Gato," she said, but her voice was a croak she doubted he could hear.

Bartholomew growled.

Gato tilted his head, banded his arms around her, and lifted.

"Put me down. I just need to catch my breath."

"Breena, my little harrier kitten, if I put you down, you will become a puddle on the floor."

"Will not." Yeah, she would.

"We are almost there." He turned onto a wider corridor and palmed open a door.

Inside, the short hall led to a living area twice the size of her expansive one. Two sofas and clusters of chairs were scattered around the room, with a massive vidscreen hanging on the far wall. She had expected a display of weapons. Instead, the walls were lined with paintings and textiles and an overfull bookcase, while a life-sized sculpture of a panther mid-leap guarded the room. Sun poured in from the outer wall's floor-to-ceiling windows overlooking Catamount's village.

Gato eased her onto the sofa, the soft leather smooth beneath her hands. She sank into it with a sigh, and he laid a cashmere throw over her legs.

"Thank you," she said. "I'm definitely not up to speed, am I?"

"You will be soon."

She was in his home, his den, and it felt strange, yet familiar and warm. Like the man. The wall hangings, the sculpture, the books— all spoke of *him*.

You are in such pain, my love. Knowing how he'd react, the words never left her lips.

"The panther is stunning," she said.

Barth meowed.

"You?"

The big cat nodded.

"Rafe is a sculptor," Gato said, "This is his work."

"It's incredible. Would you tell my guards I'm okay? They'll be frantic."

Gato winked. "Already done. Drink?"

"Do you have any coffee?"

"Bunno? Canny girl. I do." He disappeared.

Barth slipped onto the couch beside her as if this were routine. It probably was, though no scratches marred the pecan leather.

Mentally, she checked on the cubs, thankful they were physically near enough to do so. They slept, she hoped dreaming sweet dreams.

She leaned back, closed her eyes, and let out a sigh.

Rest, Barth said in her head.

"Yes."

Pots clanked from somewhere.

Her eyes flew open and snagged on the corner alter holding the gods and the Fates. Beside the kiva-style fireplace hung a portrait of his brother, an older version of the one in Arina's suite. The young man stared face forward, with humor in his eyes and a sweet almost-smile.

She lifted a photo from the end table. Two cats, one Barth. Beside it, another showed Gato and a curvy woman dancing. He wore his usual black, his boots heeled, while his partner wore a fitted red gown that flared as they twirled. They fit, and Bree fought her spurt of jealousy.

The well-used guitar resting on its stand had to be his, and she hadn't even known he played.

That small piece of knowledge made her eyes burn. Absurd, and yet she wished she'd known, wished she knew everything about him.

"Here we are." Gato carried a tray laden with a carafe, mugs, and food. He set it before her on the sofa table, taking a seat on the hassock that faced her. "Bunno is rare. You're lucky I had some."

"I am. This is lovely. You went all out, catman." She reached for a steaming mug, added honey and milk, and sipped. "So good."

She fixed him a plate of cheese and bread, knowing he didn't have a sweet tooth. But he'd included cookies and slices of cake, her favorite Eleutian ones with pistachios and banana.

After handing him the plate, she lifted the photo of him posed with the woman. "Your partner?"

"My *dancing* partner only and a great friend. Lena lives in the outer reaches of CatHome."

Bree replaced the photo. "Tell me about Arina and Taz?"

He frowned.

"Does Arina feel the same way?"

His jaw tightened. It was clear he didn't want to discuss his sister, and yet she suspected he'd talked with no one about Taz's obsession and how much it hurt him. Unrequited love was bad enough. That his cousin had twisted it into murder and betrayal… It had to tear him apart. "It's okay if you don't want to talk about it with me. It really is. But please talk to someone, voice your feelings, get them out."

"And that will make them go away?"

She squeezed his hand. "I wish. No, but it will make things better. You're not alone, Gato. How many times have you said that to me? Please don't be in this terrible place alone."

He unwound his plait, finger-combed his hair, and abruptly left the room.

Well, damn. She stroked the puma's head. "I'm glad he has you, Barth."

Always.

Gato reappeared holding a small wooden sword, nicked and battered. "Taz made these for us, one for him, one for me. As children, we fought each other and all comers with these until our fathers gave us our first true swords. Long ago, I held Taz close alongside Arina and Ahanu. He would have made an excellent Alpha."

"Would he?" she said. "Truly?"

"No, perhaps not. When Arina was twenty and I had been Alpha for a year, she told me her feelings for Taz. They wished to partner and mate, and I was shocked. I forbade their being together, and both were furious even as they knew I must refuse. First cousins may not partner or mate. It is law."

"They could have run away."

"Taz may have proposed it. Either way, Arina would never leave CatHome."

Bree leaned forward, her hand cupping his cheek. He covered it with his own.

He rose and walked to the table before the vidscreen. "Would you like to watch a show?"

She laughed. "Really, Gato? Talk about deflection. If you'd offered to play, I might have accepted." She pointed to the guitar.

The heat in his eyes made her sizzle, and he winked and picked it up.

Slow and sensual, his music wove through her, the tune evocative of Spanish guitar. Face taut, his languorous eyes focused on her, the tune meandered and swelled, intensely beautiful. It was too much.

She closed the distance between them, cradling his face and capturing his eyes. All or nothing. "You may not love me, but you're mine. No Challenge, no others. I am yours, and you are *mine*. Got it, catman?"

He put his guitar aside and crushed her to him, lifting her so they were eye to eye.

His kiss was fierce, desperate, demanding a response she was more than ready to give. She wrapped her legs around his hips, crossing them at the ankle. He tasted of honey and cedar, and his tongue dipped and probed and battled with hers. Their kiss went on and on until it felt as if her heart would burst.

Coming up for air, he held her tight, supporting her bottom and crushing her to him. He turned, pushing her back against the wall and another kiss, one hand supporting her, the other roving to her aching breast. She moaned.

He froze.

She hugged him tighter. "What is it?"

"You are not at fault." He cupped her chin. "Taz's betrayal has shaken me." He eased her back to the floor and took her hand. "We return to your suite. You need to rest."

"But—"

"Come."

Once there, he dismissed the remaining Peacekeepers and Fudge, who Bree hugged, even if she was ticked off about Bree's "escape."

Closing the door, Gato prowled toward her.

She held up a hand. "No Challenge."

He shook his head.

"Say it."

He closed the distance and gripped her shoulders. "No Challenge. *Ever*. I want you, *poosha*." He rested his forehead against hers. "I need you, Breena-mine. You rattle my world."

CHAPTER TWENTY-FOUR

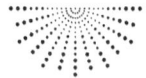

N o Challenge. He'd said it. He'd *meant* it. "You rattle my world, too."

That sexy slow smile grew across his face.

Few things were better than Gato's smile. "Make love with me?"

"You are too fragile, *poosha*."

"Then be gentle."

His eyes darkened and he snapped a nod. "I can do that."

When he kissed her, she thought she'd dissolve, his tongue and hands stroking, massaging. And her hands were busy, too, petting the muscles of his arms, his biceps, his chest, feeling his racing heart.

He carried her to the bedroom, where he banished the cubs, set her down, then locked the door.

Bree watched rapt as he drew his shirt over his head, tossed it aside, and began unbuttoning his pants.

She might have drooled. He was beautiful, carved and strong.

"Hurry up, *poosha*, I am way ahead of you."

She ripped her top off fast, like an adhesive bandage, revealing her boobs. Though she wanted to cover them, she swallowed and said, "Well?"

"Well, what?" he said.

In seconds she was naked and struck a pose.

He froze.

"You were saying, catman?"

"Your form is lovely. Perfect breasts, fabulous thighs, and sunrise hair."

"Talk about objectifying." *Perfect breasts?*

"Me? *I* am objectifying *you*? You are the one sashaying around." His clothes disappeared, and he prowled toward her. "I do not see you as separate pieces. I look at you. I see you, Breena."

She stayed put, watching his muscles flex and release, a hand fisted around his erect cock.

Her mouth dried. Scars rippled and wove across his flesh from long-ago battles, somehow making him even more sexy. Her body prickled with anticipation. When he finally reached her, she wrapped her arms around him, pressed her cheek to his chest, and inhaled his cedar and musk scent. Her fingers roamed, his flesh warm, the hair on his chest adding welcome ripples of pleasure. Touching him like this was bliss.

He clasped her tighter, his eyes searching, hopeful. "You, Breena Boadicea Balážová, are my alpha and my omega. If that is not your choice, end this now."

"It's my choice, too, Náshdóítsoh." Her words felt like a vow. "I choose you, Gato. You."

Then there were no more words.

She'd always believed a man and a woman making love was sacred, a profound joining made perfect by a oneness. But loss and drink had scarred her. This man, this loving, would be that sacred melding of hearts, minds, and flesh. Tears burned, and she nuzzled into his neck.

He lay her down and stood gazing at her, his desire obvious.

Bree felt suddenly exposed. "My breasts—"

"Are lovely. Raspberry tipped, perfect mouthfuls."

Smiling, she held out her arms, and he came to her, kneeling on the bed. He spread her legs, running his hands across her flesh, his eyes burning with need and want. He teased her with the head of his cock, and the pleasure almost made her come, her desire for this man aflame.

But desire was only part of it. Because he saw her, the real "her," minus the many enhancements she'd used as armor. With Gato she could be free.

She moaned with anticipation and he buried himself deep inside her.

This. Him, inside her, part of her, and she of him. He clasped her tight, breathing hard, and the rightness of them made her clutch him as fiercely.

"You are mine, *poosha*," he said, his voice a rusty baritone in her ear. "All mine, and unlike our wild brother and sister cats, we Cats mate for life."

He moved his hips, and the pleasure of it made her gasp. She answered the movement with one of her own and she clenched herself tight around him.

"Oh, ho, you want to play," he purred.

She winked. "Only with you. As they say, a hard man is good to find."

He laughed and buried himself deeper, grinding into her oh, so slowly. He bent to stroke her tight nipples as he began to thrust in earnest. Hands kneading her buttocks, he increased the pace again and yet again. Sweat dripped from his forehead, his face taut, eyes aflame.

She touched him everywhere, across his smooth, slick skin, roving his face, threading his hair, her hands greedy. This was more, he was more than she'd ever experienced. With each glide of his cock, she rose higher, and his hand slid between them and found her swollen clit.

A gasp, her release roaring outward and she arched, sparks of light exploding.

"There you are, my beauty," he gasped, clutching her to him, pounding into her.

Pleasure cresting, pinwheels of flame and color bursting in a night sky. "Gato!"

She held on tight as he pumped into her again and again, head thrown back until he froze, his cock deep inside her, a growl slipping from his clenched teeth. So beautiful.

He sprawled on top of her, and Bree pulled him tight as his breathing evened, and he rolled them to their sides. They lay in each others arms gasping, spent, replete.

The world felt new. She felt new, yet again. Changed once more.

"That, my sweet Breena, was much more than even I imagined."

Her lips twitched. "In other words, your imagination is epic."

"Naturally." He grinned. "But this... You are always unexpected."

She licked the tip of his nose. "I'd have to say that about all of Eleutia."

He frowned. "*All* of Eleutia?"

She laughed. "Most especially you, my catman. Most especially you."

Gato lay on his back in bed, head resting on his hands, watching Breena sleep. She was on her stomach, turned toward him, lips pursed. His *poosha*. His gift, not that he deserved such. She slept on, and he leaned close, inhaled her scent, and sighed.

He'd unlocked the door, knowing the cubs would pound on it and wake his Breena. A blue lacros ball lay in the corner of the room, the cubs' toy, and his thoughts turned to when he, Taz, and Ahanu practiced lacros, and how his little Luciana had loved watching, and how their neighbor, old Treena, would insist they stop by for soup after the game. Life was simple back then. Routine. He might fly off to fight dakos or battle goddarts, but when he returned, CatHome's soothing rhythms would again enfold him.

His lips kicked up. Derula had loved routine, while he was always seeking his next adventure. He'd had many.

Now here he was, an Alpha who always turned toward excitement, fiercely missing that calm routine. How Derula would laugh. Once war was done, the Alchemics defeated, a new reality would emerge.

Change was inevitable. He knew that. The same as he knew he would give millions of korot for a single mundane day.

The door opened, and Barth led the cubs into the room. The pair of mischief makers proceeded to sit and peer up at him, and Fortis slid a paw onto the bed. Two pair of eyes pleaded, and Gato let out a growl. "Yes, yes, come on up, you pests."

With chirping sounds, they pounced on the bed, managing to squeeze in on either side of Bree and himself.

"They're growing too fast, and soon they won't fit on the bed," Bree said with a sleepy voice.

"We will simply get a larger bed." He smiled down at his beautiful girl. "Hello, *poosha*."

"What does that word mean, anyway?" Bree said.

He wasn't about to tell her, not yet. The teasing was too much fun. Bartholomew was staring at him with mischievous eyes, and he would swear the big cat was laughing at him.

You are besotted, Barth said.

He was. Reality settled around him. He had farked the rabbit but good. He had promised her no Challenge, and he would hold to that vow. Which the Alchemics could never discover. Yet he felt lighter, more himself than he had in years. Breena, looking up at him with warmth in her eyes, made him feel full to bursting. Now all he had to do was protect her and Ahanu and his Clan from the Alchemics' fury.

Peering down at her well-kissed lips, the way the freckles danced across her nose onto her cheeks, those long, long lashes that curled at the tips, his heart flew on mistral wings. She looked sweet, innocent, eyes drowsy, with a small smile tilting her lips. He almost laughed aloud. She was his wildcat, a fitting mate for an alpha, even if he was a damaged one. With her beside him, he could repair the fractures to his Clan and become the man he had once been.

"Why now?" Breena said.

Gato propped his head on his hand. His *poosha* looked delicious, and his smile was slow. "Why now what?"

"What changed? Why after all these months are you pulling the plug on my Challenge?"

He frowned, a hand scraping across his scalp. "When you were shot, laying atop Kitlyn, the arrow, blood streaming down your arm. I knew." He frowned, shrugging. "I knew I could not give you up."

"That was weeks ago."

He nibbled her chin. "You are delicious."

"Hello? Weeks ago. Shame on you for not telling me." She nuzzled into his neck. "I should be furious." She ran a hand across his chest, sending shivers to his cock.

"Of course you should." His hand meandered across her smooth belly, lower, and her breath hitched. "Taz suspected, obviously, which is why…"

"It's all right." She kissed him, soft and swift.

"It is not. He guessed my feelings had deepened, and he knew I would never permit a Challenge. That I would keep you close."

"Because I am yours."

"Ah, *poosha*, you have all of me, as well. Body, mind, heart, spirit."

His lips moved close to hers, and he was surrounded by her scent. He breathed deep, savoring. And she teased him more, licking his lips, but not kissing him, until he thought he would go mad. He fastened his lips to hers as if she were an oasis and he dying of thirst, control snapped, and he gripped her tight, deepening the kiss. Devouring her.

His world again rocked.

Except the dust raining down on them meant it wasn't only Breena's kisses. The building had moved.

Gato leapt from the bed, pulling on clothes with precision, ice coating his veins, and his mind snapped to crystal. Bree mirrored him.

To the tune of puma howls, they raced into the corridor. Smoke billowed through the hall, people running every which way. Peacekeepers in uniform, healers, big cats and small. The kitchens. Shouts and muffled screams came from deep in the den.

He gripped Bree's shoulders. "Go back to your suite, lock the door, and gather your weapons."

"Taz?" Bree said.

He kissed her hard and raced off toward the smoke.

Calix was scared. He had found them a new nest, but terror strangled him, sure Prosa and Keplar would discover them. They would steal his Made One.

He dunked his head in a bucket of cold water, sputtering when he came up for air. He stilled, clutching a remnant of clarity and returned to the cabin.

Their new nest was deeper in the wood and was safe. He staggered, gripping the counter's edge for balance. Reason floated just beyond his grasp, his mind muddled. Whatever the cause, his condition was worsening. Calix sat down hard and scrabbled for the pages he'd written when lucid. He read, noting the hours lost since his last entry, when he'd been consumed by a fantastical fog. He crumpled the pages.

The place stank of vomit and piss so disgusting he got out a rag and bucket to clean. But...

He stood before her pod. His Made One had lost weight again and a clump of hair rested beside her head. She was dying. He reached for the sustaining elixir compound. Empty. All gone.

If in the middle of her Awakening, he lost time... He *had* to Awaken her. Now.

A wheel of fire bloomed outside. His steps led him to the door, where a yellow dakos awaited. No, not a dakos. An immense falcon flew through the trees. *His kin!* He ran after it. "Wait!"

Bree stood in the smoky hall outside her suite, her eyes watering. Gato had dived into it, but Bartholomew remained with her and the cubs, who circled them confused and frightened. Bree turned to enter her suite when prickles danced across her arms. She took a breath, knowing what she would find. She pivoted. "Hello, Taz."

The man grinned, the laseblaster he held aimed at Bree's heart. "How delightful to see you, Ma'am Breena."

She'd had it with guns being pointed at her. "Give it up, Taz. Gato knows. *Everyone* knows you tried to kill me. Why throw your life away?" Bree's left hand moved to the knife sheathed at the small of her back.

Oliver stepped beside Taz.

"Oliver. You're a healer," Bree said. "Don't do this."

Instead of answering, Oliver peered up at Taz as if he were a god. What a sap. Didn't he know all Taz cared about was revenge?

Bree's hand felt her waistband. A little further and she'd reach the knife hilt.

Barth remained silent, while the cubs formed fragmented mind words between growls and mews.

"You don't seem frightened," Taz said. "You should be." He swiveled, aiming aimed the blaster at Fortis and fired.

"No!"

Bartholomew crashed into the cubs, moving them in time, though his tail was singed.

"You *bastard!*" Bree said.

A roar from down the corridor.

Taz aimed the gun at Barth's head.

"No!" Bree's knife flashed.

Bartholomew leapt.

"Taz, no!" Oliver smashed into Taz, the gun blasting a hole in the wall while Taz toppled. Sprawled on the floor, he raised the blaster, and Oliver's head exploded in a spray of blood and light.

Before Taz could rise, Bree leapt, flattening him, his hands captured between them. But the man still gripped the blaster.

A cacophony of screams and growls, with Bree afraid to move. Taz would blast the two of them into oblivion. She pressed down on Taz's bulky frame. He was strong, and though she'd been sick, her Made One's enhanced strength allowed her to keep the pressure on.

Hoping to pull the blaster away, Bree tried to wiggle her free hand between their bodies.

The smoke worsened, and Bree began to cough. Taz was cursing and laughing and coughing, all while writhing like an eel. Bree pressed down hard, but it all could change in an instant.

Boots appeared, and she recognized a pair, felt a hand on her arm beginning to pull her away from Taz.

"Stop! He's holding a blaster. Pull me up and he'll fire."

Arina kneeled. "Taz, please give up the blaster."

"Arina-love, I cannot. You know that you are my forever."

"Do as my sister says." The Alpha took a knee on the opposite side.

The man gave Gato teeth. "Why should I?" He notched his head toward Arina. "*She* should have been Alpha. She is braver, bolder than you."

Gato held Taz's gaze. "That may well be true, but Arina chose not to compete."

"Because of you!" Taz said.

Arina cupped his cheeks. "Please, Taz."

"What do I have to live for, eh?" He turned his head toward Gato. "I might as well take your bitch with me."

Gato flung Bree off Taz as Bartholomew's paw struck out and ripped a bloody line across Taz's throat.

"No!" Arina cried.

Taz clamped longing eyes onto Arina's, his blood pooling on the stone floor. Arina pressed a cloth to his neck. "I want you to live."

"I do not," Taz weakly tried to push her hand away and failed.

"Please." Red crept across the cloth Arina held.

"It is my choice," he said with a wistful smile. "Come with me."

"To die?" Arina said. "It is not my time."

"Time. We never had that."

Tears streamed down Arina's cheeks. "No, we did not. We could not." Arina lifted her eyes to Gato.

"Come with me," Taz whispered to her.

"I cannot."

"You will." Taz arced his knife toward Arina's chest.

Bree's heart seized.

But Taz's arm fell limp beside her, the light in his eyes gone.

The next day, Breena by his side, Gato led their somber procession along a well-trod path from Catamount, four Peacekeepers carrying the bier where Taz lay. The path ran beside the Afródis, hugging the cliff that reached to the mesa above, where the reds grew and the cats roamed. The land gradually rose, and a half-hour later, caves began to dot the cliffside, the original homes of their ancient ancestors and now home to the dead.

Arina and Bree had washed Taz's body and dressed him in his military finery. Now, Taz's long hair a flowed like a banner down the bier and across the dusty earth, the ends gathering Mother Terra's soil. They'd picked fresh leaves from the Madronis tree and draped them across his eyes, and Gato had laid Taz's well-used sword in hand. Taz had fought many battles for CatHome. No more.

Tears streamed down Arina's face, and she was unashamed to mourn the man who could never accept what should not be.

Down another small depression, then rising again, they trod onward. No songs were sung, nor incense wafted, Taz having committed the primal sin of attempted murder. He was forever denied those blessings to ease his journey into the Shade.

Gato did not know if his sister still loved Taz. He had not asked, and he would not ask now.

Fates, his heart hurt, a physical pain that gripped his chest.

They halted beside a tall wooden ladder, carefully angled against the cliff wall beneath Taz's burial cave, the resting place Gato had himself dug that morning.

CHAPTER TWENTY-FIVE

*A*lmost *there, cousin,* Arina thought. *Almost gone.*

Gato began to lift Taz from his bier. "No, brother. Let me. Please."

"His weight is too much for you."

"It always was, but this I do not out of duty, but love. Lend me your Alpha strength."

Her brother's sorrowful expression made Arina pause as Clan power suffused her. Then she lifted Taz from the bier, cradling him as she had once done in life, while pieces of their youth scrolled across her mind. She began to scale the ladder. Taz was heavy, though the stiffness had left his flesh. And he was cold, something he had never been in life.

She carried only empty flesh. Not the boy who had played pinnjo with her, who had first kissed her beneath a madronis tree. Not the one who had trained with her, fought with her—always there, always present, always reaching across their widening breach in adulthood.

She had pretended their long-ago love did not matter, had taken the coward's way by avoiding him, but that had led to his obsession, his death the result. She had much to atone for.

Sweat greased her hands as they clung to the ladder. Ahanu would be devastated. He never understood her cooling affections for Taz, who Ahanu saw more as a beloved uncle than cousin. Now she must tell her brother of his death.

Climbing higher, she strained, pulling both of them up rung by rung, higher and higher, never wanting to arrive at that final rung, but knowing its inevitability.

When she reached the mouth of Taz's resting place, she pressed her forehead to his belly, wishing things had been different, though knowing, like this final rung of the ladder, they were inescapable.

The land's hush invaded her grief, stealing inside her a remembered peace. Of all the primal gods, she identified most with Mother Terra—her land and her minions. And she allowed that intrinsic bond to fill her with the strength she lacked.

Long minutes passed as she struggled with the final moment, the one that would separate her and Taz forever.

Memories flooded again, but she shut them down. Time for that when her task was complete. She lifted Taz feet first and slid him inside the cave to be embraced by the elements, and she hoped to join with Mother Terra and Father Sky. His Journey to find them would be arduous, and though much of his life had been full of goodness and deserving of aid along the way, Arina feared his final acts had sentenced him to travel alone, without comrades or weapons, a terrible thing.

Taz had loved, not wisely, but he *had* loved, and for that Arina hoped he would gain the Fates' forgiveness and aid.

When she reached the ground, she bathed her hands and face in the ceremonial bowl held by Gato.

"I go on walkabout," Arina said. Gato would not like it, but she must.

"First Commander," Gato said. "You are—"

"Not invaluable." Arina's lips bowed down. "Geo, our Second Commander, will stand in."

"He is not—"

"He is ready," Arina said. "I must, brother."

Gato nodded. "Take a cat with you. CatGuard. For how long, sister?"

"A week. Perhaps two." Arina shrugged, then strode back down the path toward Catamount and home.

No ceremony, no mourners, no memorial. As they walked back home, Bree found it strange how deeply her heart ached for a man who'd tried to kill her. And yet it did, for she could imagine how she'd feel if Gato turned away from her. The idea of his loss...

Though Taz's disgrace denied him the ceremonial final aids and blessings, Bree would light a candle for the passing of a man once brave and noble.

"Arina is gone?" she said to Gato.

"It is done when we so deeply mourn the loss of another, we must walk alone for a time."

"Did she still love Taz?"

He sighed. "I do not know."

Arriving at Catamount, she and Gato went to his suite, but a surprise awaited her.

"That's the sculpture you gave me, the one of the cubs playing. It's here."

He nodded, then vanished into the bathroom, and she heard water running.

Her turquoise cashmere throw, another of his gifts, lay across a leather ottoman.

The shower turned off, and in minutes she heard pots banging in the kitchen.

That was the pillow from her sofa, the one she'd painted.

She walked into the kitchen amidst more pot banging and lay a hand on his shoulder. "Gato, why is my stuff here?"

From the living room, the chime of the vidscreen sounded an oddly dissonant note.

Gato stiffened, his face tight. He slammed down the pot and stormed into the living room. The screen saver disappeared, revealing a florid-faced man smiling with crystal teeth, a huge blond pompadour, and wearing an outrageous cravat from an earlier Earthly century. Bree stood just inside the room, avoiding the screen.

"To what do I owe the pleasure, Fukkes?" Gato said.

The man called Fukkes frowned. "To say how sorry I was to hear about your cousin."

Gato snorted. "When have you ever been concerned about any of my people?"

"Truth be told, I am not now either." His lips pursed, his eyes cold as an eel's. "But I am concerned about you and your state of mind. Do nothing precipitous."

"I would not think of it."

Bree knew that voice of Gato's—deceptively calm, almost pleasant, yet any second he would blow.

Except he didn't.

"Was there anything else other than your..." He paused. "Your deepest sympathy at my cousin's passing?"

"When have you set the next Challenge?"

"Two months, beginning on Skyday the 7th. It will take us that long to prepare."

"Good. And Calix?"

"I have sent trackers to NoLand, and they are combing the wood. They found a cabin with signs of recent habitation they believe by Calix. But it was abandoned, and they continue to search those many thousands of acres."

Fukkes smiled, and his awful teeth reappeared. "Add more trackers. Find him."

"As you wish." Gato looked so contrite, Bree almost believed the pose. "With the passing of my cousin, I ache for my brother."

Fukkes couldn't see Gato's hand as it clenched around the wood spoon he held. The spoon snapped in two. His smile never wavered as he continued. "An idea has come to me of how I can bring Ahanu home. You have spoken of the Kestrel."

"We suspect he is unique," Fukkes said. "But we cannot be sure until we have studied him. Unfortunately, he has proven elusive."

"I am acquainted with him. As a trade for Ahanu, I will bring you the Kestrel."

Bree swallowed her gasp.

Fukkes laughed. "If we could not apprehend him, what makes you think you have the skills?"

"Ah, but you see, Fukkatsu, I have skills as well, ones that differ from yours."

"We shall see," Fukkes said. "Bring me the Kestrel and your brother will be returned to you."

Before Gato replied, Fukkes image winked out.

Gato whirled, his body rigid. "I am taking another shower. Join me?" The hand he held out shook.

Bree clasped her fingers with his. "I'd be delighted."

His large bathroom held a soaking tub, double sinks, and a shower big enough for a threesome. Mosaics of cats danced along the tiled walls, a black panther in the lead. "It's a beautiful room."

He shucked his clothes, as did she, then turned on the shower, his eyes lit with fury and hope. He was cooking up a plan, and the complex strategies he devised fascinated her.

Naked, he dragged her into the cubicle beneath the pounding spray, lifting her to sit on his lap on the wide bench. "This, *poosha*, is the one place in my suite where I am assured we will not be overheard. And, yes, the sound scramblers are active, but for this..." He held a finger to her lips, silencing her many questions.

With his face pressed close, he began to whisper.

"It is time I tell you of my brother..." He paused as if the words themselves fought their release. He began again. "Ahanu possesses a bright heart, one that always smiles and laughs, yet he is wise beyond his years. He is many years my junior, my parents' last blessing. More than two years ago when he was fifteen, the Alchemics conscripted him, claiming he had a scientific bent. Ahanu is a poet, a dreamer, but by alleging this science proclivity, by law the

Alchemics could bring him into their Clan. All done as a ploy to keep me in check.

"I deeply love my little brother." His jaw bunched. "As punishment for failing to win Kitlyn, they cut off his ear while I watched, helpless."

"Oh, gods, Gato. Damn those prickheads to hell."

"You have the most colorful swearwords." A watery chuckle erupted and just as quickly faded. "I have been conjuring ways to bring him safely home. I had always expected his recovery would take bloodshed and death, which would devastate Ahanu. To protect my brother, I have often acted against my nature. No more. The way is clear."

"You don't mean to get Kestrel for them, do you?"

He grinned. "I do, indeed."

The following day dawned deep in preparations for another journey. Though she hated leaving Fortis and Audi yet again, Bree knew it was too long a trip for such young cubs, Barth following far behind only after he settled the two. Gato looked fierce in his black fighting leathers, and he presented her with a finely crafted suit similar to his own, hers in a deep blue-gray.

He stroked a curl by her ear, her hair finally growing long enough. "I thought the color would suit your coral hair."

"You're not going to let me dye it black, are you?"

"Let you?" He laughed. "Since when have you waited for my approval to 'let you' do anything?"

What he said was true—she could do as she wished, and he wouldn't stop her. She'd always hated her hair until... "I'll be right back."

"No more cutting!" he yelled as she walked into the bath.

"I'm not!" she yelled back.

Facing the mirror, she stared at her halo of curls, having trimmed her mohawk as the sides grew. No, it wasn't Kit's gorgeous auburn. Nor was it ebony, the color she'd dyed it for years. But, objectively, its natural colors were sort of interesting—strawberry, blonde, and russet—colors she liked on other women. Why not on herself?

"Breena," Gato called. "We must go!"

"Coming!"

Bree's butt was sore. They'd been riding for two days on small, sturdy ponies—much like Icelandic ones—that were ideal for the wooded, rocky terrain. Hers was spotted with long shaggy hair, his forelock covering his eyes. How he could see, she didn't know, but he never missed a step. They'd headed for the mountains hugging the sea, and though she didn't know their ultimate destination, she trusted Gato. She hadn't a clue what he was planning, but she didn't believe he would trade Kestrel for his brother.

Since the vidcall put his plans in high gear, he'd taken no time to grieve for his cousin's betrayal and loss. She knew too well how grief could grow from a heartstone to a boulder, immovable.

"Gato, can we talk about—"

"No."

"But, I—"

"I know you. You want to discuss feelings, and that is not for here, or for now."

"Fine." The back of her neck itched, her arms goose bumping with chill. The trail was so narrow, she stared at his pony's ass and his stiff back. "Could we be attacked by goddarts?"

"Goddarts?"

"The creatures you told me about, the ones with poisoned arrows."

He pointed his arm east, to the far off mountains, their snow-capped peaks shrouded in mist. "Those are the Pellopines. The goddarts' dens are there, far, far away."

Bree rolled her shoulders. She had a niggle they were being watched, the skill she'd nurtured at sensing others for the trapeze went on high alert. The feeling made her antsy, but Gato's senses were far more honed than hers. He would know if someone was stalking them. She wore her weapons, had trained for months as Gato insisted. And he was a fighting machine who could move like mercury. Having seen his stunning displays of speed and agility on the practice field, he would have defeated Kit during the Challenge if he'd known countermoves. She massaged her neck, desperate to ease the tension.

When the path widened, Gato signaled her forward to ride beside him. "Are you well?"

"Fine." They rode on until the path again narrowed, and Gato took the lead.

Her fingers tightened in her pony's mane. She'd been glad to see Barth arrive several hours ago, but she wished he was here, rather than scouting the forest.

A wailing call from high above, and she looked up to see the raptor circling the sky swoop lower. "Holy shit! Gato, that bird is the size of a private plane! Look!"

He shaded his eyes with his palm, and grinning, raised an arm in a wave. "A friend."

"But it's huge!"

He chuckled softly. "That he—"

A creature burst from beneath the earth between her and Gato. Massive, its round head bore rows of pointy teeth, its sickly yellow eyes staring right at her. She blinked as the titanic worm rose a dozen feet above them, clumps of dirt and rock falling off its chitinous exoskeleton. The stench hit her, and her eyes watered. The thing smelled like rotted garbage, feces, and pee.

Her pony reared, and she clung to the saddle trying to bring him under control.

A bellow broke from the worm's gaping mouth and her pony flung itself backward, taking her with him. She was hurled from the saddle, bashing hard against a tree. As she lay stunned, the worm's drooling maw dipped closer and it screeched again, its foul breath washing over her.

Rolling away wasn't an option, the trees clumped too close. She snapped her body upright, but her left leg crumpled, landing her on her knees with an agonized "Fuck!"

Bree launched herself off her right leg, shaking out her left. Hoping her leg would hold, she braced herself against a tree and drew her knives.

The worm's head rose higher and higher. Eyes glittering with malevolent purpose, it paused to sniff the air.

Dammit, no fucking worm was going to eat her, especially not this creepy one.

Its head began to lower, its jaws widening.

Take the chance. She must. Blades forward, Bree bent one knee and launched herself toward the creature's eyes.

Except her ankle gave and she collapsed on the ground. *She would not fucking scream!*

A blaze of light.

Her eyes cleared to see the bloody, headless worm toppling toward her.

What. The. Fark! Gato couldn't believe that a massive bore worm had risen from the earth to attack Breena. Without thought, he threw his magical silver threads, wrapping them around the worm. He pulled, straining. The beast reared. *Shote!* Focus shattered, threads dissolving. He drew his laseblaster, dialed a narrow beam, and raised it to fire.

Except he could not see Breena or the pony. His mouth dried. No time to climb one of the trees hugging the path. He stood in the stirrups. Where was she?

Without thought, he planted his feet on the saddle and stood. There. There she was, her hair his lodestar. He aimed the blaster, but… *Now what was she doing?* She crouched for a jump, but then disappeared. Barth was close, but not close enough.

Fark this. He fired.

The worm paused, as if it didn't realize its head had exploded all over the forest. "Breena move!" he screamed.

Then the worm began to topple, thundering to earth in a cloud of dust and debris.

Standing atop his pony, he breathed hard, heart near beating from his chest. *Where was she?* Bellowing Breena's name, he leapt down and ran, scrabbling across the worm's back and sliding down to the forest floor.

Silence, and his world dimmed. The tail of Breena's pony jutted from beneath the worm. She must be under there, too, and he didn't want to see, didn't want confirmation that his Breena lay crushed beneath, her brave heart stilled.

Perhaps she could survive that. She was a Made One, stronger, faster.

But she was still flesh and blood. *The Fates, please, no.*

"Some help here!"

He collapsed to his knees, head bowed. "On my way!"

Like an old man restored to youth, he moved.

An hour later, Bree sat on a rock and watched Gato, who, for no imaginable reason, was gathering clumps of the worm's head into a sack. Her bruised leg hurt like hell, and every few minutes, her eyes were drawn to her pony's bloody tail, the only thing she could see of the poor animal.

Gato's usual silken movements were jerky. He was mad at her, though she couldn't imagine why. Loving such a mercurial man could be a challenge. She was eager for it, just not right now.

"How will we bury the pony?" she said.

"Once we are again in mobile range, I will call the den and have them attend to it." He picked up a particularly drippy piece of worm head and dropped it into the sack.

"I don't understand you. The worm attacked us. I almost died. And all you've done is pick up pieces of that revolting thing's head."

He hefted a large chunk that contained one of the worm's creepy eyes, and into the sack it went.

She pushed herself off the rock, clutching a tree to help her stand. "The least you could do is bring me some kind of stick so I can hobble around."

"No hobbling. No moving. I want you right where I can see you at all times."

"You're obviously furious. What are you mad at me about?"

He halted, whirled to face her, and dropped the sack to the ground. "You almost *died*. I have never been more afraid, not even when my cousin aimed a blaster at you. That time, Bartholomew was nearby to protect you. This time..." He went to scrub his face, stared at the glop covering his hands, and dropped them. "When the worm reared up, Bartholomew was close, but still too far away. Then when I blasted his head off, and you didn't answer..."

"I'm sorry. I was stunned. I..."

"I know, but this emotion... It is too big for me."

And she was there beside him, though she wasn't sure how. She slid her arms around his waist, resting her head on his chest.

"I cannot even touch you," he said, holding up his hands.

She wanted those hands on her. "C'mon." They gathered cloths and soap, and she leaned against him as they hobbled to the stream paralleling the trail. After shedding their clothes, Gato dove beneath the chilly water. She washed herself, head to toe, then removed the worm gunk from his leathers, and then did the same for hers.

She limped the two steps to lean against him and smiled. "What were those silver threads I saw you—"

"Hush," he whispered in her ear.

"Not more secrets again."

His breath hot on her ear, he said, "The High Magics, though how you saw them as non-Eleutian born I do not know."

"'When I'm good I'm very, very good...but when I'm bad, I'm better.' So let's be bad together." She turned her head and licked his ear.

"Absolutely not. We have far to go."

"I need to thank you properly for saving my life." She licked his chin.

"*Poosha*, there is no time."

"There's always time." She held his hips as she lowered her knees to the sandy stream bed, not easy with her lousy leg.

"What in the Sky's name—?"

"You know exactly what I'm about to do."

His hand glided over her wet hair. "*Poosha,* not now."

"Now." And she took him into her mouth.

CHAPTER TWENTY-SIX

They lounged on their sleeping bags as twilight settled around them. Bree smiled, slow and lazy, while smoothing circles on his chest. "See? There was time." And Gato never left a girl unsatisfied.

Bartholomew prowled from the trees, a dead rabbit dangling from his mouth.

"Thank you, brother." Gato rose, muscle and bone moving in sinuous harmony, long hair swinging across his naked back. She could watch him forever, he was that beautiful. And he was hers.

He took the rabbit, stuffed it into a saddle bag, then hauled her to her feet. "Come. We go."

Though it was nightfall, she began to dress while leaning against a pine.

"Do you want my help?" he said.

"Nope."

Donning his clothes with haste, he handed her an errant sock.

"Thank you."

"I want out of this cursed place. We can make the CastOuts camp by daybreak."

"The CastOuts camp. Interesting. Why?"

"For Kestrel, of course."

Not of course, not if she could stop it.

Neela didn't understand Calix's message, shocked she had finally heard from him. He used the usual code, yet the words were odd. *Must discover Fukkes rhomboid.* What was a rhomboid? *Listen at noon. Coming for us.*

Was he telling her their spying had been discovered? Calix, usually the most precise of men, sounded nonsensical. She checked her mobile. Fifteen minutes to noon. Time enough to both pack and listen.

She tossed her few belongings into the soft case, added her favorite purple tunic, and stuffed the bag beneath the bed. The last time she had spied on Fukkes, he'd caught her, and she was sure he would end her. Almost worse, he had slobbered a kiss on her, sticking his tongue in her mouth, while squeezing her breast. Even the memory nauseated her. She had scrambled from his suite fast enough to vomit in the hall. If she had spewed on him, he *would* have ended her.

Spying on him yet again was a stupid, awful idea. Yet Calix's message…

Armed with two knives and a laseball that would explode on impact, she watched as an Aspirant delivered Fukkes' mid-day tray. Several heartbeats later, she edged to the door, pressed the listening device to the wall, and tapped her earbud.

Silence.

The device would be enough. It *had* to be enough. She would not enter his rooms again.

A clattering of cutlery. Chewing. A belch.

Useless.

"Hello, Mari."

Mari. He was talking to his long-dead wife again. How sad. How crazed.

A sound, and she whirled as Darva came around the corner.

Neela slipped the listener into her pocket and brushed her hands down her clothes, trying to look natural when she didn't feel natural at all. She walked down the hall toward Darva, who broke into a smile.

The senior Alchemic looked tired, pouches obvious beneath her eyes. She was a beautiful woman and a brilliant micro-biologist who commanded the respect of all Alchemics. Her closeness to Calix surprised more than a few.

Darva raised a hand. "Neela! How are you, my dear?"

"I'm okay. But upset about the missing Made One."

"As am I," Darva said. "Walk with me."

The corridor's breeze played with Darva's loose blonde hair, lifting the golden strands. The senior Alchemic towered over her in size, but in truth, the woman was far above her in many ways. Neela could not refuse, yet she must. "I was headed over to the mechanix lab."

"Oh?" Darva hooked an arm through Neela's and squeezed. "I guess I'm feeling lonely. I am missing Calix."

They walked on, nearing Fukkes' door. "I assumed you knew where Calix was," Neela said. "You were so close."

"And I assumed..." Darva grinned, turning to face her, "you were one of us."

No no no. "One of us? Of course I am."

Fukkes' door opened. "Why, Neela, how lovely to see you, my dear."

From behind, a hand banded her upper arm and jerked. A Watcher.

Neela reached for her knife, but the man captured her wrist, twisting it. A jagged pain, and the knife dropped. He wrenched her arms behind her back, binding her wrists.

"How dare you?" she said. "I am an Alchemic. Darva, tell—"

The Watcher backhanded her.

Blood filled her mouth, and she spat it at him.

"Oh, my dear," Darva said. "Do give it up."

"Darva, help me."

The Watcher wore a grin as he pushed her inside Fukkes' suite.

"Fukkes!" she said. "This Watcher has—"

"Silence her," Fukkes said.

The Watcher shoved a kerchief into her mouth.

Neela glared at Fukkes, who only nodded, while Darva clasped her hands in front of her wearing a hungry smile.

"Good." Fukkes flicked a hand at the Watcher. "Leave."

Once the door whooshed closed, Darva dragged over a chair and Fukkes shoved Neela down into it.

She was dead. Her family would never see her again. Compass True would never know what happened to her. Neela straightened her spine. She would be brave. It was all she had left.

"You will take care of this creature?" Darva said to Fukkes.

"With great pleasure."

Fukkes walked Darva to the door, but he returned to Neela far too quickly.

"You interrupted me yet again," he said. "And I was talking with my Mari. Unforgivable." His lids drooped as he seated himself across from her and lifted the broken Essence ball, his smile, wistful. "Mari and Xenon's."

Neela's eyes burned and her lips trembled. She mustn't cry, and she began a prayer to the Fates.

"My wife and child were to join me here on Eleutia."

She nodded, assuming that's what he wanted. She puffed out her chest, trying to shake off the terror, trying to find her courage.

"For that, I will destroy your world." He smiled, teeth glinting in the low light. "Picture it—millions dead."

Clans gone, symbionts ended, along with the creatures of land, sea, and sky. She had never felt more right about her mission, nor more doomed.

He lifted the lid, and slid his fingers inside the glass. "I must take care not to cut myself." A shard of glass rested at the bottom, and he slipped a finger beneath it and closed his eyes. "Mari, my Mari."

Neela rose. Even with her hands bound, if she reached the door, she could escape. She inched backward.

Laughter halted her. Fukkes eyes had opened. "My dear Neela, do stay."

Eyes sandy, leg aching, Bree wondered how Gato kept going. But her warrior was one stubborn Cat, having walked for hours beside the pony she rode, laseblaster in hand. He hadn't stumbled once.

Bone weary herself, she admired his strength and determination. "Is the CastOuts' camp like CatHome or WolfHome?"

He smiled, chuckling. "Nothing like either."

"Like what, then?"

"Questions, questions, always with the questions. I want you to see for yourself."

She'd soon meet Kestrel and... She hesitated, but the words spilled out anyway. "Will I meet Luciana?"

"You will. But hush. Though we are on CastOut land, the forest listens."

The world grayed with impending dawn, a chilly drizzle reaching them through the thick trees. They trekked on, and she'd bite her tongue before she asked again when they would arrive.

Her stomach rumbled. "What's left to eat?"

"There are dried meat strips in the saddle bag."

She didn't want jerky, she wanted food. But as dawn filtered through the thick spruce and pine, Gato stopped and raised his eyes to hers.

"We have almost arrived, *poosha*. Hold off your questions until we are private. Agreed?"

"Sure."

He leaned close and whispered. "The CastOuts are unlike other clans, and not only because they have magic."

Magic. They were on a terrible mission, yet she couldn't help her excitement. "What kind?"

"Many kinds," he said, keeping his voice low. "Though it is rude to ask about their abilities. CastOut stories are theirs to tell. Once comfortable with you, they will be more forthcoming. Do not mention any magic or physical differences you see."

"Of course."

A few brave wildflowers, purple and yellow and blue, hugged the bases of trees near the path, a red ribbon lying atop one. Then it moved, disappearing into the earth. She gasped.

"What is it?"

"What looked like a ribbon burrowed into the ground there." She pointed. "Red, like the worm."

His eyes narrowed, and he slapped her pony's rump. "Go with her, Barth."

The pony took off at a canter up the path until a man stepped directly in front of them. Her mount balked, rearing, and Bree clung to the saddle, her left leg screaming.

"What the fuck?" she shouted.

Barth screeched.

The man calmly gazed back at her. He was the size of a mountain, a six-foot-five monolith, his angular face like a Greek god's. Bree recognized him from the road to the fair. Kestrel.

"I'm Breena, from CatHome. Gato is on his way."

He nodded. A man of few words, it seemed.

He stood unmoving, arms crossed, biceps bulging, huge sword strapped to his hip. Hard to tell if his face was a mask of indifference or patience. Like the rock of Gibraltar, immovable, yet she felt his roiling energy as if it leaked from his pores. *What* was Kestrel?

More. That was it. He was *more*, though she couldn't define what that "more" was.

After waiting what seemed like forever, Gato appeared down the trail and cruised to a running halt before Kestrel.

"Brother," Gato said, not even breathing hard. They clasped forearms.

"Brother," Kestrel replied. "You will attend to it?"

Gato grinned. "Coward."

"Why the hell did you slap the pony's butt?" she said.

"For later." He wasn't smiling as he pulled a black kerchief from his pocket and dangled it in front of her.

"A present? For me?" He got her sarcasm. Goody.

He grimaced. "You must be blindfolded the rest of the way."

"All right." She heard his sigh, relief that she hadn't argued. "You'd better make sure I don't fall out of the saddle." She leaned down for him to tie it around her head.

"Your seat is like glue, Breena-mine."

"I don't like it," she hissed in his ear.

His lips were on hers in a flash, and he dove deep for a long, satisfying moment. They eventually parted, both a little breathless.

"That helped," she said.

"I hoped it would."

She might not be able to see him, but her devil of a man was grinning.

Relinquishing the reins, she swayed as they traveled for what felt like an hour, climbing ever higher. The heat made her sweaty, her leg and ankle aching like a bitch. Sybi would say "Poor you," and get out her tiny violin.

Stars alive, Breena missed her.

She wanted to peek, she really did, and her hand crept toward her mask.

"Ma'am Breena," came a deep bronze voice.

Oops.

Blind, sounds and scents amplified, bird trills, the pony's snuffles, the crunch of dead needles underfoot, and she caught the faint scent of the Titanus sea nearby. As the day warmed, the scents of cedar and pine thickened. Soon, other smells and sounds intruded, of food being prepared and voices laughing.

Eyes heavy, soothed by the pony's swaying, she began to doze.

A hand squeezed her waist.

"We are almost there," Gato said.

Bree jerked awaked and minutes later, they halted. Murmurs came from what sounded like dozens of people.

"Lean down," Gato said. "I will remove the mask."

She did it herself, and blinked a couple times to clear her eyes. Immense redwoods surrounded the clearing where they stood, a crowd of a hundred or more staring back at them—men, women, and children. Having no clue what to do, she raised a hand. "Hi."

A few of the CastOuts waved back. Others smiled and two kids giggled.

Kestrel brushed his arm in a shooing motion, and amidst groans and laughter, the group disbursed, returning to their cook fires and mending, and when a woman entered a building, the sounds of anvil strikes followed. A female blacksmith. Cool.

Wood and stone buildings stood among the trees, perhaps homes or workplaces and shops. At the clearing's far end, a wooden lodge looked much like those Viking halls of old.

"Psst." She leaned from the saddle to whisper in Gato's ear. "Where are the rest of the homes?"

"What you see aren't houses. Many are false facades."

"Why?"

"Camouflage."

That word again. "These aren't all the CastOuts, either. You said there were hundreds. Where do they live and sleep?"

Gato's smile was slow and devilish, making her thighs clench. He held out his arms, and she slid from the pony into them.

She hesitated to press her bad leg to the ground. "My legs are like jelly. Hang onto me for a sec."

"For eternity, *poosha*," he said, his voice serious. "Beloved mine."

Bree nuzzled his neck. "Is that what *poosha* means?"

"Is it?" he whispered in her ear.

"You are my beloved, too." She caressed his cheek. "How about you show me those houses?"

He lifted her into his arms.

"You like hauling me around too much. I can walk."

"Not until their healer sees that leg." He carried her beyond the clearing into the wood. "Look up."

Tree houses perched between the redwoods' tall trunks and boughs, many connected by wooden paths that wound up and over and across the village amongst the trees. Sunlight speared through the forest, accompanied by glow lights that cast their beams throughout the village. No cobbled together structures, but graceful works of art that swooped with curving decks and roofs, strings of lights throughout. Other individual glows speckled the forest as far as she could see, their lights twinkling within the forest canopy.

Kestrel hailed Gato and pointed to a "cabin" within a cluster of tree houses. "You will stay there. I will bring the healer when you have awakened from your rest."

He vanished as quietly as he had appeared.

"There is something very different about Kestrel."

"Yes, different indeed," Gato said.

She pointed to the cottage. "How are you going to get me up there?"

"Wait and see."

Bree awakened to a warm hand smoothing her hair, and she sighed and kissed Gato's palm. "That ride on the cargo hoist was fun." She pushed up on her elbows, the large window beside their bed showing the forest beyond.

"More wonders await. The healer is about to arrive."

She groaned, wanting to stay in bed with Gato, cozy and cuddling, rather than be tortured by some healer. Gato wore clean clothes, a chamois shirt, and black cargo pants. She ran a hand down his long damp braid. He'd obviously bathed. She was desperate to follow suit.

"I need a bath. I'm disgusting."

"Later. Healing first. Marcos has tended many who were filthier. He is their Master Healer, and considered the greatest healer in the Northwest Quadrant. The CastOuts have honored you."

Greatest or not, it would still hurt like blazes. "I can't stand being this gross. Please?"

One finger slid down her cheek. "I have become pathetic and can deny you nothing."

"There's nothing pathetic about you, and you know it."

The large studio room held a kitchenette, a large sleeping pallet, and a living area with a vid screen, which surprised her. With his assistance, she stood, wincing when she put weight on her bad leg.

"Up we go." He carried her into the bathroom, complete with tub, doorless shower, and a blessed toilet.

Breena grinned. "Now I know I'm in heaven."

CHAPTER TWENTY-SEVEN

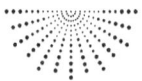

Sitting in the reclining chair in nothing but panties and a cloth over her breasts, Breena watched the huge man talking with Gato. The CatHome healers always treated her dressed, but Marcos was different. Raised scars dotted his face, his dreads bound by a colorful scarf, and a sword hung from his hip above black jeans. Definitely not CatHome's robed healers.

But the show stopper was Marcos' tie-dyed shirt that could have been from Earth. Maybe it was.

The healer's face was that of a young man in his late twenties, a near twin of a young James Earl Jones, yet Bree had no clue of his true age. Eleutians' physical aging, while slower than Earth's, wasn't noticeable until they were elderly, which meant anywhere from two- to four-hundred-years old. Now Marcos, sexy and built, peered at her with a James Earl Jones frown. Unstrapping his sword, he placed it on the dining table, then did stretches, touching his toes and flexing his hands before he sat on the cushioned hassock beside her.

"May I touch you?" he said.

Marcos' voice was very James Earl Jones, too. "Yes."

The healer took her hand in his, running the pad of his thumb across its back, staring at their clasped hands until hers tingled. He held on for long minutes, until snapping a nod and releasing her, his bright gold eyes boring into her.

"I was tuning us to the same frequency," he said and smiled, warm and open. "I will not hurt you."

If that wasn't doctor-speak, she didn't know what was.

"Show me where you feel pain, Ma'am Breena."

"Here." She ran a hand over her thigh. "And here." She showed him where she'd been shot. He might be able to fix the recurring pain there, as well as her hurt ankle.

"I can."

She jerked. *Can you read my thoughts?*

"Only your eyes." He chuckled.

He was jolly. Too jolly. "Okay, go for it."

The hand he placed on her thigh was large and scarred. She suspected Marcos had seen battle. Thought fled when his hand began to glow, spreading a surreal light, her veins gleaming like roadway maps.

When he clasped her thigh with both hands, fatigue stole over her, her eyes blinking to stay awake.

"Gato?" She sounded quivery...afraid. But she didn't know why she was afraid, and that scared her more.

A large hand wrapped around hers and kissed her palm. "I am here, *poosha*." He leaned closer "I will always be here."

An hour after his *poosha* had been healed and now rested, Gato slammed the noxious sack onto a table in the CastOuts underground lab. Two of their scientists—they refused to call them Alchemics—stood on the opposite side of the table, flanked by Kestrel and Marcos.

Gato had already explained the worm's attack, their eyes widening at his words. "The bore worm went for Breena, not me, as if he were programmed to target her."

"Bore worms are never aggressive," Kestrel said.

Marcos grunted. "And the large ones seldom enter our territory."

The blonde scientist reached for the bag, her hands covered in thin gloves. "Let's have a look, shall we?"

Two hours later, Gato's gloved hands were coated with slime, the stench near intolerable. But he was smiling.

Behind the worm's single eye lay a pinky-sized metal device. The CastOut scientists would deconstruct it, but finding the thing provided all the answers they needed.

The device that controlled the worm had nearly ended his Breena's life. The Alchemics, naturally, yet his instincts said the Anti-Made Ones had a hand in this, as well.

The small worm Breena had seen disturbed him. They were seldom on the surface, and spotting one soon after the attack hinted of devices implanted in *their* brains, too. They matured within a week, some growing to epic proportions. Another worm attack was unacceptable.

"They cross lines again and again," Kestrel said. "We must move soon."

Gato stared at Kes, a man he had known for decades. A man he called friend. A man he trusted who, like all the others, had no inkling the Alchemics held Gato's brother. To effect the exchange, he must trust Kestrel with the truth.

It went against everything in his hardened soul.

Decades ago in battle, Kestrel had accidentally revealed his greatest secret to Gato, never mentioning it again. Gato had not, either.

When he proposed his gambit, Kestrel might kill him outright, his truth that profound. Yet for Ahanu, Gato would risk everything. He almost laughed. That was no longer true, for he would never risk Breena.

"Kes," he said. "I need a private word."

He comes. Barth hadn't moved from his relaxed pose, sprawled across the bed. When Gato blew through the door, Bree's heart thrilled. It always did. Breena kept jogging in place, but she grinned. "Hello, stranger."

"I missed you," he said, walking closer.

The smell hit her. *His* smell.

"Fucking stars, you stink!"

"Is that how you greet your love?" He opened his arms wide.

"Not a chance, buster. My love smells like a dead animal. I might hurl."

"Hurl?"

"Throw up."

He chuckled softly, his eyes dancing as he vanished into the bathroom.

She opened the windows, wondering if their hosts had air freshener. Even with the stink, she was happy to see him, to show him she was herself again. It still shocked her.

Marcos was more than a healer. He was a magician. She hadn't felt this great since before her injuries and poisoning—bristling with energy and strong.

When Gato emerged, naked and splendid, he tossed his filthy clothes into the waste bin, pressed the button, and the machine whined.

"What's that do?" she said.

"CastOuts are clever, often brilliant. The bin is incinerating my clothing."

"Wow. The bins at CatHome don't do that."

"No. The CastOuts are cautious about sharing tech." He opened his arms and she went to him.

"You are well?" he said.

He held her tight, and she loved the feel of him, the way his body enveloped hers. The way his heart did, too.

She laughed. "Better than well. Better than anything."

"Marcos cleansed you along with the healing. He rarely does cleansings, as they are exhausting and deplete him of magic. A problem should an emergency arise. But he did one for you."

"I owe him big time."

"You owe him nothing but thanks."

No, more. She would think of some way to repay him. "Now what?"

"We go to mid-day meal." He cleared his throat. "There's someone I wish you to meet."

They held hands walking to the large dining hall, taking their time, and she wondered at Gato's nervousness. At least he wasn't masking his feelings, something he did with regularity. She squeezed his hand, and he returned a smile filled with love. And, damn if her heart didn't flutter yet again.

She felt giddy and euphoric. Wait until she told Kit.

A man carrying a small child walked toward the dining hall, two balls hovering above the child's tiny fists.

"Is that Kustaa?" she said.

"Yes. He has impressed Kes and the CastOuts with his talents, even at his young age. He is loved, as well."

"Jaron and Elise must be devastated."

"They are, yet they can visit Kustaa here, which softens the blow somewhat."

But not enough.

They went straight to a small corner table. As at Catamount, people filtered in and out during mid-day, moving along the food tables, though a few servers brought dishes to those she suspected weren't ambulatory. One little girl sat in a hoverchair, young enough that her three legs didn't reach the footrest. In line for food, a man stood with a small cloud, like an angel's halo, ringing his head. Feathers sprouted from another man's cheeks, yet Gato had said most of their "afflictions" couldn't be seen by the naked eye.

She and Gato stood beside their table, Gato's eyes glued to the huge open doors. A dark-haired woman appeared, and he raced to greet Luciana.

The joy at their reunion made her weepy, and she slid into one of the chairs. An instant later, the pair stood before her, grins on their faces and tears in their eyes.

Breena stood and held out her hand. "Hello, I am Breena and..."

The woman embraced her in a fierce hug. "I am Luciana, and so happy, *so* happy. You have returned my father to joy and purpose."

Luciana was still hugging her when she caught Gato's gaze.

His heavy-lidded eyes shone with a mixture of worry and pride.

Finally ending their embrace, Luciana's olive cheeks flushed a lovely peach. "Forgive me." She stared at the floor. "I... I'm not usually so effusive."

Bree clasped the young woman's hand. "I love that you were."

They sat and ate, the beef delicious, the vegetables shaped like stars with a sweet-spicy flavor, and yummy as well. Father and daughter chatted, making sure to include her in the conversation.

Luciana was beautiful, the combination of olive skin, midnight hair, and blazing blue eyes striking, her demeanor quiet and reserved.

Though he and Luciana passed on dessert, Bree dug into hers, pleased when its taste evoked her Mongolian grandfather's *ul boov* or "shoe sole cake," though this included the purple Eleutian nuts, as well.

"The cake reminds you of someone," Gato said.

"My grandfather. Did you read my mind, like Marcos?"

"Your face, *poosha*, is an emotional roadmap. Few can read minds, and I am not one of them."

Luciana grinned, and her hand slid to cover Bree's. "What papa says is true, Ma'am Breena. Your eyes tell everything." Her smile radiated warmth.

"Will you tell me more about the CastOuts? And about you?"

Dipping her head, Luciana smiled. "I would be honored. We are Eleutia's secret strength. The holders and keepers of magic and mystery. Before the Alchemics' rise, we had the ears of the Alphas. Some of us ourselves were Alphas, our special talents admired and praised. Then the Alchemics' new edicts came." Her face, so full of sweetness, hardened. "We were cast out and marked for death."

Luciana rose and looked at Gato, who nodded. "I will return."

Once she'd left, Gato squeezed her hand as if he were on his last thread. "She left so I would tell you. It hurts her to hear my pain. We placed our beloved, two-year-old Luciana on the mesa above Catamount, as required."

"You and Derula? Your mate?" Bree said.

"Derula was my partner, not my mate. A fine woman who walked into the Shade many years ago."

"I'm sorry."

He sighed out a breath. "Had we not left Luciana, the Alchemics would have killed her. At least by placing her on the mesa, she had a chance if a CastOut Finder discovered her."

"A Finder?"

"Dozens of CastOuts travel the world, hunting for those children. It is their purpose, their pleasure, and their nightmare. They often are too late, the child dead. Every few years, new Finders take their places or they would all go mad with grief."

"What a wonderful, terrible job. Why don't the Clans just tell the CastOuts when a child is left?" She watched his jaw harden. "Ah. The Alchemics forbid it."

He nodded. "Some risk it. We had more assurance than most, as Kestrel knew of our precious girl. But for her not to be in our care, not to nurture her, not to see her laugh or cry or grow…" He shuddered a breath.

Speechless, Bree rested her head on his shoulder.

"We had her for two years." His eyes twinkled through unshed tears. "She was a sprite, a minx of a child and the love of our lives. After Luciana's departure, Derula's health declined. One day, she walked out of Catamount and climbed the mesa."

"You found her?"

He shook his head. "It was as if she'd vanished into the ether. Days later, during a Clan member's funerary service, we discovered a small hole on the mesa's cliff where we laid Taz…" He hooked his hands behind his neck, closed his eyes, and leaned back. "Derula had dug it herself and was curled in a ball within the burial chamber."

Bree slid from her chair onto his lap, wrapping her arms around him. Finally she understood why he kept his heartbreaks close—they were all terrible. Ahanu's kidnapping, Taz's obsession, Luciana's loss —awful heart-shredding traumas.

Gato wiped away the tears she hadn't realized she'd shed.

"It is all right, Breena-mine. Luciana is well and she is loved. Derula was an avoidable tragedy, but she chose her path, and I respect her for that."

"I wish... I don't know what I wish other than to heal your hurt."

"*Poosha*. You have, and we are very close."

"Close?"

Luciana reappeared. "Done?"

"Impeccable timing, as always, beloved."

"Now is the good part?" Luciana blushed. "Now I can tell her?"

"You can. Let's see if my Breena believes you."

Luciana beamed. "I can talk to trees."

"Trees." Bree tilted her head. "You talk to trees? Do, um... Do they talk back?"

"Of course."

"What do they say?"

"Oh, lots. Mostly about themselves, of course. Especially whether it's safe to plant or if they need more nutrients or if a storm is brewing. At times, they tell me about the world; places I cannot go and things I cannot see."

Tolkien's trees had shepherds, the Ents. Luciana looked nothing like an Ent, but still... "Are you a tree shepherd?"

Her smiled dimpled. "No one has ever put it that way, but perhaps I am. I tell our Clan which trees are ready to be felled and which need nourishment. I know where fussy vegetables will thrive and where the trees don't wish to be planted. I like that title—Tree Shepherd. I like it a great deal."

"It suits you," Bree said. "And then they tell you about the world? How is that possible? Can they move around?"

Both Gato and Luciana laughed, and exchanged a glance of pure shared joy.

"No," Luciana said. "They cannot move, Ma'am Breena. From what my father has told me about your Earth, our world has evolved very differently. It sounds to me as though Eleutia is more alive, our species more interconnected."

"That's true, from what I've seen," Breena said. "There's nothing on Earth like the symbiotic relationship between your animals and Clans."

"As I understand, the biggest difference," Luciana said, "is that your trees are not all interconnected, as ours are."

"*All* your trees are linked together?"

"On each continent." Luciana nodded. "Through Mother and Father trees. Mother and Father are fully sentient and can move throughout our world, though they seldom do. No one has actually seen them move, yet they sometimes appear growing in different places. Their children are not sentient, not in the way the Clan animals are at least. But many are semi-sentient in their own way." She paused tapping a finger against her lips. "I will get images and sounds from my trees, though usually not words, and the sounds are mostly of nature, rushing water or a crackling fire."

"How magical."

"Hum," Gato mused. "Once we understand how magic works, we call it science. We do not see the two as necessarily at odds.'"

"That makes sense," Bree said. "Maybe that's true of Earth, too. My sister Kit and I like plants, but we have brown thumbs. Sybelle, my youngest sister, would love to meet you. She's a wonder with all growing things. It would make her so happy to hear the trees."

"I would enjoy meeting her, as well," Luciana said.

Bree bit her lip. "Could your trees tell you if they've seen her?"

"I'm sorry, no." Luciana sighed. "That level of communication, at least with me, does not exist."

Another dead end. But maybe the CastOuts could help her, especially their Finders who traveled the planet.

Gato rose. "I thought you would enjoy a day where Luciana could show you her talents."

"I would!" Bree said.

"Several of the trees are calling to me." Luciana grinned. "We will investigate."

"I must go," Gato said. "I have a meeting."

"With Kestrel?" Bree said.

He nodded.

She prayed he wouldn't do something terrible to save his brother.

CHAPTER TWENTY-EIGHT

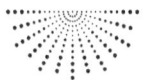

B ree walked through the village with Luciana, numerous Clan members nodding both to her and Gato's daughter. Though their dress was similar to CatHome's, all wore subdued colors— greens, browns, and dark blue.

"Do you all dress in dark colors for a purpose?" she said.

"We do," Luciana said, brushing her hand across the trees as they walked. "The Alchemics spy on us from above and occasionally attack. We do all that is possible to hinder them. Amidst the trees, our clothing hides us."

"Smart," Bree said.

Because they'd left camp, they were trailed by what the CastOuts called a Sgiath, their term for Peacekeeper, and the stern-faced man stayed well back.

Deeper into the fragrant wood, they came to a spindly spruce. "What do you need, oh noisy one?" Luciana said with a smile.

The tree Luciana spoke with was small, barely a foot taller than the young woman, yet it leaned toward her when she wrapped her arms around its diminutive trunk and whispered. The tree bent nearly in half, as if hugging Luciana back.

Birdsong had stilled, the forest holding its breath as Luciana spoke and smoothed her hand over the tree's trunk.

It was the damnedest thing. Astonishing. Even stranger than seeing Fudge breathe fire, which had gobsmacked her enough when Fudge had laughed and fire streamed from her open mouth. Their circus' fire breather was nothing like Fudge, to say the least. But the circus never had a tree talker.

Luciana moved down the slope toward a small redwood, and Bree followed.

The CastOuts—how many unseen and powerful gifts did they possess? The Alchemics hated them and wanted them dead, which made sense. With their talents, they could conquer the world.

Luciana stepped away from the red with a sigh. "He is frightened of everything—fire, knives, animals gnawing his bark." She took Bree's hand. "Come. We must assess one more."

They walked hand in hand, a furious squirrel chittering at them to stay away from his home. He was a funny thing, black and smaller than Earthly ones. Did they have chipmunks? She'd never seen one on Eleutia, but she hoped they did.

Spring was coming. Even here, tiny green shoots pushed through the forest floor still dappled by winter snow.

As they walked, the trees multiplied and grew closer together. "Do the trees sound like a chorus?"

Luciana smiled, and the trees rustled with seeming joy, though not a breath of wind blew. "Not a chorus, exactly, but there's a comforting hum always in my mind. One day, when I leave here, I want to travel Eleutia to hear all the trees' different songs."

"They sing?"

"Oh, yes. More like humming. Only Mother and Father have words."

"Have you ever talked with them?"

"No," Luciana said, and that one word held a powerful longing. "Father is far, far away, but Mother... She is sometimes nearby, near enough that she revealed herself to me once, but she did not speak."

"Maybe she will someday."

"Perhaps, but I am content."

The trailing Sgiath remained a silent presence Bree assumed Gato had assigned to watch her. Yet she felt perfectly safe in the forest with this woman, the trees ample protection. They knew and loved Luciana, bowing as she passed. Occasionally one of the smaller deciduous ones would drop a leaf on her head or chest, and she would laugh. "The young ones like to play."

"The Sgiath, do you know him?"

Luciana's cheeks turned apple pink. "He is Asher, originally from the Eagle Clan."

"His gift? Oh shit, I shouldn't have asked."

"It is fine. He will not mind, will you Ash?"

The man shook his head, but the sweet smile he offered Luciana melted Bree, too.

"He speaks seldom, but he is always listening. He can hear for many miles and can differentiate sounds, filtering out the unnecessary ones for those he wishes to hear."

"No wonder you're not whispering. It wouldn't make a diff—"

With incredible speed and athleticism, Asher leapt *over* them, sword extended, to attack something on the forest floor.

They ran to see, and a few yards away Asher stood over the remains of a twenty-inch worm, its chitinous shell and green blood speckling the pine needles. The worm was red, the same color as the one who'd attacked them.

"That was impressive, Asher," Bree said.

He gave her a thumbs up, then removed his waist pouch and flipped the worm's remains inside with the tip of his sword.

"You're a showoff," Luciana said, grinning.

It was Asher's turn to flush, but his lips twitched.

Luciana harrumphed. "He could have gone around us."

Asher placed a gloved finger beneath Luciana's chin and tipped up her head. "Where would be the fun in that, my Luciana?"

Bree almost covered her ears, his words were that loud, but their meaning was adorable. Nice that Luciana had a fella. "Why are you collecting the worm?"

Luciana answered for him. "All Sgiath have been instructed to kill and collect any worms they see. They must be checked for implants."

Asher frowned at Luciana.

"Um," she said. "Was I not supposed to say that?"

He rolled his eyes.

"Ouch," Luciana said. "I guess that horse has left the stable."

The implication was obvious.

Luciana took his hand. "There is no point in you hanging back anymore, either." She cut her eyes to Bree. "If you would not mention this to my papa, we would appreciate it. He still sees me as his little girl."

"I expect he always will." Bree winked. "Though why I shouldn't mention the worm, I can't imagine."

Luciana giggled, and Asher's eyes fixed on his sweetheart, all warmth and desire and love.

They again wove through the trees, though Bree's attention was half-focused on the ground searching for worms, as Luciana talked and touched various trees. One was a cypress with a mischievous streak, according to Luciana.

Bree halted mid-stride, almost bumping Luciana who'd frozen statue still, then broke into a run. Bree ran after her, following her to the mountain's crest. Far below, turquoise waves danced in the wind buffeting Bree's face. She inhaled deeply, almost feeling the salt spray on her cheeks.

Luciana pressed a finger to Bree's lips and kneeled facing the forest, pressing her palms to the earth. She bowed her head.

Moments passed, mist began to surround them dense as a London fog. Silence, while Luciana whispered inaudible words.

When the strange mist dissipated, the forest they faced dipped into a shallow bowl where massive trees stood trunk to trunk, like sentinels in a circle. Not redwoods, the trunks were smooth and rose ruler-straight, ending in a cone where their branches spread, the tips lost in the mist above them. Like baobab trees, though twice as large.

"The Fates," Luciana rose slowly, her face filled with awe. "For you, Breena."

"What's for me?"

"Go." Luciana shooed her forward.

Bree felt honored, though she hadn't a clue why a tree wanted her. As she neared the sentinels, a pull drew her forward, the strange feeling both gentle and tactile enough that her pulse throbbed. As she neared, Luciana's gasp sounded like a distant dream, and cool air brushed her face. Whispers. She strained to hear the words, fleeting murmurs heavy with age.

Another step forward and Bree reached the wall of trees, a gentle mist brushing her face. She pressed a palm to a sentinel, but snapped it away from the tree's burning heat. *Now what?*

Creaks and groans sounded.

"Holy moly."

The two closest trees bowed their trunks, opening a hole big enough for her to pass through. She guessed she was to climb inside the opening, so that's what she did. And gaped.

A canopy of mist shrouded the circle of trees, yet a ray of light shone down onto the small grassy rise in the center where a single diminutive tree grew. It was the strangest, most beautiful thing Bree had ever seen.

Blue frilly blossoms cascaded like a willow's, obscuring bark and branches, to trail across the earth like a woman's hair.

Come.

It was both whisper and shout, a crone's voice and a newborn's, solemn and gay as a child's.

She walked across the lush grass, whispers and laughter echoing in her head, and as she neared the tree, the blossoms sharpened into blue stars with gold centers, the scents of rose, lilac, and gardenia perfuming the air.

The tree was not far above her head, and she wondered if she should duck beneath the branches. A breeze at her back urged her onward, and she parted the blossoms and stepped forward.

Oh my stars alive.

Light filtered through the translucent blossoms, and before her lay a carpet of flowers—white lily-of-the-valley, blue roses, green jack-in-the pulpit, and yellow lady slippers. They surrounded the trunk, its silver bark inlaid with small gems—emerald and diamond, sapphire and ruby.

Shooting stars. The surrounding trees *were* sentinels, for she was in the presence of Mother, the genesis of all trees on Eleutia.

Touch.

The word echoed inside her, and Bree laid her palms and cheek against the trunk. Soothing, like standing within a cool mountain stream.

She *is here.* She *will come. Be at ease.*

Words, yet not. More like the sigh of the wind. Yet she understood. "Who will come?"

We did this. We brought you here.

"Here, you mean, to you?"

Blossoms fluttered and murmurs rose. *We whispered to the owls, who told the falcons, who spoke with Falcon to choose you three. Falcon showed you to the Evil Ones, so they would bring you.*

She *is here. She will come. Be at ease. Go.*

"Who is She?"

But Mother said no more.

Bree hugged her, the bark cool and comforting. At last she understood the meaning of "awe."

"Thank you, Mother." She backed away, unwilling to tear her eyes from Mother's beauty as she moved from beneath her boughs.

Again Bree clambered through the sentinels, whose trunks straightened when she moved beyond their circle.

They'd left after breakfast, but now the sun hung high in the sky. She'd been with Mother for hours. Up on the rise, Luciana's head lay on Asher's lap as he stroked her hair.

Bree stumbled forward, drunk with joy as she staggered up the slope to Luciana and her love.

She fizzed like shaken soda pop and couldn't wait to tell Gato. Except on their return to camp, Gato was nowhere to be found. Luciana said he would appear during mid-day, and Bree ate with her, Asher, and another Sgiath friend, saying little during the meal, her mind elsewhere. She played Mother's words over and over in her mind, still euphoric with joy. But when Gato didn't appear, worry began to nag. His plan to trade Kestrel for his brother tore at her. The trade would mean Kestrel's imprisonment and possible death.

She walked into their empty cabin, and her worry increased. Even Barth was gone. She yearned for Gato. The way he hugged her, kissed her, and swung her around with joy... *Damn.* She had to face it. Five hours away from her imperious love, even ten minutes, and she *missed* him. Oh, how Kitlyn and Sybi would laugh.

An hour later, Gato breezed into their cabin muddy and harried, and immediately began doffing his clothes.

"Gato!" Bree leapt up from the chair where she'd been reading and reached for him.

"*Poosha.*" He backed away, leaned in and kissed her. "Again, I stink."

"I don't care." She stepped forward.

He backed away. "I do."

"Sit, I'll get your boots."

"Do not. They are the worst of the mess." He hopped around removing them, then stripped off the rest of his clothes. Nasty bruises purpled his skin beneath his breastbone, on his upper arm, and thigh.

She reached out her hand. "Those must hurt. Do you have salve? What happened?"

"They are nothing." He pecked her lips and vanished into the bathroom.

Naked in seconds, Bree followed and stepped beside him into the shower. She wrapped her arms around his waist. "I missed you."

"I missed you too."

And though his cock was rod-stiff, he said, "No funny business."

She raised a brow. "What have you done with the Gato I love?"

He laughed and rested his forehead on hers, the warm water pounding them. "He is here, but barely."

305

It was her turn to laugh. "What *were* you doing?"

"Wrestling with Kestrel and his lieutenants."

"Of all things. Let me wash your hair."

He nodded and gave her his back, bending his head so she could reach the top. She began massaging the fragrant shampoo into his scalp, then his long luxurious hair, its weight a pleasure in her hands. As she rinsed and braided it into a long plait, she told him about her day and meeting Mother tree. His surprise was obvious, but he had no insight into Mother's words.

"What a gift," he said. "Few have met Mother, and she deigns to speak with even fewer. What I do not understand is *why* Mother engineered you and your sisters arrival on Eleutia."

"I can't imagine, either. I don't know who 'She' is, and it's driving me crazy. Any clue?"

"Your sister?" he said.

She shrugged. "Maybe? I've been so afraid to hope. Though I can't imagine why Sybi would be 'She.'"

They rinsed off and his eyes took on that particular heat, her body's reaction instantaneous and unsurprising.

"I find my energy has returned," he said.

"Mine's already humming."

He lifted her by the waist, hugging her tight, breathing her in.

Grinning, she wrapped around him like a monkey, her hands roaming his back.

His kiss was fierce, and Bree soon rediscovered how very energetic Gato could be.

Much later—naked and in bed—they ate cinnamon cake, licking the crumbs off each others' bellies, and Bree found the courage to speak the words troubling her. "Did Kestrel agree to the trade?"

"Kes is thinking about it." Gato lifted a piece of cake to her lips. "It is not an easy decision."

Bree licked it off his fingers, but the taste turned to dirt.

Gato ran a finger down her cheek. "If Kestrel agrees, it will work out. He will not be harmed."

"Only imprisoned."

He said nothing.

"He's a good man, Gato."

"That he is."

"How can you—"

"Trust me. *Know* me."

"I do know you, and you would do anything to save Ahanu."

His eyes darkened. "Trust, *poosha*. I vow Kestrel will be safe."

The bird-man is our friend. Trust Náshdóítsoh.

Bree startled, Barth's words a near growl.

Blinding light bathed the cabin.

Gato leapt up, shoved on his boots, and flew out the door naked.

Bree tossed on a robe and raced after him. "What's wrong? What is it?"

Gato stood on the landing, staring out at the suddenly darkened sky.

"What's happening?"

His face was stark. "The Alchemics will strafe the village with lasers." His grip tightened on the railing. "They will destroy it. Destroy the CastOuts. Us. Everything. There is no protection. Nowhere to hide." He took her hand, turning his back on beams of light soaring toward the camp.

"Come," and he tore down the stairs at a run. Once on the ground he placed his hands on her shoulders, eyes burning with fear and love and determination. "If we are to die, we do it standing on Mother Terra. I love you, *poosha*, my Breena. I would have you for my mate, for all time, in this life and in the next." He clenched her hand. "I have no ribbon to bind us, but Bartholomew is here and can call the cats. Will you take this journey with me?"

She didn't understand, but she would go anywhere with this beloved man. Three blinding balls of light soared closer and stopped. They hovered over the camp, as if the Alchemics were taunting them with their impending doom.

"I will, dear Náshdóítsoh, my Gato. I wouldn't miss our journey for the world." She wrapped him in a fierce hug, and on tiptoe, kissed him.

Barth made a loud chirping sound, like a bird's, and she heard replies, the chirps echoing through the camp, the forest, and beyond.

Bree froze, *feeling* the sound amplifying through her flesh, her mind, her heart, tuning her, realigning her. Changing her once again.

"High Magics," Gato gasped. "Forbidden and powerful."

She sagged against him. "Who cares? We're about to die, right?"

"Yes, but we are now bound together, my Breena, in this life and the next."

A cacophonous explosion. Death a breath away. If possible, Gato clutched her tighter. Though she wanted to tuck her head against his shoulder and hide, she stared into his eyes, where love and protection, fear and anger mingled.

What would it feel like? Would he truly be with her in death?

They rocked as an explosion shuddered the earth. A sudden silence, then... laughter?

A dozen observers surrounded them, including Kestrel, Luciana, and Marcos, all laughing.

The fury on Gato's face confused her even more.

"Why aren't we dead?" Bree said.

Marcos strode forward, still chuckling. "Forgive us, my friends. When the lasers appeared, we were on our way to tell you, and then... You see, we did not want to interrupt your mating ceremony. Nice ceremonial outfit, Gato."

"Why are you imbeciles laughing at us like a troop of bachons," Gato spat. "And why the fark are we not dead?"

Kestrel had the grace to look chagrined. "Our CastOut talents are many and varied."

"What Kes means," Marcos said, laying a hand on Gato's shoulder. "Is that two of our group have the ability to throw up shields. Ones that protect us from the Alchemics' lasers, which they fire at us occasionally. The farkers know we can repel them, but they choose to display their might, perhaps in the hope Peter and Elmer will tire." Marcos smiled, like a kitty who'd caught a mouse. "They never do."

CHAPTER TWENTY-NINE

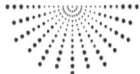

Back at their aerie, Gato began pulling on clothes, which Bree proceeded to rip off him.

His hands halted her. "We cannot, *poosha?*"

The emerald eyes focused on her burned with heat.

"Of course we can," she said. "We are mated, and I feel strange in my skin and I need you and I want you *now.*"

A bitter chuckle. "As I want you." He kissed her, and the fire inside blazed. More. She needed more. Her hands roving, touching.

He ended the kiss with a sigh. "Any minute, Clanfolk will pile into our small cabin to celebrate. Matings are rare and special."

"But...but..."

He kissed her again, and the feel of his skin touching hers was bliss.

Footfalls pounded up the steps.

Gato pressed his forehead to hers. "There is time." He buttoned his pants and slipped into a shirt. "We have forever."

"'Anything worth doing is worth doing slowly.'" And right now, she wished the rest of the world would vanish.

"Is that your Mae West again?" he said.

Bree frowned, buttoning his shirt. "Yes, though I wish I had a better quote for…for…" She waved a hand. "This!"

The door flew open on a wide-eyed man holding up a bottle of ilaberry wine. "Oops."

Gato's smile blazed. "Come in! All are welcome."

An hour later, dozens jammed their small cabin, drinking, joking, and celebrating her and Gato's mating. All except for Gato and Kestrel, who stood in a shadowed corner, their faces grave.

She feared for both of them—what would happen to Kestrel if he accepted Gato's proposal and how would Gato shoulder yet another soul-eating burden.

And yet… The trade was very un-Gatoish. He'd risk himself, sure. But risking another to reach his goal? That was out of character.

Gato had vowed Kestrel's safety. If she only knew his plan. One thing she did know—he would not betray her trust. Bree sighed. She might not like it, but she would accept Gato and Kestrel's decision and pray all would be well.

The men clasped forearms, the deal sealed. And the idiots were smiling. Gato slapped Kestrel on his shoulder and leaned in to whisper in his ear. Kestrel turned his head, eyeing her, and when the men parted, the CastOuts' Alpha walked to where she stood with her glass of purple punch and a question on her face.

Kes stared as if his night-colored eyes could see right through her, standing close enough to detect his cedar and pine scent. He was a solemn man, big everywhere, overwhelming really, yet all she felt was his warmth and a gentleness at odds with his warrior's demeanor.

"You've agreed," she said.

"Yes."

One word. An ordinary one, as if he'd agreed to a stroll in the park. "What do you plan, Kestrel?"

"Trust… It is hard," he said in that deep, melted-bronze voice of his.

Her eyes widened.

"All will be well."

"I hope so."

"Wait and see." Only his eyes smiled, but that was something.

He strode out, followed by Marcos and two other Clanmates.

The ride home was tense, and not because any worms attacked. In fact, the ride itself was uneventful except for a giant bird flying high above them.

"Will you tell me your plan?" she said.

"It is simple. I bring Kestrel to the Alchemics, and they give me Ahanu."

Simple. "It's more than that."

"Perhaps.

"What about Compass True?" she said. "Won't you be telling them what you're doing?"

"I cannot. They will wish to be involved."

"Why can't they help?"

"They would not permit the perceived loss of Kestrel."

"Perceived loss?"

He snorted. "Clever *poosha*. That is as much as I will say."

"Gurrr. I'm worried. Just tell Compass True how the Alchemics have held your brother for years. Then, when they discover the trade, they won't see it as a betrayal."

He halted his pony, though CatHome was only an hour away, and she did the same. Though his face was in shadow, his teeth gleamed in a smile, always a bad sign for their serious discussions.

"I have lived a long time in darkness, Breena-mine. The Alchemics have bent me to their will because of my brother and I have grown too comfortable in the shadows. My trust in all but a few is eroded. The exchange must proceed, and there are those Compass True members I would not trust with any of this, especially Ahanu's detention."

She bit her lip, wanting to protest, yet respecting Gato's words.

"Kestrel would not inform the counsel, either," Gato said. "He will reveal his truths in his own time, ones that will change Eleutia forever."

Gato sat on the sofa in their den, Breena at arms training and Barth with her, while the cubs nestled against him, exhausted from their CatGuard exercises. He spoke the Alchemics' code to the vidscreen and waited. And waited. And waited.

He was used to it, the arrogant pricks thinking the wait would get on his nerves, make him anxious, and then perhaps say something he should not reveal. They never tired of their experiments and games.

He poured himself another mug of steaming troff. For all their brilliance, the Alchemics were ultimately fools. Their increasing disdain and manipulation of animal Clansfolk only served to heighten Eleutians' anger.

The move with Kes would be one of the final gambits before war. Once all the players hit their marks and Compass True declared war, all Eleutia would take up arms against the Alchemics.

The war would be won with determination, cleverness, and passion, the latter an ingredient those fiends lacked. He sat back and Fortis sent him a mental picture of Breena, sword raised, lips snarling, and teeth clenched. Magnificent.

He scratched Fortis' chin. "Your first projected image to me," he said to the cub. "Impressive. That is how you see your Breena?"

Fortis nodded.

Gato couldn't wait to see her confronting an Alchemic with that look on her face. He laughed aloud.

Barth padded into the room, though Gato hadn't heard him enter the suite.

"She is done with the sword master?" he said to Barth, who nodded.

Audi sent an image of Bree in her former suite on a vidcall with Kitlyn. "Your first image, as well. Good, Audacia! You sense her talking to her sister?"

See.

"You see her in your mind?"

Yes. Audi purred.

Astonishing.

The Fates, he missed Bree, though she had been gone less than two hours. So this was mating. It was driving him moonstruck.

How was an Alpha supposed to function when his only thoughts were of his mate?

He relaxed back into the sofa. The ache was tolerable only because Breena would soon return. He must ask Rafe how he dealt with these feelings, because all he wished to do was glue her to his side.

The vidscreen chimed. Fukkes deigning to answer Gato's call.

Bree's phone buzzed, and she activated the sound scramblers before answering.

"First of all," Bree said to Kit before her sister got out a word, "things have been crazy, which is why I haven't called. I was almost killed, but I'm fine."

"Thank the Fates." Kit gasped. "You didn't take a—"

"No, I haven't had a drink. Wait'll you hear what I've learned. It blew me away."

Bree told Kit about Mother tree.

"You're saying Mother tree brought us to Eleutia?"

"Yes."

"Why?" Kit said.

"She didn't explain. It wasn't a conversation, more like a telling. But her words, *She is here,* might have referred to Sybi."

"She talked about the three of us, right?" Kit said. "Maybe that's a confirmation, though she could have told us where Sybi is."

"Mother might not know," Bree said. "She was so kind, so glorious, trying to reassure me. The words She *will come* implied 'She' was important. But if it's Sybi, what could she do?"

"Maybe it's not just Sybi, maybe it's the three of us together," Kit said.

"Maybe. I'm so frustrated."

"Me, too," Kit said, reaching for a mug and downing a sip. "I'm here at WolfHome, you're with the Cats. *Lucky stars.*"

"Mother drew me to her, she had a reason for telling me. She wanted us to *be at ease.*"

"I will be," Kit said. "Once we find our sister."

The worm story, her healing, and her stay with the CastOuts had Kit oohing and ahhing.

"Um," Bree said, forcing herself to say it. "Gato and I are mated."

"Whoa, what?"

"I know. We both thought we were going to die, and bam!"

"About to die!"

"We're fine, Kit, really. But it's strange. I've been gone for around two hours, and I'm antsy to get back to him. Can you believe that?"

Kit giggled. "I don't have to. I've experienced it. The compulsion will drive you nuts at times. Though the feeling will soften, he will always be with you at the back of your mind. A presence."

Inside, Bree could taste Gato's scent, grasp his emotion, feel his love, though she had no idea how. "He can sense me the same way?"

"Absolutely."

"It's magic."

"You are looking well, Alpha."

Fukkes smiled at Gato from the vidscreen, an arm around Ahanu's shoulders. His brother was stoic-faced. He had grown used to that face over time, but always found it unnatural. Of the siblings, Ahanu was the lightest of heart, his smile and laughter often ringing through Catamount's halls.

If Fukkes knew Gato's pain at seeing his brother's face rigid, his eyes dead, the Alchemic would cackle with glee.

But like Ahanu, he had no intention of giving anything away.

Barth uncurled from his position on the sofa and sat up, eyes glaring at the screen. His brother cat loathed Fukkes even more than Gato did.

"I am well," Gato said. "I see you are dressed in your usual sartorial splendor." Fukkes' clownish dress had become a bore, a costume he wore to annoy and incite, as were his crystal teeth. Gato often pricked that balloon. Would that he could prick the man's balls. No. Better to crush them.

Picturing it made him almost cheerful.

"I always don my best for our conversations," Fukkes said.

Gato leaned forward, hands clasped, his calm appearance belied by his roiling gut. "All is arranged. We meet in three days at Fates Peak, Kestrel by my side."

Ahanu started. "Brother, no—"

"I did not give you permission to speak," Fukkes said.

Ahanu's sweet smile failed to mask his hatred for Fukkes. "If you did not have blasters trained on me, I could speak for hours about—"

"Quiet!" Fukkes jerked his chin at someone offscreen, and another Alchemic led Ahanu away.

"He has gotten truculent of late," Fukkes said, unable to hide his annoyance. "We will be glad to be rid of him."

"Three days, at three o'clock, Fates Peak. If my brother has one scratch, you will not get Kestrel." His voice was calm, as if reciting a laundry list.

"And how would you stop us?" Fukkes smile widened.

"Come now, Fukkes. Let us make this more cordial, as we have done numerous times. You have always been fair." What a crock of *shote*. "Let us continue in that vein. Consider, I am bringing you a treasure beyond compare."

Fukkes lids drooped. "As you have done before. Tell me, Alpha, how are your preparations for The Challenge coming along?"

"Well."

"Excellent. Now, to the more taxing task—have you found our missing Alchemic?"

They had not found Calix, though he had sent Peacekeepers to search for him. "Unfortunately, no. I have made every effort, even searching CastOut territory, at much risk to my life. While on the hunt, I almost lost our Made One to a bore worm attack."

"Fool to bring her with you." Fukkes eyes widened. "Is she well?"

"I made short work of the thing, but it was quite odd. A *very* peculiar-acting worm."

"Mindless creatures can be like that," Fukkes said. "Stupid and without reason."

Which was how Alchemics thought of Eleutians. "They can, indeed."

For mid-day meal, Bree joined Fudge and Ax at their table, Fortis and Audi nestling at her feet, with Gato joining them after his vidcall. Ax would know the day Gato planned to complete the exchange. All she had to do was squeeze it out of him.

She'd hadn't seen Gato for hours, and it felt like the time she'd given up smoking, her craving for nicotine an itch beneath her skin. Only worse.

The stir fry of snow peas, carrots, and slivered almonds, normally tempting, failed to appeal. The mood she was in called for PB&J, which she ordered, and then pushed her plate aside.

She couldn't help it, she was still worried about Kestrel. Gato knew, because their mating had changed everything, honing their need for each other to a diamond-hard point, not to mention how the Clan now treated her.

Everywhere she went, all remarked on their mating. Five minutes ago a Sequestered wearing a winged helmet had stopped her, greeted her with affection, and *sniffed* her. After which the woman said, "Ha ha, you have mated with our Alpha. Congratulations. He is a good man."

Gato *was* a good man, and he would never sacrifice Kestrel without a positive endgame, no matter that she couldn't see it. She might be able to tease it out of their bond… Whatever the gambit, it would be dangerous, and their mating had heightened her fears.

Bree took a bite of her sandwich, followed by a sip of milk.

"You are mated," Ax said, his beaming smile getting under her skin.

She snorted. "You, too? I assume Fudge told you."

He elbowed his mate. "She did *not,* and she should have done so."

Fudge elbowed him back. "You are as subtle as a goddart, Ax."

"Ow!"

"Oh, dear one, that was a love tap!" Fudge said, batting her eyelashes.

Poor man. "It's my smell, isn't it? How *do* I smell?"

"Like yourself." Geo, the temporary First Commander, slid onto the seat beside her.

"It's more than that," Bree said.

Fudge lowered her voice. "You also smell like Alpha. Your scent is a combination now, of yours and Gato's, which is how we know you mated. Why did you perform the mating away from Clan? It's a big celebration. You cheated us out of a party!"

"Sorry about that, kiddo," Bree said, and explained about their mating. "Now, with Gato not here, I feel…"

"Like you're missing a body part?" Ax said

"Pretty much. It's uncomfortable."

"There's an easy way to fix that." Geo, the most serious of men, offered a poorly done wink, more like a twitch.

"Oh, really? And how is that?" She waggled her brows.

Geo's blush crept from his neck to his forehead. Sort of like watching a sunrise.

"Come on, fella. Tell me. How?" She was being bad, but it was fun poking the bear, er, cat. But he wasn't *her* cat, and hers was the most fun of all to poke. *Dammit.* She wished he'd hurry up and get there.

"By…" Geo's face grew redder. "By being with Gato, your mate."

"I see." Too much fun yanking his chain. "So what if I want to get out of this thing, this mating?"

"You could." Fudge nodded, all serious. "Death. You could kill him. I suspect you have wanted to at times." Then she giggled, spoiling the whole effect.

"You wouldn't!" Geo said, his face shocked.

"Of course I wouldn't. But shame on you for following me, Geo."

"I..." His Adam's apple bobbed.

The snort from Fudge made the cubs raise their heads, curiosity pouring off them.

"Nothing's happening, kids," she said. "Relax. Our new First Commander has been given babysitting duty. For such an accomplished man, you seem awfully uncomfortable with your latest assignment."

"I was supposed to be stealthy," Geo said.

"I guess that kitty cat is out of the bag." She would *not* laugh.

His confusion almost made her smile. She patted his hand. He was a decent guy, and she was giving him a hard time. "Sorry. An Earth expression that I guess doesn't translate. You might be First Commander, but I wouldn't add 'spy' to my resume, if I were you."

"I wasn't spying on you, Alpha."

"Alpha?" Bree said.

"You and Náshdóítsoh are one. Two Alphas."

Shit. Now she was Alpha, too? The mating thing kept getting stranger.

"As noted," Geo said. "I am not spying. The worm almost killed you." He shuddered. "I am to protect you, Ma'am Breena."

She *should* be annoyed, but instead she was touched. "I'm glad to have such a fine protector."

Bree stacked her dishes at the bin when her phone vibrated and she answered.

"Go to your vidscreen, Made One. I have something to show you."

The caller clicked off. Bizarre, but intriguing. Whoever he was, he sounded intense and purposeful. She'd heard that voice before, though where eluded her. Shooting stars, he might have news of Sybi.

Gato and Barth were still gone when they returned to their suite, the cubs curling up by the hearth. She poured some kamla, barked "Vidscreen on!" and settled on the couch.

Her catman always laughed at how she shouted at the screen. She sniffled, eyes burning, hating these absurd feelings. But the Fates, she missed him.

The vidscreen coalesced with the usual scrolling rundown of the happenings at CatHome, while Fortis and Audi crawled onto the sofa. They were full of questions, and it astonished her how she knew that.

"A mystery man is calling," she said to them.

Audi chirped.

"We'll know soon enough."

The screen dissolved to reveal Kestrel cradling an infant in one massive arm, the child asleep. She sat up straighter. The cubs did, too.

Gato had to have put him up to this. She waved at the beautiful man with a commanding presence and the face of a Greek coin. "Hello, Kestrel."

He nodded. And said nothing. From her time with his Clan, that didn't surprise her. Kestrel chose his words with deliberation.

The Alpha raised the child and kissed his forehead, then returned his attention to Bree. "This is Bartok, formerly of the Simian Clan, now a CastOut. His eyes glow. We do not know why yet, but that was enough to force his Clan to cast him out."

The baby woke up waving his arms. A leather tie on Kestrel's vest drew his attention, and he clutched it in a tiny fist.

An image of her holding her baby popped into her head, with red hair and emerald eyes, two men without faces tugging at her child to steal it. She shivered. "I can't imagine giving up a child."

Kestrel drew the tie from the baby's mouth and substituted his finger. "Their parents want these children and some try to hide them. When they fail, which they always do, the sadists rip the child from its parents' arms and destroy it."

Swallowing hard, she recalled Gato telling her the same. "I see."

"You do not. Many have an excess of magical talent, which is due to the Alchemics, who created many of us."

"By the Alchemics. This isn't a rumor, is it."

"It is truth. We are the results of their many experiments. They use Clan eggs and sperm, often combined with animal DNA, and manipulate it. A CastOut is the result. Do not speak of this." His black eyes intensified.

With that one look, Kestrel could terrify. Lucky she wasn't easily scared. Much. "I won't. If they're creating you, why don't they take their creations to Alchemic City for study?"

The infant began to fuss, and Kestrel disappeared, returning in moments without the child. He rested a hand on the hilt of his sword. "Most Alchemic experiments using Eleutian DNA include releasing our children into the wild, where they can be studied *in situ*."

"But they're left to die."

"Many do, yes." His robotic stillness was perfect, but his white-knuckled sword grip and blazing eyes betrayed his passion for this cause.

"Within my Clan," he said. "We have many gifts. Our curses outnumber them. Those without arms or legs, one who can fly but is blind, a seer with no memory of his own past. Many are barren. Several have male *and* female genitalia. Physical deformities, mental aberrations, ill health—they stalk our people. Our creation must stop. My trade for Ahanu is our opening salvo."

"I understand, sort of. But trading for *you*? That I don't get."

"You do not. But I appreciate your willingness to accept. You are accompanying your mate on this mission?"

"To meet with the Alchemics? No."

She'd offered, but Gato had declined. They both knew how hard it would be for her to watch Kestrel become a prisoner.

"You must. Our seer proclaimed it."

Their *seer*? "You have a psychic?"

"He has never been wrong."

"Gato won't want me to go."

"You are essential, though you cannot tell him I asked."

Save her from psychic pronouncements. "I'll consider it."

"Vow it."

"No."

"Think of Mother's words," he said. "'She *is here*.' Vow."

She hadn't told Kestrel about Mother. Though Luciana would have, she hadn't heard Mother's words and Bree hadn't told her. Whew. Kestrel was more, and she couldn't help wondering what all that "more" was. "I will go. I vow it. Why can't I tell my mate about our talk?"

"Rudolfo says telling Gato would alter the Fates."

How stellar to have gods and psychics pulling her strings. "This is like some Greek tragedy."

"Not a tragedy, Made One." His lips twitched, eyes warming. "Perhaps a comedy. I will see you again. Ah, yes. One last thing."

"What?"

"Bring your knives."

The screen blackened.

"Opening salvo" eh? For all he'd told her, he hadn't revealed how he planned to escape, the one thing Gato had said only Kestrel could reveal. Thanks a lot, falcondude.

Why were they barreling ahead with this cockamamie idea? Whatever Kestrel's secret was, it had to be a big one. Now he insisted she go with Gato. And she was to bring her knives, no less.

She hugged Fortis and Audi tight, burrowing into their warmth. "What a mess, kids. A big fat mess."

She found Ax, who had taken over the cubs' CatGuard training, and left the pair with him. Returning to their suite, she zoomed inside. "Gato?"

He appeared from the kitchen, long hair unbraided, his black t-shirt and pants covered by...an apron? White puffs that looked like flour dotted the apron, his shirt, and hair.

He scowled, striding toward her. "What's wrong?"

Her hands cupped his face, and she kissed him. He tasted like the finest springwater, like a summer's day, like home.

His arms banded her so tightly she squeaked. But she didn't break the kiss. Neither did he as he carried her into the bedroom, *their* bedroom, where they began to strip each other with frantic motions.

Both naked in bed, he slid inside her. "I have missed you, *poosha*." He moved with agile grace atop her, his eyes fastened to hers, his hand tenderly roving over her.

"I missed you, too, catman. Can you tell?"

His laugh, punctuated by a strong thrust, sent her to that place where all she felt, all she knew, *all* was him. Bree clutched him tighter and tighter, his thrusts increasing along with her moans and his growls until pleasure surged over her. He kissed her, all lips and tongue, his thrusts speeding up until his back arched, and he gained his own release.

Hugging him close as they slowly spiraled back to earth was almost as good. Sweaty, giddy with pleasure, she nuzzled his warm chest. "Why are we now both covered in flour?"

"Because we just made love?"

She nipped him on the shoulder. "You know what I mean."

He laughed, emerald eyes intense. "It was a secret, a surprise for you."

"Flour?"

Gato licked the tip of her nose. "A cake, *poosha*. A *chocolate* cake."

She gasped. "But chocolate is rare. To use it in a whole cake...for me?"

He grinned, the cocky one where his eyes crinkled at the corners and sparked with humor. "Fudge assured me it would please you. Never leave me, *poosha*."

"Leave you? You're part of me, catman." She tried, she tried really hard, but a single tear escaped her burning eyes.

CHAPTER THIRTY

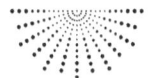

Her one tear gutted him. They had made love in the most beautiful way, and she had not even had her cake yet. Her lips trembled, and his *poosha* valiantly fought a deluge. She was killing him. He folded her in his arms, whispering soothing nonsense and rubbing a hand up and down her arm.

"Why are you sad, love?"

Her eyes blinked rapidly, her lips trembling. "Because I love you."

"As I love you. Does that not make you happy?"

She nodded, biting her lower lip. He raised her chin. "And...?"

"But you're going away, and... Since our mating, my feelings ricochet from joy to terror to longing. I'm out of control."

"No, sweet *poosha*. Our emotions will eventually settle, but our feelings share energy now, so it is to be expected at first. I have an idea. I will devise a tether, one tied around each of our wrists. That way, my Breena will always be near." She would hate the idea, but it would make her laugh.

"Perfect!" she said. "What shall we use?"

Understanding the mysteries of his Breena would take years upon years. He could not wait.

An hour later, Gato left his *poosha* nibbling her third piece of cake. Lopsided it might be, but she assured him it tasted "heavenly." He loped down the hall toward the stables to finalize plans for the exchange in two days.

Kestrel did this trade as a gift to Gato, and by doing so would reveal much that he was. A daring move and a profound kindness.

The Alchemics' reaction would be incendiary, and the Clans must be prepared to handle their response, whatever it was. Fukkes would first be astonished, then confused, then furious, but Gato could allay the problem and buy Compass True time, because he had done as promised—delivered Kes. It was that simple and elegant.

He had first met Kes between their battles with the dakos, when he and Rafe had taken some much needed rest. Kestrel was not part of their flight squadron, but led ground troops, and the two forces seldom mingled. Yet at a pub in Bear country, Rafe had greeted Kes with deep joy, their friendship obvious.

At first, he found Kestrel stolid, his speech slow and deliberate. But then the man had told a joke, one so sly and clever few at their table understood. Gato did, and his laughter and the answering glimmer in Kestrel's eyes began a friendship that now was decades long and had only deepened with time.

Gato arrived at the stables to find Bellerophon out of his stall and waiting with his usual impatience, the stable master, Franklin, wearing concern like a shroud.

"How is he?" he said as he approached, then reached down to lift the hoof injured in a training exercise.

"See for yourself."

What his taciturn stable master lacked in civility, he more than made up for it with his skilled handling of the stables.

Bell's curly fetlock had been shaved, and to his relief, the deep cut had healed well. Thank The Fates. But when the mistral set the hoof down, he still favored the leg.

Gato walked Bell up and down the barn's long aisle, his eyes focused on the injured leg. He definitely favored it.

He slipped Bell a peppermint and returned to Franklin. "Bell will not do."

"No, he will not."

Nor could he fly Pegasa, who was at Rafe's WolfHome stable for breeding with Daybreak. Gato needed to fly to arrive at the meeting in time.

"Take a hovercraft," Franklin said.

"Too slow." All across Eleutia, Clan techs worked to override the Alchemic's checks on hovercraft speed. They had yet to succeed. He scratched Bellerophon's muzzle, his affection immense for the big beast, then returned him to his stall.

The stable master shrugged and walked away.

Gato's frustration boiled as he called the vetrina to have another look at Bell. He could either borrow a mistral from Rafe, who would want to know why, or take ponies. Ponies it was, and with the travel time increased by two days, he must push back the meeting. Plus, given the inherent dangers, he would have to take CatGuard with him.

He laughed aloud. It couldn't get any worse, yet he was sure it would. *Fark.*

When Gato had left, Bree had donned her leathers, cleaned her weapons and laid them out on the bed, then packed her go-bag. The cubs sat on the floor as she bustled around, her nerves twitching. Both watched her with sad eyes. Like her pups on Earth, they knew she was leaving again.

She fixed a glass of kamla, set it on the coffee table, and crouched down in front of the cubs.

They were beautiful, Audi black and Fortis gold, their faces meltingly sweet, love shining from their eyes. She stroked their heads, then hugged them, the pair filling her to the brim with love. "I'll be back soon, guys. Then we'll go on a big jaunt to the top of the mesa where you can chase mice and squirrels to your heart's content. I love you."

They purred, their tongues licking her neck.

"Such good cubs. Such good Fortis and Audi."

Gato breezed in, snapping his phone closed as he entered the living area, and stopped. "Why are you wearing your leathers?"

She rose. "We're leaving to meet Kestrel for the exchange."

"*I* leave to meet Kestrel. You are not coming."

Surprised? Nope. Though she had backup plans, she couldn't cave too easily. "Of course I am."

"No, you are not." He advanced on her, his arms outstretched to enfold her.

She skittered backward, bumping the table. "Wait one minute. I am invested in this. Kestrel matters to me. *You* matter to me more, and I don't want you doing this alone."

He held his arms wide as if pointing out the obvious. "I will have CatGuard with me, both men and cats. Kes will be fine. I will be fine."

"I'll stay, but I wish..."

He wrapped his arms around her. "I am sorry, *poosha*. It is too dangerous."

"I understand." She did, too, and she hugged him tight, though she had every intention of going. Knowing her as he did, he would anticipate her rebellion. No matter, she would find a way.

The following morning, Bree waved Gato off, as he and nine CatGuard—six men and three pumas—left CatHome on sturdy ponies. Though her jaw was clenched, she made herself smile. She didn't want a frown to be his parting memory of her. With so few CatGuard accompanying him, she hadn't been able to replay her fair deception.

She could saddle up and follow, but if she stayed well behind them, she'd be traversing miles of dangerous territory on her own. Not smart. If she revealed herself, Gato would simply send her home with one or two CatGuard, reducing his numbers. Not an option, either.

She had vowed to be there. *Needed* to be, according to Kestrel's psychic. Gato took ridiculous risks, diving into danger before any others—he put a leader's obligation to lead into practice.

A hovercraft wasn't fast, but it would get her there more safely than a pony. All she needed was to figure out how to drive one. How hard could it be?

Atop their ponies, Gato's troop filed eastward, through soft-rolling desert hills and scrubby forests, headed for the peaks of the Druzy Badlands. There, they would meet up with Kes, whose own method of transport would remain a mystery to most.

In two days, he would again hug Ahanu, see his smile, hear his true laughter, not a vidscreen simulacrum. He leashed his anticipation and resumed scanning their surroundings for attack.

CHAPTER THIRTY-ONE

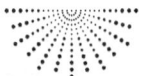

A day later, Bree remained stuck at CatHome. As she'd expected, two CatGuard trailed her everywhere. Not their fault. Now she poured over the topographic map she'd gotten from the library. She didn't trust those damned Alchemics. They might try to keep Gato, along with Kestrel. They might kill him. For all Gato had been blackmailed into helping them, he was a thorn in their sides.

A ping. She'd activated the vidscreen's monitor that coupled with the front door's camera, enabling her to eavesdrop on her two chatty CatGuard. Gato's group was headed east, and her two guards speculated on where. Instead of horses, they'd taken ponies, meaning the terrain must be rough. But eastward lay the high desert, a vast area in which to find seven men and three mountain lions.

"Fudge!" said one of her guards through the vidscreen. "Can I have a piece?"

The screen showed her friend holding a cake.

"No," Fudge said. "It's for Ma'am Breena and no one else."

Bree opened the door to find her friend batting her eyelashes at one of the men, who'd flushed beet red.

"Come on in!" she said.

She and Fudge talked about inconsequentials as they downed thick slices of cinnamon bread and drank milk. When Fudge said she was going to wash up, she instead clicked on the sound scramblers one after another, her finger pressed to her lips. Then Fudge leaned in close. "I'm going after Ax. He's with Gato. Want to come?"

Her friend had shocked her, Fudge's timid soul and gentle heart was at odds with her coloring outside the lines. "I'm in, but are you sure? Gato will be furious. Ax might be, too."

"I know." Her lips trembled. "I do not like breaking rules. But if I lost Ax… He put things in place so that if something happened to him on this mission, I would be safe here in CatHome. He's never done anything like that before. I am scared. But I can help." She straightened and thrust back her shoulders. "I am a Bear, after all."

"Yes, you are." Bree was scared, too, but Fudge's resolve made her smile. "So how do we do this?"

Fudge's eyes twinkled. "I have friends in high places. In an hour, Nightfall will arrive."

"One of Rafe's mistrals?"

"Have you forgotten I train them?"

"I had, actually, but still… Mistrals are beyond valuable, and he's *lending* you one of his?"

"Radulfr owes me. And he trusts me."

"Do you know where they're going?"

"I know nothing, except that it is very dangerous."

An understatement. "How will we find them? I've been pouring over the map. They're heading for the high desert. The area's huge."

"I stole a tracker from tech." Fudge flushed.

"You stole…"

"I put it in Ax's saddlebags."

"You are wonderfully evil."

A smile stole across Fudge's face, slow, like the rising sun. "I guess I am."

"Onward."

· · ·

A half-a-dozen CatGuard rode beside him, including Ax and Geo, along with Barth and three CatGuard pumas. Rafe had called about a Compass True issue right before they'd left, and Gato added Rafe to his worry list. The Alpha trials had come down to intelligence and stamina, and from the exhaustion in Rafe's voice, he was running low on the latter. Gato sent prayers to the Fates that his friend had the reserves to win through. He had almost asked Rafe to join them on this gambit, but the exhaustion in his friend's voice doused the thought.

They rode twisting paths trod by deer and antelope, mountain lion and bear. The air grew crisp and cool, the terrain covered in graceful meadows and scrub pine.

Gato missed his mate, and with each mile, he missed her more. Would that Breena could have come. Her humor, warmth, and pithy comments would have lightened the journey, and he would not feel as if he were minus a limb. But he would never risk her. He hoped she would forgive his refusal, but was glad he hadn't relented.

His cat senses active, he sniffed the air and signaled for his troop to gather close.

Whoever was following them would attack soon.

Bree and Fudge flew high and fast, though Nightfall carried two of them, as well as their arms. The huge black stallion had flown rider-less to CatHome, which shocked Bree. Fudge had explained that mistrals, though not symbionts, were semi-sentient. When she'd asked about the mistral's return, Fudge told her of Nightfall's deep devotion to his sister Moonrise and his bond with Rafe.

"Almost there," Fudge shouted above the howling wind.

Bree's gut tightened. Gato would murder her.

They attack. Now.

Bartholomew's warning came as Gato's cat senses screeched high alert. His blood thrummed, while his head cooled, and he drew both sword and laseblaster after confirming his knives and flying stars were easily accessible.

Raising his sword high, he shouted, "To arms!"

The sky blackened, and a shroud of insectoid legs hovered above them, their cacophonous clicking rattles like undead screams. The cloud split apart, the bugs' iridescence reflecting the light, blinding him. He blinked, his eyes clearing. Hundreds of hovercraft-sized beetles with immense stingers streamed toward them.

The largest battle beetles grew to two feet. These were at least six feet long, their stingers exponentially as large.

"Beware the stingers," Gato shouted. "They're—"

He broke off as he swung his sword, cleaving a bug in half.

Too many. Way too many.

Bree and Fudge dove downward faster and faster, except instead of the ground, she saw an undulating mass of shimmering colors. *What the...*

"What is that?" she shouted over the wind.

"Bugs!" Fudge said. "Huge ones. They are unnatural!"

Gato and the CatGuard were down there amidst those monstrous things.

"Hand me the sack on the right!" Fudge shouted.

"The food?"

"No! The other one."

Clenching Nightfall with her thighs, Bree struggled to unbuckle the small sack. Stars alive, they would be massacred.

She tore the sack loose, almost lost it, and swung it up toward Fudge.

The sack flew off as Fudge unwrapped a bottle, pulled out a cork, and drank.

"What are you doing?"

"I need to moisten my throat! I know, counterintuitive!"

Bree drew her knives as Nightfall dove impossibly faster, the undulating mass parting enough for her to see Gato's and the

CatGuard's flashing swords. Laseblasters fired in bursts, but they weren't enough.

A boulder reared above the rippling mass. "Fudge! Get low enough and I can jump!"

"Into the beetles?"

"Onto that rock!" She pointed, then holding her knives, she planted her fists on Nightfall's withers, drew up her legs, and rose high enough to set her feet on the saddle. In the crouch, her butt bobbed with the rhythm of Nightfall's wings. "Get me over there. I can land on it."

"You're crazy!"

"I've done this hundreds of times from the trapeze. I can do it!"

"But there's no net!"

"I'll land on my feet," Bree hollered. "Just get me there!"

Fudge laugh boomed out. "Will do."

Down they went, closer, closer.

Now.

Bree thrust upward, twirled, and spun, landing hard on her feet. Except it was atop a beetle, and she flatted it with an *"Oomph."* She scrambled off and headed for a wild-eyed pony frozen amidst the chaos. Then she was vaulting onto the pony and entering the fray. Above her, Fudge was drinking again, and in-between sips yelling "Fark!" over and over.

"I'm coming for you, catman!" Bree shouted.

A beetle scrabbled toward her and rose on its back legs, its mandibles dripping blood, teeth clacking. The fucking thing had *teeth.*

She hung onto the pony's saddle with her right hand, leaned sideways, and stuck a knife into the beetle's gut, her hand near buried in it searing ichor.

The beetle screamed, a disturbingly human sound.

"Fuck you!"

A twist of the knife, as she'd seen others do, and the beetle toppled backward. Bree swiped the ichor off on her leathers. *Damn, that hurt.*

On her left, a beetle swooped in to sting a guard fighting two more of the creatures. She kicked her pony hard, squeezed her thighs tight, and charged forward to stab the beetle's gut and twist.

Satisfying. Then she was in the fray, slicing and cutting, so juiced she ignored cuts, bruises, and the burn of the ichor. Their toothed jaws clacked, wings a high-pitched hum, while men's shouts of victory or pain punctured the air.

She peered around, scanning, searching. *Where the hell was that infuriating man?*

The scent of cabbage, and hot breath bathed her neck. She whirled, slicing both knives into the eyes of the beetle about to sink its teeth into her, its death cry horrid.

She couldn't find Gato. Surrounded as she was by three CatGuard, their swords blazing, she stood in the stirrups.

A troop of soldiers far in the distance galloped toward them, friend or foe she couldn't tell.

Fucking stars! Four of the beetles legs had clamped onto Gato and were lifting him from his pony. Blood dotted his shirt while he struck out with his sword. But for every beetle he killed, another swooped into replace it. He was almost out of the saddle.

"Here I come, you bastards!"

She stood on the saddle and leapt, arms thrust out, knives pointed forward, and thudded into the flying cluster, slashing and stabbing as she began her descent. What she wouldn't give for wings.

The ground thundered up, but Gato was free, even if her landing would cripple her.

Whomp!

Ax stared at her, holding her close, covered in beetle glop, and grinning like a fool.

"Fudge would kill me if I allowed her best friend to break."

He set her gently on the ground and dove back into battle.

"Gato?"

Ax pointed to Gato, who was back in the fray, sword flashing. He was okay, thank the stars, and Bree twirled, trying to find her pony, striking out at any nearing beetle as she climbed atop a pile of dead ones.

A dust cloud surrounded the troop she'd seen earlier, yet they were close enough she caught Arina's banner of white hair leading at least forty men and cats. Friends, but still too far away to destroy the beetles in time.

Barth flew though the air, his claws taking out a beetle.

"Bree down!" Gato yelled.

She dove into a valley between two mountains of dead bugs, a stinger piercing the air where she'd stood. Surging to her feet, Bree sliced off the offending stinger, then stabbed into the beetle's gut and twisted. The thing stood on two of its legs, wobbling.

"Farking finally!" screamed Fudge, waving the bottle as flames erupted from her mouth.

Holy shit! Swaths of fire poured from Fudge's lips across the beetles, toasting them into crispy critters, the smell horrible.

The teetering beetle she'd stabbed toppled. Bree jumped, but not fast enough. The creature slammed her to the ground, its legs still moving, burning ichor seeping onto her from its wounds. She rolled, pushed, shoved, but the thing wouldn't budge.

Pain seared deeper and deeper, and her struggles became frantic. She screamed. All went dark.

A day later, Bree still felt the effects of battle in protesting muscles and sensitive skin, even after the CatGuard healer had mitigated the damage. She was one of the least injured, and the poor man had worked through the night, aided by the healer who had come with Arina. Now, as they climbed a steep rise, Breena leaned forward on her pony, who must have glue for hooves.

During the beetle assault, one of the CatGuard had fallen and two were badly injured, as was one of their cats.

Gato's joyful reunion with Arina had turned explosive when he insisted she and her troops return to CatHome. Gato won the argument, and they departed, taking Gato's dead and injured with them, while three of Arina's men and one cat remained as replacements. Bree stayed, as did Fudge, and Gato hadn't even argued about it. In fact, he hadn't spoken a word to her since the battle.

Their troop reached the crest to find Kestrel awaiting them, and they stood atop Fates Peak facing the Druzy Badlands. And badlands it was, a chilling place of deep sandy washes rising to scarred fossil summits, bare of grass or trees. Naked, the jagged hills undulated into sharp peaks, only to plummet downward to deep valleys. Maze-like wrinkles rippled for miles until they blended into the distant hazy desert. The place invited nightmares as the view shifted again and again with the fading light. A banshee wind howled, perhaps mourning the inevitable.

A somber group waited for the Alchemics. Fates Peak was aptly named.

In the day it had taken them to reach the peak, Gato hadn't spoken to her, though she'd overheard him grilling the healer about her injuries. She didn't blame him, and knew well enough to let him seethe in peace.

Once, she would have railed at him for not appreciating their aid. Fudge surely deserved accolades, as her flames had decimated the beetles. But Bree also knew her love—he wasn't speaking to Fudge, either—and he was grieving their fallen comrade.

As they crossed the promontory, Bree got a clearer look at Kestrel—a god in his embroidered white robe, a wreath of feathers crowning his head.

Gato hugged his friend, and after talking for fifteen minutes, Gato raised his head to stare at her.

She slid off the pony, clenching her teeth to stop from saying "I'm sorry for coming." She wasn't sorry, though she felt like a guilty child. Gato's eyes were hooded, his face blank, but she knew her mate's fury when she saw it. Kestrel smiled and avoided her burns as he hugged her.

"Thank you," he whispered.

"Are you well?"

"I am."

That was all they had time to say before a movement over his shoulder made her gasp.

The dot in the sky she'd first thought a bird had grown epic in size. No bird, but a walled city floated across the desert's ridges and valleys, reminding her of those giant alien ships from *Independence Day*.

Kestrel whispered, "Alchemic City."

"We have no idea how they move it." Gato stepped closer. "No idea as to when or where it will next land. That is our biggest hurdle in bringing the fight to the Alchemics—discovering the location of their city. They do not want all-out war. That is clear. Yet whether they wish it or not, war is coming to them."

The city was white, its walls curving upward like a saucer-shaped champagne glass, with crenellations and windows breaking up the walled facade. Four immense red hands secured the bowl to a stem beneath, its base flattening outward. Buildings soared high above the wall, with dozens more peeking above the rim. In the center, a jagged tower glowed blue, like a damaged obelisk. Creepy. Adding Sauron's flaming eye would complete the picture.

Gato stepped behind Kestrel and bound his hands.

Fudge gasped, while CatGuard murmured and frowned, a few turning away. No one uttered a word.

Kestrel's eyes were molten in the setting sun. Or perhaps his eyes had actually changed color. It wouldn't surprise her. She stood on tiptoe. "Take good care, please."

The CastOut stared back at her and nodded.

As the city neared, it seemed almost a hallucination, too massive to float. Yet it did.

The city halted with a shudder. A metal slide emerged from its belly to glide downward, coming to rest on a mountain peak in a puff of dust. A hovercraft followed the slide down, and when it reached the ground, it raised its snout and flowed up and down the russet cliffs, closer and closer.

More grumbling from the Guard, while Gato stood beside Kestrel, both men solemn.

If Bree could only pull a rabbit from the hat, say a *Voila!*, and save Kestrel, all while rescuing Ahanu. Instead, tears welled from a deep sorrow for what he was about to sacrifice. She hoped whatever the two had cooked up worked.

She fought the urge to turn away, she'd be damned if she would, but her pony grew skittish. Soothing him with words and touch, she mounted, though her eyes never left Kestrel.

A hand reached up dangling a handkerchief. Gato, of course. "Thanks."

"Made One." Though Kestrel's lips didn't smile, his eyes held laughter. "Are all your sisters as tender-hearted?"

She chuckled a watery laugh. "I'm the tough one."

His lips twitched.

The hover landed on the crest of Fates Peak, and the doors whooshed up. Two men emerged dragging between them a young man with white hair, more beautiful in person than images portrayed. Ahanu's hair was unbound, his missing ear covered. Behind them, a middle-aged man dressed in clownish clothes approached. Fukkes, the Alchemic Gato had spoken with on the vidscreen call. A fourth man followed, a laseblaster in each hand pointed at their group.

Fukkes smiled at her. Gods alive, those crystal teeth gave her the shivers. He laughed, this disgusting monster who traded in human lives. The eyes he turned on Kestrel hungered.

Gato stepped forward. "I will speak with my brother before the trade, Fukkes."

"Be my guest." Fukkes waved a hand.

As Gato strode toward Ahanu, the Alchemic moved to Kes, examining him as a buyer would an object.

Kestrel remained stoic-faced—tall, imposing, fearless.

The Alchemic's absurd clothes, his arrogance, the way he examined Kes, it was too much.

Bree was glad she'd remained on her pony, so she could look down on him. Her throat tightened, blackness encroaching, and her breaths coming in pants. Forcing her fingers to unclench the reins, she closed her eyes and breathed deep. She would *not* have a panic attack in front of this monster.

An outpouring of strength and calm shocked her.

You are ours. Bartholomew said. *Of the pack. Mated.*

A deep breath later, and she opened her eyes and smiled, putting all the snark she could muster into it.

"One of you Made me, didn't you?" she said to the Alchemic.

His eyes flashed to hers. "You will address me as Fukkes. And, no, 'one' of us did not Make you. *I* Made you."

"Where is my sister, Sybelle?"

"You are disrespectful, Made One."

She rolled her eyes. "Who am I supposed to respect, *you?*"

Those crystal teeth gritted. "I *Made* you."

In a flash, her insecurities roared back. But she shunted them away. If Eleutia had taught her one thing, it was that she, Breena, was good enough. She grinned, dismounted the pony, and got in Fukkes face. "You made me? Ha! My parents gave me life. *I* made me into who I am." She flicked a hand across her body. "All you did was steal me for some science experiment of flesh and bone. You didn't make me, fool."

Fukkes flushed apple red. "How dare you speak to me thus?"

"Why the fuck not?" she said. "You brought me here without my consent. You're all ego and no humanity."

"I Made all three of you," Fukkes said, nostrils flaring. "And I can unmake you as easily."

A thrill rippled through her at the confirmation Sybi was on Eleutia. Bree crossed her arms, feet spread. "You don't get it. The only one who can unmake me is me."

"What ingratitude!" Fukkes said.

"Who is ungrateful?" purred Gato, joining them.

Bree's eyes narrowed. "You've lost my sister, haven't you?"

Fukkes didn't blink, but in those eyes, along with entitlement, she read confirmation.

"Well?" she said.

Fukkes collected himself and shot Gato a haughty frown. "Alpha, can you not control the Made One? You, Made One, should be preparing for The Challenge."

"I thought," Gato interrupted, his voice honied ice. "Ma'am Breena should meet you, Fukkes."

There will be no Challenge, asswipe, she almost blurted. "And I will prepare for The Challenge once Ahanu is safely home."

Fukkes took a step closer to Breena, his breath metallic, near enough to catch patches missed by his spray tan. He clamped a hand on her chin. Any second Gato would combust.

"I do good work." Fukkes released her.

Bree almost kneed him in the balls. Then Gato would have gone at Fukkes, and they'd be blasted to smithereens.

Fukkes pivoted to Gato. "We do the exchange now."

The entire time, Kestrel had watched, saying nothing, revealing nothing. Gato walked to him, and Kes gave him teeth and growled, as if the exchange was against his will. The Alchemic holding the lasers stepped sideways, aiming both at the Falcon.

Grumbles came from the remaining CatGuard until Gato cut them a look. The men holding Ahanu brought him forward and Gato pushed Kestrel to stand before Fukkes.

Bree threaded her hands together, knuckles whitening. It was like a play, one she couldn't exit.

"Be very sure you wish to do this, Fukkatsu," Kestrel said.

"Be silent," Fukkes replied.

Kes laughed, the sound chilling.

The men were exchanged, and Bree tensed, her skin tight, mouth dry. Kestrel was led to the hover.

Fukkes followed, climbing the hovercraft's first step. He paused, a hand gripping the hatch door, turned to Breena, and smiled. "Two alive out of three isn't bad, now is it?" He ducked inside the craft, the hatch closing on a whoosh, and the hover lifted and took off, hugging the landscape. It seemed even the Alchemics' hovercraft couldn't fly more than six feet above the ground.

Bree stared at the departing craft until it climbed the ramp and entered the city.

. . .

Gato and Ahanu talked late into the night as they rode toward CatHome, and Gato held himself in check. His many questions must wait and at some point, he must tell Ahanu about Taz. But not yet.

He stared at his brother, unable to stop reassuring himself that Ahanu was really here and whole. He had matured into a handsome, well-formed man, almost as tall as Gato, with broad shoulders and defined muscles. Seeing him on the vidscreen had never been enough, the reality infinitely better. His eyes burned yet again. "You are well?"

"Brother," Ahanu said, a hint of exasperation in his voice. "You have asked me a dozen times. I am fine."

"And I will keep asking until you give me the truth."

Ahanu shook his head, his smile warm. "Where is our cousin?"

Gato peeled away from the group, signaling Ahanu should follow.

"Where is Taz?" Ahanu said. "Our cousin is always with your cohort, brother."

A buckle on Gato's saddle pack had come loose, and he tightened it.

"Brother?"

"He is gone," Gato said. "Dead."

The old Ahanu would have wept. "How?"

"Let us wait until we return to CatHome to—"

"Let us *not*."

Ahanu was right, of course, though the steel in his voice shocked Gato. Change was to be expected, but he wasn't sure who this new Ahanu was. He gave his brother the bare bones of Taz's betrayal and attack.

"Did he go at you because of Ma'am Breena or Arina?"

"How did you—"

"You are mated to Ma'am Breena," Ahanu said. "I also knew of Taz's desire for our sister." He sighed. "Had I been there, I could have tempered his more violent tendencies."

So Ahanu knew. But he had never spoken a word. Gato should not be surprised, yet he was. "Perhaps you could have, though I doubt it. In the time you were away, his obsession for revenge increased. We were not mated when Taz poisoned my Breena."

"Poison? A despicable thing for a man who was once a fine warrior."

An un-Ahanu response, a worrying one. "He died a traitor to all CatHome honors."

"Tell me," Ahanu said.

Gato explained about the cubs, their bonding with Breena, and how they had often spilled her tea. "That is the only reason I believe she lived. They smelled the poison, but they could not convey that to Breena. Shote, Ahanu, what is wrong? You have not wept for Taz."

"I made a decision to put tears behind me. That was approximately twenty months ago."

"I see." Gato could *not* think about what they had done to him, would *not* imagine it. "I wept for our cousin, the waste of it all."

"Who killed him?"

"Barth."

Ahanu glanced down at Bartholomew, who padded beside Gato's horse. "Why?"

"He held a laseblaster and would have shot and killed one of us."

"I am glad neither you nor your mate died."

"As am I." *Ahanu, talk to me. Let me inside.*

His brother tipped back his head and stared at the stars. "I am free. It will be good to be home. Makena?"

"She remains Sequestered."

"When we return, I wish to increase my arms training."

"Of course. Whatever you want. Your piano, your journals are all waiting for you, just as when you left."

"At first, I thought much about all I had left behind. Now that no longer matters. All that does is killing Fukkes myself."

CHAPTER THIRTY-TWO

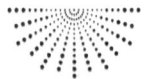

Later that evening, Gato rode beside Breena, drawn by her pale face and stiff posture. "Sybelle is not dead. Fukkes was lying to hurt you."

"I'm sure you're right," Bree said.

He wished he could give her true assurances.

"I shouldn't have gone off on Fukkes," she said. "I'm sorry. I could have messed everything up. But I'm not sorry about the battle, even if you're still furious with me. You are, right?"

"Of course I am! You could have died." He gave her the side-eye, unable to keep the warmth from his eyes. "But angry or no, I love you, my Breena."

She turned to him wearing the sweetest smile, and his love for her deepened yet again. The hand she held out to him beckoned, and he took it and kissed her palm.

"I love you, too, catman."

They rode for days, hearts heavy, and only sentries noted their late-night arrival through the gates of CatHome.

The next morning, the Clan began preparations for a festival the following week to celebrate Ahanu's return. Yet sorrow over the CatGuard's death and Kestrel's bondage hovered over CatHome. Through it all, Gato continued to assure Breena all would be well.

It was a lie. An emergency meeting of the Compass True council had been called for two days hence. Though unstated in the missive demanding they meet, all would have learned of Kestrel's trade and Gato's part in it. If the meeting went as planned, Gato would live. If not, he would face a death sentence.

He would fly Bellerophon to the CastOuts' village, their time away having fully healed the mistral's hoof. He wanted to sleep for a week. Maybe a month. But a warm rightness filled him with Ahanu's return. No longer the lighthearted boy who had been taken by the Alchemics, nonetheless beneath his steely exterior, the sweetness remained. Gato prayed to Mother Terra and put in place protocols he hoped would restore Ahanu's spirit.

Packing two days later, warm arms banded his waist from behind, Breena's body pressed to his. "*Poosha,*" he said. "Love. I must pack."

"*We* have to pack," she said.

He thumbed on the sound scrambler beside the bed. "Yes, we do."

Breena jerked.

"So you had best get started." *Ha!* He had surprised her. "You will not be allowed to attend the meeting."

"No problem. Good thing you're not leaving me behind, catman."

Would that he could. But he was too weary to rekindle that battle. He turned and held his Breena, burrowing his head in her neck and inhaling her rich, heady scent.

The stroke of her hand soothed him.

"I know how exhausted you are, my love," she said.

He squeezed her shoulders, then resumed tossing garments into his pack. Having fired the first salvo in their war on the Alchemics, he had hoped to rest and regroup until Ahanu's celebration. He slid his laseblaster into his shoulder holster. "We may be attacked in the air."

She rolled her eyes and sat at the end of the bed. "I'm getting used to it. Go on."

His knives in place, he moved his sheathed sword aside to include a dozen throwing stars. "The CastOuts know the trade was entered with Kestrel's full cooperation. That being said, some will nonetheless blame me, and..."

Breena bit her lip.

"You blame me, as well."

"I don't. Truly. I'm worried about Kes, is all. You know."

Taking her hands, he pulled her flush against him. "The CastOuts won't touch me. It's you I worry about."

Her sad smile hurt his heart. "They're good people. I'll be fine."

"Yes, they are good, but as with all Clans, bad fruit exists."

She pressed her forehead to his. "We'll watch out for each other."

He gave her a wicked grin. "Perhaps we have time to do a bit of 'watching out' right now."

Bree thrilled at flying Bellerophon to the CastOuts' village, the huge mistral's wings beating with authority as they soared above the treetops. Barth, having refused to be draped across the mistral's back, would arrive later that day, as would half-a-dozen CatGuard. The cubs had been a problem at their leave taking. Fortis considered himself near-grown, and he pitched a fit that he couldn't accompany them. Audi's demure and sorrowful chirps hurt worse. With Gato's help, she'd gotten them settled with Fudge, but they were maturing, having more independent thoughts, and each day they grew bigger and bigger. Time for that larger bed.

Gato picked a grassy knoll to land for lunch and rest Bellerophon. As Bree unpacked their picnic, Gato was strangely silent. He spread his cloak on a bed of pine needles, and after they ate, they made slow, exquisite love.

Yet desperation clung to his caresses as they lay in each others arms in the sweet aftermath.

"What aren't you telling me?" she said.

He played with her shaggy hair and remained silent.

"You know I'll worm it out of you, catman. This is about more than the CastOuts' anger."

"Yes." He sighed as he stood and began donning his clothes. "When I tell the council about the trade they will learn of my past association with the Alchemics." His words were tight, as if reading a script.

She pushed onto an elbow. "And…?"

"All may not go well."

"What the hell is that supposed to mean?"

"As you know," he said. "Barth and three CatGuard will arrive later today. Do as they say."

"Basically, you're telling me something bad may happen to you at the meeting."

He stretched out his arms, head tilted back, and laughed. "What can they do to me, the most powerful Alpha on the planet?"

"This is a thing you do when you don't want to answer me."

"And what is that, *poosha*?"

"You put on your Alpha-arrogance cloak."

He bowed. "That's me, Mr. Alpha Arrogance."

"Stop it, please," She leapt up and stalked toward him. "That's not who you fucking are."

He whistled for Bellerophon. "You swear quite a bit when you're agitated."

"Answer me, dammit!"

"Yes, well." He wiggled his eyebrows and grinned. "The council may vote to expel me."

"Bullshit. That's not all of it."

"Or end me."

"What? We're turning around. Going home."

His eyes flashed. "No. At last, I have brought Ahanu home. The Alchemics no longer control me, and I am free to wage war. On *them*." His fist tightened. "For that, we need Compass True."

Bree was shaken. They might *end* him?

"Ahanu likes you very much," Gato said. "We have spoken, and he will see that you are honored and cared for."

That did it. He was arranging things in case of his death. "You're nuts. *This* is nuts. Like I would give a shit about anything without you?" She cupped his cheeks. "You are everything to me. If you're gone, I won't want to li—"

"Do not say it. You can. You will. I must attend this meeting, Breena. It is the culmination of all we have worked for."

"Was it worth it?"

"Yes. A key door we needed to open to begin our rebellion to save Eleutia."

He was all that mattered to her. She whooshed out a breath. That wasn't true, but for him to walk into a place where he could die... Gato was right, though, and she wrapped her arms around him, her cheek pressed to his heart. "I won't fail you."

"You are strong, my Breena."

"Tough as nails."

Oh, the lies she told.

The vibe of the CastOuts village was subtly different from their previous visit, colder and more reserved, though the few awake to greet them hadn't been actively hostile. Gato had wanted to talk with Rafe prior to the meeting, but they'd arrived too late at night. Marcos appeared while they were unsaddling Bellerophon and the healer walked them to their same treehouse cabin.

"Whatever was done," Marcos said, hands clasped behind his back. "We know it was at Kestrel's behest. Nonetheless, some are..."

"I am aware," Gato said.

"Are you?" Marcos stopped dead. "Can you possibly understand our loss? The cost to the CastOuts? The price paid by my friend?"

"He can, Marcos," Bree said, softening her voice. "Kestrel was his friend, too."

"Breena," Gato said.

She wasn't about to shut up. "As Alpha, Gato knows only too well what a leader's loss means to his people."

Marcos burst into a low chuckle. "With an advocate like her, old friend, you are well cared for."

"That I am."

In bed, they held each other tight.

"It will be fine," she said. "We will make it through."

"Nothing will be fine, *poosha*, until the Alchemics are swept from our world."

At dawn, Gato left for the meeting, his face grim. They'd made love and she'd smiled and kissed him goodbye. Like another day at the office. Except terror chewed her gut, like a rabid dog.

She took a deep, cleansing breath. No time for pity parties. She would do what must be done.

They would meet in a room off the main dining area. Though she told Gato she would find Luciana, Bree had every intention of protecting her mate.

Outside, across the square, Peacekeepers circled the dining area, while down below, Gato marched to what could be his death. Rafe met him halfway, slapping him on the back in greeting. They paused for long moments, heads bent in conversation, Gato nodding, while Rafe talked. Gato shook his head, and Rafe pulled him in for a hug. Her heart squeezed.

The two men turned to peer up at her window. She waved, hoping they could see her.

She sat down hard in the chair. Gato always saw her.

Knowing what she had to do, she folded her legs and meditated for ten minutes. Then she prepared.

Bree gathered the listening device she'd gotten from CatHome's lab, along with the necessary earwig, too. She was pleased how well bribery worked across worlds, as she'd traded the tech art lessons for his son, a boon, not a burden. Bree pulled on a turtleneck and a jacket for the cool mountain air and wore her weapons of choice, including her claws.

Minutes later, she sat beneath the boughs of a large pine, her heart beating triple time. When she'd tried to enter the council room to bring Gato some troff, the Peacekeeper had turned her away. As expected. But not before she'd stuck the listener to the wall.

Next she scoped the building and found a good entry point, ticking boxes for what she'd need, and gathered a few more items.

They might kill him! shrieked in her mind. Her panic rose, and she denied it and buried it deep. Centered as she was, she would not have an attack, not with the surprising help from Gato's bond. Like a warm wave lapping her, she was calmed.

Beneath the pine, she pressed in the tiny earwig and took a breath. *Here goes.* She tapped it on, and leaned back against the trunk to listen. And heard only a soft hum.

Fuck.

That was the hum emitted by a sound scrambler. Of course the council would use one. Duh.

She ran toward the dining hall.

Gato surveyed the room. Multiple skylights bathed the hall in watery light shining on the round table set up for the council. Servers bustled about carrying water pitchers and glasses and setting them at the nine seats for the attending members and a tenth for Tilde, the little redhead who was once again speaking. All the usual suspects were present, some with their symbionts. All but Kestrel. Kes was fine, but Gato's small nag of worry was a distraction.

A bell chimed and they took their seats, his between Rafe's and the Deer's, the room's energy electric with foreboding.

Rafe would stand by him, and the ancient female Bear Alpha was a friend, though she could surprise him. The Deer First Commander might be young with a spine of steel, but he was not one to color outside the lines. Both the Falcon Alpha and the Ferret Chief Armorer were hotheads, neither a friend of his. He knew little of the newest members—the Sequestered, a gentle soul who seldom spoke; the Tiger Alpha, with his striped hair and quiet demeanor; and the

Dolphin, a soft-faced blond man whose gills allowed him to breathe beneath the sea. Marcos stood in for Kes.

How would they react to his tale? He'd prefer to face a wing of dakos.

Rafe banged his gavel, quieting the group. "We have news. Tilde?"

The little redhead rose, more wan than he remembered. She shook a bit, as she had the previous time, but her eyes sparkled. The council quieted.

"As you know," Tilde said, "the problem we Eleutians face is a lack of potable water to reverse the chemicals that inhibit our women from bearing healthy female children."

"I still do not understand why we cannot reverse engineer those chemicals," the Deer said.

"While our laboratories are improving daily," Tilde said, showing remarkable patience, "They are makeshift. We have neither the facilities nor the knowledge to do that." She peered down at her notes. "Since we last met, our laboratory network has been working on the potable water problem. My mouse friend has, too. You remember, the guy who helped me with the mice and opossums?" She grinned.

"Get on with it, woman." The Ferret Chief Armorer crossed his muscled arms.

"Gee," Tilde said. "If you're mated, I pity her."

The Ferret half rose from his seat, but the Deer shoved him down. "Shut up. You are discourteous."

Tilde's eyes laughed as she pressed her hands on the table and leaned forward. "We have got the potable water."

As surprise rippled around the room, the Dolphin leaned back in his chair and smiled.

"How?" said the Falcon Alpha, disbelief written across his face.

"By using a combination of methods for differing locales. The only way we can be sure we are not drinking tainted water is by desalinating seawater."

The Falcon laughed. "Desalinated seawater? In quantity? Patently absurd."

"You are incorrect," Tilde said, voice snippy. "We have devised methods of reverse osmosis which—"

"The energy consumption alone is prohibitive," Falcon said.

"Shut up, you arrogant blarter," the Tiger said. "Let her speak."

"Who the fark are you calling a blarter?" The Falcon puffed his chest.

Marcos rose and bellowed, "Quiet! This is a council meeting, not a Challenge match."

With the Tiger and Falcon shooting dark looks at each other, Tilde continued. "We've devised a way to use solar power to effect the reverse osmosis."

"That will work well in cloudy environs," someone mumbled.

The girl cleared her throat. "For those in less sunny climes, we will use geothermal desalination. My mouse friend came up with that one. He's very clever when he chooses to communicate."

"You are saying we can really accomplish this?" the Bear Alpha said, her lined face taut.

"We have been," Rafe said, twitching an almost-smile. "At Wolf-Home. We Wolves are the test subjects, and to date, the water is eminently potable."

"But you won't know for months if girl children will be born," the Ferret said.

"True," Tilde chimed in with a smile. "There is no way to speed up *that* process. But we used the treated water the Wolves drink on opossums and mice, as well. Their births have leveled off at fifty-fifty, male/female, as we expect the Wolven ones will. We can do this."

Murmurs as the council members' excitement grew. Rafe had told Gato about the desalination project. The tainted water was the major roadblock to war with the Alchemics. Every Compass True council member knew that. Eventually, Made Ones would no longer be necessary. That gave him pause. If there had been no Breena... He could no longer imagine life without her.

Tilde thanked the council, and left.

Gato stood. "This is what we have been waiting for. It is time."

The Bear rumbled to her feet. "I still do not see a way. If we go to war, the Alchemics will switch off our tech, while theirs will remain active."

"You are correct," he said. "Which is why we have built our underground labs. That tech they cannot reach."

"Ours don't come close to their tech's capabilities and sophistication," the Deer said.

"True," he said. "But if we do not go to war, we lose our world." *Here it was.* Time to reveal his greatest disgrace. All was in place for Breena's safety. She had Bellerophon and soon the CatGuard and Barth would arrive. Though Gato had not revealed the danger of this meeting to his brother, Ahanu had promised he would guard and honor Gato's mate. If Gato lived...

Drawing on his cat sense, his battle calm descended, and he described Kestrel's trade for Ahanu.

Anger perfumed the air, with even Rafe giving him the side eye. At least his friend had not joined the accusers who said he had sacrificed Kestrel for personal gain. In part, they were correct.

Their animals were on high alert, too, growling and hissing. If Bartholomew were here... But by the time he arrived, all would be over, for good or for ill. He finished his recitation amidst growls and yammering, and sat.

"You have lost all sense," the Bear said.

"I have not, Alpha," Gato said. "In fact, I have recently regained it." He smiled, took in each of the councilors. "You see, I have an inside track on them." Then he told the council of his conversations with the Alchemics, making eye contact with each member to show he was not ashamed. He prayed to the Fates they saw that.

His eyes held Rafe's when he said, "I abandoned friends, hurt my Clan, perhaps some of you. Those are my regrets. But I would not change a thing." Rafe shuddered, the man valiantly trying to contain his anger.

While Gato had talked, he noted the passing of time. His concern grew. The scenario was getting out of hand, but all would be revealed soon. It had better be.

"You have colluded with the enemy," the Ferret said as he rose to his feet.

"It was not collusion," Gato said.

The Falcon banged a fist. "You have given Kestrel to the Alchemics."

"Which Kes agreed to," Marcus said.

"Who knows?" The Ferret peered around the table. "Who here knows what the Cat Alpha held over his head? You die." He surveyed the room. "Agreed?"

"Agreed," said the Falcon.

"Agreed," chorused the Tiger and Deer.

Gato betrayed nothing, but his and Kestrel's plan was disintegrating, the vote too swift, the anger too hot. And though he did not want to fight, it appeared he would be left no choice. He hoped some of the others would fight with him.

"Denied," said the Bear.

"Denied," echoed the Dolphin.

"Denied," said Marcos.

"Denied," said Rafe.

Four to four. Death or life.

All eyes turned to the Sequestered, who sat arrow-straight, her hands beneath the table.

An arc of lasefire blasted from where she sat and the Tiger exploded, while everyone else dived for the floor. Several councilors raised the table as a barrier and pushed it forward.

Knives flew toward the Sequestered, but one of the servers pulled out a blaster and aimed it at Rafe.

Gato released his knife, striking the server in the shoulder as he turned. But it had served its purpose.

Who were these people. Anti-Made Ones? Alchemics? Both?

He leapt for the Sequestered as she rounded the upright table, raising her blaster at the Ferret.

Farking Fates! He scented Breena. *No!*

A crash, showers of glass, a rope dropping from the roof. All stared upward as Breena swung down from the roof, turned two somersaults, and landed on the Sequestered.

She was Nixana come to life. He tried to say her name, but his breath wouldn't come. When he'd seen her twirl from the ceiling...

The women began fighting, and the Sequestered's partner raised his blaster toward the pair, but the Ferret leapt upon him.

Gato ran toward Breena, who was grappling and losing to the Sequestered. A knife in the robed woman's hand sliced a breath away from Bree's throat.

Time. He needed time. He jumped.

A sharp pain in his side, and he drew a bronze thread as he spun, aiming at a third server. The man skittered away and raised his blaster at Bree.

Gato threw the thread, slicing off his arm. Fark, he shouldn't have done that. But Breena...

She was on the ground amidst a tangled pile of Bree, Sequestered, and Bear, the Sequestered raising her arm to stab his mate.

He reached for his final knife.

Beneath the pile, a clawed hand ripped out the Sequestered's throat. The woman's helmet flew off as she collapsed on Breena. She was a he.

He staggered toward his mate.

"Stop!"

Peacekeepers poured into the hall, subduing the final server, while others helped the bloodied and injured councilors. But in the shadowed doorway, a man paused, his powerful stance one of authority. The councilors froze and Gato snickered, more like a wheeze. Better late than never.

All knew who it was. No one believed it.

"What is the purpose of this fight?" Kestrel said.

Gato's smile was bloody. "What took you so long?"

Kestrel's lips twitched. "I was busy."

CHAPTER THIRTY-THREE

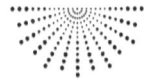

"This is some kind of trick." The Falcon's chest heaved with indignation.

Gato staggered toward his mate. Reaching her, he tried to lift the Sequestered's body off, but spots danced before his eyes. The Dolphin ran up, removing the dead Sequestered to reveal the elderly Bear.

"She is alive," the Dolphin said.

"Good. Get help." His Bree was entwined with the Bear, both smeared with blood.

Legs like tree trunks appeared, then Kestrel gently lifted the Bear off Breena.

His mate was covered in blood, and he couldn't tell how much was hers. He took a knee. She was unconscious, her eyes closed, but thank the Fates her chest rose and fell. Please let her be all right.

"Breena mine," he said.

Her eyes fluttered and opened.

"*Poosha.*"

She grinned, teeth red. "Not one of my best landings, but who gives a shote!"

"You are swearing in Eleutian." He chuckled, even as dotted suns chased each other across his vision.

"Gato!" She rolled to the side and kneeled. "You're hurt! Where are you bleeding?"

"Humm?" The world undulated, and tiny sparks danced in space, dark crowding his vision.

He toppled.

Bree stood beside Gato's cot while he was patched up, along with all the other councilors who'd been injured. They'd taken his shirt, and she gripped his hand, her jaw clamped tight, as the doctor cleansed the horrible burn in Gato's side. He, on the other hand, laughed and chatted with the doc, whose medical healing would be followed by a psychic one. But her catman's lips had whitened, his breath swift, jaw bunching. She gripped his hand tighter.

When the doctor cleansed the deep burn, Gato closed his eyes, hers starting to ache from holding back tears. If Gato could bear this, so could she.

After they bandaged him up, Marcos appeared and did his mojo, which was equally hard to watch, the pain of the healer's working severe.

Finally, they were done. Gato was pale, but he washed and donned a fresh shirt, then insisted they return to the hall where the Council would conclude its business.

"Why don't we go lie down, hum?" She wrapped an arm around his waist.

That imperious brow shot up. "And miss all the fun?"

"Are you twelve? You need to rest."

He leaned in close. "*Poosha*, I must go. No councilor can see my weakness. They are sharks who would devour me alive."

Politics. She hated politics, but nodded. "I'm coming, whether it's in the rules or not."

.   .   .

Bree sat between Gato and Rafe, surrounded by councilors who looked like wounded warriors from an old Revolutionary War poster. They were all idiots, posturing as if they were fine, while each one ached for his or her own bed.

The blood and bodies were gone, and someone had doused the room with cinnamon and rosemary, which covered death's scent. Mostly. Fresh chairs had replaced broken ones, the table righted and adorned with flowers, the mood festive in the way of those who'd escaped death.

When they were all seated, a grim-faced Marcos stood. "As you know, the Anti-Made One faction has become increasingly violent. While you were seeing the doctors and healers, Kestrel and his men discovered the remains of our four CastOut servers. We have also lost two of our councilors, the Tiger, Justees, and the Sequestered, Lana, whose body was found in her cabin."

Murmurs and outrage. Not only had they lost councilors, but a precious Eleutian woman.

Marcos tapped the gavel. "From the villains' tattoos, the series numbers on their weapons, and other indicators, we are certain their purpose was to end the Compass True council. That was obvious. But we have also learned that this Anti-Made One operation was aided by the Alchemics."

"That makes no sense," the Dolphin said. "They hate each other."

"They do, Dolphin," Rafe said. "We doubt the Anti-Made Ones knew their 'helpers' were Alchemics."

"Which coincides with Rafe's belief," Marcos said. "That the Cabal of Eleven Alchemics plans to accelerate Eleutia's death or to destroy her themselves. I mentioned blasters. Theirs were a new iteration and unlike those possessed by the Clans. The serial numbers confirmed that. More telling, a body lay by their hovercraft hidden in the wood." He heaved a breath. "An Apprentice Alchemic named Neela."

"No," the Ferret said, his voice hushed.

Gato bowed his head.

"You knew her?" Bree said, lacing her fingers through his.

"She was a spy in Alchemic City for Compass True. Young and earnest."

Bree sighed. War wasn't coming. It had arrived.

"Why would the Alchemics wish to destroy our world?" the Falcon said.

"Perhaps..." Rafe said, and paused. "Perhaps they plan to leave Eleutia and find a fresh world to experiment on."

"I do not see it," the Dolphin said.

The Falcon rose and pointed at Kestrel. "How did you escape the Alchemics, CastOut? Your arrival was convenient. Almost as if it had been prearranged with our attackers."

Kestrel's face betrayed nothing, but his black eyes glittered with fire. "Do you wish to die?"

"You could try," the Falcon said with more bravado than sense.

"Shut up, Falcon," The Bear said, her arm in a sling, head swathed in bandages. "You couldn't defeat Kestrel with one arm tied behind his back. Constrain your temper."

The Falcon flicked a hand at Gato. "What about him? We were voting to execute him. He must be punished."

"For what?" Rafe said, a snap in his voice.

Marcos spread his hands. "Falcon, we are Compass True. Kestrel is returned. Gato has fought for our cause longer than I have been alive. Your jealousy does not become you."

"Laws matter," Falcon said. "And by our laws, he dies."

She'd had it with these poseurs, full up to the tip of her head. "How *dare* you?" She leapt from her seat.

His Breena stormed toward the Falcon like an Earth Valkyrie, flaming hair like a crown, weapons raised, eyes intense. Joy shot through him. She was *his,* and the Fates, how he loved her.

Breena got in the Falcon's face. "I repeat, how dare you?"

The Falcon's eyes widened, as if he didn't believe what he was seeing. Alphas could be twitchy and prideful. He should know. The Falcon was a dangerous beast with a hair trigger.

"You act like a hatchling," she continued. "One who's not getting his way."

The man drew his sword.

Kestrel rose to his full height, gathering his power, his quiet profound. "Put away your sword, Falcon."

"Ma'am Breena," Marcos said. "Please step back. You should not be here."

"Fark that!" She whirled. "Are you going to haul me out, Marcos? Or you?" she said to the Ferret, "with your big mouth and small heart? You may not know it, but he protected your sorry ass."

Rafe shook his head, and muttered, "You are *just* like your sister."

"No way." Bree laughed. "She doesn't swear much and she's a lot nicer."

"I object to that statement," Gato said.

Bree turned, her eyes soft, and he was again laid low.

Rafe leaned in. "How in the Fates' name did she get by our Peace-keepers?"

"When she came from the ceiling? I imagine she swung through the trees."

"You can't be serious." Rafe snorted.

Thinking of his *poosha*, his smile grew and grew. "Oh, I am very serious. With my Breena, you never know how she will surprise you."

"As I said, like my Kitlyn."

"Too much talk," Kestrel said. "We vote again." He seemed to grow larger, more magisterial, power pouring off him like ilaberry wine. "To *dismiss* all charges."

Kestrel had uttered "dismiss" like a command, and not a single counselor balked.

"As it should be," Rafe said, banging his mug on the table. "Compass True has one purpose and one purpose only, to defeat the Alchemics and rid our land of them. Now we talk war."

Fists pounding, mugs raised, the counsellors cheered for a war long anticipated, one they must win to survive.

. . .

Servers flowed into the hall, thankfully none carrying laseblasters, but rather the expected platters of food and drink.

Breena watched Kestrel, who sat directly across from her, his expression flat and closed—an enigma wrapped in a mystery, a profound one. During the meal, it was laughable how many approaches the councilors used to worm from Kestrel the secret of his escape. Always a man of few words, Kestrel said little, yet deflected beautifully.

How had he escaped? Gato knew, and he'd better tell her. Kestrel finally shut everyone up with, "You will understand in time. Now, let it be."

To her surprise, the councilors did, unlike their talk of war that went on...and on. She tried to keep alert, she truly did, but her eyes kept drifting closed.

The meeting adjourned at three a.m., and she and Gato walked exhausted to their treehouse, the cool breeze waking her up enough to ask, "How *did* Kes escape?"

He kissed her on the nose and laughed. "Ah, but sweet *poosha*, Kestrel would kill me if I told. Considering I wish to live, I'm afraid you will have to ask him."

"That's exactly what I'll do."

Five days had passed since the council meeting, and those same councilors who wanted to lynch Gato now danced in his home. Ahanu's party had been raging since ten that morning, and, boy, could these Cats party. Before her, while revelers clapped, two-dozen-plus men danced together, a combination of Highland fling and Ukrainian hopak, with Gato at the center and Ahanu beside him.

Much to her surprise, Arina hooked an arm through Gato's, the other through Ahanu's, and kicked high. The First Commander was thinner than ever, and though she didn't smile, she appeared to be healing. Bree hoped so.

When Rafe joined them halfway through, he wore a huge grin,

perhaps because a day ago the Wolves had anointed him their Alpha, or maybe it was simply the evening's joy as the men kicked and leapt, twirled and crouched. Individuals were highlighted, Rafe on fire, but when Gato leapt, with arms and legs extended, then crouching and kicking one leg out, then the other…

Oh, my—she could barely keep herself from hauling him off to their rooms. She fanned her face, resenting that they must remain until the party's conclusion.

"I could use one of those, too," Fudge said. "Look at my Ax."

"We could haul both off and go play," Bree said.

"If only," Fudge said. "I see your sister. Oops, lost her. I'll be back."

Even if tomorrow's war council changed their lives forever, tonight was for celebrating. And learning Kestrel's secrets. She had looked for him earlier, but he still hadn't arrived.

Kit squeezed through the crush to Bree, sloshing the two mugs she carried. "For you,"

"Thanks," Bree was parched, and Kit would have dipped into the non-alcoholic bowl for her drink. Her cravings for liquor had subsided to a small thrum, for which she was grateful.

"This is great." Kit looked around. "You look tired, Bree."

"I've had easier weeks. Isn't the dancing wonderful?"

"I love it," Kit said. "The Wolves do similar dances."

"I want to haul Gato to bed."

Kit flushed. "They are beautiful, aren't they?"

Gato stood beside Rafe and Ax, chest heaving, head thrown back in an exuberant laugh. A thrill rippled through her. Each time she saw him, each time he walked into a room or awakened from sleep, she felt the same thrill. She suspected she always would. "They are *very* beautiful."

Her sister elbowed her in the ribs. "You're drooling."

"True. Your mate is almost as fine as mine."

"Almost? Lucky stars, look at the man. He's…Apollo!"

Bree laughed. "Then Gato must be Hades. A very gorgeous Hades."

Someone tapped her on the shoulder, and she turned to find

Ahanu holding three cupcakes, Bree's contribution to the party. The Cats head chef had been curious when she'd described them, for they knew nothing of cupcakes. They did now.

Gato's brother handed one to Kit, then Bree, and she was charmed by the whimsical star tattooed on his wrist. She missed her own tattoos and would get a new one. A cat, naturally.

"These are unique," Ahanu said, his shy smile making a rare appearance. "And delicious. I cannot stop eating them." He nibbled the edges of his red-frosted chocolate one.

Kit bit a huge chunk of hers, but Bree licked off the rich buttercream first.

Ahanu tilted his head. "Why do you do that, sister?"

He was such a serious young man, quiet and curious, with the demeanor of an ascetic. So unlike the laughing, joyful prankster Gato had described.

"I always lick off the frosting before I eat the cake. I do the same with my Oreos, too, eating the centers, except you don't know what those are, do you?" Bree bet the chef could make those, too.

But Ahanu had paused, his eyes tracking a Sequestered in a pale blue tunic and pants, her face hidden by a woven-straw helmet festooned with stars. Makena. So tall she nearly matched Ahanu's six feet, she was Compass True's newest counselor, having replaced the murdered Lana. Makena raised her hand to wave, revealing a neon blue forearm tattoo that matched Ahanu's. He waved back, his eyes following until the crowd swallowed her up.

"Makena's a friend?" Bree said.

A poignant smile briefly lifted the corners of his lips. "From long ago."

Gato swooped in and took Bree with a fevered kiss, and she sank into his embrace. Even sweaty, he was delicious. She savored him, his lips, his taste, his scent. Better than any high. When they parted, it appeared Rafe and Kitlyn had followed suit. Sybi would make so much fun of...

She froze, squeezing her eyes tight. Tomorrow was for worry about Sybi. Tonight, she would hold the joy close.

"Where's Kes?" Bree said.

Gato frowned. "He was eager for Ahanu's celebration and assured me he would attend."

"I'm concerned."

"No worries, *poosha*. Kes is where he should be. He always is."

"That sounds ridiculous."

He kissed the tip of her nose. "It does, matter of fact. Kestrel has a preternatural sense that puts him at the right place at the right time. He is a man with many hidden talents."

"Ones you won't tell me about."

He nuzzled Bree's neck.

"I'm certain of one thing," Rafe said, leaning close. "He will not miss tomorrow's council meeting."

"No," Gato said. "He has worked too hard for too long. He will not."

A rubbing on Bree's leg made her look down. Fortis blinked up at her, his eyes bright with excitement. She scooted down. "What is it?"

She is found.

For the first time, Fortis spoke in a complete sentence. Wow. "Who, Fortis?"

SHE!

CHAPTER THIRTY-FOUR

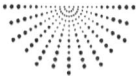

C alix had begun spitting up blood, as if he were melting inside, his world a kaleidoscope of colored lights and jarring sounds. His death was near, and he wept.

His last act must be performed without delay.

When he Awakened the Made One, she would have to deal with a dying madman. He squeezed his fists, his nails biting his palms, and slapped his face hard. Good.

What seemed like hours later, he had the vials for Awakening laid out, including the precious palladious. Exhaustion made Calix weave on his feet, but he leaned against the hovercart and pressed the "On" button, pushing the Made One's pod outside into the sunshine. He peered up at a cloudless sky.

The palladious rested in his palm, the final element in the infusion, and a rainbow on the faceted crystal caught his eye. He turned it this way and that. Mesmerizing.

Hard. This was so hard. All he wanted was sleep.

But he must complete his task.

The circle of trees loomed, casting inky shadows, the clear sky transforming to gray. Scents of juniper and pine filled him, wind cooling his fevered flesh.

As he sank into madness, his beautiful girl would Awaken and never know the true Calix. He pulled out the notes he'd written long before the psychosis had sunk its claws so deep and laid them beside her.

Once he found a splash of sunlight, he set the hovercart and checked the table for the glass, pitcher of water, and sheet to cover her when she Awakened. Gabin said Earthlings were self-conscious about nudity, and he did not want her to feel embarrassment.

Her flesh glowed in the light, and he waved his hands above the pod. Calix had never seen her original hair or breasts, as Fukkes had tinkered with her. Alchemics always perfected a Made One's health and enhanced their strength, and other things such as visual acuity. But Fukkes had done what was anathema—altered her for what he called "aesthetic" reasons. His adjustments infuriated Calix and demeaned the Alchemics' sacred covenant, a document Fukkes had long abandoned.

Calix checked the calibration once more, then allowed his tattered Falcon sense to enfold him. He flipped the infuser switch. Blue liquid spurted from the vial, snaking through the tube and port and into the Made One's body.

Almost there. His stomach cramped and he coughed, red flecking the pod and grass.

The wind increased to scatter leaves and bring the sounds of...

No! He swiped a hand across his mouth, turned his body to obscure the infuser tube, and drew his blaster.

Keplar stepped into the clearing wearing a feral smile. "What are you doing?"

His words sounded muffled. "I am giving the Made One some sunshine. Vitamin D."

Keplar neared, and though Calix kept the blaster against his thigh, his finger twitched. Prosa was here, too. Somewhere. "Go away."

Keplar stared into the pod filling with blue vapor. "No wonder you didn't want us to see her. She's a beauty. For a Made One." He spat on the pod.

"How dare you?" Calix said.

Keplar snorted. "Made Ones are disrespectful. They insult all of Eleutia."

Calix rubbed his forehead. There was a group. Their name...? His muzzy mind finally puzzled it together. "You are an Anti-Made One fanatic."

"Fanatics?" Keplar laughed. "You Alchemics are the fanatical ones. Creating things which don't belong on Eleutia. Say farewell to your Made One."

Calix raised his blaster. "Leave now."

A sharp prick on his spine. The point of a knife. The scent of Prosa.

"Have you Awakened her?" Prosa whispered in his ear.

"Not yet." A lie, and Calix fired, blasting Keplar's body in half.

Pain shot through him, Prosa's blade. He howled.

"You fucking asshole," Prosa said. "I'm going to make you suffer for killing my friend." He twisted the knife.

Calix screamed again, his legs failing, but he clung to the pod. He had to look, had to see. She was lovely, his Made One. *Farewell. Mother Terra help me.* In a final burst of strength, he snaked his arm behind him and blasted Prosa to the Fates.

Kestrel ran through the wood at a speed no normal Eleutian could match. He'd run for miles, something he did often to expend his excess energy, though flying to Ahanu's celebration would have been swifter. As he ate up the miles, he again fixated on the elements the Alchemics had used to create him. He had learned many—his mistral bones, his kestrel DNA—but others remained elusive. He *needed* to know.

Shouts. A scream. A howl.

His Falcon senses slammed into his consciousness, and he pushed his body faster.

. . .

Pain blasted Calix as he strained to reach the knife in his back. He slid from the pod, landing with a soft whoosh on a bed of leaves. The smells and sounds of life surrounded him—trees and birds, grass and rock, chirps and sighs, growls and...

Hyla stuck out her tongue and waved. Typical younger sister antics. She walked toward him, arms outstretched, and he greeted her in the silence.

Her eyes flared open. She blinked rapidly, so tired, as if she'd slept overlong. Her nose was stuffy, her muscles aching. She blinked again. Smoky blue wisps surrounded her and obscured a faint sun. She lay on her back—why? She never slept that way, and she raised her arms to stretch. *Ow.* They had hit something.

She pressed her hands against the clear ceiling, but the thing wouldn't budge, so she ran them up and down the sides. She lay inside a clear, curved chamber.

The smoke dissolved in patches. Her heart sped up, her breaths, rapid. A coffin. She was in a clear coffin.

Her breath stuttered, but her sensei's training asserted itself and she breathed deep. The air was thin, as if she were at altitude. No. Maine was at sea level. Where were Kit and Bree? Terrible pressure on her chest. It built, pressed down like a vise.

Couldn't breathe. *Breathe!*

Had to get out get out get out get out.

She screamed.

The blood spattered the clearing, its scent fresh. In a swift assessment, Kes scanned the glade—the glass cylinder, a hovercart, three dead men, no apparent threats. Sword drawn, he closed in to peer down at a man minutes dead. He and Calix were of the Falcon Clan, and Calix had been vital to Compass True, yet his dishevelment spoke of a severe disconnect—unshaven, shirt torn, pants stained, odiferous. When he had last seen the man, Calix had looked fit and healthy, hefting a heavy lasepipe on his shoulder.

A conundrum for another time.

He avoided the fogged capsule, knowing he would find a desiccated Made One, sheathed his sword, and considered the remaining two bodies. He knew neither man.

A muffled cry for help snapped his head around.

The cylinder. Inside, a woman pounded at glass that wouldn't budge.

He tried to lift the lid, locked, the keypad near flush with the glass. No time to sort out a combination. Smashing the glass would injure her further, and she was running out of air. He slipped his sword from its sheath and raised it, angling his body to slice parallel to the pod.

Gripping his sword in both hands, he calculated the trajectory and arc. Off a centem, he would kill her.

The woman's fearful eyes widened.

He lowered his blade with immense thrust.

Sparks shot from the lock and died, and he flung back the lid. "Breathe."

Her skin had turned bluish-red, her gasps relentless.

He cupped her shoulders. "Slowly. Breathe."

Panicked eyes captured his, hers the color of a turquoise sea. He slid his arms beneath her shoulders and hips and lifted her from the pod. "You are safe."

Patches of moonlight-blonde hair fell from her head, but her breathing had slowed, the blue tinge leaving her skin.

"Good," he said.

She shivered.

More bones than flesh, she was slight in his arms as he supported her weight and wrapped a sheet around her, eyes huge in her skeletal face.

She licked her lips, croaked something, and pointed to the pitcher.

He poured her a glass of water and held it while she sipped.

"I will get you warm soon," he said. "Food, as well."

"I'm not hungry," she said in a rusty-sweet voice.

"What is your name, Made One?"

Moments passed, her restless movements and rapidly blinking eyes reflecting her stress.

"It matters not." He carried her from the camp before she could spot the bodies.

"It matters." She touched her fingers to his chest.

A chime jolted his heart, and the kestrel within sounded a clarion call.

Kestrel had imagined. Had hoped. Now, he *knew*. She was theirs.

"Kes didn't show," Bree said to Gato, who was tuning his guitar in the living room. She tossed her party clothes in the hamper, slipped on a robe, and nuzzled her cubs. They slept on, curled together on the bed.

In the kitchen, she poured some chilled water, and brought glasses into the living room, handing one to Gato.

"No, he did not come," Gato said with a shrug. "He often has an agenda—things we cannot imagine—that trumps all. I have a surprise for you."

"A surprise? A good one?"

"Of course!" He set down the guitar and disappeared, returning with a large brown bottle. "I believe this will please you."

"And it's...?"

"Hair dye. The foundation for the color change. My chemist will mix it to any color you wish."

Oh, wow. She ruffled her hair, a lock now long enough to hold up to the light. She had always loved her black hair. It was who she was, right? Her small boobs looked more sprightly than usual, too, Gato's fault for giving her such a silky robe.

If she changed back—black hair, big boobs—would Gato still love her?

He'd begun to play and looked up, eyes narrowed. "What?"

He would. Nothing physical could change that. If Gato were bald or crippled or… She would love him.

What a grand gift he'd offered her, a gift simply to make her happy.

She set the dye jar on a table, rose, and slid into his lap, wrapping her arms around his shoulders.

"I cannot play this way," he said.

"Sure you can, catman, just not the guitar."

Bartholomew, lounging before the fireplace, chuffed.

"You still like my red hair, catman?"

"I do." He squeezed her tight. "But you do not."

She nuzzled his neck. "You've given me a precious gift. The hair dye is a choice, and choice is precious. For now, I'll leave well enough alone. You never know what your chemist might cook up. My hair could turn green."

"*Poosha*, he has tested the mixture. It will not turn your hair green."

"But I might like green. Yes, bright neon green."

He laughed. "What if I like it? Then you would be forced to always dye it green to please me. One rule—no more mohawks!"

"Rule?" She snorted and kissed his cheek. "No more, promise. I think I'll keep the red. It doesn't bother me much anymore. And you like it."

"It is my sunrise and sunset."

"Then I'm keeping it and my tiny boobs, so no need for a boob expander, okay?"

His laughter bubbled up, his kiss infusing her with his joy, which was when his mobile buzzed.

Swearing beneath his breath, he sat her on the chair and disappeared into their bedroom, Barth trotting after him.

Bree followed to find Gato pacing their bedroom while he talked. Tomorrow's meeting would be a humdinger, a terrifying call to arms. She sat on the bed, the cubs running their heads under her hands in search of pets. Her beloveds. She stroked them, her eyes on

Gato as he ended the call. He began removing his clothes. Few things were more pleasurable than watching Gato get naked.

"Why are you smiling?" he said in imperious tones, hands on hips.

Her smile widened, and he stepped towards her.

The buzz of his mobile came *again*.

"You should sew the damned thing to your ear," she hissed.

While he paced during the call, something about seating arrangements, she moved to wrap her arms around her naked mate.

He ended the call, flipped the phone closed, and tossed it on the bed. Turning to face her, his lips and hands began to roam.

"Take a short break from calls?" Bree kissed his shoulder, nibbled his neck.

"Short?" His lips meandered into a slow smile. "Never short, *poosha*."

She laughed. He always made her laugh. "You complete me."

"As you do, me."

"It's a line from a movie." She pulled him onto the bed. "I always thought it was ridiculous. But it's true. You do."

Her robe vanished, and she melted into his caress.

Fortis' paw banged her nose. Gato growled, which should have sent the cub into retreat. Instead, he chirped, *She is home,* and Audacia chimed in, too.

"Stop!" Gato flashed his eyes to Barth. "Tell them."

"Wait, love," Bree said. "Fortis referred to 'she.' At the party he said, 'She is found.' Could he mean Sybi? Please let it be Sybi."

SHE!

Bree slapped her hands over her ears, though the blast was in her head. "He's screaming at me."

"About what?" Gato said.

"About *she!*"

Fortis lay down, rested his golden head on his front paws, and stared at her.

A settling inside her, as if a last puzzle piece snapped into place, the feeling profound. "He means Sybi. I'm sure of it. My sister is *here*. And the cubs know where she is."

THANK YOU! AND NEWSLETTER

Thank you for reading *Changed*!

Reviews mean everything—they're an author's lifeblood as readers find us through your reviews. If you enjoyed *Changed*, leaving an honest review would be a kindness.

Would you like a free book? Do sign up for my newsletter and receive my bonus novel, *Body Parts*. My monthly newsletter contains info on The Made Ones Saga, the Afterworld Chronicles, life in L.A., and lots more yummy stuff.

Come visit with me... VickiStiefel.com
Facebook • Instagram • Twitter • BookBub

AWAKENED, BOOK 3, EXCERPT

THE MADE ONES SAGA

Wakeupwakeupwakeup

Stop it!

The voice in the head was relentless, driving her near mad.

She wanted to go back to sleep, but she couldn't. How could she hear the voice?

A woman's voice. Low and deep and heavy with age.

Like mist on a sunny morning, the voice dissipated.

She slept.

Wakeupwakeupwakeup

Not yet. She was so comfy, clouds of dreams luring her to faraway places. She was of the ether, dancing and swirling like the Firebird in Stravinsky's magical ballet. The lotus eaters welcoming Odysseus and his men. Then Daphne, pursued by Apollo, while laurel branches grew from her fingers, her torso's bark rising to encompass her.

Wakeupwakeupwakeup

Shouting!

Her eyes flared open, dry and crusty. She blinked rapidly, still tired, the kind where you wanted to sleep forever. Her nose was stuffy, her muscles aching. She blinked again. Foggy blue wisps surrounded her, and above their swirls, a faint sun. She lay on her back—why? She never slept that way—and raised her arms to stretch. *Ow.* She'd hit something. How odd. She pressed her hands to the clear covering and pushed. The lid didn't budge. She smoothed her palms up and down the curved surface.

A patch of fog dissipated, and her heart sped up, her breaths coming faster.

She was in a transparent coffin.

Starry skies!

She breathed deep…and gasped. Pressure on her chest, a boulder crushing her.

Tried again. Couldn't breathe. *Breathe!*

Had to get out get out get out get out.

Her fists pounded the ceiling over and over, and she gasped out a scream, twisting, rocking.

A shadow above. Growing to monstrous size. A horrible screech.

The coffin lid disappeared, the blue fog dispelling.

"Breathe," the deep voice demanded, backlighting the man who blocked the sun.

Cool, crisp air filled her lungs, and she gulped it down faster and faster.

Black descended.

Leaning over her, the man cupped her shoulders. "Slow down and breathe."

Apollo, the angles and planes of his face beautiful and terrible to behold. Strange hair fell forward as his black eyes bored into hers, asking…

No.

Arms slid beneath her, lifting her.

Her chest rose up and down, faster and faster and…

ACKNOWLEDGMENTS

Thank you, my readers, for your inspiration each and every day! You're the best.

Many thanks for those who helped shepherd *Changed* through to the finish line. Once again, my incomparable editor, Aria Jones, worked her magic. Thank you! To the extraordinary Camille Cotton —this book wouldn't exist without you. To the amazing Rosemary Hill, whose friendship, aid and insights are both invaluable and inspirational. To Monica—for your fantastic blurb help. To Lorelei Owens, whose help with circus "speak" and moves made Bree's flying real. To my much-loved Betas—Wayne, Ro, Genevieve, Pilar, and Meri—for their invaluable critiques and friendship. To Lorelai —who keeps me smiling through the sweat and tears.

To my exceptional cover artist, Mirela Barbu—you turn dreams into reality, including mine. Thank you! And to Blake, my brilliant graphics sounding board.

To Eileen Shapiro, for all your terrific assistance. You're a peach!

To Award-winning Master Karen Darabedyan of KD Mixed Martial Arts Academy. You are one of the kindest gentlemen I've ever met. Thank you for your martial arts help.

To the Illuterati group and my Facebook pals who inspire me

with warmth, humor, and truth-telling. To the Warrioresses, who soothe my heart. To Norah, Ro, and Karen for your friendship, support, and knitting expertise. To Sheila Ryan, for her beautiful love, and Marc Ryan, who inspires me daily. To Andrea Urban, Suzanne Hendrich, Pat Murphy, Donna Cautilli, CJ Williams, Linda Windels—love you. To Cindy's Knitters for the many stitches we wove together. To Betsy Bair, Georgi Mueller, and Karen Waxman for your love and friendship. To Cynthia Michaels, for your friendship and your Cranberry love.

To Peter, Kathleen, and Summer—your love and profound support mean the world. Love you! Finally, to my beloved boys, Blake and Ben—for all that you are, for all that you have gifted me, and for your abiding love. I'm the luckiest mom in the world.

Any errors or screw-ups are mine alone.

ABOUT THE AUTHOR

Award-winning author Vicki Stiefel's romantic science-fantasy series, The Made Ones Saga, launched with *Altered*. Vicki continues work on her Afterworld Chronicles, a five-book series begun with *Chest of Bone*. Her mystery/thrillers feature homicide counselor Tally Whyte, and Vicki's knitting love produced *Chest of Bone The Knit Collection* and *10 Secrets of the LaidBack Knitters*.

Having grown up in professional theater, Vicki planned to become an actress. Instead, she slung hamburgers, managed a scuba shop, and taught at Clark U. She's a mom to two wonderful humans and is currently playing with her pup, Penny, her grand puppy Bash, staying safe, and pounding the keys on Book 3 in the Made Ones Saga, *Awakened*.

Come visit with me...
www.vickistiefel.com • vicki@vickistiefel.com

ALSO BY VICKI STIEFEL

The Made Ones Saga

Altered

Changed

Awakened (coming 2021)

The Afterworld Chronicles

Chest of Bone— Also on Audible

Chest of Stone

Chest of Time

Chest of Fire (to come)

Tally Whyte/Homicide Counselor Series

Body Parts • *The Dead Stone* • *The Grief Shop* (DAPHNE DUMAURIER AWARD WINNER) • *The Bone Man* (DAPHNE DUMAURIER AWARD FINALIST)

Nonfiction

10 Secrets of the LaidBack Knitters

Chest of Bone The Knit Collection

Visit with Vicki:

Website • Facebook • Instagram • BookBub